PROPHECY

To Dong
Best wishes!

[signature]

August 2007

Also by Paul Mark Tag:
Category 5

PROPHECY

A NOVEL

PAUL MARK TAG

iUniverse, Inc.
New York Lincoln Shanghai

Prophecy

iUniverse books may be ordered through booksellers or by contacting:

iUniverse
2021 Pine Lake Road, Suite 100
Lincoln, NE 68512
www.iuniverse.com
1-800-Authors (1-800-288-4677)

Because of the dynamic nature of the Internet, any Web addresses or links contained in this book may have changed since publication and may no longer be valid.

This is a work of fiction. All of the characters, names, incidents, organizations, and dialogue in this novel are either the products of the author's imagination or are used fictitiously.

ISBN: 978-0-595-43444-2 (pbk)
ISBN: 978-0-595-68236-2 (cloth)
ISBN: 978-0-595-87771-3 (ebk)

Printed in the United States of America

ACKNOWLEDGMENTS

Many people contributed to the research and proofing that went into the completion of this novel. Foremost among them is my wife, Becky, who offered patience, encouragement, insightful readings, and constructive criticism. Beyond her, my overwhelming thanks go to my primary reader, Robin Brody. I wish to acknowledge a host of secondary readers, in alphabetical order: author Arline Chase (my mentor), Peggy Dold, Myra Golphenee, Michael Guy, Kris Hoffman, Fran Morris, and Ann Schrader.

I am grateful to the National Park Service, particularly the staff at the Johnstown Flood National Memorial: Mary Anne Davis, Mindy Kuzminsky, Doug Richardson, and Terry Roth. They allowed me access to the grounds and building, and answered my numerous questions.

Two books provided important reference material:

From the editors of *Scientific American. Understanding the Genome.* New York: Warner Books, Inc., 2002.

McCullough, David G. *The Johnstown Flood.* New York: Simon and Schuster, 1968.

All persons and materials listed above provided invaluable, accurate advice and data. Any errors that remain in the manuscript are mine.

AUTHOR'S NOTE

Prophecy is a work of fiction. All of the characters, names, incidents, organizations, and dialogue in this novel either are the product of the author's imagination or are used fictitiously. That said, I have attempted to create an interesting story set within realistic scientific, theoretical, and geographical boundaries.

Except for the scenes set in Cairo, I have personally scouted the geographic locations for all chapters in the book and have imagined the action occurring there. I determined the GPS coordinates using a Magellan Meridian Platinum handheld GPS receiver. The reader can view these locations using Google Earth, software that allows one to view Earth locations using satellite imagery. Type into your computer browser "Google Earth" and follow the directions for loading the software. Then type in the chapter GPS locations to see where the action in the book occurs. In some instances, the resolution of the images provided by Google Earth is inadequate. Others, such as all settings in Washington, DC, are amazingly detailed. As an example, consider the location where Senators MacDonald and Thurston have offices. Type in the following: 38 53 32N 77 00 28W. Google Earth will position you at the front entrance to the Russell Senate Office Building.

Blair Aviation, the Branding Iron Restaurant, the Cairo sites, Carmel Bay Motor Lodge, Columbia Pines Lodge, Comstock Aviation, Thurston's Emporia, Kansas, and Georgetown residences, and Weaverman's detention apartment are fictional locations. Nonetheless, these buildings and facilities are imagined to be located at the GPS coordinates provided.

All times given at the beginnings of chapters represent daylight saving time. For example, times in Washington, DC, occur in eastern daylight time, while those in Monterey, California, take place in Pacific daylight time. All chapters and scenes move forward either simultaneously or sequentially in time.

Please use the glossary and the "Cast of Characters" section at the end of the book. Information there, if needed, will assist the reader as the action unfolds. Information concerning the Naval Research Laboratory organizations, the Johnstown Flood National Memorial, the Human Genome Project, and Celera come from their Web sites.

PROLOGUE

LAST WILL AND TESTAMENT

Johnstown, Pennsylvania, USA
40° 19'37"N latitude, 78° 55'19"W longitude
Friday, 4:00 PM, May 31, 1889

Augusta whispered softly to herself, knowing that her family would not understand the words. "Augusta, you are a strong young woman, no matter what others would say. You alone know that truth. God will forgive you." She walked proudly, head high, having no fear that others would recognize her in attire suitable only for churchgoing Sundays. She drank in her surroundings, remembering breakfast with her family—all the while knowing that what would happen in the next thirty minutes would be her final experience in this lifetime.

What had to be would be. She held tightly the handwritten sheets, the envelope she would use to store them, and the corked bottle that would protect its precious contents, all the while struggling with an umbrella against the unrelenting rain.

Augusta entered by way of tall oak doors and looked high to the rafters. Rain poured steadily against the tin roof. It had done so all night and into this Friday, the day after yesterday's successful Memorial Day festivities. The town and its inhabitants accepted their yearly consequence as Providence; Johnstown, Pennsylvania, often experienced springtime flooding.

Slowly she walked toward the sanctuary of the old German Lutheran church. Though it was Friday and the weather dreadful, she wore a pink taffeta dress with hand-embroidered roses sewn around the bottom of the skirt. She had borrowed the dress and matching bonnet from her sister. Most would agree that the combination was a bit festive for a place of worship. Moisture from her eyes ruined her rouge and powder, cosmetics that had taken a month to save up for and buy—secretly. With the house to herself this afternoon, she had taken a bath, washed her hair, carefully applied the makeup, and put on her sister's corset. She'd done her best to make herself presentable to the Lord, to make one last attempt to curry his favor.

Augusta quickened her pace. There was little time. The metal safe to the rear of the church behind the chancellery was the safest place. The church kept important papers and money there.

At the altar Augusta knelt to pray, to ask for mercy for her town—and herself. Augusta didn't deserve the fate she now felt helpless to stop. But she had decided to make one last stand. She could save herself, but for what? A lifetime of guilt? *No!* She would face her destiny with courage and strength—standing alongside the townspeople who knew nothing.

Augusta thought back to the morning, to her family. At breakfast she had made a point of telling them she loved them dearly. Nineteen years old, the eldest of three children, with a sister and brother one and five years younger, Augusta already possessed the wisdom of an elder. Perhaps her parents had instilled in her that maturity. More likely, she thought, it had sprung full-grown from her curses, both of them—although it was the latter curse that had brought her here today. Her parents, Heinrich and Frieda Schmidt, devout Christians, honest to a fault, God-fearing, would not—could not—have understood. She would not have dared to broach the topics.

"What's wrong, dear? You look so sad," her mother had intoned.

"It's nothing," she had lied. What could she say? Should she have warned them? They wouldn't have believed her anyway.

There had been no one for Augusta to talk to. Her pastor? He, as well as her parents, would accuse her of communing with the devil—and that was a deed to be avoided in this religious community, under the threat of everlasting fiery brimstone. Their pastor held little tolerance, seeing evil everywhere, especially in people's hearts, and even in such simple pleasures as dancing. Such activities were the stock-in-trade of Satan, he often thundered from his Sunday pulpit, tools for converting innocent souls to his side of the heaven/hell divide.

No, there had been no one.

Augusta made one final attempt. "Dear God, save us from thy fury. Save us sinners who live here. Have mercy on us. Have mercy on me." And then she recited the Lord's Prayer. "Our Father, who art in heaven ..."

Augusta finished, stood, breathed deeply, and glanced around, absorbing the moment and the gravity of what was to come.

Could it be? The rain had abated. Perhaps God had heard her prayers. But then the wind picked up, and she felt the large wooden structure heave a mournful sigh. Her eardrums ached as the air pressure rose and fell. It seemed as if God himself had breathed out and in.

Augusta ran behind the altar and opened the wooden door that fronted the safe. She fumbled for the key, which was hidden inside. She knew the location because she had watched her father on many a Sunday lock up the receipts to await deposit in the bank on Monday morning.

At once, she heard a roar in the distance, like the beating of horse hooves. She stood and peered over the altar toward the front doors, to the north from where she knew the onslaught would come. At that instant, she recognized that she would die. God, if he existed, had ignored her prayers.

There was little time. She knelt on one knee, thrust the key into the lock, opened the door, took a final look at the two pages she had written the previous night, and stuffed them inside the envelope. She licked and sealed the envelope and squeezed it inside the bottle, forcing the cork tight against the neck. Augusta squinted as she held the bottle close to her eyes to make sure all was inside, and then she thrust it inside the safe. *The devil will know what he sees.*

She slammed the metal door shut. As she turned the key to its locked position, a vibration from the old church's floor made its way through Augusta's feet and up her body. Her hand lost contact with the key. She gasped, tried to stand, and fell backward. Her shoe had caught in the hem of her dress.

Augusta made one final attempt to escape her destiny. She rushed down the aisles between the pews but stopped short, halfway. She looked ahead at the tall wooden wall and its circular stained-glass window. On most days, a brilliant harmony of colors blazed through the array of glass. But now it revealed only darkness—no light, only the blackness of hell.

Augusta watched as the front wall of the church strained against the torrent of water and then exploded before her eyes. The church's timbers and siding planks danced through the air, swept away by a forty-foot wall of water.

CHAPTER 1

LIABILITY

Northbound on I-495, west of Washington, DC, USA
Wednesday, 4:45 PM, July 22, 2009

James Weaverman glanced again into his rearview mirror. Sweat beaded on his face, even with the AC dialed to max and the fan speed one click from the top. Damn Washington heat! The white Ford Fusion had held its position, a dozen or so cars back, for the past thirty minutes. As if they thought he wasn't smart enough to see them. He had changed lanes, even exited at one interchange and then driven back onto the freeway; no doubt about it, they were tailing him. Had been, ever since he had departed Overlook Avenue and the Naval Research Laboratory at 4:15, his normal quitting time. He glanced down. There was still time, and his gas tank was a quarter full. Time enough to escape—or make one final phone call.

Weaverman pulled the tab on another pack of Marlboros, his single concession to Wall Street's image of manhood. As if he fit *that* mode. When conventional pressure had failed at convincing him of the error of his ways, his supervisor had used that against him, too. Bastard! And finally, he had resorted to money as a bargaining chip. Weaverman had thought about it—for about a millisecond. His personal integrity and scientific ethics weren't for sale.

Of course, the signals had been there—ominous warnings that told him to back off and not insist on publishing his findings, to do as his supervisor suggested, to classify as Top Secret his three years of research and make his work inaccessible to the public, and maybe even to himself. The higher-ups had decided that was best. For national security, they said.

No, he wouldn't do that. Even under continuous pressure from Dennis Rafferty, his bastard supervisor, Weaverman had not backed off. Truth be told, he felt rather proud of his act of confrontation, his balls, as they would put it. The research was his, discovered by him. Why should he bend to the overbearing, inept, stab-you-in-the-back son of a bitch he worked for?

Still, Weaverman understood their motives. He hadn't graduated number five in his class at Stanford by being stupid. His work hadn't yet produced absolute proof, but the signs clearly pointed to the conclusion. The evidence so far was suggestive and titillating at worst and downright revolutionary at best. Fucking damn near explosive, to put it in the vernacular.

A Nobel Prize wasn't at all out of the question. NRL had one of those, but only one, from 1985. Jerome Karle and Herbert Hauptman had both received the Nobel Prize for Chemistry for their use of X-ray diffraction analysis in the determination of crystal structures. Of course, their work was so esoteric that Joe Citizen wouldn't appreciate its significance. Weaverman was sure that would not be the case for what the world would soon judge to be the most significant discovery of the past century.

Weaverman needed more data to confirm his suspicions, more comparisons for gene sequence number 326, to prove to all those experts deciphering the human genome that he was on to something. Further exploration would require some unorthodox science. Much of society, particularly those of the Christian and Muslim faiths, would scoff at what needed to be done, digging into the dirt of centuries past.

Weaverman, with his minuscule budget, had made the connection— not the HGP, the government-funded Human Genome Project, or the privately funded Celera teams, with their untold millions of dollars of seed money. He alone had stumbled upon a gene mutation responsible for an unusual hereditary anomaly, unrelated to diseases linked to genetic predispositions—a genetic aberration that could prove fundamental to several of the world's religions.

Weaverman glanced at the gas gauge. He had continued clockwise around the Beltway and was heading south, close to Andrews Air Force Base. He had to decide soon.

What would they do when they caught him? Kill him? Unlikely, but not out of the question. Confine him to a cell where not even relatives could find him, building a case for spying as the FBI did to Wen Ho Lee, the Los Alamos scientist accused of surrendering missile secrets to the Chinese? Possibly.

Either way, his work would remain confined to the decision makers in the military. The scariest part was that he had shown Rafferty his data. A noted biologist in his own right, Rafferty could continue development himself. Weaverman cursed his own stupidity.

Weaverman took the Andrews exit from 495. He had access to the base because he was a member of the 121st Weather Flight, an Air National Guard unit that conducted its monthly drills there. His coworkers found it odd that a well-known biologist would spend time forecasting the weather as well. During his years in the Guard, he had made many friends. One of them, a Navy scientist with impeccable credentials, stood foremost in Weaverman's mind, a friend with connections who might be able to help.

The Fusion followed him off the exit and pulled up behind him at the controlled entrance. Noticing the decal on the windshield, the sentry at the gate waved Weaverman through. The Fusion stopped but only briefly; the outstretched wallet displayed to the guard had its desired effect. The car then accelerated until it caught Weaverman's Volvo. He continued driving across the base, the Fusion on his tail.

It was time.

Weaverman glanced at his watch. It was still early on the West Coast. He grabbed his cell phone and accomplished two actions in sequence. First, he sent a text message that he had prepared for this occasion. Second, he hit the speed dial to the office of a Dr. Victor Mark Silverstein. As he had feared, his call connected only to an answering machine. Weaverman made his point quickly.

Having accomplished this final act of defiance, Weaverman pulled over and waited. Two men ran to his vehicle and ordered him out.

CHAPTER 2

BOLT FROM THE BLUE

Naval Research Laboratory, Monterey, California, USA
36°35'34"N latitude, 121°51'17"W longitude
Friday, 8:45 AM, July 24, 2009

Silverstein returned the phone to its cradle, reconsidered, picked it up again, and punched two buttons for the in-house intercom. He briefly thought about the implications of his earlier call, which had gone unanswered.

"Kipling! Get your butt down here." He was agitated and not shy about letting his assistant know it—although it would have been only a twenty-foot walk to her office.

Dr. Victor Mark Silverstein, the Navy's preeminent meteorologist, a genius by everyone's acknowledgment (including his own), did his best to calm himself before his faithful assistant entered. He wasn't angry with her; even so, she would take the brunt of his exasperation. He leaned back in his Leap chair and took in deep, purifying breaths, the kind a yoga instructor had advised. On his third inhale, he glanced up to see Kipling's smiling face.

"What is it this time, you old blowhard? Is your testosterone-fueled Porsche knocking on one of its cylinders?" Kipling understood Silverstein's ways and never flagged at any opportunity to fan incipient flames higher.

Silverstein grunted in disgust. With all that they had been through together, he thought she'd give him a little more respect. Of course, he had to admit that he owed her his life. The incident at the Fort Collins Mountain High Inn two years earlier had established beyond doubt her credentials for bravery. Although he had plenty of life's rewards—adulation from the scientific community and money—it shouldn't have been too much to ask that Dr. Linda Kipling, his principal colleague, treat him with deference and understanding. He had feelings, too. Well, enough of feeling sorry for himself.

Silverstein had calmed down enough to know his complexion would appear normal to his assistant. Although his chocolate skin hid his emotions from most people, Kipling had been around him long enough to detect subtle tinges of scarlet.

"I'd like to bring you in on something. I need your help." Silverstein stared intensely in her direction, making sure he had her attention.

Kipling continued her onslaught. "Have I ever denied you anything?" She smiled.

Silverstein grimaced in response and stood. "There was a message waiting on my phone yesterday morning when I came in, from Wednesday afternoon." He paused. "If I hadn't left for a dentist appointment, I would have been here to take it."

Kipling, her interest aroused, grabbed the guest chair and sat in it backwards. "Who called?"

"You wouldn't know him. He works at NRL DC." The Naval Research Laboratory in Washington, DC, represented the corporate headquarters for the Marine Meteorology Division in Monterey, California.

"Try me."

"Dr. James Weaverman. Biologist. The only reason I know him is that he's also a meteorologist for the Air Force—a weekend warrior for the Air National Guard, actually. Does his drills at Andrews Air Force Base. Five months ago, I spent a weekend there as a courtesy to an old Penn Stater who's the commanding officer for his weather flight. I got to know Weaverman fairly well. We hit it off. He's one sharp cookie."

"And this is the first you've heard from him?"

"Yup. Wednesday, out of the blue, he leaves this incredibly troubling message on my machine."

Kipling sat up straight. "Trouble? What did he—" she cut herself off. "First, tell me why you're so upset. You've had twenty-four hours to absorb the significance of his call. Why the delay?"

"I repeatedly called his home and office yesterday; no answer. Today I called his boss, a guy named Rafferty. I made it sound official, told him I was calling from NRL Monterey. He told me that Weaverman had gone on a temporary leave of absence. I called his home again. Still no answer. I hung up, just now. The fact that I can't reach him is disturbing … in light of his message."

"Okay, I'll bite. What was the message?"

"Hang on. Before I tell you that, let me tell you about Weaverman. The guy's gay, okay?"

Kipling grimaced. "That doesn't bother you, does it?"

Silverstein's face flushed. "Hell no! I'm trying to make a point."

Kipling seemed satisfied with Silverstein's response. "Okay, sorry. Make your point."

"The point is that Weaverman's boss, Rafferty, has no idea that I know he's gay."

Kipling looked back at Silverstein, incredulous. "You sure have a back-handed way of getting to the point."

Silverstein feigned anger and sat back down. "For crissake! Will you just let me finish my story? I'll listen to anything you have to say then."

"Okay, okay. I'll behave." Kipling folded her arms and took on a mockingly somber look.

Silverstein spoke his first words slowly. "The *reason* that it's important is that Rafferty made a serious mistake during our conversation. When I asked him if he knew when Weaverman would be back or where I could contact him, he said his absence had something to do with his family."

Silverstein leaned back and interlocked his hands behind his head. "When I heard that, I decided to set a trap. I knew I was taking a chance because he could have been referring to Weaverman's parents or siblings. I said, 'Is it his wife? The last time I saw her she was in poor health.' I expected a pause at the other end … and I got it. I listened carefully for his response because, depending on his answer, I decided I might be able to tell if he was lying." Silverstein pointed his index finger to the ceiling. "And therefore whether he was part of the problem Weaverman referred to in his message."

"What problem?" Kipling pressed.

Silverstein was on a roll. "I'll get to that later. The way I see it, the fact that he paused meant one of two things. Rafferty could have known that Weaverman *was* gay and wondered how I could possibly think he had a wife. More likely, because I said I had met his wife meant that, although he knew Weaverman's secret, he was surprised to discover he had a wife."

Kipling held up her hand. "There's another option. Rafferty may have no idea that Weaverman's a homosexual but also knows he has no wife. What mistake did Rafferty make?"

"The safe reply was for him to say he didn't know. Instead, the fool agreed with my statement. That was a stupid response, and one he probably regretted after our conversation."

"Okay, okay! I'm getting lost here. So what you're saying is that Rafferty is lying." Kipling took a deep breath. "I can't take it any longer. What the hell did Weaverman say to you on your machine?"

Silverstein folded his hands in front of him. "Here's what he said, verbatim. 'Victor, it's me, Jim Weaverman, from the 121st. Remember what I told you during our visit? I haven't proved it yet, but I'm making headway. But the shit's hit the fan. If you don't hear from me soon, I'm in trouble.'"

Kipling seemed to understand Silverstein's dilemma. "He never called you again … *and* Rafferty's lying! That's why you're upset."

"You got it!"

Kipling rose from her chair and started pacing. "Sounds ominous. What did he tell you when you last saw him? Something classified?"

"No, it wasn't secret, or at least it wasn't back then. What he said was so preposterous that I'd forgotten about it. He admitted that it was far-fetched. In the months since our meeting, he obviously did more work to convince himself of the results." Silverstein paused. "And if what he postulated bore fruit, and he told his boss, I can imagine higher-ups would clas-sify his work Top Secret in a heartbeat. The implications of what Weaverman told me are staggering."

"You wouldn't have called me down here if you weren't going to give me the scoop. What did Weaverman tell you?"

"You know about the Human Genome Project, right?"

"Not much, even though my bachelor's degree's in biology. They're trying to decipher the human genetic code. Getting to the roots of disease and birth defects, that sort of thing. Right?"

"You better sit down."

Silverstein sat on the edge of his desk and continued. "Indirectly, Weav-erman got involved in gene sequencing. I don't pretend to understand any of it. He's convinced that he's discovered a gene sequence that's so rare it gets activated only once every couple hundred million or so births."

Kipling's back straightened. "That's more than just rare; that's extraor-dinary!" She paused. "Okay! I understand. What—"

Silverstein cut her off. He couldn't wait any longer. He had to tell someone. "Let me put it in a way that a layman would appreciate. He thinks there *is* such a thing as a clairvoyant. He thinks that a person born with this gene sequence can see into the future."

CHAPTER 3

REINS OF POWER

1221 Rural Street, Emporia, Kansas, USA
38° 24'47"N latitude, 96° 11'16"W longitude
Friday, 10:50 AM, July 24, 2009

The Merchant Street exit from Interstate 35 was a welcome sight for U.S. Senator Samantha Thurston. Her early morning flight home from Washington had been a tiring one. The drive from the Kansas City airport to Emporia, two hours to the southwest, was drearier than usual. The anticipation of upcoming events had drained her mind of energy; actions and accompanying reactions would come quickly now. As Caesar had so succinctly put it, *the die was cast*. She looked down the brick-inlaid street, one of the few that remained in Emporia, toward her stylish white brick house.

Although scarcely five months into her husband's remaining Senate term, her frequent flights back to her constituents were taking their toll on the Kansas Republican. They were boring, too. Power had its rewards but also its obligations. Thurston yawned and fought off fatigue. It would be a short weekend, then back in the air come Sunday evening. And there was much to do before then, beyond her usual duties. Back in Washington, Tuesday's call from Clifton MacDonald indicated that the wheels had been set in motion. Packets had gone out. Her husband would have objected strenuously to MacDonald's plans. She still missed him, naive wuss that he was.

Thurston pulled into her driveway and the open carport, dragged her bag from the trunk, and plodded to the back porch. She glanced around the yard, comforted to know that the gardener had finished his weekly cutting and pruning; a Virgo required that all ducks march forward in order. She let herself in the back door. Her head turned sideways as she sensed a whisper of a sound. Since birth, she had been blessed (or sometimes cursed) with an incredible sense of hearing, particularly at the higher frequencies. She walked straight through the kitchen toward the stairs. The man sitting on the sofa looked up inquiringly, as if she had disturbed him. She *had* heard something: his movement on the seat of the sofa.

"Who the hell are you?"

A stranger, reading a magazine, sat comfortably on the sofa. He looked up. Had she stumbled across a prowler? Even with the possibility of violence at hand, Thurston held her ground. Since childhood, fear had been a foreign concept.

"My name's Dick Jamieson. I work for MacDonald. Weaverman's in custody."

Thurston understood the significance of the intruder's reply. Nonetheless, his sudden appearance twelve hundred miles from the office where she had first met his boss caught her by surprise. "Dick?" *You don't say.*

Two weeks earlier, following a Senate session on Medicare, Clifton MacDonald, Republican senator from Wyoming, had followed her back to her office for a closed-door session, the second since her husband passed away. Maxwell Thurston had died a sudden death six months earlier— only forty-two years of age and five years her senior.

The governor of Kansas had seen fit to appoint her as her husband's replacement, to complete the remaining three years of his term. None of the Kansas congressional delegation had offered any encouragement for her to accept, but then again, they hadn't stood in her way, rumors about her personal life notwithstanding. The appointing governor hadn't had much choice in the matter either. Samantha Thurston had made sure of that earlier. She inherited her husband's office in the Russell Senate Office Building.

"I'm worried Weaverman's going to spill the beans. That's not what we need just now," MacDonald had insisted earlier.

Seven months earlier, MacDonald had briefed Thurston's husband on new research that had intoxicating implications. He insisted that the information be held closely, that Weaverman's supervisor was the only other link in the information chain. MacDonald erupted in anger when he discovered that Maxwell had violated that stipulation. That betrayal of confidence had taken place with Senator Thurston's wife. Upon his death, Samantha Thurston made clear in her first face-to-face meeting with MacDonald that she expected to be a partner in his newfound venture. MacDonald, taken aback, reluctantly agreed. Her powers of persuasion left him speechless.

That MacDonald, the Republican chair of the Senate Committee on Commerce, Science, and Transportation, had gained access to the original information was accidental and fortuitous. Realizing the potential of Weaverman's discovery, Dennis Rafferty, Weaverman's supervisor and an acquaintance of MacDonald, brought it to his attention. The implications for national security (and beyond) led MacDonald to urge Rafferty, and hence Weaverman, to keep a lid on further dissemination of this scientific breakthrough. As he proceeded with his research and became ever more confident about its validity, Weaverman became a problem. He thought it wrong not to share his research with other scientists. MacDonald concluded he had no choice but to resort to threats.

Thurston dropped her bag, crossed the room to the wet bar, removed a bottle of California Chardonnay from the refrigerator, uncorked it, and poured a glass. She glanced back toward the sofa. "Do you care to join me?"

Jamieson shook his head.

"Are you sure?" Thurston tilted her head down, her red bangs framing delicate facial features that highlighted a mole on her right cheek. She saw no further response but liked what she saw.

Thurston crossed the room, settled herself into a stuffed chair, legs uncrossed on purpose, and stared at the man who had violated her private sanctum. She assessed him as young, late twenties; naive; blond, slicked-back hair; and a pale, bleached complexion that belied his sturdy, fit physical frame. She swirled the wine in her glass and took a swallow, letting the alcohol linger on her tongue. "How long can we keep him this way … quiet, that is?"

"As long as we have to."

"How're you going to do that? Unless we declare him an enemy combatant like they did back with al-Qaeda and send him somewhere like Guantanamo …" Jamieson's stern, forceful demeanor sidetracked Thurston's thoughts. She regained her composure. "Won't that be a problem?"

"MacDonald has friends in the right places."

Thurston nodded, again swirling the wine in her glass. "I thought he was a fag who hadn't come out of the closet yet. Threats didn't work?"

"Apparently not. Money didn't either."

Thurston sighed. "What's the world coming to when the usual methods of blackmail don't work anymore?"

Thurston, assuming that her initial offer had been rejected, crossed her legs and wondered what MacDonald's underling had in mind. "I assume you've come to give me something. Otherwise, you could have called." She paused. "Why didn't you just come by in DC?"

"MacDonald prefers that these matters be handled away from the capital." Jamieson leaned to his left, set his briefcase flat on the floor, and opened the lid. He removed a manila envelope, rose to his feet, and walked across to Thurston. Thinking that he may have been slow on the uptake the first time around, she uncrossed her legs as he approached. As she reached out to accept the envelope, she made a point of locking eyes. Jamieson nervously cleared his throat and returned to the sofa.

Thurston stood, ripped open the sealed envelope, and walked to the window to take advantage of the morning light. She knew what the folder contained. She didn't need her 160 IQ to figure this one out. MacDonald had told her that significant funding would be necessary—to allow Rafferty to complete the remaining research independently of NRL funding.

She skipped to page two. MacDonald wanted two million dollars from each of six investors—including MacDonald and Thurston, but excluding Rafferty, the seventh participant, who didn't have the money but was an indispensable member of the team. The other participants hailed from the private sector. One owned a certain biotech company crucial to providing facilities for the next phase of development. Thurston would have no problem writing her own check. Her husband's insurance had paid off handsomely.

The twelve million would allow Rafferty, under MacDonald's supervision, to complete the remaining research. In movie terms, Rafferty would play the role of director for the upcoming research, but MacDonald was the producer. In exchange for that sum, each investor would be privy to the promise and expected riches of the designer gene.

The investors, carefully selected, were friends or acquaintances of MacDonald. He had explained to Thurston that each had to agree to the strict terms of his or her contract, written to ensure that each participant understood not only the benefits but also the risks—and threats—implicit in their signing. Thurston's connection to this project had come through her husband, who had been a close colleague of MacDonald. Thurston's husband hadn't seen eye to eye with MacDonald regarding the proper way to proceed. As it happened, his unfortunate death made his conservative concerns irrelevant.

With no other body movement save her eyes, Thurston glanced over at Jamieson, sitting patiently again on the sofa. *Finally, some reaction.* She caught his eyes taking in her breasts. Before he noticed that he had been busted—and to give him a better look at her other assets—she turned around and studied the documents further.

After his experience with Thurston's husband, MacDonald understood that he needed extraordinary measures to keep his investors in line. The explosive potential of the research that they would sponsor to its conclusion was such that they could tolerate no further leaks. For that reason, each member of the team received a document identical to the one Thurston was reading now, identical except for the information on page three, specific to that person—information that, if released, could potentially ruin the career or life of the individual involved. It was through the threat of that release that MacDonald intended to control all parties involved.

Thurston turned, surprised that Jamieson was now on his feet, staring without embarrassment. It was time. She couldn't wait any longer. Her impulsiveness, whether responding to physical or emotional needs, was her weakness.

She dropped the document to the floor, walked over, placed her left hand behind Jamieson's head, pressed her lips to his and, at the same time, moved her right hand slowly down his chest to his abdomen. She slid his zipper as far down as it would go and slipped her hand inside, relieved to know that her new acquaintance had the wherewithal to appreciate someone of the opposite sex.

An interesting thought occurred. Maybe she could bend this young man to *her* purposes. As quickly as that notion crossed her consciousness, she filed the concept away to the intellectual reaches of her mind. The visceral portion of her brain required stimulation just now.

A few minutes earlier, Thurston had blinked but otherwise provided no further reaction to the specific words in her document—words meant to keep her true to MacDonald's intentions. Facing away from Jamieson, she had smiled. MacDonald didn't know her very well. The potential of this project was enough to ensure her loyalty. But beyond that, the threat of exposure contained in the explosive words written on that third page would fall short in stopping her from doing whatever she wanted or found necessary. Samantha Jane Thurston had no fear.

CHAPTER 4

EXCAVATION

Naval Research Laboratory, Monterey, California, USA
36°35'34"N latitude, 121°51'17"W longitude
Friday, 9:05 AM, July 24, 2009

Silverstein waited for Kipling's response to his bombshell.

"That's unbelievable! Is Weaverman nuts?"

"I've got to tell you, that was my reaction when he explained this back in Washington. But he's no dummy. He's published and well respected. He doesn't come off as a kook."

"You realize what this would mean if it turned out to be true?"

"I have my ideas, but I'd like to hear your thoughts."

"First, it would throw religion into chaos." Kipling stopped to think. "Or maybe not. One *could* argue that this was God's way of interjecting superhuman individuals, prophets, into the mix. It could be God's subtle attempt ..." She held up her right index finger. "Which worked by the way ... of suggesting to humanity that something does exist after death, an afterlife. Or," Kipling giggled, "it could also be his little joke on us, a monkey wrench thrown into the mix, an experiment to see how humans would—"

Silverstein interrupted. "A logical concept, but the religious right could never live with either idea. They'd say that God would never attempt something so rational—or humorous." He could feel his rancor rising. He had little sympathy for points of view that deviated from logic. "For crissake, no pun intended, some Christian fundamentalists can't even accept the idea of evolution ... as if that would be an affront to God's nature, that it would be beneath his godliness ... if we knew what that is ... to design the human race from a rational, scientific point of view. It all happened in seven days, and so on."

Silverstein continued his diatribe. "And if you think I'm only pointing a finger at the Christians, let me go on record to say that it's the religious right in all religions. Look at the grief the ultra-Orthodox Jews in Israel cause. Don't get me started."

Kipling appeared nonplussed and shook her head. "I've got to figure a way to bring you out of your shell, to know what you really think."

Silverstein smirked.

Kipling continued. "Remind me to bring up religion at our next holiday party. You could liven things up fast."

Silverstein laughed. *Holiday* party—it had come to that today, lest any non-Christian be offended by the term 'Christmas party.' Even his status as a card-carrying Jew hadn't prevented him from appreciating Christmas. The Christians beat out the Jews by a mile when it came to holiday music. And he missed their parties from the old days. They had had some good fun then. Their skit using helium to raise their voices in a rendition of the chipmunk song had been priceless.

"That's all right. I did my share when I dressed up as Santa Claus. I make enough trouble around here."

"You've got that right. I think that some of the white kids who watched your performance are just now getting out of therapy." Kipling winked. "But let's flesh this out further. Setting the religious aspect aside, the second thing I was going to say is scarier."

"Yeah, go on. What could be more frightening than the religious right?"

Kipling laughed. "Can you imagine what would happen if word of this got out, if the general public believed there were actual soothsayers out there?"

"Quite a few already believe it. Have you forgotten Psychic Hotline? But you bring up an interesting point. Remember what I said that Weaverman postulated, that this genetic aberration would arise only once every couple hundred million or so births?"

Silverstein turned to his computer, brought up Google, and typed: *How many people in the world?* A few more clicks of the mouse brought up some interesting figures.

"Listen to this, Linda. There's around six and a half billion people on the earth right now." He clicked some more. "At year one, when Christ was alive, estimates range from 170 million to 400 million people." He did some calculations in his head. "Using 200 million as a round number, this means that the population of the earth was only 3 percent of what it is now. Interesting, huh?"

Kipling broke out in a smile. "We've gotten too prolific, if you ask me."

Silverstein grinned. "Let's do some arithmetic. What would you say the average life span was back then?"

Kipling looked at the ceiling. "From my anthropology course, I seem to remember that life expectancy throughout most of history was around twenty. Of course, that doesn't mean that some people didn't live to be old. There was a high infant mortality rate."

"Doesn't matter. A birth is a birth. Let's assume a figure of twenty. That means, to sustain a population of 200 million, you'd need 200 million births every twenty years. Right? Extrapolating, that means a billion births every hundred years."

"Yeah. So using Weaverman's assumption means you would have five clairvoyants born every century. Assuming that half of them died young, you'd be left with two and a half. And back then, with the population so diffuse and with most people illiterate, you'd be lucky to have one that could cause enough commotion to be written up in history."

Silverstein leaned back in his chair and reflected. "One clairvoyant every hundred years. About the right number to cause a stir."

"Yeah, but remember the world's population has increased a lot since then, and so has our life span. Don't forget, even though my parents raised me in a Colorado commune and both sides of my family came from Germany, I grew up Roman Catholic. My religion has had more mystics and saints than you can shake a stick at."

"What's a mystic?"

"Ah, that's interesting in itself. The word *mystic* comes from a Greek root that means *mystery*. In Christianity, it refers to someone initiated into the mysteries of Christ's death and resurrection. Those who achieve that state are close to God and often acquire supernatural abilities: to conduct miracles, to heal people, to—"

Silverstein interrupted. "To look into the future?"

"Perhaps."

Silverstein's back straightened. "You can't beat us Jews when it comes to clairvoyants. We called them prophets, and the father of them all was Moses. If I remember right, there are fifty-some prophets in the Old Testament, the Scriptures, as we Jews see them. Maybe Weaverman's figure is too conservative."

Kipling turned serious. "This religious discussion is very interesting, but we ... you ... have a bigger problem. What do you propose to do now, about Weaverman?" She hesitated. "On the other hand, from the message he left you, he didn't ask for help. He just gave you information."

Silverstein tilted his head. "You really believe he wasn't asking for help?"

Kipling responded sheepishly. "Nooo."

"Okay, then."

"So the ball's in your court. What're you gonna do?"

"What would you say if I called Lopez?"

Kipling blinked. "Hector? Your friend in the CIA? And tell him what? That a potentially mad NRL scientist who might turn religion on its ear called you and is in some kind of trouble? That'll go over real big! The CIA isn't much interested in something unless it has international implications, right? Spying, espionage, that sort of thing. That's why Hector helped us two years ago with your Egyptian friend, Ghali ... who blew out the back of his head right in front of our eyes. Thanks for making me think of that again!" She let out a breath. "This problem is more in the FBI's line."

"Maybe, but I don't know anyone in the FBI. But ... there's one more thing that Weaverman told me, a necessary component to completing the proof of his theory ... a component that would give it an international spin ... and thus a reason to involve Lopez."

Kipling grimaced. "You pull this sort of thing on me all the time."

Silverstein thought about how to explain it, to reformulate Weaverman's words. "Do you understand how they relate genetic sequences to diseases and that sort of thing?"

"Not really. They must do some kind of matching."

"That's right."

"Tell me more."

Silverstein leaned across the desk with his hands folded. "In a nutshell, here is what I know. The genome is nothing more than a sequence of four letters: A, C, G, T; but there are billions of combinations."

"Stop! Start with something I've heard of, like a chromosome, okay?"

"Right! You remember Mendel, from the 1800s. He's the guy who grew the sweet peas and showed there was something to the idea of heredity, that there were *units of heredity* that got passed on from generation to generation. About a half century later, a biologist by the name of Hunt gave these units the name 'genes.' Hunt worked with the fruit fly and located these genes on chromosomes in the cell nucleus. This was sort of the official start to what we now call genetics."

Kipling spoke slowly. "These details are coming back to me. Remind me how this ties in with DNA."

"Well, as Weaverman explained it, chromosomes are mostly made up of DNA molecules that are coiled up to facilitate cell division. And genes are short, specific sections of these DNA molecules. Now, remember this term, 'base pair.' When Watson and Crick figured out the structure for DNA in 1953, what they showed was that each DNA molecule is composed of millions of base pairs. Genes are sequential sections of these base pairs. So, compared to the billions of base pairs, there are only thousands of genes, maybe twenty to twenty-five thousand, something in that range."

"How—"

Silverstein held up his hand. "Wait, one more point! When you determine the complete series of all the base pairs in an organism's DNA, you've mapped its genome and, by the way, every organism has its own unique genome. Bacteria and viruses have the simplest genomes, and so they were sequenced first. Getting back to your chromosome question, the forty-six chromosomes that we have are made up of about three billion base pairs."

"How do you relate disease to these genes? Do you understand that?"

Silverstein placed his hands flat on the desk. "Weaverman explained that what scientists are really after are the proteins produced by the genes. Apparently, proteins make up most of the human structural mass; they affect and control nearly everything going on at the cellular level. So, if biologists recognize that a gene sequence has somehow mutated from the normal, they can possibly control the disease at the cellular level by altering the protein that is expressed by the genes. 'Expressed,' that's another term the geneticists are fond of."

Kipling seemed to be getting bored. "Okay, okay. Back to my question. How do you relate a given gene sequence to a disease?"

"Weaverman talked about that at length, but the only way it made much sense to me was by doing a comparison. Let's say that, however they do it, they know that a certain protein correlates with cancer. They then look for a gene sequence which produces that protein. They can then compare that sequence between the cells of healthy and diseased people. If they see a difference in the gene sequences, a mutation has occurred. You could then design a test to detect that protein, to see if someone's susceptible, and maybe do something about it before the disease strikes."

Kipling pressed her hands to the sides of her head. "Before my brain explodes, let's bring all this back to Weaverman and his hypothesis. How could he possibly determine in the laboratory that a given gene sequence, or its proteins, relates to being a clairvoyant? Your comparison method won't work. It's not like we have DNA for a hundred clairvoyants lined up to compare to us normals."

"That's right, we don't. But what Weaverman did have was some data from mice."

"Mice, as in Mickey?"

Silverstein smiled. "If I were you, I wouldn't be so quick to put the big mouse down. It turns out, from a genome standpoint, that mouse and human genes are similar. Many of the gene sequences are the same."

"Yeah, keep going. Are you suggesting there are clairvoyant mice?"

"Linda, I've got to hand it to you. In essence, you're right. Weaverman said that he picked up on some research out of Russia. As often happens, the discovery was accidental. In the Russian experiments, they had mice running mazes, testing some drug they thought might improve memory. They noticed that one mouse always completed the course quicker than the others did, even when they kept changing the maze. That meant that the mouse knew ahead of time how to make his way through the turns."

"So how do you correlate that ability with a genetic change?"

"Good question. Apparently, there is a way to compare the proteins from different samples of tissue. In this case, all the mice had been bred identically and were of the same age. When they compared the expressed proteins, they isolated one particular gene sequence. When Weaverman read about this work, he extrapolated the results to the human genome. He recognized that gene sequence and went about looking for the same thing in human DNA." Silverstein paused. "Remember what I said, that many of the sequences in mice are the same as in humans. In all his comparisons, he found that this gene sequence was inactive, that no protein was expressed."

"Yeah. That protein may never appear in human DNA. The only way you could prove otherwise would be to test DNA from someone who supposedly had clairvoyant skills, and see if they expressed that protein."

Silverstein nodded. "That's what he said."

"Right! Just put an ad in any paper, and you'll get plenty of responses."

Silverstein laughed. "Actually, he considered that but also decided that he might not live long enough to find a match."

Kipling stood and began to pace. "Since no one's made the news recently that I've heard of, anyone fitting that description is long dead." She turned and smiled. "Is he suggesting a little grave-robbing is in order?"

"I don't know. I told him that if any digging needed doing, I was glad it was he, and not I, doing it." He hesitated. "He laughed hard when I said that."

CHAPTER 5

BLADE OF THE SINAI

Headquarters, Sphinx Petroleum, Cairo, Egypt
30°05'44"N latitude, 31°22'60"E longitude
Friday, 7:50 PM, July 24, 2009

Mohammed Abu Saada, strategist and interlocutor, fourth in command within the Blade of the Sinai's hierarchy, drummed his fingers on his huge desk. And a fine piece of furniture it was. The position of chief financial officer for Sphinx Petroleum had its perks.

"He's in captivity, been kidnapped, you say. Are you sure? And why?" Abu Saada needed to hear the words again; they made no sense. The Americans had somehow bumbled their way into this latest gambit by the Blade. Their foray was disturbing, and discouraging. And from what he understood, the Americans in the know consisted of only a few individuals.

Abu Saada's underling, Caliph Ishmael, a rising star within the organization's ranks, responded. "Yes. You know that our spy is reliable. Weaverman's out of the picture, but that's not important."

Abu Saada became impatient and strained to control any outward show of irritation. "Not important, you say?"

Ishmael responded. "We already know that Weaverman duplicated what our Russian comrades accomplished. They've isolated the gene sequence. The Russians are as surprised as we that the Americans caught on so quickly." Ishmael paused and smiled. "Knowing that the infidels are on to this has been a gift from Allah. May his name be praised."

Abu Saada, annoyed further by the naiveté of his younger compatriot, replied with cynicism. "It may have been a gift from Allah, but hardly one we would ask for. And now, this information about Weaverman. You may think it's not important, but I'm not so sure. How will they continue the genetic testing?"

Abu Saada looked across his desk into the face of a true believer, albeit a brilliant one. He himself had long since concluded that the Russians' original, state-defined concept of deity held more legitimacy than that of his own fellow citizens. After Gorbachev's embrace of détente and the collapse of the Soviet system, atheism was beginning to lose its hold on the Russian people. That was the problem with democracy. It gave citizens too much free time to ponder such nonsense.

Abu Saada accepted the sad fact that the Islamic zealots in the Middle East received their motivation from a religion not that different from Judaism or Christianity. If the devil was the antithesis of a peaceful God, and religion was the medium by which humankind praised their maker, Abu Saada had long ago concluded that the Supreme Being had inadvertently left open another point of entry for the devil's campaign—by way of the fanatics in the religious right of all religions.

"From what we understand, Weaverman's boss, a man named Rafferty, is completely capable of continuing the science. Besides, coming back to your earlier concern, I think you're taking too pessimistic a view of the Americans' involvement. It is true that up until now we thought we had the inside track on the Russian research …"

Abu Saada blanked out the rest of Ishmael's words and reflected on these surprising developments. The Blade of the Sinai, a shadowy organization that operated out of the mainstream, was always on the lookout for new technology that might prove useful for its purposes.

Because of the recent advancement of one of their own into the upper reaches of the U.S. government, they had known for weeks that the Americans had usurped their discovery of the rodent experiments out of Russia and that Weaverman had uncovered the genetic link. But why would they remove him from his work, the scientist who made the discovery? Such a report was troubling—and confusing. Were there competing factions within the American government? The American psyche could be every bit as baffling as that of the sword-wielding Arab.

The Blade had paid handsomely for the privilege of being alone (until now) in knowing that an exceedingly rare human gene sequence could be responsible for endowing someone with psychic powers. Of course, Abu Saada knew that accepting such a premise could make a mockery of organized religion, especially Islam. Ishmael had already rationalized that paradox by assuming that the prophet Mohammed had powers far beyond what a simple gene sequence—even if the Russians' theory turned out to be true—could bestow upon humankind. Abu Saada wasn't so sure that other Muslims would accept that sort of thinking. Besides, Allah himself had sent Mohammed to this earth, Ishmael would say. He tended to spin data to his liking—a skill the Americans had turned into a fine art.

"… and so maybe I will yet have my revenge on the infidels who took my brothers. If I get the chance, I'll kill that black Jew with my own hands." Ishmael leaned back in Abu Saada's expensive recliner and seemed pleased with his arguments.

Abu Saada's head jerked upward. "Your words are blasphemous, Caliph! You must forgo your hatred, or it will destroy you. Remember that your brothers lost their lives through negligence, not by anyone's hand. Revenge is not our objective, Caliph. Our goals are righteous; we are honorable men."

Ishmael's back stiffened. "You've said that for years. I suppose that our operation to sink Washington, DC, with a monster hurricane two years ago was honorable in your mind?"

The creases on Abu Saada's forehead deepened, and his breathing quickened. "You know better than that! That was an unfortunate situation. We had no choice." He held out his hands. "The Blade pays for research that we feel can give us leverage in solving the Middle East's problems. We don't go around with bombs strapped to our backs like Hamas or Hezbollah."

Abu Saada understood Ishmael's hatred and realized that he himself might feel the same if he walked in his shoes. Their operation in 2007, using the brilliant hypothesis of the American, Cameron Fitzby, to grow and steer a hurricane using a laser from space, had proven to be a costly disaster. When they determined that the Russian satellite would lose its strength after just one hurricane season, the Blade's hierarchy reluctantly decided to deviate from their original, more measured, plan.

Every organization had its hawks, and the Blade proved no exception. In contrast to the common practice in Western corporations, the hundred million dollars they had spent could not be written off. They had to have something to show for it. And they had come so close, so very close. Had it not been for the black Jew from America, Victor Silverstein, a navy scientist, they would have succeeded. Abu Saada had learned these details from the Russians who had operated the laser during those final hours.

Not only had they lost monetary resources, but four of the Blade's faithful had given their lives to the operation, one by his own hand. A second had disappeared but was presumed dead. The other two, the Ishmael twins, had been Caliph's brothers.

The suicide had been the hardest for Abu Saada to accept: his best friend, Ghali, a fellow Egyptian. In battle, years earlier, Ghali had saved Abu Saada's life. Abu Saada regretted that he would never have the opportunity to repay that debt.

In retrospect, Abu Saada should have seen it coming. During the final weeks of the operation, when the Blade had authorized the Washington target, Ghali had confided to him that he had serious reservations. Nonetheless, he would do his duty. The Russians later reported that Ghali had killed himself. Abu Saada personally interviewed one of the Russians who, while employed by Fitzby, had never let on that he spoke English. He relayed the final moments when Silverstein diverted the hurricane. And for some reason that still confounded Abu Saada, the Americans had never gloated over their successful interdiction. Their press had remained silent.

Abu Saada forced his mind to the present; the past held too much sorrow and failure. Although he hadn't been listening closely, several of Ishmael's words resonated in Abu Saada's consciousness after the fact. "My mind went blank a minute ago, and I missed something you said. Repeat what you just said about the Americans."

Appearing to regret his temporary burst of vehemence, Ishmael reacted deferentially to his superior. "I went on for some time. What part are you referring to?"

"The part about an existing psychic."

Ishmael relaxed his posture and softened his words. "Yes, I remember. The reason it's an advantage for the Americans to be involved is that they have more resources than we do."

"Go on."

"Even if it is technically possible, it'll be some time before we or the Americans figure out a way to create the gene sequence artificially. Long before that, we may discover someone who has acquired that quality naturally. And the more people looking, the better."

Abu Saada realized why Ishmael remained optimistic while he felt despair.

Ishmael completed his thought. "We've never before had someone in such a favorable position to feed us information." He paused and grinned. "Just because the Americans happen to be the first to find such an individual doesn't mean they'll be the first to take advantage of him."

CHAPTER 6

SNAPPED

Downtown Johnstown, Pennsylvania, USA
40° 19'41"N latitude, 78° 55'18"W longitude
Monday, 11:55 AM, July 27, 2009

Fred Cannon labored along the perimeter of an excavation one story below street level. Their noon break couldn't come soon enough. Sweat bathed his body. The carved-out hollow where he and his coworkers toiled made Pennsylvania's summertime heat feel all the worse. What little breeze nature provided had no chance of making its way into the pit. He had nearly completed his part of the project, digging trenches for the new building for which Goliath Construction had made the winning bid. They would begin pouring concrete into the pilings in a few days.

Cannon blinked the sweat from his eyes and squinted to bring an unexpected image into focus. He abruptly let up on the controls to his backhoe. He looked ahead, straining to identify what had revealed itself with his last extraction of dirt. He stepped down from his tractor, walked over, removed his sunglasses, and crouched to get a better look. He dug with his hands around what appeared to be a metal box, rusted and now scratched from the last pass of his scoop.

Cannon yelled over his right shoulder to his supervisor, bent over his construction plans. "Herb, take a look at this!"

Herb Smith, construction supervisor, noted that Cannon had stopped work. He set his plans aside and stepped over to join him.

"What's going on?" Smith crouched next to Cannon.

"You tell me." Cannon pried it from the ground. "It's heavy." He rubbed his gloved hands across the box's sides to clear the dirt.

Smith got down on his knees, wiped away the remaining dirt, and scanned the outside of the box. "There's nothing much left to identify it. Mostly rust. Wait! Look at the indentations here. This side looks like a door of sorts." He pointed. "Here's what's left of a keyhole. This is a safe, a strongbox." Smith rubbed his hands together and stood.

Cannon took off his hard hat and ran his fingers through his hair. "God knows how long it's been here." He glanced over at Smith. "The building they just demolished here—how old was it?"

"The cornerstone was set in 1932. This box is at least that old, probably older. It makes no sense that a safe would have been lost during the construction of a building. It must have been hidden under dirt that they never excavated."

Cannon took off his work gloves, stored them under his left armpit, and glanced about the site. "We've been digging far beneath the original foundation."

Smith brought his hand to his mouth. "You don't suppose, do you …"

"Suppose what, Herb?"

"You know the history of this place, right?"

"What history? I've been here six weeks."

Smith shifted his weight from one foot to the other. "I grew up not far from here, so I learned about it in high school. You and Marilyn need to take a visit to the Flood Memorial, about ten miles northwest of town, off 219. The Park Service did a good job, fantastic movie. You can get a flavor of what happened here."

"Flood? What flood?"

"One of the worst environmental disasters in U.S. history happened right here, back in 1889. Biggest thing in the nineteenth century after Lincoln's assassination." Smith turned and pointed to the north. "A dam let go and killed more than 2,200 people. A sportsmen's dam, owned by the

Pittsburgh elite. Caused quite a scandal. Town was wiped clean. Catastrophic devastation."

"Twenty-two hundred people?"

"Where we're standing right now was smack dab in the center of it all. It's altogether possible this safe has been here since the flood." Smith looked around the site. "Look how far down we've dug below street level. They never went this deep during construction back then."

"What should we do with it?"

"I'll make a call to the Memorial. I'll bet you they'll be interested."

Cannon knelt and flipped the box so that the apparent lid faced upward. He looked closely. He jumped up and ran back to his rig, returning with a wire brush. He used his fingers to remove more dirt from what looked like a keyhole and then gently applied the bristles to the same area. Slowly, a few layers of rust flaked off, and he could make out more detail.

"What is it, Fred?"

Cannon looked up. "Take a look for yourself."

Smith stooped over the box and stared downward. "What are you looking at?"

"Look carefully at the keyhole. That isn't just rust covering the hole. That's a piece of metal sticking out. I'll give you odds that's what's left of a key that broke off."

Smith extended both hands, palms up. "That makes no sense. Why would anyone leave a key in a safe ... unless they had no time to remove it?"

Cannon replaced his hard hat. "My thoughts exactly."

CHAPTER 7

AUGUSTA'S LEGACY

Johnstown Flood National Memorial, South Fork, Pennsylvania, USA
40°20'59"N latitude, 78°46'17"W longitude
Tuesday, 2:00 AM, July 28, 2009

Peggy Sue Houston stared at the two handwritten pages and read the words yet again. The envelope and paper were old and delicate but undamaged. Remarkably, the glass bottle—the only solid object inside the safe—that contained the letter was unbroken and the cork intact. The handwriting was in an old-style cursive, meticulous, refined, not something you'd see these days. Her eyes followed her index finger as it moved down the ledger of the flood dead. The initial discrepancy Houston had noticed was probably just an oversight, a typo. It was easy enough to forget the last letter on a name.

Was this a hoax? Had she become prey to some magician's trick? Was Mr. Smith, the man who had transported the strongbox to her office, part of that hoax? No, he didn't seem the sort. Houston peeked at the clock on the wall and couldn't believe the time. She lowered her head to the workbench and adjusted her sitting position to avoid the bruise. Although she was mentally and physically exhausted from the previous evening's activities, sleep wouldn't come. With her mind fully alert and cascading between alternate theories, the day's events marched through her mind like the parade that had occurred the day before the letter was supposedly written.

*   *   *   *

It had been about one in the afternoon on Monday when she received the call. A construction supervisor in downtown Johnstown reported finding what appeared to be a safe in the excavation pit for a new building. Not that it was that unusual for bits and pieces from the flood to appear now and again, even though it had been well over a century since the disaster. That said, Houston couldn't remember anything of substance discovered in the twenty years since the visitor center opened, when she had taken on the position of curator.

Mr. Smith offered to deliver it himself later that afternoon, once they raised it by crane from the trench where a backhoe operator had discovered it, far below street level. The excitement of a new discovery took hold and made the afternoon wait a long one.

Houston stood by the lower-level entrance to the building that visitors knew; it included the movie theater and various flood displays. Inside the door, a room that housed the heating system also served as space for her role as curator. From their earlier conversation, she knew that the metal container measured about twenty inches square and was heavy. Houston watched as Smith and another worker carried the dirty, beat-up box to her workbench. They seemed honest enough.

Her first task was to identify exactly what now sat in front of her. It was probably a safe, heavy, with what appeared to be a door with two hinges on one side. Although dents and scratches marred the sides, the container had no holes and was intact. Depending on how tightly the door fit, the contents might have escaped damage. Moisture and time had erased any exterior markings that existed when the box was new. Still, there were indications that the original color was black.

Mr. Smith had positioned the box on the workbench with the door facing up. She inspected the perimeter and wondered whether the door would open if she could unlock the lock. Although dirt and rust filled the grooves between the door and frame, such deterioration might not prevent her from opening the door.

Mr. Smith had pointed out what looked like a broken key still in the keyhole. Houston checked the time. All her staff had departed for the day, and it was probably too late to call a locksmith. Even so, what would she have him do? She reached to the rear wall to retrieve an old crowbar, noted its heft, and set it aside. If she could somehow disengage the lock, the crowbar would be her next tool of choice.

Houston took a screwdriver and ran it along the sides of the door, tearing away at the rust and deterioration. She placed a canister vacuum on the workbench and sucked out the remnants as she scraped. The soil and a century's worth of metallic decay came away surprisingly easily. By the time she reached the area next to the lock, she ran into something solid. It was the bolt from the lock. No sophisticated locking mechanism here: a simple deadbolt. That answers that question, Houston thought. *No point in using the crowbar quite yet.*

Having been a tomboy as a child and her mechanic-father's helper, Houston knew a thing or two about mechanical devices. First, she brushed away as much rust as possible from the stub of the key that remained. She wiggled it with her fingers but felt no give. She then reached for a can of Liquid Wrench, a penetrating oil her father had often used to free up rusted bolts and nuts. She squeezed a few drops into the void around the key and watched the liquid seep away. She repeated the procedure two more times. Before setting the can aside, she allowed a few drops to settle upon the bolt she had revealed and the hinges.

While she waited for the fluid to do its job, she inspected what was left of the key. It was tempting indeed to take a pair of pliers, grasp the key, and twist back and forth until she opened the lock. There was a big downside, however. Because the strength of the metal might have degraded with time, her only reward might be for it to twist off in her hands.

From the shape of the shank, Houston deduced that the key rested vertically within its hole. This meant that the smart course of action was to first pull it straight out. It might still break off, but the chances were less so than from a sideways action. If this tactic proved successful, she would clean the key, lubricate the keyhole, reinsert the key, and carefully twist until she sensed movement.

Houston waited another ten minutes. She poked gently at the stub of the key with her pliers and was pleased to note that it seemed solid. Then she took her pliers and clamped down over the stump, allowing as much of it as possible to contact the grooved sides of the pliers, anchored her elbows to the safe for stability, and lifted vertically in a direction perpendicular to the opening. No luck. Houston released her pliers and examined the results of her effort, relieved to see that the metal remained intact. It was now a question of applying more force, and to do that she needed to rotate the safe to a position with the door facing her. She leaned against the front of the safe, grabbed the back edge, rotated it toward her, and let it settle back to the workbench. So far, so good.

Houston opened a drawer and fumbled around for a replacement for the pliers. In the back, she found what she needed. *Always keep a Vise Grip available in your toolbox*, her father had coached. *That together with duct tape will serve you well.*

Thinking that the key shaft was strong enough to handle the heavier tool, she carefully adjusted the opening down to a smaller size. She squeezed. Nope, too big. She turned the screw adjustment one more turn. She squeezed again, this time harder, and heard the audible snap that meant she had good contact. She pulled gently at first, to confirm that the grip held tight. She pulled harder, but the key still did not budge. The strength in her one arm was not enough.

Houston wiped at the sweat now gathering on her forehead. The room had too little ventilation. She grabbed a two-foot length of two-by-four and nailed it securely to the front edge of the workbench, creating a lip so that the safe would not slide off.

This time she grabbed the tool with both hands, still being careful to pull straight. With her left foot set back to provide stability, she pulled harder. Still nothing. The next step was to lift her right foot to rest against the first of two storage shelves beneath the workbench. With this position providing additional advantage, she tried again. Still no give.

In a final effort to provide optimum leverage, she raised her right foot still higher, to the second shelf. Other than placing both feet on that shelf, this was the best she could do. But knowing that she didn't have the patience to wait until morning, Houston pulled with all her strength. When the key finally let loose, her left leg had forgotten its job of maintaining stability and contributed to the force transferred through her stretched-out arms. Houston shot backwards, flying across the small room, and landed on her butt.

Even before she hit the ground, and before the pain from the hard fall reached her brain, she turned the Vise Grip in midair and stared. The key remained intact.

*   *   *   *

Houston stirred in her sleep. The pain in her hip shot upward through her back. Damn! The gunman had gotten the drop on her and fired his weapon in her direction. She ducked around the corner of the tavern and winced from the pain, hoping he hadn't hit anything vital. At once, confused, she heard an airplane and glanced upward. There were no aircraft back in the 1800s! As happened often, her action-oriented dream evaporated into the mist of semiconsciousness. She had heard the furnace fan kick on.

Houston sat up straight and focused on the clock, surprised to see the hour hand creeping past five. She reached to her rear to rub her bruise, winced, and remembered the successful conclusion to her earlier task of opening the safe. The soreness woke her to reality and to the mystery of the missive lying in front of her.

She read it yet again:

> *Thursday midnight*
> *May 30, 1889*
> *Johnstown, Pennsylvania*
>   *My name is Augusta Schmidt, and I am nineteen years old. I live on*
> *Jackson Street with my parents, Heinrich and Frieda Schmidt, along with*
> *my eighteen-year-old sister, Annabel, and my fourteen-year-old brother,*

Thompson. Papa is a supervisor at the Cambria Iron Company, and I work with him there on occasion. I have an older half brother, William, who lives in town and is Papa's son, too. His mother died giving birth. He works full time with Papa at Cambria Iron.

If you find this letter—no doubt days or weeks from now—you discovered it in the safe of the Trinity Lutheran Church where Papa is an elder. More importantly, as you read this, my family and I are surely dead, the result of a terrible flood that will destroy our town tomorrow afternoon.

Today I tried to think of some way of tricking my family into leaving town but could think of nothing that would achieve a satisfactory result. I could have told them the truth—what I knew would happen—but they wouldn't have believed me. And besides, I would have had to warn the entire town.

I considered saving myself alone. Tomorrow I could walk across town, climb up the side of the hill, and watch the flood play out in front of me. But Papa always tells me that we must place ourselves in God's hands. For that reason, tomorrow afternoon I will walk to our church and make one final plea to our Lord and Savior. My curses, both of them, make me a freak of nature. I know that I will not be going to heaven. I want to die along with my family. Once my family has left this world, I would not want to live anyway.

The reason I know about the flood is that I have a curse, an ability to see the future. In my lifetime, I have had many visions. The ones that I could verify have all come true. Most of the time I can't predict when my visions will actually play out. But right now, I see the destruction of our town tomorrow.

I once asked our minister in Sunday school if there were people who could predict the future. He said that if there were such a person, he or she was possessed by the devil and would go to hell, as surely as the Lord Jesus Christ stood at the gates of heaven. Knowing that my soul is doomed to an eternity of fire and brimstone, and realizing that if I told my parents they would have driven me from the house, I never brought up the subject again. Rather than take my secret to the grave, I am writing this letter. Because my family will be dead, I can take some comfort in knowing they will avoid the shame of a child condemned to hell.

I see many things in my mind's eye. I see many graves, mine among them, high on a hill above the town, and the town rebuilding itself. I see our country involved in large wars that will kill many. In one of these wars, I see a cloud shaped like a mushroom, and it suffocates everyone and everything in sight.

Sometimes I believe that the things I see are only the product of a vivid imagination. Colored, moving pictures that appear on windows, boxes that talk, and large silver birds that are big enough to carry people. Far into the future, I see two of these birds flying into the Towers of Babel, which fall and kill many people. Most of what I see is so scary that I pray it never comes to pass.

Beyond the silver birds, I see many things I cannot understand. But as consolation for my isolation at this moment in my life, I take comfort in seeing someone, far in the future, searching for me, hoping to find me, thinking that I am someone special. I see him standing at my grave. From what I can make out, he may be the devil, having come to claim his due. With this letter and bottle, I open my soul to the future, leaving a part of myself for posterity. The devil will know what he sees.

Any other relatives that I have are in Germany, far away. I have no other family here, so you needn't look.

I ask only that whoever finds this letter takes a moment to pray for my soul, because I am among the damned.

In Christ's name, I sign this letter in the name I cherish as my own, Augusta Schmidt.

The fluorescent lights buzzed above her head. Houston rested her face in her hands and drew in air warmed by her skin. The mystery of what lay in front of her burned in her mind. She reached for her ledger and scanned once again the names of those lost from the flood.

No! It was unlikely that this correspondence represented a trick or forgery—because one name from Augusta's letter did not appear on that list. For whatever reason, that person survived the flood. Unless the perpetrator of this letter was a descendant of the Schmidt family, it could not be a hoax. No one else would have known that Augusta Schmidt had a half brother named William.

CHAPTER 8

WHEELS IN MOTION

Russell Senate Office Building, Washington, DC, USA
38° 53'32"N latitude, 77° 00'28"W longitude
Tuesday, 7:00 PM, July 28, 2009

"I'll see you in my office then, in twenty minutes. Don't keep me waiting."
Clifton MacDonald returned the phone to its cradle, stood, and stretched
the kinks from his six-foot-five frame.

His staff had gone home for the night. Senator Clifton Ashton Mac-
Donald paced the floor, contemplating his strategy and trying to predict
the outcomes of the wheels he had set in motion, not the least important
of which was the kidnapping of a prominent scientist in the government's
employ. It was unfortunate that so many players were part of his plan, but
he needed the cash. Clandestine actions, especially ones requiring scientific
technology, didn't come cheap. He might even have to ask his investors
for a second installment, a sum they would balk at, but would pay nonetheless.

MacDonald, forty-nine years of age, divorced, grandson of one of Wyoming's original nineteenth-century land barons, had learned from his
father early on that you never accepted risk without insurance. The indem-
nity he carried on each of his investors was knowledge, scraps of information he had garnered over many years in office, consigned to his private
stash of collateral, waiting for a day when these tidbits might prove useful.

Anyone in a position of power such as his would eventually stumble across such secrets. Some had been random discoveries; more often than not, they came about from deals consummated, favors rendered, and occasionally, need (theirs, not his). Such specifics, if released publicly, would cause serious harm to the individuals involved and were so sensitive that MacDonald knew he had each of them securely by the balls.

All except one, that is: Samantha Thurston. He wasn't as certain as with the others that grabbing her in such a sensitive part of the human anatomy would have the desired effect—even if she'd had the appropriate genitalia. In Thurston's case, he knew of her sexual dalliances with various high-ranking government officials, whose reputations would go into free fall if word leaked. Of some concern was his sense that Thurston would not react as expected if threatened with the release of such information. Control was everything to MacDonald, and he wasn't about to share it with some conniving bitch who had usurped her husband's power after his untimely death. He cursed himself for also falling for her feminine charms. He wasn't about to let that happen again.

Although unfortunate (because MacDonald did admire the man), Maxwell Thurston's death did have its benefits. Having been privy to the same information as MacDonald, Thurston had a different take on the use, or exploitation, of biologist Weaverman's results—as relayed through Weaverman's supervisor, Rafferty.

Poor Maxwell, bogged down with puritanical ethics that bordered on the absurd, had no appreciation for the serendipity of their private discovery and the potential, monetary and otherwise, of their find, if nurtured and controlled in the proper manner. MacDonald had to admit it was also possible that nothing would come of their efforts. Why should taxpayers shoulder the expense of a project that might come to naught? Even more reason to fund the research privately. Alternatively, if their efforts did prove fruitful, they alone should reap the rewards.

Although MacDonald worried about Thurston's wife for other reasons, she had none of the ethical hang-ups of her husband. That such a dichotomy of characters had ever married in the first place was remarkable, he thought.

A solid knock across the room drew MacDonald's attention. He pulled open the door to look into the repulsive face of Rafferty, another of the necessary evils MacDonald had to endure. "Come on in, Dennis."

MacDonald waved Rafferty into a side chair and continued to his own behind the desk. When he looked back and caught Rafferty's eye, his appearance hadn't changed. Rafferty was butt-ugly and someone with little sense of personal hygiene: overweight, with belly fat protruding through a missing shirt button (sans T-shirt) beneath an unbuttoned blue blazer that had long since passed its prime; greasy hair that outlined beady, cold eyes and a square face; and large ears that stood out in mock opposition to his smallish facial features. These physical attributes did nothing to complement the intellect housed within his skull. Rafferty reacted as if he had seen MacDonald's stare a thousand times.

Beyond his physical appearance, Rafferty had another annoying characteristic. As if his maker had had an especially bad day when he created Rafferty, he gave him a further unusual attribute, an aural one. Rafferty had the most unusual high-pitched sneeze, similar to that of a woman but higher still on the decibel level. When it came—and fortunately for those around him, he gave ample warning (as the blast usually didn't let loose until the third or fourth inhale)—those in the know either turned away or, sometimes, discreetly put their fingers in their ears. MacDonald saw one coming and rotated 180 degrees away from the discharge.

After the resounding echo dissipated, MacDonald turned back. "What's the latest? Have you made sense of Weaverman's work?" He held Rafferty's eyes in check.

Rafferty fidgeted, his fat belly resonating in sync with his jittery movements. "I'll get to that directly … but you should know that people are asking about Weaverman. I don't know how long I can hold them off." His eyes drew down to smaller slits. "Is Weaverman dead? If so, it might be useful for his body to show up somewhere. That would take the heat off me."

MacDonald stared across his desk, appreciating the fact that the son of a bitch *did* have the stomach for what might lie ahead. "You're forgetting that I need to keep track of the bigger picture here." He shook his head.

"No, he's not dead! He's our only backup if you can't pull off your part of the bargain."

Rafferty sniffed. "He should be. But you needn't worry. I'll keep up my end."

"Where do we go from here?"

MacDonald recalled that Rafferty kept insisting that he needed DNA from a recognized clairvoyant. Even then, the combined sum of their data might not satisfy the reviewers of a scientific journal, he said. No matter. They did not intend to publish these results.

MacDonald smiled inwardly at the thought of searching for a clairvoyant. Until five months ago when Rafferty had first detailed Weaverman's supposition, MacDonald had been a card-carrying follower of the Amazing Randi, the magician turned cynic who made a profession out of debunking the supernatural. In fact, no one had yet laid claim to his offer of one million dollars to anyone who could demonstrate in a laboratory setting (designed and administered by Randi to prevent cheating) the ability to divine random symbols on a hidden display.

To MacDonald, all talk of the paranormal had been bunkum. A sophisticated, learned individual like himself didn't fall prey to such nonsense. That Rafferty and Weaverman could convince him otherwise amazed him. The mouse results out of Russia, together with Weaverman's assertion that the genetic anomaly was so rare that it occurred only once in every couple hundred million births, had grabbed his attention and excited him like nothing had in decades.

"I've validated Weaverman's data," Rafferty responded to MacDonald's question. "I've checked his computations. All we need is a human genetic sequence that matches the one from the mouse. Once we have that—"

MacDonald cut him off. "Tell me again. Why can't we just skip that part and go right to the step where we genetically alter that sequence in a human?"

Rafferty's face contorted. "I've told you before. Although the human sequence is similar to that of the mouse, it's not quite the same." He paused. "We're moving into unfamiliar territory here. We need to test someone who claims to be clairvoyant. Considering how rare this sequence is, I can make the case that if we discover one individual who's clairvoyant … and then, if his or her DNA matches that of the mouse, that would be something we could take to the bank."

Rafferty's logic had begun to gel in MacDonald's mind. "Okay. You've convinced me. Earlier, you suggested we limit ourselves to Catholic saints."

Rafferty folded his hands across his protruding stomach, noticing that he was missing a button. "We'd be better off with prophets who, almost by definition, could see the future. Unfortunately, prophets haven't been around for a while. Since I'm Catholic, I know there are a lot more saints that are recent. That said, the miracles attributed to saints don't always include clairvoyance. Still, some claimed to have prophetic visions. St. Patrick comes to mind."

Rafferty paused, perhaps to form his next sequence of words. "It won't be easy. But that comes down, ultimately, to whether there's anything left from which we can sample the DNA. Our techniques are so sophisticated these days that we can extract it from almost anything even remotely biologically intact. It wasn't that long ago that you needed the root ball from a hair to extract DNA. Today, a snip of hair gives us almost as much. But after a couple of centuries in the ground, there may be nothing left to sample, period."

MacDonald decided he had heard enough and stood. "Well then, I suggest you get on with it."

Rafferty remained seated, either ignoring or not picking up on MacDonald's cue that their conversation had ended. "And how do you want me to handle Weaverman's absence? Last Friday and again today, I received a call from a Victor Silverstein. He's an NRL employee too, out in California. Says he's an old friend of Weaverman's. I don't think I handled his questions very well, and I think he's suspicious."

Choosing a more obvious way to make his point, MacDonald walked to the door, opened it, and waited for Rafferty to respond. "Stonewall him, don't take his calls … I don't *care*. You figure it out. We have enough to keep us busy right here in Washington. Someone three thousand miles away is hardly a concern to us."

Rafferty gave no indication that he wanted to leave. He looked up and caught MacDonald's eye. "I beg to differ. Silverstein is either big trouble ... *or* the answer to our prayers."

CHAPTER 9

MOUNTAIN TO MOHAMMED

Naval Research Laboratory, Monterey, California, USA
36°35'34"N latitude, 121°51'17"W longitude
Wednesday, 9:05 AM, July 29, 2009

Silverstein was sitting at his desk, long-faced, dead tired, hands folded in front of him, when Kipling strolled in. He looked up, knowing that his bloodshot eyes and apparent lethargy gave away the fact that he hadn't slept well. "Good morning."

Kipling appeared to commiserate but then responded to the contrary. "You look worse than what the cat outside was dragging around this morning."

He winced. "Thanks, I needed that."

"Any more thoughts on what to do about Weaverman?"

"I've been losing sleep trying to figure out how to proceed, looking for a tree I could shake. And then, yesterday afternoon, through serendipity, an opportunity presented itself, and I seized it." He touched his wrists together and leaned his chin between them for support. "I've stirred the pot and expect it to start boiling any time now."

Kipling pulled up a chair, sitting backwards as usual. "What happened?"

"I called Rafferty again. I wanted to yank his chain ... unearth *something* that would tell me what to do next, to help Weaverman."

"Yeah. What did you say?"

Silverstein stood, locked his hands behind his head and stretched, making cracking noises with his fingers. "He apparently remembered my tricking him during our earlier conversation and said nothing … at first. I asked him if he'd heard *anything* because it was imperative—I used that word—that I talk to Weaverman. He said he'd heard nothing more. Then he made his second mistake."

Kipling laughed. "What did you pull on him this time?"

Silverstein sat down. "You know me too well. Rafferty asked why I needed to talk to Weaverman. Sooo … because I know things he doesn't know I know, I decided to rattle his cage."

Kipling's mouth dropped open. "You didn't?"

Silverstein opened his mouth to speak.

Kipling held up both hands as if she were stopping traffic. "Wait, don't tell me! Let me think. What's the most incendiary thing you could say?" She stared back hard. "I know how you think."

Silverstein folded his arms in front of him and waited. He never ceased to be amazed at the way she seemed to see right through him.

Kipling stood, paced back and forth twice, plopped herself down again, put her right hand to her forehead, and did a respectable imitation of Carnac, Johnny Carson's psychic character who could divine answers to questions hidden inside an envelope. "Here's what you said, more or less. 'Weaverman brought me in on his project months ago, asking for our help here in Monterey. He told me to call him the instant I received the samples. Well, I've got them.'"

Silverstein responded open-mouthed. "Kipling, you astound me. That's pretty damn close." *How does she figure these things out?* "In response to my question, Rafferty paused, his second mistake. This guy may be a brilliant scientist, but he's not one to think on his feet."

Kipling interrupted and smiled. "I bet he's ugly, too."

Silverstein ignored her comment. "The pause meant that he knew what Weaverman was working on; otherwise he would have responded immediately. Guess what he asked me to do? And Linda, I swear to God it sounded like he was hyperventilating. He tells me to mail the samples, and he'll make sure Weaverman gets them."

Kipling beamed. "So what did you say then?"

"I told him that's impossible, that it would be too risky, considering their value to the project, and that Weaverman said he would fly out and pick them up personally."

Kipling laughed like a kid. "You *fox*. What did he say then?"

"He said he'd make sure to tell Weaverman when he got back."

Kipling, still grinning, leaned back with her hands grasping the bottom of the chair. "I've got to hand it to you. He now thinks that you have the DNA samples that would prove Weaverman's hypothesis. Remember what you told me Weaverman said: 'I haven't proven it yet, but I'm making headway.' If Rafferty is connected to Weaverman's disappearance, no doubt he'd want that same proof."

Kipling turned serious, apparently realizing there was little humor in this from Silverstein's point of view. She backpedaled. "Your problem is solved. You can get some sleep now. If Mohammed can't go to the mountain, let the mountain come to Mohammed. When you jerked Rafferty's chain you put us smack dab in the middle of this mystery. How long do you think it will be before the phone rings, and you look down to see that the origin is Washington, DC?"

Silverstein capitulated. "What did you mean when you said *us?* Weaverman means nothing to you."

Kipling smirked. "After the trouble you got us into two years ago, do you think I'd let you tangle with malcontents all by yourself?"

Silverstein stared back approvingly. "That's what I hoped you'd say."

With that comment, he turned his head to the electronic warble behind him and stared at the caller ID. The 202 area code wasn't that unusual; Silverstein often received calls from NRL headquarters in Washington. But Silverstein had seen the remaining seven digits less than twenty-four hours earlier.

He stared up at Kipling. "Bingo."

CHAPTER 10

FOREBODING

Detention apartment, Wisconsin Avenue NW, Washington, DC, USA
38° 54'14"N latitude, 77° 03'45"W longitude
Wednesday, 12:15 PM, July 29, 2009

It had been a week since his capture, and Weaverman was bored out of his mind. Although his accommodations were acceptable, nothing could change the fact that he was being held against his will. House arrest was too generous a term. He had a window that allowed some exterior light but no view, only the bricks of an adjoining building. No television, no radio. His jailer had finally granted his request for some newspapers and magazines. Was anyone looking for him? His only real hope lay with his friend Victor Silverstein.

Weaverman mused to himself. If he could wave his magic wand—go back and conclude that, in fact, there was no such thing as a special gene tied to clairvoyance—would he do it? The answer to that question would be *no*. From a scientist's viewpoint, a discovery of this magnitude was so rare that it made winning the lottery seem like child's play. He was damn proud!

Weaverman alone had made the discovery—not the likes of the HGP and Celera. They were interested in genetic gold mines, solutions to human conditions for which people would pay a fortune. Human frailties represented the reason why those companies had received such mammoth funding, and why drug companies lay in wait, like vultures, to develop—and patent, if the courts allowed—their chemical miracles. Everyone wanted to live forever, to discover that magic cocktail of gene-expressed proteins that could conquer the physical maladies of humankind. It was all well and good to spend huge resources on such cures, assuming that one could ignore the six million children who failed to reach the age of five every year due to lack of basic medical care.

After an altogether different initial premise, a fortuitous siren had beckoned Weaverman down a strange detour, searching for a human quality that no respected scientist would dare suggest existed, a characteristic that humanity had witnessed, or at least suspected, since the beginning of time. Dr. James Peter Weaverman, PhD, discovered the link that no one had considered. And now his superiors, or more likely their superiors, higher still on the bureaucratic food chain, wanted to silence him. All research under the auspices of the Department of Defense was eyed with a military bent, to provide an edge over the enemy. He shuddered at the thought. His findings had ramifications that staggered the imagination.

That Weaverman had been given the green light to conduct his study at all was remarkable. He had made his presentation to the RAC, the Research Advisory Committee of NRL, for a *new start*, a new line of research that normally lasted up to three years. His proposal to piggyback on the Genome project had taken everyone by surprise.

NRL had minimal interest in medicine or disease. To make his case, he had underscored the obvious: that the military could ill afford to inoculate its soldiers with vaccines that later proved dangerous. The drug cocktail that the military had administered before Gulf War One in the early 1990s had proved a disquieting example. The jury was still out on the possible harm caused by the vaccine, with veterans groups continuing to contest the study results. Weaverman had made a convincing argument that gene mutations initiated by the drugs used in the inoculations could be determined beforehand. It wasn't until the second year of this research that an unexpected spin-off became evident.

Now Weaverman's only hope to bring his discovery to light—and get himself rescued—was his friend Victor Silverstein, a weatherman. Back in the early 1970s, there had been a good reason for Weaverman's interest in weather. Dreading the thought of dying in Vietnam, he had enlisted in the Air National Guard. After basic training at Lackland Air Force Base in Texas, where he had expressed some interest in weather, they shipped him off to Chanute Air Force Base in Illinois. Remarkably, the military saw no use for his distinguished degrees in biology.

At Chanute, they taught him the basics of weather observing and forecasting. Because he had grown to enjoy the monthly outings, he continued his affiliation after his six-year stint had run its course in 1978. Now a lieutenant colonel, he had many friends in the Guard and in meteorology. Silverstein was one of them.

Weaverman flinched at the sound of the key in the door. Had they finally gotten tired of providing him room and board? Had they concluded that he would be better off dead? Those thoughts entered his mind every time he heard the turn of the key.

Weaverman looked up to the sight of his midday meal. He could count on at least one more day among the living, he figured.

CHAPTER 11

ESCALATION

Watergate Hotel, Washington, DC, USA
38°53'57"N latitude, 77°3'22"W longitude
Wednesday, 8:00 PM, July 29, 2009

Senator Clifton MacDonald took a sip from his second glass, the alcohol speeding its way through his empty stomach. He did his best to ignore the pale skin that grew ever darker as it descended into the shadows of the plunging neckline seated across from him. He had trouble concentrating and tried to get his mind back on track, focusing on Thurston's extraordinary suggestion just moments earlier. As if the previous night's meeting with Rafferty hadn't given him enough to worry about, her recommendation only seconds into their meal provided additional unease.

He had met with Thurston only twice before. Their last meeting had been memorable. Following her repeated statement that she would be taking over all aspects of her beloved husband's affairs, she seduced him right there on her official, opulent senator's desk. Although a pleasant juxtaposition, he would have preferred a traditional, male-dominated seduction. He had had the opportunity for many of those during his twenty-four years on the congressional payroll. As she responded to him and he to her, MacDonald witnessed a combination of danger and anger skulking in those eyes, lurking amidst a steamy sensuality.

Thurston's call this afternoon suggesting dinner had been unexpected, and unwanted—considering Rafferty's revelation the previous night and the complications that his new information presented. Although Mac-Donald's last meeting with Thurston had intoxicated him for days afterward, this wasn't the time for him to lose focus.

"I have a proposal, one you'll want to hear, I guarantee it," she had purred over the telephone. He had no choice but to follow through. He intended to listen patiently, reject whatever silly notion had come into her head, and extricate himself from the cat's lair as hastily as possible. He could hardly have prepared himself for the words that would escape her luscious lips. They played right into the mystery that lay behind those eyes.

$$* \qquad * \qquad * \qquad *$$

MacDonald's mind wandered, still reeling over the previous night's conversation. Rafferty's bombshell—and the way he chose to reveal his new information—had pissed him off. An honest person would have blurted out Silverstein's comment about the samples immediately after entering the room. Instead, Rafferty held on to the information, waiting until the last possible moment. *Controlling bastard!* And before he finally left the office, Rafferty demanded that Weaverman be dealt with, with little ambiguity as to what he meant.

But beyond being upset over Rafferty's juvenile behavior, MacDonald now had a serious problem. Rafferty had been correct on one point. Silverstein represented either big trouble or their salvation. Or both.

Who was this Victor Mark Silverstein, and why would Weaverman have gone to *him* for help with his project? It made no sense. Spurred on by Silverstein's shocking admission, Rafferty had hurriedly checked him out (before his meeting with MacDonald) and determined that he was who he said he was, an NRL employee in California, a meteorologist, apparently a famous one—but *only* a meteorologist, for God's sake. Why would Weaverman, a biologist, go to a weather-guesser for help?

Nevertheless, Silverstein's declaration that he possessed the samples Weaverman needed overshadowed the puzzle of his involvement. Rafferty told MacDonald that he'd had the good sense not to question Silverstein unnecessarily.

Consequently, what was supposed to be a twenty-minute meeting with Rafferty didn't end until much later. The questions bandied between them took various forms. Did Silverstein have DNA from a recognized psychic? Why would Weaverman go to him for help? Did Silverstein know everything about Weaverman's research? Was Silverstein a friend? Had they collaborated on the research? Would Silverstein surrender the samples to Rafferty, rather than to Weaverman? And if not, how could Rafferty get them?

Stimulated by these questions, MacDonald had two concerns. To what length would he allow himself to go to retrieve the samples from Silverstein? And second—of equal importance to the bigger picture—how would he deal with this new, loose cannon on the deck of his project? Five partners were plenty. He didn't need the complications of a sixth, someone he knew nothing about and had no control over.

The import of these concerns overshadowed the connotations inherent in the earlier questions. During their discussion, MacDonald was careful to keep his own counsel. Rafferty's game-playing aside, the last thing MacDonald wanted was to make the son of a bitch think he was part of the brain trust. Rafferty was an employee, paid handsomely for his technical talents. Nothing more. After more than an hour of conversation (MacDonald chastised himself for having spent so much time with the surly bastard), he came to his senses, took control, and issued the order. "You're a clever man, Dennis. Use your wiles. Call Silverstein and convince him to send you the samples. I'm counting on you." This time, when MacDonald held open the door, Rafferty obliged.

*   *   *   *

With that final remark to Rafferty resonating in his mind, MacDonald heard before he felt the vibration of his cell phone inside his jacket pocket.

He checked the source of the call and made his intent known to Thurston. "Sorry. I need to take this."

Thurston nodded.

"Talk to me."

The drone of Rafferty's voice seemed even more irritating on the digital phone. "Bastard won't budge, sir. He says Weaverman's the only one he'll relinquish the samples to."

The dull headache that had plagued MacDonald all day intensified. This Silverstein was going to be a pain in the ass. There were two options, and both involved coercion, the first with Weaverman and the second with a complete stranger whom MacDonald had nothing on. He might persuade Weaverman to call Silverstein. But that could get nasty because Weaverman would refuse once he knew that the objective was to provide Rafferty with the very data Weaverman had been searching for. The second option, although fraught with unknowns, would prove more straightforward. They would pressure Silverstein to turn over the biological samples.

MacDonald ended the conversation as tersely as it had begun. "I understand." He terminated the call, pressed the speed-dial number designated for occasions such as this, and waited through two rings for the requisite code word that signaled a proper connection.

His response was brief. "Dick. MacDonald here. Six tomorrow morning." The conversation ended. No need to specify a location. The party at the other end knew the drill.

MacDonald returned his attention to Thurston, who had done an admirable job of projecting disinterest during the interruption. Neither chose to be the first to end the silence.

The waiter inadvertently broke the ensuing tension. "Is anything wrong, sir?" he inquired respectfully.

"No ... thank you." The question returned MacDonald's attention to the food in front of him: the filet mignon; steamed green beans flavored with olive oil and a touch of garlic; Caesar salad (which he preferred to eat with his dinner, not before, not after); and the Beringer Cabernet that offered a hint of black plum and red currant flavors (according to the label). Since Thurston's disturbing suggestion concerning his investors, MacDonald had tasted only the Cab and not the food.

By contrast, the implications of Thurston's proposition had little impact on her own appetite. "You've hardly touched your food." While staring at MacDonald and seeming to formulate a thought, she played with the fork in her hand. "Surely I'm not suggesting something foreign to you. You wouldn't have gotten this far without a little backbone. If this pans out the way you say, why give away the farm? They can't touch you, right? Judging by my contract, I assume you have dirt on each of them. Screw them." She paused and spoke reflectively. "I sense that you and I are much alike … much more so than my late husband. So much potential, so little ambition. Poor Maxwell."

The words *poor Maxwell* came out only milliseconds before a large bite of her own filet mignon went into her mouth and, simultaneously, her right foot edged its way up MacDonald's calf, with no revealing expression or movement to give away her naughty shenanigans. He hadn't experienced anything like this since high school and marveled at the single-mindedness of this rebel. Would he fall for her charms yet again?

Thurston's toes crawled slowly and deliberately up MacDonald's leg while she continued eating unabashed. *She must be out of her mind. She has no business telling me how to run this project.* Would she politely accept his rebuke? On the other hand—now that he thought about it—she'd made a good point. If this project worked out the way he thought it would, why share the results with anyone?

The long tablecloth hid everything from view. The conversations from neighboring tables grew faint as MacDonald succumbed to her touch.

CHAPTER 12

INITIAL PRESSURE

Branding Iron Restaurant, The Village, Carmel Valley,
California, USA
36° 28'48"N latitude, 121° 44'05"W longitude
Friday, 7:55 PM, July 31, 2009

Silverstein loved living on the Monterey Peninsula. He had moved here after earning his PhD from Pennsylvania State University in 1982. Whenever his meteorological soul lamented the absence of apparent seasons on the central coast of California, he reminded himself of the frigid winters of Pennsylvania and the steamy summers of his native Atlanta. No, thank you! Cool in the summer and warm in the winter provided all the seasonal variation that Victor Mark Silverstein cared to enjoy. If he wanted to experience winter's cold and snow, he could trek to the slopes of the Sierra Nevada. If he missed the heat of summer, ninety-degree temperatures could be had for the price of a twenty-minute drive up Carmel Valley.

To quell that nostalgia for the Georgian heat of his youth—but without the humidity—Silverstein would occasionally patronize the Branding Iron Restaurant, a thirteen-mile drive eastward from Highway 1 and the ocean, up Carmel Valley Road. The Branding Iron, an eclectic French restaurant that also served traditional American favorites, lay within the confines of The Village, a tiny, quaint, rural assortment of houses and businesses whose residents ran the gamut of cultural variation. You'd be just as likely to run into a cowhand as you would a business tycoon, rock star, or artist. Remarkably, this intellectual, artistic, and monetary diversity suited everyone there just fine, thank you.

"What strikes your fancy this evening?" Silverstein looked across the table at Kipling, who was absorbed in the fine print beneath each of the evening's entrees, which changed weekly (it was that kind of restaurant). As a rule, he preferred not to socialize with fellow workers, except on business trips. He occasionally made the exception with Kipling. When he did so, as often as not, he left his cherished Porsche in the parking lot at work. Riding second saddle on Kipling's BMW motorcycle represented a concession to her obsession with manly toys. This indulgence stood in stark contrast to her more feminine virtues.

Kipling was a vibrant, attractive female with more than her share of personality and wit—and courage, as he could attest from 2007's experience with the Egyptian terrorist Ghali. Having been divorced for some years now, Silverstein occasionally considered making a move on her.

In terms of physical attributes, there was nothing not to like about this 43-year-old female: five-foot-ten, 125 pounds, long lean legs with just the right amount of muscle, blond hair, and a spectacular figure. The fact that she was white and he black made no difference. Adopted as a baby by white Jewish parents and raised in racially mixed Atlanta, Silverstein saw the world less in black and white than did the average citizen. Shades of gray proved far more interesting to his mind.

"I'm leaning toward the salmon; it's in season. You're not supposed to eat farmed salmon, you know." With that comment, Kipling looked first over her right shoulder and then her left.

Is she looking for someone? "Who says so?"

"The Monterey Bay Aquarium, that's who." Kipling reached inside her purse and removed a small folded pamphlet. She pointed. "See, you're supposed to avoid farmed salmon. The farming is harmful to the environment."

"If the aquarium says so, then I believe it." Silverstein smiled, but he respected Kipling's concern for nature. Her stint as a ranger for the Forest Service in Colorado had given her a perspective on nature that most people lacked. Besides, the Monterey Bay Aquarium, one of the world's finest, had an excellent reputation.

Kipling looked up with her devilish grin. "It hardly matters. You'd never pick salmon." She ran her finger down the list of entrees. "Let me see … I predict the rib-eye is more to your taste."

Silverstein winced. "Well, you're wrong for once! I'm having the pork chop stuffed with apples and raisins." *How does she do that?* He had had his heart set on the steak.

The waiter came by, and they placed their orders. "Yes, sir. The 2001 Bernardus Merlot is an ideal choice." Silverstein knew from experience that Kipling preferred red wine, even with fish.

Silverstein leaned back and tried to appreciate a week that had had both its disappointments and merits. He knew that he'd caught Rafferty's attention when Rafferty had initiated the call back to Silverstein to make another request for the samples. "I'm getting worried again. It's been two days since Rafferty called, and nothing's happened. I'm making no headway in finding Weaverman."

The waiter returned, uncorked the bottle, poured a small amount, waited for Silverstein's nod of approval, and poured two glasses. "Will that be all for now, sir?"

"Yes, thank you."

Kipling, sampling the wine from her glass, suddenly pivoted in her chair and looked around the room as if she had noticed something. She then refocused her attention on Silverstein. "What more could you do?"

"I could go to the authorities back in Washington."

Kipling sighed. "We discussed this before."

Silverstein bit his lower lip. "I think it's time to call Hector. Besides, he owes us big time and the CIA can—"

Before he could complete the sentence, Kipling pushed back her chair, stood up, turned completely around, and again scanned the room.

"Linda? What's wrong? Talk to me."

She stared down at Silverstein. "I'm fine. Will you excuse me for a minute? I need to powder my nose." With that comment she grabbed her cell phone, shoved it into her pants pocket, and headed toward the restrooms, located opposite the entrance to the restaurant.

Silverstein sat confused, his eyes following Kipling. *Powder her nose?* Kipling never used, nor needed, makeup. He watched as she paused briefly before the hallway that led to the restrooms, the kitchen, and the rear of the restaurant. A brief look of recognition appeared on her face before she disappeared. Another woman, African-American, and dressed in blue jeans with a white blouse and leather jacket, followed.

Silverstein turned back to his wine. *What's going on?* His certain knowledge that Kipling rarely did anything without a purpose made the hairs on his neck stand on end. *Think! Use that photographic memory you were blessed with!*

Silverstein closed his eyes and scanned the mental images from the preceding days, looking for any clue he might have ignored that Kipling hadn't. Going back and forth to work, the visitors at work—only the usual. But wait a minute! His mental slide projector came to a halt. Tonight he and Kipling had left for dinner directly from work. They had parked just inside the gate to the complex that included the NRL buildings. They had walked directly from Building 704 across the street to the parking lot. As they made their way to Kipling's motorcycle, he had noticed a couple standing between a sedan and a minivan on the street, casually looking into the compound. A blond-haired man—accompanied by a *black female* in a white blouse and jacket! Silverstein opened his eyes, ready to sprint after Kipling—and looked directly into the face of the blond who now sat in Kipling's chair.

The stranger folded his hands in front of him. With poor timing, the waiter approached, two salads in hand, obviously puzzled that a man had replaced the lady. The stranger looked up toward the waiter, leaned forward to remove his wallet, extracted a $100 bill, and stuck it between the fingers of one hand and the plate. "I trust you could delay Dr. Silverstein's dinner for a few minutes." The waiter nodded and walked away.

"I'm here to pick up the samples. Weaverman sent me."

Silverstein stared across at this pissant kid who had the nerve to interrupt his dinner. He reacted internally to the fact that he had wanted the pot to boil and that his wish had come true. *Be careful what you wish for*, his father had admonished. "Who are you, and who do you work for?"

"My name's Dick and, like I said, I work for Dr. Weaverman." He reached inside his left coat pocket, removed a pack of Camels, shook one loose, and placed it between his teeth, bobbing it up and down.

Silverstein's demeanor changed to one of irritation and resentment. "Well … I don't much appreciate your approach to customer relations. And Dickey …" Silverstein reached across the table, tore the cigarette from his mouth, ripped it in half, and placed it on the table. "You're in California now. We don't allow smoking in restaurants. And furthermore, *Dickey,* you can tell Weaverman that I took him at his word, that he was the only one I was supposed to give the samples to. Pick up your coffin nail and get the hell out of here."

Silverstein hoped that his open display of bluster would have the desired effect, notwithstanding his concern about Kipling. *What was happening in the restroom?*

Dickey remained composed, with his eyes unflinching, breath even, and hands steady. This could be trouble, thought Silverstein. Such composure meant that he was used to this sort of thing. Silverstein waited for the other shoe to drop. It wasn't long in coming.

"Even as I speak, your assistant has left the building with Myra, my capable associate. She will remain under our protective custody until I have the samples. Unless Myra hears from me, and soon, she has orders to do whatever she wants with your friend. And I must tell you, My is a little different from most of us. She has a mean streak."

Dickey hesitated, removed a second cigarette from his pack, and resumed in a mocking manner. "Am I doing an adequate job of getting my point across to you … or do I need to explain further?"

✳   ✳   ✳   ✳

Linda Kipling knew from the moment she entered the Branding Iron that all was not well. And before she entered the hallway to the restroom, when she had looked back across the room behind Silverstein, she saw a blond-haired man sitting at the bar—the same man who had been standing outside NRL earlier. *This can't be good!* She'd alert Silverstein by text message using her cell from the bathroom.

Separate restroom doors for men and women stood on the left side of the hallway across from the entrance to the kitchen. A screen door that opened to the back parking lot followed. Kipling turned into the second of the two doors. She reached down to lock the door to the small bathroom. Before she had the chance, the door was pushed open, and a woman in blue jeans forced herself in and closed the door behind her.

Kipling recognized the woman immediately as the companion to the man she had seen outside NRL. "I beg your pardon! I think this room is a little small for both of us."

The demeanor of the intruder made clear to Kipling that her actions were intentional. With her left hand, she pushed backward against Kipling's chest while simultaneously raising her right arm. Off balance and before she could react, Kipling recognized a nine-millimeter pistol. "Believe me, I don't want to hurt you. Just play along for an hour or two, and you'll be free. For now, you're going to go back into the hallway, out the back door, turn left, and walk toward the blue minivan. You'll enter the sliding door on the driver's side, and I will follow. Do you understand?"

Kipling recalled that it hadn't been all that long ago when the terrorist Ghali had said similar words to her at the Denver airport. At least this time, her assailant didn't have a poison-filled syringe tucked against her shoulder.

Kipling maintained her composure. Back in Colorado, as a game warden, her giving a mountain lion a fighting chance by not firing until the rabid male was in midair leap had earned her the nickname "Ice"—which represented the frozen version of what her Forest Service colleagues assumed surged through her veins.

"Whatever you say … who are you, by the way?"

The attacker seemed to be enjoying the physical encounter a bit too much. As she slid her left arm upward across Kipling's chest and to her neck, Kipling caught the woman glancing down at her breasts. *Oh God!*

thought Kipling. *First a Middle Eastern terrorist who had never before encountered an independent female, and now a lesbian who probably prefers the type.*

"My name's Myra. But because of our really close relationship, you can call me My."

"Okay, My. You're the one calling the shots. Lead the way."

"That's cute. Just do as you're told."

Myra backed up, pulled her arm from Kipling's neck, and motioned to the door with her gun. Kipling briefly considered disarming her attacker during her move to the door but decided otherwise. She hadn't forgotten her martial arts training from her forestry days. Wait for that solitary moment of vulnerability; make sure all conditions are optimal, her instructor had taught her. The space was too confining, with too little room to maneuver.

Kipling opened the door, looked right, turned left as instructed, walked down the empty hallway, and exited, all the while sensing My's presence close behind. They entered the parking lot into the dimming evening light. Except for the employee cars, the lot stood empty. Most patrons parked in the ample front lot.

It didn't take a rocket scientist to understand what was happening, that Rafferty had sent them to bring back the samples. Silverstein had wanted things to happen, and happening they were. Kipling's abduction was undoubtedly part of their plan to pry the booty from Silverstein.

"Keep moving!"

On purpose, Kipling walked slowly, considering her options, number one of which was to disarm Myra and escape. Afraid that Myra might have gone to the same school of abduction as Ghali, Kipling considered the remote possibility that a tranquilizer might be waiting—or worse, that a second party waited in the van.

As they approached the van, the side door opened automatically. Kipling turned her head.

"There's nothing back here for you to look at. Get in!"

The opening door meant one of two possibilities. Either Myra had triggered it remotely with her key fob, or she had an accomplice. The latter would be bad news. As Kipling looked into the obviously vacant van, she recognized Myra's moment of vulnerability.

*   *   *   *

Silverstein looked across at his adversary, a professional who had covered his bases. A sickening feeling overwhelmed him. *He had done it again!* He had inadvertently placed Kipling in harm's way, just as he had two years ago. It wasn't long before Silverstein's nausea was replaced with a determination that told him, this time, he would control the sequence of events. He would either make Dickey wish he hadn't made this trip to California or go down honorably in battle.

Silverstein responded as he figured Dickey would want him to. "You've made your point. They're back at my house. Let's go."

*   *   *   *

As Myra entered behind her, Kipling made her move. Instead of sliding butt first across the seat, she instead moved headfirst with her hands on the seat supporting her body weight. She looked back briefly to focus her aim. Kipling dropped prone on the seat, left leg on the floor for stability. Her right leg, which had slid forward across the seat, suddenly shot backwards. Kipling's boot caught Myra's wrist perfectly, smashing it against the door. The audible crunch of bones in Myra's wrist was more than Kipling had hoped for. More importantly, she saw the weapon fall to the floor. Myra screamed.

"You bitch!" Myra was livid and lunged for Kipling without thinking. Unfortunately for her, a now useless right hand gave the advantage to Kipling, who quickly subdued her, forcing Myra to her stomach on the seat, Kipling's right knee on her back, with Myra's good arm ratcheted up behind. Myra whimpered as the pain from her broken right hand made its presence known. Kipling reached behind her and closed the sliding door.

"Did Rafferty send you?" Kipling shoved Myra's arm upward.

Myra groaned in pain but did not reply.

Kipling angled the arm still higher. "If you don't respond to my questions, instead of six months of therapy, you'll have more recovering to do from a dislocated shoulder. I speak from experience. Both of your arms will be useless, and someone will have to feed you. Is that what you want?"

Myra replied grudgingly. "I don't know."

Kipling, until now patient and the model of controlled anger, suddenly remembered that Myra's partner posed a threat to Silverstein. Rage rose in her throat and involuntarily transferred itself through her arms. Kipling knew she had pushed a little too far when she heard the cartilage in Myra's shoulder tear. Simultaneously, Myra stopped moaning. She had passed out. *So much for that line of questioning.*

Kipling released her grip and glanced back to the third-row seat. There lay a roll of duct tape that Myra had obviously planned for Kipling.

Although it was unnecessary, Kipling's irritation prompted her to use a third of the roll before stopping to make a complete circle around Myra's head, covering her mouth.

Kipling completed her task, took a breath, and considered her options. *What was going on back in the restaurant? Was Victor still there, or had the blond-haired stranger convinced him to cooperate?* She looked up and glanced through both the front and back windows of the van, relieved to see that no one had heard their commotion.

Myra moaned and opened her eyes.

Kipling reached down to retrieve the gun. After a moment's further consideration, she realized she had no choice. A backup strategy seemed wise. She would follow through with Silverstein's earlier suggestion.

Kipling opened the door to the van, stepped outside, slid the door closed, did a quick scan of the parking lot, removed the cell phone from her pocket, and dialed. The number was one she had made a point of memorizing.

CHAPTER 13

FOREIGN INTEREST

George Bush Center for Intelligence, McLean, Virginia, USA
38°56'06"N latitude, 77°08'46"W longitude
Friday, 11:35 PM, July 31, 2009

As happened all too often in his line of work, it was nearly midnight when Hector Rodriguez Lopez, Jr., senior investigative officer in counterintelligence, took the call at his Langley desk.

"A Linda Kipling for you, sir. Do you wish to take it?" the operator inquired.

"Yeah, Janet. Thanks." Lopez held up his index finger to signal Marc Miller, his principal assistant, that he would be a minute. Miller nodded and went back to studying the electronic chatter they had garnered in past weeks. Intriguing stuff.

Of course he'd take the call. Memories from 2007 that culminated in Silverstein and Kipling saving Washington, DC, from an environmental disaster were still fresh in his mind. The CIA's presence at the end had been mere window dressing. Kipling and Silverstein, along with Hector's own wife Barbara, all NRL employees, had provided the nerve, muscle, and smarts in their harrowing flight to Bermuda (in the midst of a hurricane) and the final confrontation with a lunatic mastermind and his Egyptian sponsor. It was a damn shame they could never receive official acknowledgment for their heroic deeds. The upper echelon of the federal government decided that it wouldn't do anyone any good to know that a terrorist organization had come that close to repeating an event comparable to 9/11.

But there was more to Lopez's obligation to Silverstein, stemming from the early 1980s when they had attended Pennsylvania State University together. Lopez owed his life to the stranger who had taken on a pair of street thugs—at considerable risk to himself—intent on making an example of a young Hispanic who had the nerve to attend college. Lopez had never told anyone, including Silverstein, the hateful comments rained down upon him before Silverstein arrived to save the day. At the time, his misshapen leg had prevented him from running away. Two sessions of corrective surgery had later corrected most of that deformity. More than a quarter of a century had passed since that night, and Lopez still hadn't had the opportunity to repay that debt.

Lopez listened for some five minutes to Kipling's story. Afterward, he stared across at Miller, who was still engrossed in their latest data. Brow furrowed and eyes squeezed tight meant that he was deep in thought.

Lopez mentally replayed the salient points from Kipling's call: Silverstein's brief association with the NRL scientist Weaverman, Weaverman's astonishing research and theory, his subsequent phone call and disappearance, Silverstein's clever trick to turn up the heat to locate him, and now the two heavies Kipling thought had been sent by Weaverman's boss—a guy by the name of Rafferty—to pick up the samples that Silverstein claimed he had. Lopez made a mental note to ask Barbara if she knew either Weaverman or Rafferty.

Kipling explained that she had disarmed her female assailant. That she had done so hardly surprised Lopez. Silverstein's account of how Kipling had saved his life in Colorado had etched her credentials for bravery indelibly on his mind. Heaven help anyone who crossed her.

Kipling told him her concern now was how they would react once they learned that Silverstein had no DNA samples to hand over.

Lopez's closest human assets lay half a continent away from California. He could only plead with Kipling that she not do anything stupid. Lopez saw no need to remind her that Silverstein's assailant would be pissed as hell once he discovered that Silverstein had lied. Kipling could not know, during Lopez's admonishment, that he was praying that Silverstein would follow that same advice.

Lopez cursed the fates. Once again, Silverstein had stumbled into harm's way. And even with the considerable resources available to him, Lopez could do nothing about it. His lifelong obligation to Silverstein would have to wait.

Their conversation had ended with Kipling promising to call back.

Lopez had hardly reacted (he wondered if she found that strange) to Kipling's initial mention of clairvoyance, extrasensory perception, or whatever you wanted to call it. The public had no idea that the government had been testing psychics for decades. Over the years, the CIA had tested many of them. If there were such a thing, the military wanted to be the first in line to use this ability.

All psychics who presented themselves to the CIA eventually made their way to be tested by the Mensa team, an Agency branch that all CIA divisions could draw upon. The CIA had chartered Mensa back in the early 1990s to develop novel technology for use either in the field or at home. Their success in 2007 with the tracking transmitter embedded in the scalp of the terrorist Ghali had the Mensa crowd crowing.

However, it wasn't because all Mensan had genius mentalities (which they did) or because they were all scientists of one form or another (which they were) that the Agency entrusted the psychics to Mensa. It was because several of their resumes included the words *professional magician*. As those among their small number were quick to point out to their skeptical colleagues, you can't trust the skills of a scientist to validate a psychic's talent.

In general, the magicians claimed, the smarter the scientist, the more easily fooled. The non-magician Mensan took offense to this seemingly nonsensical statement. They accepted the conclusion more easily after the magicians assured them that it was their wealth of knowledge that made them susceptible. The more intelligent the victim, the more ways that victim could rationalize a deception to be legitimate, the more ways for the tricked to come to the desired conclusion instigated by the swindler. Anyone doubting the ability of a professional magician to fool the public into believing in psychic powers had only to remember the Israeli spoon bender, Uri Geller.

So far, the magicians in Mensa had a perfect record. Not one purported psychic had passed their rigorous tests. Not that some methods used by the impostors hadn't been damned clever.

For these reasons, Lopez took Kipling's initial comments in stride. Before she had finished her account, Lopez found himself listening intently.

Miller stirred. "What's up? Did I hear you mention Kipling and Silverstein?" Miller had assisted Lopez in Colorado and Bermuda and knew them both.

Lopez leaned into his desk and composed his thoughts before he spoke. "All the chatter we've been following may be more than hype. It turns out that the rogue scientists in the Blade aren't the only ones who think there's such a thing as a psychic."

CHAPTER 14

PLAN B

***Branding Iron Restaurant, The Village, Carmel Valley,
California, USA
36°28'48"N latitude, 121°44'05"W longitude
Friday, 8:41 PM, July 31, 2009***

Kipling pressed the disconnect button on her cell phone, jogged to the door she had exited earlier, tiptoed down the hall, and sneaked a look. As she expected, Silverstein and Myra's accomplice were gone. Kipling hurried past their table. Two glasses, an unfinished bottle of wine, and two salads remained. A torn cigarette lay on the table. Before leaving the restaurant, she asked the maitre d' for two items. He obliged with both.

A quick walk to the front parking lot revealed the only good news. Their attackers hadn't bothered to disable her bike. She still had transportation.

Before departing, Kipling's conscience kicked into gear. She rode to the rear parking lot to check on Myra. She didn't look very comfortable, but was conscious and seemed okay.

"Take good care of yourself, My. Don't get up on my account."

With that adieu, Kipling stuffed her hair into her helmet, straddled her BMW, pulled down her visor, and accelerated away, leaning into the turns as she roared back down Carmel Valley Road. The speedometer on the BMW R 1200 GS slipped past the 80-mile-per-hour mark (more than double the posted 35) twice before she tore into the right-hand turn onto Laureles Grade Road, a shortcut back to Highway 68. As the tachometer sped repeatedly toward the 7,000-RPM cutoff in the lower gears, Kipling reviewed her plan of action.

Not much twilight remained. Dark was good. What Kipling had in mind was best accomplished without much light.

*   *   *   *

Silverstein gripped the wheel of Dickey's Nissan Altima as they approached the crest of the ridgeline that separated Carmel Valley from the Highway 68 corridor that connected Monterey to Salinas, nineteen miles inland. Dickey rode in the passenger seat. Surprisingly, he hadn't bothered to brandish a weapon. It hadn't been necessary. Dickey's threat had had its desired impact on Silverstein.

Back at the Branding Iron, after settling the bill, they had simply strolled out the front door, stepped into Dickey's rental, and driven off. Silverstein told him that he kept the samples at his house in Halcyon Heights, a private gated community in the hills above Highway 68. Dickey ordered him to drive.

"Since you're going to get what you want, tell me at least if you work for Rafferty. Did he send you here?" Any additional information could be useful later. Despite Kipling's earlier reluctance, Silverstein had decided it was now time to call his friend at the CIA.

Dickey's tone didn't change. "That's none of your concern, Dr. Silverstein. Just hand over what I want, and both you and your associate will remain unharmed." Dickey turned to face the driver. His demeanor turned colder. "And afterward, it would be in your best interest to forget this whole affair."

Silverstein snapped back. "That's easy for you to say. What about my friend Weaverman?"

Conciliation followed. "That's fair. I can assure you that Dr. Weaverman is alive and safe."

Silverstein reflected on his situation. Earlier Dickey had threatened him, saying that unless he reported back to Myra, she would have her way with Kipling. Silverstein considered the obvious; while he could probably overcome Dickey, could he convince him to make the call to free Kipling? *What now, O brilliant one?*

Silverstein chose to play a mind game on Dickey, albeit premised on the truth. "What would you say if I told you there are no samples, that I only told Rafferty that to get his attention?" He turned to judge Dickey's reaction.

Dickey's voice remained even. "That would mean I made this trip for nothing, and I would be very unhappy. Beyond that, I wouldn't believe you. You couldn't be that stupid."

That stupid, huh?

Suddenly, what looked like a single headlight appeared in the rearview mirror. Silverstein took note of it but did not react. Motorcycles were common on the Monterey Peninsula.

This one was coming on fast and showed no intent of slowing. Silverstein knew many motorcyclists to be foolhardy and overconfident. Instead of slowing down, the machine blasted by on the left side twenty to thirty miles per hour faster than their car.

Silverstein had little time to focus on the reddish-colored bike. *Linda? Is that you?*

*   *   *   *

Kipling recalled the Nissan parked in front of NRL. As her headlight caught the tail of the car ahead and she recognized the color, she chose to pass as quickly as possible, to give Silverstein's assailant no time to consider the possibility she had escaped. A peripheral glance confirmed the make of car. To maintain control, Myra's partner had likely asked Silverstein to drive. Kipling's plan hinged on that fact.

Before she departed the Branding Iron, Kipling had inferred Silverstein's likely course of action. His blond assailant would have threatened him with her abduction. Kipling knew that Silverstein still felt guilty because Ghali had nearly killed her, and Silverstein hadn't been the big hero to rescue her. *Stupid male dominance thing!* Kipling knew that he would do everything to protect her and would accede to anything the stranger asked. This course of action begged the question of what Silverstein would do later, since he had no samples to deliver.

Only one question remained: where were they going? Silverstein's office or his house? Kipling took a glance into her rearview mirror, confirming that she had lost them, braked hard, and turned left into the rear entrance to Bay Ridge, the gated community adjacent to Halcyon Heights where Silverstein lived. Her plan rested heavily on Silverstein choosing this direction of travel.

*   *   *   *

Silverstein felt sweat form instantly on his palms against the wheel. Had Kipling escaped? That was *her* motorcycle, no doubt about it. Silverstein stole a glance to his right to see if Dickey had reacted. He hadn't. *Thank God!*

But what was Kipling up to? She knew he would recognize her bike. Had she done this just to let him know she was off the hook? That was why she had passed so fast, to not give Dickey a chance to suspect it was she.

Silverstein sucked in a slow breath. *Okay, Dickey, the game's changed— and you don't even know it. You sorry son of a bitch!*

*   *   *   *

Kipling rode swiftly through the forested area that preceded the Bay Ridge gate. At the most, she would have about a minute. The minimally lit area surrounding the center island provided a reasonable location for her plan to evolve. She had to do two things before Silverstein and company arrived.

First, she drove her bike to the left of the road, hiding it behind a tree. No one would see it from the Laureles Grade direction. Kipling peered up into the darkening sky.

So far, so good. Kipling sprinted to the automated entry area. There were two ways that residents and visitors could open the gate. Visitors could look up the gate code for a resident and call him or her from the attached telephone; the resident would then open the gate by pressing "9" on his phone. Residents either had a remote clicker or flashed an encrypted card before a scanner to open the gate.

A short ledge rested beneath the telephone keypad. She removed the sheet of paper she had borrowed back at the restaurant and the pen she always kept on her motorcycle.

*   *   *   *

Silverstein made the turn from Laureles Grade Road into the wooded area leading to Bay Ridge. He had to decide when to jump Dickey. Doing it inside the car made no sense. Assuming that he didn't pull a gun, Dickey would provide easier prey once they exited the car. That opportunity would come at Silverstein's house.

As they approached the entryway to the gate, Silverstein lowered the driver's side window.

"What are you doing?" Dickey seemed confused.

"Haven't you ever been to a gated community?" Silverstein leaned forward, removed his wallet, held it up for Dickey to see, and removed the white gate card—available to Halcyon Heights residents as a courtesy to drive through the adjacent Bay Ridge community.

As his window lowered, Silverstein rolled forward slowly and extended his left arm so that the sensor could read the card. The audible beep indicated that the accompanying computer had authenticated the card's code as legitimate. The creaking metal of the center-closing gate signaled its opening.

This gate opened slowly, Silverstein knew. To his left, beneath the keypad, he noticed a sheet of folded paper nestled against the back panel.

Nothing unusual, he thought. Residents often left notes for arriving parties. But this one wasn't taped to anything. A gust of wind could easily blow it away. He glanced over and, for the second time since leaving the restaurant, caught his breath. Despite the dim light, he recognized Kipling's printing.

*　　　*　　　*　　　*

Kipling waited behind a tree on the side opposite her bike, fifty feet back from the entry. If anyone looked back, they would see her. But the two men in the car faced forward. Assuming he had seen it, she knew that Silverstein was now processing the information on the note she had left. "BACK UP, GET OUT, AND RUN."

In the recesses of her mind, Kipling had the sudden, sickening sensation that Silverstein was not thinking as he should.

*　　　*　　　*　　　*

Silverstein had to make a decision, and soon. The gate had nearly opened. Kipling was sitting back there, waiting to jump Dickey when he exited the car to chase Silverstein. But what of the risks? Although he hadn't brandished a weapon, Dickey obviously carried one. Kipling had nothing and might or might not be able to disarm him in time. Before Silverstein could attack from the opposite side of the car, it might be too late. Was that a chance Silverstein wanted to take?

I think not! I'm sorry, Linda.

Silverstein drove slowly through the now-opened gate.

*　　　*　　　*　　　*

Kipling crouched to the ground, the nine-millimeter dangling from her right hand. "That son of a bitch!" she cursed to herself. *He knew I was back here and decided not to take the chance. Damn!*

Kipling gathered her wits and scurried back to her bike in time to go through the gate before it closed. Time for Plan B. She felt for the back pocket in her jeans to make sure she still had the other item, an envelope, she had requested back at the restaurant.

CHAPTER 15

HAIRBRAINED

Halcyon Heights home subdivision, Monterey, California, USA
36°33'30"N latitude, 121°46'29"W longitude
Friday, 9:10 PM, July 31, 2009

They parked in front of Silverstein's garage on the lower level of his home. Silverstein tried to buy some time by questioning Dickey further on the status of Weaverman. He proved no more responsive than earlier and ordered Silverstein from the vehicle.

Perhaps because he now felt vulnerable, Dickey chose to supplement his threats to harm Kipling with hardware reinforcement. Silverstein turned and saw the drawn gun as they walked from Dickey's car to the leftmost of Silverstein's four garage doors. Dickey's instruction to leave the headlights on ensured that his target remained adequately illuminated.

The numeric keypad on the exterior wall allowed entry to the garage without the remote normally stored inside Silverstein's car. He could have driven to the upper driveway and entered via the front door, but he decided that the garage entry and their ascent up the long stairway to the main floor had its advantages.

There was one important upside to Kipling's note. He knew that she had escaped and was safe. Unfortunately, his choice back at the gate had a serious downside. Although his choice not to take chances with Kipling's life represented a morally defensible position, she would not see it that way. She would be pissed as hell.

*   *   *   *

The gathering darkness had leached all light from the sun's last rays as Kipling weaved her way through Bay Ridge to Silverstein's house. That was his obvious destination and only about a mile beyond a second gate that separated Halcyon Heights from Bay Ridge.

The cool night air blowing from Monterey Bay only partially lowered the temperature as measured by Kipling's internal thermostat. *Did he think she hadn't thought her plan through? Had he no respect for her physical skills after their adventure in Colorado?* Be calm, Kipling willed herself. *Be calm, hell! If the blond hadn't killed Silverstein by the time she got there, she might decide to do the job herself!*

*   *   *   *

Silverstein considered his options. Dickey was expecting Silverstein to hand him an envelope, box, or whatever. Had Rafferty given Dickey any information? All Silverstein had told Rafferty was that he had the samples. Besides hair, Silverstein imagined that DNA could take many biological forms, depending on whether the donor was alive or dead. For the latter, bone came to mind. *Oh what a tangled web we weave*, his mother had once reprimanded an adventurous, and occasionally devious, youth.

"Stop! Where are we going?" Dickey demanded clarification of Silverstein's intent.

"In case you haven't figured it out yet, Dickey, we're going inside my house."

The gun pointed at Silverstein's backside posed a complication. During college, Silverstein had made a good showing in the heavyweight division at the state level for the Golden Gloves championship in Pennsylvania in 1978. Nonetheless, compared to Kipling, who had trained in law enforcement and the martial arts, Silverstein knew his fighting skills had limitations. He accepted as fact that luck would play a role in his plan for Dickey.

*   *   *   *

Kipling pulled over well shy of the stop sign below Silverstein's house. She sprinted along the road to the stop sign, turned left up the hill, and continued running the last hundred feet to the lower driveway.

Kipling had visited Silverstein's home often enough to remember the basic layout: garages below, above which lay the living area. A long, straight set of steps connected the two. Silverstein usually entered the house from the garage when he drove.

A row of *Myoporum* trees lined the left side of the drive, and Kipling ran behind them to give her more cover than the natural darkness provided. Fortunately, this rural neighborhood had no streetlights to contaminate nature's nighttime blackness. The leftmost garage door stood open, with the headlights from the car and fluorescents from the garage illuminating portions of the driveway. The car she had passed earlier sat empty.

From the shadows, she peered into the open garage door.

*   *   *   *

Well, it's now or never, Silverstein thought as they ascended the steps. If they reached the top of the staircase, he would be out of options. There were no samples to give, and he would be standing face-to-face with Dickey, hardly a position from which to exert influence or achieve surprise.

Halfway up the stairs, Silverstein stopped and turned to face Dickey on his right, expecting immediate eye contact. His intent had been to look Dickey in the eye, ask an innocuous question, turn as if he intended to continue up the steps, and instead crouch down and throw his legs backwards, surprising him and throwing him off balance. It wasn't a great plan, but it would have to do.

In the instant that Silverstein turned, an alternate strategy presented itself. Dickey had not expected that Silverstein would stop moving. In the fraction of a second during which Silverstein recognized his opportunity, he reacted instinctively.

Silverstein's right arm snaked back to seize the wrist of his surprised victim. In doing so, his weight shifted so he now stood off balance and leaned down the steps toward Dickey. With Dickey's wrist firmly in his grasp, the weapon provided Silverstein's only real concern. For that reason, as he pivoted on the step ready to push Dickey down in front of him, Silverstein's left hand came to the assistance of his right. Two strong arms trumped one. Silverstein held on to Dickey's right wrist as they fell backwards, Dickey square to the steps and Silverstein at an angle.

As Silverstein forced Dickey's arm downward with both hands, Dickey's reaction, instinctive or otherwise, was to pull the trigger. The gun exploded in the confined area of the steps. The projectile flew harmlessly into the drywall to the left. Silverstein figured that unless Dickey knocked him out with his left hand, he had control.

The bodies of both men tumbled down the steps together, with Silverstein trying to remain on top. Unfortunately for Silverstein, it didn't work out that way. Before they crashed together on the landing, they had rotated a full 180 degrees, and Silverstein took the brunt of Dickey's weight, nearly knocking the wind out of him. With both of Silverstein's hands coping with the gun, Dickey's left fist delivered a glancing blow off Silverstein's head. On the second try, Silverstein saw stars.

Praying that his left hand had the strength to control the gun, Silverstein reciprocated with a punch to Dickey's face, accompanied by a satisfying crack.

Dickey dominated Silverstein. His right arm had better leverage and was overcoming the upward pressure from Silverstein's left hand. To make matters worse, Dickey pushed down with his left hand and pressed his thumb into Silverstein's eye. Instinctively, Silverstein closed both eyes as tightly as he could. Silverstein now found himself fighting blind.

*   *   *   *

Kipling heard the explosion and ran to the door at the base of the stairs. She cracked it open just in time to see Silverstein struggling to control the weapon in the assailant's hand.

Kipling opened the door wide and jammed the barrel of Myra's gun into the right ear of the man on top. "Drop the gun. Now!"

*   *   *   *

Silverstein couldn't see a thing but heard the words clearly. The thumb jammed into his eye slowly released its pressure. He opened both eyes but saw only a blurred background with the right eye. He impulsively blinked to try to bring the eye into focus, but he knew from a personal incident in his teen years that it would take hours before the eyeball achieved its earlier shape. He looked up with his good eye to see Dickey's weapon slipping to the floor.

Kipling reached down and retrieved the handgun.

Silverstein crawled awkwardly and pulled himself from beneath Dickey, twisted around on the floor, and looked up into the welcome face of his colleague. She didn't appear any too happy.

*   *   *   *

Silverstein spoke first. "It's good to see you, Linda. Dickey here was making a good showing for himself."

Dickey, huh? "I assume that all this trouble is over Weaverman's DNA samples."

Kipling looked down first at Dickey and then at Silverstein. "It's not worth it, Victor. Why the hell didn't you just give them to him?"

Dickey rolled onto his back. Kipling placed her left boot on his stomach. "Although I'm tempted to turn your sorry ass over to the police, I'm not sure what I'd tell them. But I'll make you a deal. If we give you the

DNA, do we have your word that you'll get out of here and leave us alone?"

Dickey, his nose bleeding, coughed, and replied softly. "You have my word."

Kipling removed her foot, looked back at Silverstein, and made her case in a convincing manner. "From where I stand, I say we give him the samples. Do you agree?"

*   *   *   *

Silverstein, weak from exertion and his fall down the stairs, didn't have the strength to stand. Instead, he crept up the steps above Dickey. With his right eye closed and his left blinking steadily, he looked toward Kipling and wondered if one of Dickey's blows to his head had shaken something loose. Her words made no sense.

Between a mental fog and not understanding her question, he replied. "Yes, but—"

Kipling cut him off and repeated her question more forcefully. "Victor, I've had it! I'll make the decision for both of us. You told me you put the samples in your bedroom safe. You're obviously in no condition to walk right now. Give me the combination. While you keep an eye on Dickey, I'll get them. Do you understand what I'm saying?"

Silverstein finally had Kipling's face in focus and sensed she wanted an answer in the affirmative. "6-45-91"

With that response, Kipling thrust Dickey's gun into Silverstein's hands and looked at him directly. "If he moves, Victor, I want you to shoot him. If once doesn't do it, shoot him again. Do you think you can do that?"

Silverstein nodded and took hold of Dickey's weapon with both hands. He slid himself upward two steps to put more distance between them and concentrated on Kipling's direct order. He wasn't feeling too well—complicated by the fact that Kipling had obviously lost her mind.

Dickey stirred on the floor, seemingly gathering his wits at the same pace as Silverstein.

It wasn't long before Kipling came striding down the steps. "Okay, Dickey, we're keeping our end of the deal, and we expect you to do the same."

Dickey rose slowly to his feet and took the envelope that Kipling offered. "Can I have my gun back? That's Myra's too, isn't it?"

Kipling responded. "Fat chance! Now get out of here."

Dickey turned to the door and started to leave.

"Dickey!" Kipling yelled when he was out of sight.

He retraced his steps and stared back at Kipling.

"Give me the envelope." She wrote something on it and gave it back. "That's my cell number. When you leave here, make a left at the stop sign. That'll take you back to Highway 68. You need to drive back to the restaurant and pick up Myra. She'll need some medical attention. Take her to Community Hospital. The exit is marked from Route 1 north. If you get lost, call me."

Kipling paused. "One more thing. Don't lose what's in that envelope. You have no idea what it took to get those hairs."

*   *   *   *

With these instructions, Dickey struggled to his car, his left hand holding his face. Kipling followed him down the driveway and watched his taillights disappear as he turned at the stop sign.

Kipling returned to the steps to discover Silverstein missing. She climbed to the top, heard the toilet flush down the hall, leaned against the wall, and waited for his return.

He was a sorry sight. He limped. His right eye was closed and swollen. As much as she wanted to feel sorry for him, she was angry because he had ignored her instructions at the gate.

Silverstein spoke. "What was that all about? Where did you get the hairs you gave Dickey?"

Kipling smirked. "Use your brain, Victor. Where do you think I got the hairs?"

Silverstein's mouth dropped open, and his right eye opened, if only for an instant.

CHAPTER 16

NEEDLES

Russell Senate Office Building, Washington, DC, USA
38°53'32"N latitude, 77°00'28"W longitude
Monday, 9:15 AM, August 3, 2009

Senator Thurston hung up the phone, her mind mulling over new information from MacDonald. She looked up when she heard the knock on the large mahogany door. Cynthia Grafton, the senator's executive assistant (and previously her husband's), entered Thurston's private office, situated just off the front office where visitors entered and stated their business.

Other than the metal detectors that screened visitors to the Russell Senate Office Building, Grafton represented Thurston's only line of defense. When her days turned hectic, Thurston could predict almost to the second the time between her hanging up the phone and the subsequent knock. Cynthia could tell from the damn phone lights when Thurston had concluded a call.

"Don't forget your ten o'clock." Grafton, an attractive woman in her forties with dark European features, smiled appropriately.

"I haven't forgotten, Cynthia. Give me a moment, will you."

The tall door swung back to its closed position.

Thurston leaned back, crossed her arms, and reflected on her earlier conversation. Dick Jamieson, MacDonald said, had returned to Washington. Moreover, he had been successful in retrieving the DNA samples from the NRL scientist, Silverstein. Thurston knew of Jamieson's planned trip to California because MacDonald had spilled the beans following their little tryst at the Watergate the previous Wednesday. MacDonald had explained that DNA from a recognized psychic would bode well in their search for confirmation of Weaverman's gene sequence.

Judging from his tone on the telephone, MacDonald could hardly believe that their fortunes had turned in such a favorable direction so easily. Their plans might progress more quickly than he had originally thought, he said. They had found the needle in the haystack.

The proverbial needle, huh? Thurston didn't believe either in finding needles or in fortuitous good luck. First, needles were sharp, pointed pieces of metal that any child learned to avoid. And second, if it was so hard to find such an object, how did MacDonald stumble across one on his first try? Was MacDonald being played for a fool? Thurston was reminded of another saying: don't count your chickens before they're hatched. They hadn't yet tested the sample.

Trying to rein in her cynical nature, Thurston concluded that the worst-case scenario had no real downside. If Rafferty determined that the DNA sample did not possess the special gene, no harm was done, was it? But that result would lead to the obvious question of *why*. Why would a Navy scientist offer up a bogus sample? Who was this Silverstein, and what was his relationship to Weaverman? Thurston made a mental note to query MacDonald further.

Thurston checked her watch. Forty minutes. She lowered her head to take in the details of the Social Security legislation she would be discussing with Republican colleagues. Before long, her office computer gave its distinctive sound that indicated an instant message from Cynthia. Cynthia used this form of communication, rather than the phone, when she didn't want the visitor to hear her words. *What now? I told you I'd be there.*

"Senator, a Mr. Jamieson to see you," Thurston read. "Says it's important. Should I send him away?"

Jamieson? Thurston drew a shallow breath, started typing, changed her mind, and then backspaced over her first words. She had no choice. "Send him in," she typed.

Cynthia's face showed itself first, followed by the figure of the buff-looking Jamieson.

"You can go, Cynthia. Thank you."

Thurston's eyes rose to the face of the man standing in front of her. Her reaction occurred too quickly to hide it from Jamieson. "What the hell happened to you?"

Jamieson seemed annoyed. "Never mind that! I've decided to take you up on your offer."

Oh. This time she thought quickly enough to make sure that any lack of understanding didn't translate into noticeable facial confusion. Obviously, Thurston's powers of persuasion back in Emporia hadn't let her down. *Welcome to the winning team, Dick.* What Jamieson didn't know was that his being part of that team would likely prove of no benefit to him.

CHAPTER 17

BLASTOFF

Naval Research Laboratory, Monterey, California, USA
36°35'34"N latitude, 121°51'17"W longitude
Monday, 8:00 AM, August 3, 2009

Silverstein braced himself for the upcoming outburst. Following Dickey's departure Friday night, Kipling had stomped out the door without a further word. She was pissed, and knowing her capacity to hold a grudge, he could feel a storm brewing. She hadn't called over the weekend, and he had been afraid to contact her, much as he wanted to hear how she escaped from Dickey's partner.

Embarrassed to do otherwise, he continued looking at his computer monitor when Kipling walked through the door. But knowing that the grenade had been tossed into his foxhole and that she was waiting for eye contact—which he, thankfully, had recovered enough to give—Silverstein sheepishly turned in his chair.

Kipling didn't hold back. "Well, what do you have to say for yourself?" she demanded. Simultaneously, she threw a manila folder on to a side table.

Silverstein figured that logic represented his best line of defense. "I made an on-the-spot decision that the risk was too great."

With hands planted on her hips, Kipling shot back. "Victor, you've known me for some time. From my stint with the Forest Service, you know I understand weapons. I even shoot bow." Her eyes lasered into his. "I bet you didn't know *that*, did you? You also know I don't make snap decisions without thinking them through. I set up a perfect ambush. And instead, you ignore my help and almost get yourself killed in the process."

He blinked. "You shoot bow?"

"In college. I was on a team."

Good! Maybe an opportunity to change the subject. "I shot for a while. Now it just sits in my guest room closet."

"Don't try to change the subject. I'm still mad at you."

Silverstein knew that his next statement was a bit of a stretch, but his male ego required it just the same. "I just about had him, thank you."

Kipling rolled her eyes and made no attempt to stifle her laugh.

"Just about had him, huh? From where I stood, it looked like you were down for the count."

"Looks can be deceiving, you know. Didn't your parents teach you that?" Knowing that he was foundering in quicksand, he changed tack. "Besides, backing up, you're forgetting one thing ... and you owe me this."

"What's that?"

"When I left you at the gate, I had no idea you had a gun. If I'd known that, it would have been different. Without a weapon, it would just have been you against him, one on one, until I ran around the car. By then Dickey could have smashed your head in, or worse. Remember, he *did* have a gun."

Kipling continued her assault. "Did you know *he* had a gun back there at the gate?"

"Well, no."

"Well then."

"Well then, what?" Silverstein was sinking fast and knew that his initial strategy had been best. "Can't you see that after what I put you through in Colorado, I had no choice?"

Kipling's boastful attitude subsided, and she pulled up a chair. "That's real sweet, Victor. But if there's ever a next time, I expect you to give me the benefit of the doubt. Do we have an understanding?"

Silverstein drew an internal breath of relief. The thunder had become less threatening; he could see the storm receding over the horizon. "I understand."

Kipling focused on Silverstein's face. He could detect a degree of sympathy there, however slight.

"How's your eye?"

"Better, thank you. It's the bruises on my back and legs that hurt now."

Silverstein sat quietly, and Kipling did the same, both avoiding eye contact. Given that she had made the first move toward reconciliation, it was his obligation to reciprocate.

The reason he had wanted to call her all weekend bubbled to the surface. "Give me details! I've been waiting since Friday to learn how you got away."

Silverstein leaned back, hands folded behind his head, and listened to Kipling's story of her escape from Myra, Dickey's cohort. "And you broke her arm and left her tied up in duct tape? Damn!"

"It was her wrist actually, and I didn't mean to. It just sort of happened."

Silverstein reminisced. This display of bravery was no different from when she'd saved his butt in Fort Collins. He continued. "And then, at my house, I can't believe how clever you were. Dickey fell for it, hook, line, and sinker."

The crimson in her face finally receded.

Kipling held out her palms. "It was the only thing that made any sense to me. I couldn't see any benefit in turning him over to the police. For your friend Weaverman's sake, I figured it was important to keep our channels open with Raf—"

Silverstein interrupted. "And how did you know I had a safe in the bedroom?"

"I didn't. I made that up. All I did was walk around the corner to prepare the envelope with my hair." Kipling's eyes narrowed. "You have a safe in the bedroom?"

Silverstein nodded. At the time, he had taken for granted that she somehow knew that. In fact, he had given her the correct combination.

"Don't you agree that we had nothing to gain by holding Dickey?"

Silverstein nodded again. "You did the right thing."

He started thinking, doubly relieved that their relationship had returned to normal. He needed her to help figure out this mess. "That's the hell of it. All this started with Weaverman's call. Dickey's arrival means I sure stirred up the pot when I told Rafferty we had the samples. And we know even less where your clever subterfuge will lead. It seems like we're back to square one. Although … I expect we're going to hear from Rafferty after he tests the DNA and discovers that it's normal. Until then, what do we do?"

Kipling stood and started pacing.

"Let's summarize what we know. First, Weaverman's been abducted; he could even be dead, but—.

Silverstein cut her off. "Wait! One thing that Dickey did say was that Weaverman's alive and safe."

Kipling nodded and continued. "Second, *everything* Weaverman told you earlier is probably true. Sending professionals like Dickey and Myra requires resources, which means there's serious money behind this operation." She stopped and turned, looking exasperated. "There's nothing new. We knew that much after we learned Weaverman was kidnapped."

"Never mind. How can we get them to shake loose Weaverman?"

Kipling hesitated before answering. "You know, don't you, that all of this means that there's a lot more at stake here than just Weaverman's life, not that that isn't important." Her voice increased in volume. "Think about it! The reason Weaverman's been abducted is because someone wants to keep all this secret."

She pointed her finger at Silverstein. "Knowing what we know, would you want knowledge of this find controlled by a few individuals with unknown intentions, maybe with a maniac in charge who may stop at nothing to maintain control of this discovery? It's not the same, but imagine if Hitler had been the first to discover the atom bomb. Let's face it. You and I are privy to information that has significance well beyond Weaverman."

Silverstein arched his eyebrows. "I think we need help."

"We now have it."

"Have what?"

"Have help."

"From whom?"

Kipling smiled. "I would have told you long before now, but I wanted you to come crawling first."

"That hurts!" Silverstein looked back with the most pitiful expression he could muster. "What do you mean?"

"You can lose that wounded little boy look. It doesn't work on me."

Sometimes I just can't believe this woman. "I repeat, what help?"

"I left out one tiny piece of my story that happened before I rode up on my red stallion and rescued you from Dickey."

Silverstein couldn't take any more. "Please spare me. I'm crying uncle already."

Kipling continued. "Back at the Branding Iron, after I duct-taped Myra, I called Lopez. Believe it or not, he was still at work. It was late his time."

Silverstein blinked. "You called Hector? That's what I suggested, and you pooh-poohed the idea."

"Yeah, well, that was before we ran into Myra and Dickey."

"What'd he say?"

Kipling returned to her seat. "It was an interesting conversation. We didn't talk long, but I gave him the gist of the story from beginning to end. I figured that's what you would do." She hesitated. "When I got to the part about there being a psychic born every so often, his interest suddenly peaked."

Silverstein responded. "Anybody's would. That's a given."

Kipling's next words came slowly. "I know what you're saying, but it was more than that. It was like I hit a nerve. Maybe it was my imagination, but it was as if I had just told him something he'd heard before."

"So you think he knows something?"

"Could be."

Silverstein leaned forward. "Is that it?"

"No, he regretted that he couldn't help us and told me to be careful. When I arrived home from your house, he called back. I told him what happened, including my bit with the hair, and he seemed relieved. He said he needed to talk to you and would call today."

Silverstein stood and took in the moment, enjoying the fleeting thought that help might be on the way. "Good. All of our cunning and ingenuity here in Monterey can get us only so far. Did he say when he'd—"

Both heads rotated toward the phone.

Silverstein took note of the number on the caller ID and winked. "Houston, we have liftoff."

CHAPTER 18

CONFIRMATION

Johnstown Flood National Memorial, South Fork, Pennsylvania, USA
40°20'59"N latitude, 78°46'17"W longitude
Monday, 11:15 AM, August 3, 2009

Less than a week had passed since Peggy Sue Houston read Augusta's letter. After word of the safe and its remarkable contents leaked from the Flood Memorial, the local press came to do an interview. Once the story hit the wires and far-flung newspapers printed it, she spent most of her time on the telephone. Half the calls were nasty, accusing Houston of having staged the whole thing to gain personally from the publicity. The rest of the calls covered a variety of personalities: fortune-tellers who assured Houston that they too possessed Augusta's unique abilities; spiritualists who insisted that her discovery signaled the end of the world; amateur magicians who were convinced she had staged a practical joke and wanted to know her secrets; radio and television personalities who wanted interviews; Park Service personnel concerned about the organization's reputation; and on and on.

The one rock to whom Houston could cling during this commotion was her supervisor, who provided total support. He believed her and was a logical thinker. He said he knew someone at the Smithsonian Institution in Washington, DC, who could age date the paper in the letter and envelope. That would be a first step, he said, in authenticating the safe's contents.

One of the telephone calls Houston received turned out to be extremely relevant. It came from a grandson of Augusta's half-brother, William Schmidt. Peter Schmidt—now in his 70s—corroborated what Houston had surmised, that William had survived the flood. In fact, he had lived until the early 1950s, and Peter remembered him, along with his stories of the disaster. Peter confirmed that William's father and stepmother, and their three children, had perished in the flood and were buried in Grandview Cemetery, overlooking Johnstown. As soon as time permitted, Houston intended to pay her respects.

In Houston's conversation with Peter, she hoped that he could resolve the single discrepancy that made absolutely no sense. Unfortunately, he corroborated what Houston had seen on the list of the flood dead. There had been no typographical error!

CHAPTER 19

ORDER DIPTERA, FAMILY MUSCIDAE

George Bush Center for Intelligence, McLean, Virginia, USA
38°56'06"N latitude, 77°08'46"W longitude
Monday, 11:25 AM, August 3, 2009

Hector Lopez returned the phone to its cradle and stared across at Miller, who had listened to Silverstein's side of the conversation through the speakerphone. Lopez leaned back, the fingers of both hands drumming the desk.

"What's your take, Marc?" He hoped that Miller had caught something he hadn't.

Miller sighed. "He didn't add much to what Kipling told you Friday night."

"Except that this time, he came right out and asked me for help for his friend Weaverman."

Following Friday night's conversation with Kipling, Lopez hadn't spent the weekend doing nothing. Using in-house sources, he confirmed Weaverman's existence and his employment at the Naval Research Laboratory. Barbara, Hector's wife and an NRL employee, had never heard of him; this was not surprising, since there were well over two thousand employees at the Washington campus.

Miller responded. "So what do we do? Although we now have a foreign connection to this mess, it's not like we can go busting into a national laboratory and ask what's happened to one of their employees."

Lopez understood. Most citizens knew that the CIA's mission concerned *foreign* intelligence, with the domestic side under the purview of the Federal Bureau of Investigation. It said so right on the Agency's Web site: *the Director of Central Intelligence (DCI) serves as the principal adviser to the President and the National Security Council on all matters of foreign intelligence related to national security.* That didn't mean they couldn't contact their friends (and they had a few) at the Bureau to look into the matter, although they would say that a missing person was hardly within their jurisdiction either, and was something best left to local police. Worse, their FBI contacts might ask why this was important, and that wouldn't do just now.

Lopez changed tack. "Let's forget Weaverman for the time being. If there's something to this prophecy gene, then—."

Miller interjected. "Prophecy gene. I like that."

Lopez blinked. "What I was going to say is that if there is something to all of this, then the last thing we want is for the bad guys to get hold of it."

Miller's eyes betrayed his thoughts. "Wait a minute. Are you saying you're going to leave Silverstein out in the cold again?"

"Goddamn you, Miller." Lopez shot from his seat, veins bulging in his neck, and turned his back on his friend and colleague.

What struck Lopez so hard was that what Miller had said was true. Two years ago, when Silverstein had wanted more information than Lopez could give, he had stonewalled Silverstein and had given up his store of data (and even then, he hadn't told him everything) only after two henchmen and then an Egyptian terrorist—and a not so insignificant hurricane off the coast of Bermuda—had come crashing down on Silverstein's head. To top it off, after it was all over, Silverstein and Kipling provided him with more information than he gave them in return. And Lopez couldn't let himself forget that, in the process, he had also put his own wife in danger.

Lopez faced Miller. "What is it you expect me to do, Marc? Congratulate him on discovering 10 percent of a visible iceberg when we know where the remaining 90 percent lies hidden? Maybe I should just swear him in and give him a CIA access card? Am I making any sense here?"

Miller placed his hands over his face, sat forward in his chair, and faced the floor. "Silverstein saved your life in college. Now he's facing something that's way over his head, and you're turning a deaf ear." Miller held up both hands. "Don't get me wrong. I remember how you agonized over this the last time around. I don't want you to make a mistake you're going to be sorry for later. He's asked for your help, Hector."

What made the problem so intractable, as Lopez recognized the instant Kipling brought it up, was that her information confirmed that scientists both inside and outside the United States had stumbled upon the unusual gene sequence. While scientists made discoveries every day, they usually became public by way of scientific publications or the press. Contrarily, private companies seeking to patent their results held their secrets tight.

Weaverman worked for the U.S. government. The citizenry who paid his salary held title to his find. Silverstein said he was sure that someone had silenced Weaverman—implying that others wished to keep the information hidden. Government personnel who shouldn't be keeping secrets were doing so. That was bad enough, but when that same data came by way of a Middle Eastern group that had tried to devastate the nation's capital with a Category 5 hurricane in 2007, Lopez had to take it seriously. Lopez's job at the CIA involved counterintelligence—which in recent years correlated directly with counterterrorism.

Lopez chose to force the issue. "Okay, Marc. Since you were kind enough to remind me of my moral predicament, I want you to tell me how we ... I ... get out of it?"

Miller sat up straight. "You're making too big a deal of Silverstein's lone request. All he wants is to be able to respond to his friend's plea for help. He may have a fleeting interest in the genetic work, but that's not why he's involved. I know we can't do anything directly, but that doesn't mean we can't shake the bushes. Silverstein tried, and Kipling's ruse with the hair was damn clever. It didn't get Silverstein anywhere, but it sure kept him in the loop."

Lopez responded. "If I haven't mentioned it before, Silverstein is a certifiable genius, comparable to our Mensas."

Miller cringed. "You have! But don't sell us short. We're not exactly lightweights. Remember my personal credo: better products and service through chicanery."

Lopez laughed. "So tell me, what do we do to find Weaverman, assuming he's not already dead … and in the process, help our own cause?"

Miller smiled. "I thought you'd never ask."

Lopez rolled his eyes.

"Here's what we do. Let's face it, this secrecy, if that's what it is, extends higher than Weaverman's boss, Rafferty. Do you really think that an NRL biologist would have the motivation or wherewithal to kidnap an employee? I say that we reach for fruit that's a little higher off the ground."

"And how do we do that?"

"We do that by doing things we're good at, by using the innovative technology we're known for."

Lopez covered his eyes and forced back his recurring thought of pulling out his service revolver and blowing away his partner. Miller did this all the time, getting to his point through a series of mazes that left the listener wanting to scream for mercy. Despite his urge to off his partner, Lopez looked up with interest. "Can I assume that you're talking about something more elaborate than bugging his phone and using a tail? We're known for doing quite a bit of that."

Miller placed his hands on his knees. "Not a bad thought, but I'm thinking we can be a little more sophisticated these days. Sound is good, but video is better. I'm thinking of the latest Mensa invention."

Lopez had to stop and think. The Mensas had come up with some doozies, including the amnesiac-spiked knockout spray and the tracking chip they had used with success against Ghali in Colorado. "You're not proposing that we kidnap Rafferty and sew a chip in his scalp?"

"Don't be silly. We know *where* he is."

Lopez was taken aback. *He's calling me silly?*

Miller stood up to make his next point—or what Lopez hoped would be the clinching argument. "Have you already forgotten last month's seminar?" He wavered. "I'm referring to the first part, not the second. I missed the second."

Lopez thought back to the briefing, the more interesting second half having to do with a new method for extracting information from an unwilling participant. He then caught himself and almost choked when he remembered what Miller was referring to. "You're not suggesting we activate a Romguard?"

"Why not? The Mensas are anxious to give it a try, and Winston's already checked out. Remember that you volunteered him because of his flying experience. It'll give us a front-row seat on Rafferty's day-to-day activities. We'll have pictures of his contacts. You saw the demonstration. That sucker worked like a champ."

Lopez squinted and shook his head. "Under test conditions only, I might add. One wrong turn and, what was it, $200,000? Down the drain."

Following their briefing on the latest contraptions they had invented, Lopez concluded that most of the Mensan were, in fact, lunatics. They patterned themselves after Q, James Bond's weapons designer, admirably played by the actor Desmond Llewelyn until he, ironically, died in a car accident in 1999. The Mensan, however, didn't restrict themselves to weapons design or ejection seats. Their ideas exceeded the limits of reason. And the Romguard, named after its designer, Peter Romguard, a wunderkind in mechanical engineering, biomechanics, and miniaturization, stretched that frontier to its outer reaches.

During the briefing, Romguard himself had demonstrated the abilities of his mechanical device. All of the attendees marveled at its capabilities, given its size—and became dizzy watching its gyrations about the room. Lopez couldn't argue that the list of attributes for this invention wasn't impressive: remotely controllable using electromagnetic frequencies that could penetrate most buildings; the ability to operate either while hovering or sitting in place; onboard video and audio transmitted back live to the user; and a one-week life span, based upon eight hours of activity every twenty-four hours, depending on how much flying and image transmission proved necessary. The downside was that each one cost a small fortune to build, test, and deploy, and required a trained operator to fly, which was particularly difficult in any sort of wind. And while in operation, it needed a data transfer facility within a block or two of its location.

Miller continued. "Remember Romguard's final comment. 'This device could revolutionize field work.'"

Given Miller's enthusiasm and the two weeks that Lopez had invested in John Winston's training, he acquiesced. "I guess there's no harm—unless we get caught. You know that we're not supposed to spy on our own citizenry."

"This isn't really spying, is it?" Miller winked.

Lopez raised an eyebrow at that comment.

"Besides, Hector, don't you remember that each one has its own self-destruction device? Practically fail-safe. Two chemicals separated by a flimsy glass partition. When they mix, they go boom. Although the operator can activate the mechanism manually, any extreme movement will break the separation and set off the tiny explosion. Peter says there's precious little left to examine. There'll be no wiretaps or bugs to come back to haunt us. We'd be killing two birds with one Romguard, so to speak. We need on-the-spot intelligence, Hector." Miller paused. "I recommend that we move ASAP. If Weaverman's in danger, there's no point in waiting."

Lopez lifted his phone to call Winston but stopped to snicker. "I can't believe we're going to trust our intelligence-gathering to a souped-up housefly."

CHAPTER 20

SIX FEET UNDER

Naval Research Laboratory, Monterey, California, USA
36°35'34"N latitude, 121°51'17"W longitude
Monday, 8:25 AM, August 3, 2009

"Well, you couldn't have put it more directly," Kipling declared after listening to the conversation between Silverstein and Lopez.

Silverstein's eyebrows rose. "What do you mean? Asking for help to find Weaverman?"

"Yeah."

"Well for God's sake, he's in a better position to do something about this than we are. Besides, don't you think he owes us a favor or two after what we did in 2007?"

Kipling leaned back, the front legs of her chair lifting off the floor. "I agree, but I can hear him right now. 'It's not in our jurisdiction,' he's saying. 'We have no right to investigate something internal to the United States, particularly when it involves government employees.'"

"Hector wouldn't do that to me, Linda. He'd help me if he could."

Kipling shook her head. "You may be smart, but you're also naive!"

Silverstein reacted. "Why do you say that?"

"Look at how things played out in Bermuda. Even after all was said and done, do you think Lopez told us any more than he had to?"

Silverstein conceded the point. "He hardly told us anything."

"Exactly. And did you wonder why he swore us to secrecy? You were a goddamn hero and never got one bit of credit for it."

With that comment, Silverstein bristled and chose to set the record straight. He had played a role, maybe a big one, but it had taken the three of them to pull off their miracle in Bermuda. "I don't deserve any more credit than you or Barbara! It took the three of us to get the job done." Silverstein shrugged, his lips pursed. "But you're right. Lopez told me that, for national security purposes, our whole escapade had to remain secret."

Kipling slid her hands forward over her legs. "That's why I don't think we can count on him. If he does anything to help, it won't be because of Weaverman."

Silverstein sighed. "Thanks for dashing my hopes that we were making progress. So what do we do now, short of flying to Washington and confronting Rafferty directly?"

Kipling leaned forward. "You can be sure you'll hear from Rafferty—."

"When he realizes the hair is bogus?"

"That's right."

Silverstein considered his options. "I could come right out and tell him that we tricked him, that I didn't appreciate being pressured, but that we still have the real samples."

Kipling stood up. "That's an idea. You could also threaten him. Tell him that unless he frees Weaverman, you're going to the press with an announcement that NRL has discovered … let's call it the prophecy gene."

Silverstein's eyes opened wide. "Prophecy gene; that's good. If Rafferty's in cahoots with someone, that'll get us some reaction." He smiled. "I wouldn't be surprised if we see Dickey and Myra again."

Kipling winced. "Dickey maybe, but it'll be a while for Myra."

"A broken wrist won't keep her off the job that long."

Kipling's face contorted as if she had just sucked on a lemon. "Myra has more problems than her wrist."

"What else did you do to her?"

"When I knocked her down and had my knee in her back, I may have been a little too energetic in trying to extract information."

"Energetic?"

"Let's just say that I now know what a human shoulder tearing apart sounds like."

Silverstein cringed and turned his head. This description of Myra reminded him of what Cameron Fitzby, the mastermind of the Bermuda operation, had looked like after Kipling had run him down. Silverstein never had the nerve to ask what she had done to him.

Silverstein strained to get his thoughts back on track. "I like your idea. Whoever is behind Rafferty wants to keep this secret. If we push some more buttons, maybe something'll happen. On top of that, we should get some reaction soon from the phony hair sample."

"Okay." Kipling headed toward the door. She twirled on her heels, reached down for the folder she had brought earlier, and handed it to Silverstein.

"Take a look at this. I cut it out of today's *New York Times*. You'll find it interesting."

Kipling left the room, leaving the door ajar.

Silverstein opened the folder and read:

Augusta Schmidt, Johnstown flood victim: fact or fraud?

JOHNSTOWN, PENNSYLVANIA—Local reporters have been investigating a story that has captivated this Pennsylvania town. Peggy Sue Houston, curator of the Johnstown Flood National Memorial, claims to have acquired a letter written hours before the devastating flood of May 31, 1889, in which more than 2,200 of Johnstown's inhabitants perished.

In that letter, the author, a 19-year-old girl named Augusta Schmidt, said that she could foresee the future, including the destruction of Johnstown less than 24 hours later. She also foresaw other future events, including descriptions that are undeniably those of the atom bomb and, incredibly, the Sept. 11 tragedy in New York City.

The letter was discovered intact in an old, rusty safe that was recently excavated far beneath the foundation of a building whose cornerstone was set in 1932. Speculation is that the safe had lain there since the 1889 flood.

Interviews with the construction crew who unearthed the safe suggest their story is authentic. Any suspicion lies with Ms. Houston, who opened the safe alone with no witnesses. The letter has been sent to the Smithsonian Institution in Washington, DC, for age dating.

Silverstein squinted and stared up at the ceiling. He reread the article a second time, folded it, and put it into his wallet. As he did so, he sensed a presence in the hallway. Kipling's head peered around the door. He beckoned her inside.

Kipling spoke first. "Are you thinking what I'm thinking?"

Silverstein responded. "I don't know what you're thinking, but the first thing I'm wondering is whether my old friend, Jimmy Travers, still works at the Smithsonian."

"And if he is, and he confirms the age of the letter, then what?"

Silverstein responded with no hesitation. "Then my second phone call will be to Peggy Sue Houston in Johnstown, Pennsylvania. She'll know whether Augusta Schmidt's body was recovered and where she was buried following the flood."

"Eureka! All great minds travel in the same track."

Silverstein laughed aloud. "There's a corollary to that statement, you know."

"What's that?"

"All fools think alike."

CHAPTER 21

YE OLDE SOB

Russell Senate Office Building, Washington, DC, USA
38°53'32"N latitude, 77°00'28"W longitude
Tuesday, 7:00 PM, August 4, 2009

MacDonald was working late. The duties of a U.S. senator, at least while living in Washington, seemed endless. Committee meetings, conferences on the Hill, concerns from home state constituents, photo opportunities, staff administration. All of these ate up hours and left little time for what could prove much more important.

Rafferty had just called from his NRL office and said he was on his way over, that he had news, good news, news that MacDonald would be anxious to hear.

MacDonald pumped his fist in the air. He wanted to yell out at the top of his lungs but couldn't—it was a rare night when someone wasn't working down the hall. Besides, those who held the privilege of serving as a U.S. senator—any of whose off-the-cuff utterances could find their way into the *Washington Post*—were not the type who should yell out in seeming abandon. Nor were governors, as one by the name of Howard Dean learned when he ran for the Democratic nomination for president back in 2004. Instead, MacDonald pulled open a drawer, reached to the back for his flask, threw his feet up on the desk, leaned back, and took a healthy swig. One was enough. He had learned that lesson early in his career.

Rafferty hadn't actually told him that the DNA sample obtained from Silverstein had provided a match for the gene sequence in question, but his words and the tone in his voice suggested as much. Rafferty had wanted to come right over, saying that what he discovered had exciting and unexpected significance.

MacDonald could imagine the exciting part, but not the unexpected.

George Bush Center for Intelligence, McLean, Virginia, USA
38°56'06"N latitude, 77°08'46"W longitude
Tuesday, 7:05 PM, August 4, 2009

They had just gotten the call. Hector Lopez and Marc Miller raced down the hall and entered the makeshift command center for controlling the Romguard. John Winston sat at his console.

"What's up, John?" Initially skeptical, Lopez had become as excited as the others on this maiden voyage of their camera- and microphone-laden insect.

"Take a look. Rafferty's on the move." Winston pointed to the screen.

On the large plasma wall screen, Lopez could see a hallway disappearing behind him. The image appeared amazingly smooth and clear. "What's happening?"

"Rafferty's been in his office most of the afternoon, and we just picked up this telephone conversation." Winston reached over and flipped a switch.

It's me. I've got news, some of it you're expecting to hear, and some of it that'll surprise you, that'll knock your socks off. Can I come over? ... I'm on my way.

Lopez marveled at how well this operation had progressed. Following their decision yesterday to utilize a Romguard—a miniaturized electronic flying device identical in size to a housefly—they had moved quickly. Because of the uncertainty involved in flying the device into a strange building, Peter Romguard suggested that they position his bug outside

NRL and ride Rafferty to get inside. The plan had transpired successfully eleven hours earlier.

Winston continued. "Rafferty's excited about something. We followed him all day, back and forth between his office and his laboratory. Other than a few greetings to his colleagues, Rafferty kept to himself. What you just heard are his first words of significance. He's discovered something and can't wait to tell someone."

Marc Miller interjected. "Could you get a read on the call by sight or sound?"

"No. He used an automatic dialer, and even if the touch-tones were audible, we couldn't pick them up."

Lopez's eyes rose in time to see the door to the building close behind Rafferty. "Where are you sitting on Rafferty's body?"

Winston turned briefly toward Lopez, all the while keeping an eye on the video image. "Peter recommended that when we were in hitchhiking mode, we position it on his lapel behind the neck. It'd be nice to set it on the front of his body, but that's too risky. Here, let me show you."

Winston reached down to his controls and moved one of his toggles. The video image rotated. "Notice that I can move the camera in any direction I want. I'll angle it down. See how it looks like we're about six feet off the ground."

"That's amazing. Are you reading the signals directly from the bug?"

Winston raised an eyebrow. "You must have missed that part of Romguard's briefing. The transmission power is too small. Hansley's sitting in a van outside NRL. He has equipment that receives the signal, amplifies it, and then broadcasts it back here. Our return signals go first to Hansley's van and then to the Romguard. Averill did the initial tailing and will continue to follow Rafferty, staying as close as he can so we maintain control."

Lopez looked back at the screen. They watched as Rafferty left the building and walked across a parking lot, presumably to his car. Suddenly, the image began to vibrate and then disappeared. "What the hell?"

Winston remained cool. "We're okay. We're picking up some flutter from the wind. When the vibration gets too big, the camera goes into a lock position and automatically stops transmission. It'll start up again once the wind dies down, probably when he's inside the car."

"Could it get blown off?"

"Not to worry! It'd take more than a stiff wind to dislodge our bug. It has small pincers that look like needles that lock onto the fabric underneath—a trick Romguard says he learned from the Mensa magicians." Winston laughed. "What I have to remember is to release the pincers before I take off."

Lopez and Miller watched in fascination. Sure enough, as soon as Rafferty entered the car and shut the door—which they could hear through the Romguard's microphone—the image returned.

Winston tended to his controls. "Our view is limited because we're looking backwards, probably right at the head restraint. I'm going to rotate the camera to see where to fly, release the pincers, and take off to get a better view."

Lopez fidgeted. "Isn't that a little dangerous? Why not stay put?"

"You're right, but there's also some danger in staying where we are. If he moved the wrong way, we could get squished."

Winston deftly manipulated the controls while talking his observers through his actions. "First, I'm rotating the camera to the side to make sure we have a clean egress path." A clear image appeared, looking toward the passenger door. "Looks clear. Okay … I've just released the pincers and have added a little power to lift off from the fabric." Winston nodded toward a power display on the lower left corner of the screen. "See how I've increased the wing flap speed. As you probably recall, the propulsion for the Romguard is very similar to that of an actual fly. We need about 25% of maximum power to take off."

Lopez watched as the power display rose steadily. At a few ticks above that critical value, the video image moved, probably signifying liftoff, he thought. "Can he hear it?"

"No. Peter's testing has shown that the wing movement isn't audible to most humans until about the 90% power level." Winston paused. "I'm going to fly toward the passenger seat and make a right turn. We'll ride out the rest of the trip sitting atop the backseat. Once we're stable, I'll rotate the camera forward." He chuckled. "I could ask Hansley where we're headed, but it'll be more fun to figure it out ourselves."

Events unfolded the way Winston described. Once the camera faced forward, they had the same view as would a rear-seat passenger sitting in the middle.

Lopez recognized the landscape visible through the windshield. "I know the area around NRL. He just left Overlook Avenue and is heading north on 295."

Winston removed his hands from the controls and relaxed. "This is going to be interesting. Where do you think he's headed?"

"My guess is to some Beltway bandit, a contractor dealing in genetics or something like that." It made sense to Lopez that a government employee would team up with private industry—because that was where the money was.

[The sound of honking horns.] *Get the fuck out of my way, asshole!*

Everyone laughed aloud, with Winston the first to respond. "Your friend's in a big hurry and has a bad disposition, I'd say."

"He's not *my* friend." Lopez squinted at the screen. "He's exiting and getting onto 395." Minutes ticked by as all in the room watched from their backseat perch. "Who the hell's he meeting?"

They watched as the scenery changed. Finally, Miller chimed in. "I know this area. My wife's a Capitol tour guide, and I often meet her there. He's on 1st Street, headed north to Constitution. See the Supreme Court to the right. The Senate Office Buildings are ahead, Russell to the left, Dirksen to the right."

After they watched for another minute, Winston inched his hands back to the controls. "Okay; it looks like he's going to park. I've got to get us back on his body somewhere."

Lopez watched as Winston steadied his hands. But just as he prepared for liftoff, the car came to an abrupt stop. Faster than Winston could react, Rafferty opened the door, climbed out, and slammed the door shut—all before Winston could fly the Romguard back to the front seat.

Winston breathed out audibly. "I can't believe it! We just got ourselves locked inside the goddamn car."

Lopez watched as Winston did a quick rotational scan of the inside of the car and the windows, an obvious egress point. In the heat of Washington's summers, people often cracked their windows. As luck would have it, the left rear appeared to have about a half-inch gap.

"Okay. There it is." Winston took the situation in stride. He flew the Romguard toward the open window and judged the distance. "I think I can make it through. Hold on."

Winston flew the Romguard ever so slowly. Fortunately, the video image held still, meaning there was no wind blowing through the narrow opening. If the video camera shut off, it would have spelled disaster. But within fifteen seconds from the time the front door had closed, the Romguard exited into the fresh evening air.

Lopez had begun to hyperventilate. "Where's Rafferty?"

Winston immediately ramped up the power to 60%. "I'm going to ascend vertically and see if we can locate him."

Miller responded, equally excited. "I think he started to walk to the right."

Lopez experienced vertigo as Winston rotated the camera quickly about the landscape. "There he is, straight ahead." Rafferty wasn't all that fast and hadn't gone far.

Winston pushed the throttle lever to 100%, and all viewers could sense the acceleration. "At full throttle and no wind, I can hit 25 miles per hour."

Lopez watched as the distance between the flying device and their target decreased to zero. Winston reduced power and flew straight into the center rear collar of Rafferty's jacket just as he entered the building they had all but ignored in the excitement of keeping their eyes locked on Rafferty.

"Pincers activated." Winston rubbed his face with both hands and let out a sigh of relief.

Lopez noted that everyone in the room exhaled at almost the same time. "No harm done. Now where the hell is he?"

Miller responded. "I know exactly where he is. That's the entrance to the Russell Senate Office Building."

*   *   *   *

MacDonald paced back and forth. "What the hell's keeping him?" he muttered under his breath. Rather than soothing his nervous tension, the earlier drink had put him on edge.

The knock at the door played on his nerves in opposite directions, calming him down because he would now receive the latest information on the hair samples, but also exciting him because the next phase of their operation lay at hand.

MacDonald jerked open the door. Sweat beads glistened on Rafferty's brow, and his breathing seemed labored. "Come on in, Dennis."

MacDonald gestured to a seat and returned to his desk but did not sit down. He saw the warning signs. The burst of sound and air came through on the third heave. By then, MacDonald had stuck an index finger into each ear and turned away. Because Rafferty had never learned to cover his mouth, MacDonald knew that not only sound but also spit was on its way.

CHAPTER 22

SACRED EXCREMENT

George Bush Center for Intelligence, McLean, Virginia, USA
38° 56'06"N latitude, 77° 08'46"W longitude
Tuesday, 7:42 PM, August 4, 2009

"What the hell's going on?" Lopez noticed it the same time as the others. "Did that guy just put his fingers in his ears?"

The Romguard had ridden Rafferty through the entry into the Russell Senate Office Building, past security, up the steps, down the hallway, and through an office door. Two clues alerted those watching the video that they had neared their destination. Movement had stopped, judging from the video they received looking sideways alongside Rafferty's jacket. Simultaneously, the Romguard's microphone picked up what sounded like a knock on a door. Winston had informed Lopez of his intent to fly away from Rafferty the instant he arrived at his destination. He wanted to avoid any possibility of Rafferty removing his jacket, something Winston said he should have thought of earlier.

The instant the camera appeared to pass the threshold of the door, Winston released the Romguard's pincers and flew vertically. Making a quick scan of the area, he flew in place to Rafferty's left and immediately focused in on Rafferty's host. But before they had a clear visual, that figure rotated away from his guest, fingers in his ears.

Lopez watched as Winston moved his video toggle to see if Rafferty could provide a clue to what was happening. But before the camera had rotated back to Rafferty, the image whirled about the room, and a pop came through on the speaker.

"Damn! We've picked up some kind of turbulence. The Romguard's stalled out, and we're in a spin." Winston started working the controls.

Lopez understood Winston's alarm because he had actually paid attention during that part of Peter Romguard's briefing. The way Peter described flying his invention, it sounded much like flying an airplane. After college, Lopez had taken flying lessons in a single-engine Cessna 150. He had learned then that once an airplane, any airplane, stalled (meaning insufficient airspeed to provide lift to support the aircraft), the next step in its descent was called a spin. And unless the pilot could recover from this rotating spiral, fire, destruction, and death lay at hand. Lopez remembered stalling his 150 on purpose, under the watchful eye of his instructor, to understand the process. At least in the Cessna, recovery was straightforward if you knew what to do. Lopez prayed that Winston had trained on that maneuver. At the very least, they needed to identify Rafferty's host.

"I've got it." The Romguard had fallen dangerously close to the floor. Even as light and small as the Romguard was, a bump into a solid object would spell disaster. Winston let out a sigh of relief that preceded the same reaction by Lopez and Miller. "Let's gain some altitude and see what's going on here."

Lopez watched the video, which thankfully was now steady as the Romguard lifted vertically, this time to near the ceiling. For the first time, they looked down on both men in the room. "Okay, there's Rafferty. Who's the other guy?" He could see the lips move, but there was no audio. "Turn up the volume, will you?"

Winston switched toggles back and forth and turned a dial clockwise, with no change. "Something's happened. The guy on the left who put his fingers in his ears did that for a reason. Whatever it was, I think the blast blew out our microphone."

Russell Senate Office Building, Washington, DC, USA
38°53'32"N latitude, 77°00'28"W longitude
Tuesday, 7:43 PM, August 4, 2009

MacDonald turned back, the last of the echo from Rafferty's sneeze gone. He motioned Rafferty to a chair and sat down as well. "Talk to me."

Rafferty mopped his brow with his handkerchief before answering. For the first time that MacDonald could remember, Rafferty exuded excitement.

"First of all, there's no question that the DNA from the hair replicates Weaverman's gene sequence."

"Yes!" MacDonald pumped his fist in the air. "That was fast. I thought it would take longer."

"We've developed some new sequencing techniques that we're going to patent."

Based on their earlier conversation, MacDonald knew there was more. "This is what we've been hoping for, but you said there was more."

Rafferty appeared to hyperventilate. "You're not going to believe this! The person whose DNA we have?"

Rafferty waited, as if for a prompt. MacDonald obliged. "Yeah? What else do you know about him?"

"First of all, he's a she. And further, she's alive! The hair samples we received couldn't be more than a couple of weeks old, maybe days. One of the samples had the root ball connected, and that gives us DNA that's more robust."

MacDonald's mouth dropped slack. He thought about their earlier conversations. "Remind me why we care about whether he … she … is alive."

Rafferty's eyes seemed to glaze over. "Just because we have a DNA match doesn't mean that we have a clairvoyant! If she's alive, we can determine, once and for all, whether the gene sequence that Weaverman postulated, I repeat, *postulated*, based only on the mouse results—has any relevance to our species. If there's a human match out there, we need to find her." Rafferty paused and slid his hands forward over his pants.

MacDonald took in Rafferty's words and reflected on their significance. If Rafferty needed personal confirmation of clairvoyance before going forward with the more tedious second phase of genetic manipulation, they now had a lead far superior to the alternative—locating the DNA of someone from the past, long dead, who may or may not have been a clairvoyant.

MacDonald saw no need to continue the conversation. "Then I suggest you call Silverstein and locate that woman."

Without further coaxing, Rafferty hurried to the door, with MacDonald bringing up the rear. MacDonald leaned against the doorjamb, his eyes trailing Rafferty down the hall. He realized there was more to say. "One more thing!"

*   *   *   *

Other than the loss of audio, the Romguard had suffered no ill effects from its aborted death spiral. Following the seating of both men, Winston repositioned the device on the wall on a line perpendicular to the two and halfway between them. Non-setting glue (on the feet of the device) similar to that used on self-sticking paper held it in place. Because they no longer had audio, this position afforded them a sight line from which they could observe both sets of lips. Lopez soon realized that their view from this position was worthless. The Agency's lip readers would need to observe head-on to have any chance of making out the words. "This is no good."

Winston made the request. "Okay boss, you choose. Which one?"

Lopez considered his options. Since Rafferty was the one bringing information to the other, it made sense to read his lips. They already had an adequate visual of the man seated at the desk, enough to identify him. "Go for Rafferty."

Winston gave the Romguard a spike of power to break the bond of the sticky glue, lifted away from the wall, and flew to the window, a position behind the man seated at the desk, affording a clear, lighted view of Rafferty's face. "I'll zoom in on the face."

From what Lopez had picked up in casual office chitchat, even under the best of circumstances, lip readers could assess only one out of every three words. But considering their bad run of luck, beggars couldn't be choosers.

Only minutes expired before Rafferty rose and walked to the door.

Winston rattled off his demand. "Stay or go?"

To Lopez, the answer was obvious. They had arrived farther up the food chain, exactly where they wanted to be.

"We stay and then follow."

Winston nodded. "Yes sir."

*   *   *   *

Rafferty accepted MacDonald's advice and took his leave. As objectionable a human being as he was, Rafferty had certainly proved useful. And what good fortune it was, to have located a live human being who possessed Weaverman's gene sequence.

That understood, MacDonald remembered Jamieson's description of Silverstein and the difficulty he'd had in acquiring the DNA samples in the first place. If Silverstein should prove equally intransigent the second time around, things could get messy. No matter, thought MacDonald. He had committed too much to back off now. His final comment to Rafferty, an ultimatum for Silverstein to consider, would hopefully give Silverstein the encouragement he needed. If not, MacDonald had a backup plan. Dick Jamieson remained on call, ready to take the next plane out of Washington.

*   *   *   *

Winston flew the Romguard to a safe position high on the wall near the entry door. They watched as their newfound quarry retreated to his desk, immediately dialing a number on a cell phone. The conversation lasted only a minute.

"Do you recognize this guy?" The face was not familiar to Lopez.

Miller cleared his throat and spoke. "I've seen him somewhere, but I can't place him."

Winston manipulated his controls and repositioned the Romguard's video so that it occupied the left half of a split screen. "Things happened pretty fast during our entry. I'm going to rewind the video and play it in slow motion. Remember, we were looking sideways as Rafferty walked through the door."

Lopez watched as Winston rewound the video, returning to the point where Rafferty knocked on the door. He then reversed directions and moved forward a frame at a time.

Lopez and Miller reacted simultaneously, Lopez verbally. "Stop! Right there!"

Although the image was fuzzy and they looked at it sideways, the name-plate on the wall proved sufficiently clear to make out: *The Honorable Clifton MacDonald, Wyoming.*

"Holy shit! What the fuck have we gotten ourselves into?"

CHAPTER 23

DRAG

Naval Research Laboratory, Monterey, California, USA
36°35'34"N latitude, 121°51'17"W longitude
Wednesday, 8:00 AM, August 5, 2009

Silverstein had hoped that he would be the first to initiate contact. The caller ID suggested otherwise. He wondered how to handle it. Threaten Rafferty, as Kipling had suggested, exposing him and his accomplices to the press?

Rafferty's obnoxious voice was decidedly curt, more so than in previous calls. "This is Rafferty. I want you to tell me who she is and where she lives."

What? They had completed the DNA analysis already? "Who are you talking about?"

"Don't be cute. We'll find her. You tried to stiff us once. I'd hope you've learned your lesson."

"Why the hell do you want her? She has nothing to do with any of this. I'm the one who can get you what you want."

"I'll make this short. Weaverman's still alive. You have forty-eight hours."

Silverstein heard the click. *What was that all about? Do they think that Kipling has the prophecy gene? That's rubbish. The only other possibility is they determined that the hair was bogus and wanted to get to me through Kipling. Bastards!*

On top of that, he had threatened Silverstein with Weaverman. Rafferty knew he could use him as leverage—ransom for the DNA that Silverstein had foolishly claimed he had. *And I was just thinking how damned clever I was.*

Silverstein shook his head. Seconds passed before he jerked out his address book.

He hadn't spoken to Jimmy Travers in years and hoped he still worked at the Smithsonian. He'd been Silverstein's roommate during Travers's senior year at Penn State. Unlike many of his friends, Silverstein had spent his entire undergraduate life in the dormitories, moving downtown to an apartment only for his postgraduate work.

Silverstein dialed the number and glanced at his watch. Not quite lunchtime back in Washington.

"Travers."

The voice was a welcome memory. They had gotten along well during their year together before Travers left for Boston University, opting for a master's degree in anthropology to complement his bachelor's at Penn State. Silverstein, having completed his undergraduate requirements in three and a half years, chose to continue graduate school at Penn State. "Jimmy, Victor here. How the hell are you?"

"This couldn't be *the* Victor Mark Silverstein, the Navy's scientist extraordinaire."

"Yeah, it's me, Jimmy."

"What have you been up to? It's been a coon's age." Travers's upbringing in the hills of Tennessee came through often, not only in his accent but also in his colloquialisms.

"Oh, the usual." Silverstein cleared his throat. "But I'm calling because I need your help."

"You name it, old buddy. Anyone who could tutor a dummy like me to pass statistics deserves my undying loyalty. Without you, I'd never have made it."

"You haven't changed a bit, Jimmy. You've always underrated yourself." Silverstein paused and prepared himself. "Do you know anything about that letter that came in from Johnstown, Pennsylvania? I read about it in the paper."

Travers laughed. "From the kook who could foresee the future?"

"You know about it then."

Travers replied. "Hell's bells! You called the right place. I'm the one who did the dating analysis on the paper. The day before yesterday, as a matter of fact."

Silverstein swallowed hard. "Are you saying that the paper isn't old enough?"

"No, I'm not saying that at all. Whatever magician pulled off this stunt had the good sense to use paper dating from the late 1800s, both for the envelope and the letter. I give credit where credit's due."

Silverstein let out his breath. "Then why are you so sure it's a hoax?"

"Come on, Victor, you don't believe in stuff like that, do you? Besides, there's something else that gives it away as a prank."

"What's that, Jimmy?"

"What did the newspaper article tell you?"

Silverstein summarized the clipping. "It said that a young woman, Augusta Schmidt, wrote a letter before the Johnstown Flood, foretelling the disaster and seeing other things in the future."

Silverstein could hear the chuckle on the other end of the line. "That's right. But whoever tried to pull this one off forgot one important piece of new technology that's available now."

Silverstein brought his hand to his forehead. "I'm missing something, Jimmy. What is it you have besides dating the paper?"

"Haven't you ever watched *CSI?* We have DNA, pardner, with testing methods far more sophisticated than when that show started back in 2000."

Silverstein's heart raced. "Jimmy, what are you saying? Where the hell did you get DNA? Surely you can't extract it from fingerprints on the letter?"

"No, we're not that good yet, but it's a piece of cake to get it from the saliva when the envelope got licked."

Silverstein began to hyperventilate. "You have the DNA for the person who sealed that letter?"

Silverstein reflected on the magnitude of this statement. If they had Augusta's DNA, they could determine if she possessed the prophecy gene.

He tried to keep his voice steady. "Jimmy, this is very important. Do you still have that envelope?"

"Sorry, buddy. I mailed both the letter and envelope back to Houston. Along with a note telling her that whoever tried to pull this off forgot one minor detail."

"Jimmy, I'm in the dark here. What could possibly be in the DNA that would tell you the letter is a fraud?"

"Elementary, my dear Watson. I didn't do much of an analysis, but I did do one thing. Whoever licked that envelope forgot one thing."

Silverstein's patience had reached its limit. "Dammit, Jimmy, spit it out!"

There was a pause before Travers responded. "Your words are unusually appropriate. It was a *male* from our species who licked the envelope, Victor. I found a Y chromosome. If Augusta was the one who licked the envelope, he was a he and not a she."

CHAPTER 24

UNDERCOVER

Senate Dining Room, U.S. Capitol, Washington, DC, USA
38° 53'26"N latitude, 77° 00'32"W longitude
Wednesday, noon, August 5, 2009

Thurston sipped at the Senate Bean Soup (a gastronomical tradition since the early twentieth century) and then pushed the bowl away, all the while trying to convince herself that she'd had no choice but to react immediately. From the information MacDonald had given her the previous evening by phone, events were transpiring rapidly.

"So Rafferty is sure of this, is he?"

MacDonald had no corresponding lack of appetite. Quite the opposite. "Rafferty is a well-respected scientist. And at this point, he has as much at stake as we do." He took a bite of his ham and cheese sandwich. "Besides, from his scientist's viewpoint, he's more excited about this than I am."

Thurston nursed her iced tea. It would be nice to have confirmation to justify her decision last night. "So the next step is to find this woman who has the special genes. What will you do when you find her?"

"Rafferty tells me he'll feel a lot better about this once he confirms she's psychic. He says there are standardized tests to determine that sort of thing. When he's convinced she's the real McCoy, we'll have the proof we need to move forward with the gene manipulation."

"And why do you think she'll even agree to such a test?" Might as well cover all the bases.

MacDonald huffed. "Hell, I don't know. We'll make her feel special. Tell her she's an important part of some experiment. What woman wouldn't fall for that?"

Thurston felt her blood pressure soar upward. The idea of a quick romp following lunch had suddenly lost its appeal. To calm herself, she concentrated on the practicalities of this operation, something MacDonald seemed to take for granted.

"You're counting a lot on Silverstein's cooperation. From what you said, it took some coercion on Jamieson's part to get what you have." Thurston chose not to let on that, from her private conversations with Jamieson, she knew more about what had happened in California than MacDonald did. If it hadn't been for the common sense exhibited by Silverstein's assistant—obviously influenced by the fear of God that Jamieson had put into the two of them (Jamieson had recounted his heroics in detail)—they would never have obtained the hair samples, and thus the DNA.

"Rafferty's my interface with Silverstein. I suggested that he play our ace in—."

"Weaverman?"

MacDonald's eyebrows arched. "Yes, I do mean Weaverman." He hesitated before his next words, seemingly caught off guard by Thurston's abruptness. "Weaverman's the reason Silverstein called Rafferty in the first place. At first, he seemed concerned only about Weaverman's whereabouts. As it turned out, there was more to it. He needed to reach him because he had the DNA Weaverman had requested. Either way, Weaverman is important to Silverstein."

Thurston drummed her fingernails on the table, a habit that seemed to annoy MacDonald. Although she had taken action based on MacDonald's latest information, the details he gave weren't very comforting. "I don't know, Clifton. Things seem to be just a little too neat here. Doesn't it strike you as odd that this Silverstein fellow was able to find this DNA that's—what—one in 200 million? And on top of that, she just happens to be alive."

MacDonald pushed away the remains of his sandwich and started on the cheesecake with blueberry topping. "I'm not going to question our good luck. If Rafferty says that the DNA is what we've been looking for, that's good enough for me. You know the old saying. Don't look a gift horse—"

Thurston blocked out the rest of MacDonald's words. *Gift horses are a hell of a lot more common than this bitch's DNA.* Thurston looked across into the vacant expression of someone who had obviously not gotten to his station in life from sheer intellect. Politicians honed personal and public manipulation to a fine art; deep analysis and understanding were not pre-requisites.

Thurston's attention returned to MacDonald's words: "—you worry too much." He smiled but then jerked. He pulled the cell phone from his belt and read the screen. "It's Rafferty."

MacDonald listened for a moment and replied. "I understand. That'll give me time to set things in motion. Bye." Obviously concentrating on the message, he folded the cell.

"Rafferty called Silverstein and gave him an ultimatum. He said he subtly brought up Weaverman's name. Knowing Rafferty, I doubt he understands the definition of the word. I predict that we'll know the name of our mystery woman pretty damn quick." MacDonald seemed pleased with himself. "I talked to Jamieson this morning and made sure he was ready to take on another assignment."

Thurston was inwardly pleased. Poor fool that MacDonald was, maybe she shouldn't be so hard on him. He really couldn't help it. No reason not to use him to full advantage. Her stocking foot under the table signaled her intent.

MacDonald might have talked to Jamieson this morning, but she had spoken to him last evening following MacDonald's call. Even as they ate together in the official dining room of the U.S. Senate, Dick Jamieson was winging his way to the Golden State. Thurston had no idea what Jamieson had meant by one of his comments and considered it wise not to ask. For whatever reason, he'd said that Silverstein and Kipling were in for a little surprise on this go-round. Something about there being a small debt to repay.

CHAPTER 25

CONTEXT

George Bush Center for Intelligence, McLean, Virginia, USA
38° 56'06"N latitude, 77° 08'46"W longitude
Wednesday, 1:45 PM, August 5, 2009

Less than a day had passed since Lopez and his team had gotten their first shock in this bizarre investigation—the discovery that Clifton Mac-Donald, senator from Wyoming, was connected to Rafferty, and probably to the prophecy gene.

It took two rings before he reacted, since his eyes were glued to the video screen. "I can't fucking believe this! Would you look at that?" Lopez exclaimed to no one in particular. Miller and Winston needed no reminder that what they were witnessing by way of their electronic insect could get them all thrown into jail.

Lopez answered the phone between looks back at the screen. Winston's hands remained glued to the controls for the Romguard, which didn't need any attention just now. The video was working just fine.

"Yes, Margaret ... sure ... come on down."

The evening before, following Rafferty's departure from MacDonald's office, the senator made a cell call and then went home. Because the Romguard's microphone was still on the fritz, the best Lopez could hope for was a successful report from the Agency's lip readers. Margaret Sanfold, the best of the lot, had been assigned to both Rafferty's face-to-face meeting with MacDonald and MacDonald's cell call.

The Romguard's piggyback ride on MacDonald's coat back to his townhouse in Georgetown, with Hansley following in the van, had been uneventful. Winston chose to play it safe once they got there and stationed the device in a secure location inside the door—on top of a picture frame that offered a panoramic view of the room—awaiting MacDonald's departure the following morning. There had been enough near-disasters in the mechanical fly's short lifetime. Although Lopez had no intention of trusting anyone else to fly the Romguard during this critical stage, Winston had volunteered for the all-night vigil. He activated the onboard infrared motion-detection system and demonstrated the alarm that the motion sensor would trigger. Lopez felt confident of its ability to stir Winston from sleep. A cot allowed him some shuteye until the device reported motion. Hansley slept in the van outside MacDonald's residence. Lopez and Miller departed CIA headquarters around ten.

Still awake at four o'clock, Lopez realized that Winston was getting more sleep than he was. When he arrived back at Romguard Control at six, Winston was snoring away on the cot. And apparently Miller hadn't been able to sleep at home either, although he was doing better here, slouched in a stuffed chair he had appropriated from the lobby.

Two hours later, MacDonald left his apartment with the Romguard (and Hansley's support van) in tow. He spent the morning in his office in various meetings. Lopez made the judgment call *not* to listen—which at this point meant not taping the lips of any of the participants—to *any* of the conversations. Their being there at all placed them on thin ice. The Constitution and those employed to make sure its tenets were adhered to would take a dim view of their actions. No need to compound the problem by recording conversations that likely had no bearing on the prophecy gene. Afterward, the Romguard hitched its way to the Senate Dining Room and then to its present location.

Lopez responded to the knock at the door and led Sanfold to chairs at the rear of the room. She casually looked back at the screen and did a double take. "You know, fellows, watching this sort of thing can get you fired."

Lopez grimaced. "You're more right than you know."

After several more glances from Sanfold, Lopez repositioned their chairs to face away from the video. "Okay, Margaret. Talk to me."

Lopez saw the translation in her hand and reached for the sheet of paper. She drew back.

"What do you know about speech-reading?" Sanfold seemed serious.

Lopez assumed she meant lip-reading. "Nothing."

Sanfold relaxed in her chair and began a tutorial she had probably repeated a thousand times to nonprofessionals like him. First she explained that "lip-reading" is the old term, that "speech-reading" is the modern expression. English is not a particularly easy language to speech-read. The best estimate is that only 30 to 35 percent of English sounds can be speech-read. She explained that the reason is that too many of the sounds come from the middle and back of the mouth. To be understood, the sound must be formed on the lips or at the front of the mouth. Also, many English words look the same coming out of the mouth but have different meanings; they're called homophones. And if that wasn't enough to complicate the process, while the average person displays 13 to 15 speech movements per second, the human eye can observe only 8 or 9. We miss a lot of speech because the brain can't keep pace, she said. The recorded image made up for this by allowing repeat analysis. Finally, to put him in his place, Lopez figured, she also emphasized that women were usually better at speech-reading than men were.

Sanfold concluded. "So as you can see, it's hardly an exact science, if you want to call it that. Your guy, Rafferty? Not an easy read. He moves his mouth less than the average person."

Sanfold concluded her explanation and handed over the typed sheet. It was even worse than Lopez had expected.

Transcript, Rafferty, August 4, 2009

First of all——————she. ——further she——. ——————sample we received——be more——————————weeks——maybe days. One——————

*——sample—————ball————that————A——more
robust.*
RAFFERTY PAUSES
*——because we————A match————that we——
voy——. ——she——we——determine once——for——whether——
—————quince that weave——pos—————repeat pos——
based only—————mou results————relevance to————.
—————————match——there we—————her.*

The frown on Lopez's face betrayed his disappointment. Sanfold slid her chair closer, took back the sheet of paper, and elaborated.

"Before you get too discouraged, listen to me." She held back her next words, seemingly to make sure she had his attention. "When you're looking for something, whether in words or some other form of clue, it often doesn't take much at all to make the connection. I'm pretty good at what I do and, believe it or not, I've memorized Rafferty's entire mouth sequence."

What's she saying? If there's more, why hasn't she given it to me? "What are you trying to tell me?"

Lopez could tell that he was trying her patience. "What I'm saying is that I need context. If you can give me some clues, I can discover and create words that I couldn't otherwise pick out."

That makes sense. "Okay, Margaret. What I'm going to tell you can't leave this room."

Sanfold made a face and smiled. "How many times have I heard that? And beyond that, I won't even tell anyone that the second person whose lips I read and"—she turned her head—"whose face is on the screen behind us, is Senator Clifton MacDonald from Wyoming."

Lopez's face flushed scarlet. "How the hell do you know that?"

"Remember that my profession is looking at lips, and"—Sanfold gestured with her hands and smiled—"lips are usually connected to faces. Besides, you don't know I'm from Wyoming, and I would probably have voted for the guy if I still lived there." She paused. "Who's the chick? I can only see the back of her head."

Lopez shook his head and continued. "Okay, I can't tell you everything, but I can tell you what you need to know."

"Shoot."

"Their discussion may have something to do with genetics and"—Lopez didn't want to say the word but decided he had no choice—"psychics."

To Lopez's surprise, Sanfold's look remained professional, without judgment. She rested her face in her hands and cradled her body with the sides of her arms. A full thirty seconds transpired before she came up for air.

"Okay. This makes some sense now." She handed the sheet back to Lopez. "Where you see an A by itself I think he's saying *DNA*."

Lopez nodded. *Fantastic!*

"But there's one other part that made no sense until now." She pointed to the sheet and the segment, *voy*. She seemed satisfied with herself. "He's saying ... I'm positive of it now ... *clairvoyant*."

With that word, Lopez shot out of his seat and bent his head back, looking at the ceiling. As much as he had needed to confirm that MacDonald was conspiring with Rafferty, he had hoped for the opposite. Now he had proof that a connection existed and that he would have to proceed—in what way he did not know.

Lopez took his seat and looked further at the translation. He had been so disappointed in not seeing a faithful reproduction of each word said that he hadn't taken time to realize how much information the scraps could give. Context was important. He looked up. "Could *Weave* have been *Weaverman?*"

Sanfold closed her eyes, thought for a moment, and blurted out her reply. "Yes, that's it. See what I mean about things being in context?"

"Okay! What about the cell conversation for MacDonald? Where's the transcript for that?"

"There is none."

"Why?" Lopez squinted.

"I need to have a full-on view of the lips and face. I can't perform miracles. Most of the time, he had his head turned sideways. It was hopeless. You should have moved the camera."

Although the tidbits from Rafferty were useful, Lopez had hoped to get something extra from the cell call. The fact that MacDonald had called so quickly after Rafferty's departure—and used a cell phone rather than a landline—likely meant something. Lopez looked up, noticing that Sanfold wanted to say something.

"I almost forgot. The cell call. There was one word that I've gotten part of. Maybe you can make sense of it."

"What was that?"

"I'm pretty sure that he said something like *versteen*."

Lopez blinked in disbelief. "Could the first part of the word have been *sil*, like *Silverstein?*"

Sanfold snapped her fingers. "You got it."

Silverstein had obviously gotten himself noticed even at this level of the operation.

Sanfold grinned and turned around, staring at the screen once again. "See! What did I tell you? Context is everything. Even for those two whooping it up in that bed."

CHAPTER 26

DÉJÀ VU

Naval Research Laboratory, Monterey, California, USA
36°35'34"N latitude, 121°51'17"W longitude
Wednesday, 11:47 AM, August 5, 2009

Silverstein rested the phone in its cradle, having completed the two calls he needed to make. He and Kipling would leave first thing tomorrow morning.

It had been over three hours since the baffling conversation with his Smithsonian contact, which followed the more disturbing call from Rafferty. Silverstein glanced at his watch. His stomach growled from neglecting breakfast. Both calls had left him confused. First, why would Rafferty threaten Silverstein by way of Kipling? That made no sense. And second, was the Johnstown story indeed a hoax as Travers suggested? However, the reality that DNA did exist on an envelope from which Travers could test for the prophecy gene was too much to ignore. Silverstein wanted to talk to this Houston person face-to-face to assess her sincerity for himself and to ferret out an explanation for Travers's unexpected discovery about the letter's author, Augusta Schmidt.

Silverstein reacted to the high-pitched squeak from his office door. Kipling's sparkling blue eyes protruded at the five-foot-eight level. "I sense that you're famished and wouldn't mind being treated to lunch at Chef Lee's."

He smiled. "You're more of a mind reader than you know." With that comment, Silverstein's brain clicked, and his head jolted upward, smile disappearing. *No, it couldn't be!* He rewound his conversation with Rafferty. Silverstein *had assumed* that Rafferty was referring to Kipling because he was incensed over the bogus hair, using her as a wedge to get to Silverstein. *But Rafferty had never said that, nor had he mentioned Kipling's name. Had they completed the DNA testing? Did Rafferty mean to imply that the hair sample had tested positive for the prophecy gene?*

Kipling entered the room and reacted. "Are you okay? You look like you just saw a ghost."

Silverstein paused and responded awkwardly. "Sorry." Waves of prior discussions with Kipling came streaming back. *This very situation, where she seems to know things she has no way of knowing, has happened before.* He had written it off to Kipling's intelligence and her ability to tie together disparate pieces of information. He could feel the blood draining further from his face.

Kipling, aware that something was wrong with her boss, ran over and grabbed him by the shoulders.

Silverstein, realizing that this was not the time to tell her of his discovery—if it were really true, he'd have to think this one through some more—recovered quickly. "Back off, *Kemo Sabe*. I'm fine." The lie he was about to tell had to be a good one. Well, maybe he could get by without a lie. She might be able to sense an untruth. "You won't believe the conversation I had this morning with my old roommate who works at the Smithsonian."

Kipling retreated but seemed unconvinced. She pulled up a chair and sat stiffly. "It must have been a doozie if your reaction lasted this long. I thought you were having a stroke."

Silverstein, to deflect further questioning, continued. "I have good news, bad news, and good news. First, the good news."

"Yeah?" Kipling remained on guard.

"Travers verified that the envelope and paper from the Johnstown letter came from the nineteenth century."

Kipling's heightened alert subsided, and she slouched in her chair. "That is good news. What's the bad?"

"The DNA says that Augusta is male, not female. Jimmy's convinced that proves the whole thing is a hoax, that whoever set this up didn't know how accurate DNA testing is these days."

Kipling's eyes widened. "DNA! What DNA?"

Silverstein pursed his lips and nodded. "I had the same reaction. That's the second good news. Whoever Augusta is, whether male or female, she, he, licked the envelope to seal it. According to Jimmy, saliva on the envelope is enough to do a DNA analysis."

Kipling couldn't sit any longer and started pacing. "That means we could test for the prophecy gene. No more worrying about digging up bodies."

"You got it."

"Can Jimmy run the test?"

"That was my first thought. I asked him if he still had the envelope. He said he had mailed it back to Houston, along with a note describing how the perpetrator had screwed up."

Kipling stared. "So what do you want to do?"

"You and I are headed to Pennsylvania, to Johnstown. I just spoke to Houston. She received Travers's letter and is very upset. I tell you, it wasn't easy convincing her to see us. Since the newspaper article, life's been hell for her. But she's expecting us tomorrow." Silverstein pointed, at the same time glancing at his watch. "But I also talked her into overnighting the envelope back to Washington. I called Jimmy back, telling him to expect it tomorrow. And I sent him the e-mail."

Kipling shook her head. "What e-mail?"

Silverstein realized he hadn't given her all the pieces to the puzzle. "Right! I forgot to tell you. In Weaverman's phone message, he told me to check my e-mail."

"Yeah?"

"What's there looks like gibberish, but according to Weaverman, it contains the human genetic sequence and related proteins for the prophecy gene. I'm hoping that Jimmy can figure it out and apply it to the DNA from the envelope." Silverstein squinted. "Does that make sense?"

"Sure. How bright is this Jimmy fellow?"

"Very! If anyone can figure it out, he can."

Silverstein leaned back and reflected on their plan of action. "I apologize. I should have checked with you first. There's no way we can justify this trip on government time. Do you mind using some vacation time?"

"Not a problem. When do we leave?"

Silverstein smiled and realized that for once he had been able to predict Kipling's reaction. "I figured you'd say yes, and I've already booked our flights. We leave first thing tomorrow morning."

"Sounds good. We can talk over lunch."

He grinned. "If the money's coming from your pocket, I'm game."

Silverstein rose and grabbed his jacket. The morning stratus clouds hadn't yet broken for the day, and the air was probably chilly. Kipling led the way out the door. They made their way down the hall, down the flight of stairs, and toward the door that exited to the parking lot.

Halfway to the door, Silverstein pulled up, realizing that he had lost Kipling. He looked back and saw her standing at the base of the stairs, a questioning expression on her face. "Did you forget something?"

"No, something odd just occurred to me. It's nothing."

What was that all about? Just like at the Branding Iron.

Outside the door, the stairs led down to the service road that circled the compound, which lay inside a six-foot-high chain-link fence that corralled this secure area. The only gate lay dead ahead, controlling entering and exiting traffic. On days when the security threat was high, a guard stood duty. No sentry stood watch today.

No sooner than their feet touched the sidewalk below the final step, they stopped and stared ahead. Both sets of brain synapses probably clicked at the same time, thought Silverstein. Through the chain-link fence, they saw an automobile parked outside the compound, and beside it stood two individuals looking across. As the former baseball manager and practicing philosopher Yogi Berra was wont to point out, *it was déjà vu all over again.* Their simultaneous memory registered from scarcely five days earlier.

Kipling's verbal breakdown of the situation matched his own. "This can't be."

Silverstein stared as the female of the duo lifted a phone to her ear. A moment later, he heard the Hallelujah Chorus, the music Kipling had chosen for her cell phone ring. He remembered that it wasn't that long ago that Kipling had given her cell number to the male member of the team. Kipling pulled out her phone and listened. Silverstein watched as the woman concluded the call and folded her arms across her chest.

"What did she say, Linda?"

Kipling spoke slowly, radiating discomfort from her normally imperturbable demeanor. "She said, 'My name's Vi. You probably remember my twin sister, My.'"

CHAPTER 27

OPTION THREE

Naval Research Laboratory, Monterey, California, USA
36°35'34"N latitude, 121°51'17"W longitude
Wednesday, 12:07 PM, August 5, 2009

Silverstein stood dumbfounded. The presence of Dickey and My's look-alike across the street was too much to absorb. Kipling would want answers. He hadn't yet mentioned to her his earlier conversation with Rafferty, and in light of his deduction that Rafferty's call suggested that Kipling possessed the prophecy gene, he probably shouldn't. But could he hold back this information? And further, if he lied, could she tell?

Kipling broke into his train of thought and rattled off her questions in staccato. "Why are they back? Are they that pissed off because we gave them a bogus hair sample? And can you believe it, My has a twin sister?" She seemed perturbed.

Silverstein chose Plan B. Plan A, his inclination to turn around and walk back into the building, would solve nothing. "Can I borrow your phone, Linda? Please."

He stared at Kipling, looking for a clue that she knew more than she admitted. From her expression, she seemed to genuinely lack understanding. *She doesn't know that Dickey has come to get her. Plus, if she has unlimited psychic abilities, she would have recognized that gift long ago. Maybe there are degrees of psychic ability.* Ironically, while Kipling stood confused beside him, across the street Dickey had no idea that the *her* he was after was Kipling. Rafferty's words reverberated in Silverstein's head. "This is Rafferty. I want you to tell me who she is and where she lives … Weaverman's still alive. You have forty-eight hours." Silverstein's brain clicked. *Why had Dickey returned so quickly when Rafferty had given Silverstein two days to come through on his own?*

Silverstein opened the flip phone, identical to his own, punched his way to *Received Calls*, and pressed *Send* for the last entry. He watched the female respond. "This is Silverstein. I need to talk to Dick."

Vi handed over the phone. Since Kipling could hear his side of the conversation, to keep what he knew from her he had to choose his words carefully. He started safely, playing dumb. It would serve two purposes. Dickey might confirm Silverstein's suspicions and perhaps provide additional information. "What is it you want? We gave you the hair samples, just like you asked. You promised to leave us alone. I'm beginning to question your integrity."

Kipling nodded. So far, so good.

Silverstein mentally did the same when Dickey confirmed his suspicions. "I apologize for that, Dr. Silverstein. But you must understand that I made that promise under duress. Your partner did the right thing. I hope you have no hard feelings over our little tussle. I've forgotten it already. Now, I need you to tell me where the hair samples came from. Once I have that information, you'll never hear from me again."

Silverstein looked at Kipling. "And what would you do with that information?"

Kipling mouthed the words, "What information?"

This wasn't going to be easy.

Dickey answered Silverstein's question directly. "No harm will come to the donor; that's a given. From what I understand, Rafferty wants to confirm he has the right person by taking another DNA sample. He'll then run a few standardized psychological tests. You, of all people, know how scientists think."

Yeah, that's all, all right. And for the next step she'd be quarantined and used for God knows what. The fact that Weaverman remained under lock and key supported that prediction.

Where to go with this now? If Silverstein said much more, Kipling would become suspicious. His butt rested squarely between the proverbial rock and a hard place. In any event, he had to protect Kipling, which meant getting the hell away from Dickey. And recalling Kipling's description of her little episode with Myra, there was one other person outside the gate who might not be as magnanimous as Dickey.

What choices did he have? Option one: he could lie to Dickey, sending him off searching for a nonexistent person. That would buy some time. Option two: ignore Dickey and play out the consequences. They would fly east to Pennsylvania tomorrow, as discussed minutes earlier. Would this option force immediate retribution on Weaverman? Unlikely, but could Silverstein take the chance? Both options had downsides. With that in mind, there was option three, although not the most attractive of the lot. He could tell Dickey some of what he wanted to know.

This was one of those times when he needed to bounce his ideas off Kipling. But now was not the time. How would she react to the news that she had the dubious honor of being the one in 200 million they had discussed just days ago? Would she freak out?

Beyond the uncertainty of Kipling's reaction, another fact blared out to Silverstein in mind-numbing subwoofer frequencies. Even if Kipling discovered this truth, *no one else in the world must know!* Silverstein recalled his boyish escapades with his best friend, Larry Janowski. When something critical was at stake in their make-believe games, and they needed to act, he would always ask Larry the same question. At what cost should their action be accomplished? The answer would always be the same. *At all costs!* They would laugh at the gravity they assigned to the imaginary worlds they created, where Western marshals, James Bond-like spies, and intergalactic warriors all fought against darker forces. In this real-life situation, he asked himself the same question. At what cost must he protect Kipling's secret? The correct response: *at all costs!*

Knowing this obvious, indisputable fact, he had to make a choice. Kipling, and the duo across the street, expected it of him.

Dickey continued. "I assume you know who she is. Am I correct?"

Think, Victor, think! "I think I know, but I'm not sure." In a court of law, that would hold up. Kipling claimed that she'd put her own hair into the envelope, but he hadn't actually witnessed it.

Oh, hell! Kipling's pupils had widened. His last statement was a mistake. *She's wondering what I'm talking about and maybe two seconds away from figuring out the whole mess herself.* With or without the prophecy gene, Kipling was no dummy.

Dickey's voice projected disappointment. "You didn't get the sample yourself?"

This part would be easy. "Of course not. Do you think I have time to go running around the planet looking for something like that? I was Weaverman's intermediary. All I did was make phone calls."

Silverstein's ploy seemed to work. "Okay, then. What would it take for you to find out that information? And remember, Weaverman's fate is in your hands."

"You needn't worry. Your boss, Rafferty, made that clear to me." Silverstein hesitated. Something didn't make sense. "I'm surprised you're here so soon. Just this morning, he told me I had two days to provide him the information. It seems to me you're jumping the gun. Why did you come so soon?"

A moment's hesitation. *Oh, Dickey, you stupid son of a bitch!*

"That's none of your concern, Dr. Silverstein. How soon can you locate her?"

Something's rotten in Denmark. Has Dickey gone off to work for himself?

Time to tell the truth. "I received Rafferty's ultimatum this morning. My assistant and I are flying east tomorrow, to locate the source." Silverstein paused. "Who is it that I should stay in touch with? You or Rafferty?"

No indecision this time. "Call me on Vi's cell. And ... when exactly are you flying, and where?"

With that final question, Silverstein responded truthfully and watched as Dickey handed the cell back to Vi. They talked briefly, returned to their vehicle, and drove away.

Silverstein breathed deeply. The rabid dogs had backed off, at least for the moment. But another predicament, one requiring equal finesse, stood nearby. He turned in Kipling's direction, afraid of what he would encounter.

Her response could have been harsher. "You drive. I need you to explain some things to me."

CHAPTER 28

SHARED INTEREST

Headquarters, Sphinx Petroleum, Cairo, Egypt
30° 05'44"N latitude, 31° 22'60"E longitude
Wednesday, 10:10 PM, August 5, 2009

Caliph Ishmael stared across at his superior, a top official in the Blade. "I say we move now. Waiting will gain us nothing."

His mind considering both the pluses and the minuses, Mohammed Abu Saada stared into the night at the airport lights. Although less impetuous than his inexperienced underling, Abu Saada had to agree that waiting would hardly be advantageous. The Americans had found someone, a woman, who possessed the genetic aberration.

Until his death in 2007, Clement Warner had been the go-between for Cleopatra, the code name for their infiltrator in the U.S. government. Abu Saada became Warner's replacement, an obvious choice since he had originally recruited their government spy. Cleopatra reported that Rafferty, the biologist who had taken charge once they diverted Weaverman, had acquired the DNA sample from another government scientist named Silverstein—the *same* Jew who had thwarted the Blade's efforts in 2007. Abu Saada was astounded that this same man was again at the center of a Blade operation. And how had he obtained such an extraordinary acquisition? Rafferty was now asking Silverstein to identify that person, using Weaverman as a pawn. It was unclear whether Silverstein would be cooperative, since some intimidation had been necessary to force him to turn over the DNA sample in the first place.

What Ishmael was suggesting was that they go after Silverstein, to be the first to apprehend this woman. There were considerable risks involved, but tremendous gains if they proved successful. Blade scientists emphasized that they could save a lot of time if they possessed someone with the special gene.

"Who would you recommend for this assignment, Caliph? Our operation two years ago was a disaster. We lost four of our best Western operatives. And Warner had penetrated the highest levels of the military." He paused. "There's Sidki, of course, but I wouldn't trust him in charge of this kind of operation."

Ishmael fidgeted in his seat. "I'd like this assignment for myself."

Abu Saada did his best to control his outward expression, although he admitted to himself that he had been expecting such a request. Ishmael's father, who had lost his life in pursuit of the Blade's interests (although his family was led to believe he had passed away naturally), would want Caliph protected. Never before had the Blade sent the youngest Ishmael into the field on a major assignment. Not that he wasn't qualified. The Blade had spent considerable resources training him, as they had the Ishmael twins, his male siblings. Four years at George Washington University in Washington, DC, had taught him fluent English. He had earned an engineering degree and understood many of the scientific aspects of the projects the Blade had taken on. The two years Ishmael spent in Syria training with weapons and learning the intricacies of field operations did make him an obvious choice.

Abu Saada expressed his trepidation aloud. "I've been expecting such a request for some time. You are your father's son, and if he had lived to see this day, he would be proud of both you and your sister." He paused to reflect. "On the other hand, I am thankful he was spared the loss of his twins."

"He and my brothers now share their existence with Allah, drinking milk and honey."

Abu Saada willed his eyes not to betray his thoughts to the contrary. "No doubt. However, you know I am concerned that you want this assignment to avenge your brothers' deaths. If I should grant your wish, what assurance can you give that you will pursue the Blade's interests above all else? If you cannot put aside your quest for revenge, you will not only threaten the success of our mission but place yourself in danger as well. I needn't remind you how much we've invested in you, Caliph." Abu Saada paused and reflected before he spoke. "I've seen men make foolish judgments under the influence of revenge and hate. For the sake of the Blade's interests, this assignment may not be the best one for you."

Ishmael sat up straight, his face displaying humility. "I will live with the loss of my brothers until my final days. I have committed my life to the interests of the Blade."

Abu Saada leaned back, one hand behind his head and the other hanging to the side, his eyes drawn to the ceiling. Besides operational considerations, the ramifications worried him. How would his Muslim compatriots react when told that the Prophet Mohammed's unique abilities, including his predictions as detailed in the Qur'an, stemmed from a genetic anomaly that had been duplicated in a woman from the Western Hemisphere? Chaos and confusion could erupt in the Muslim—and Christian—worlds. On the other hand, if the Americans were on the verge of this discovery as well, there was no turning back.

Abu Saada returned to the issue at hand. Would Ishmael do as he said—put aside his feelings toward Silverstein—and carry out the mission with only the Blade's interests in mind? Abu Saada doubted it. But then, did he have a choice?

Abu Saada leaned forward, his look stern and focused, and issued his orders. "Notify Sidki. He will be your partner. I will advise Cleopatra of your intentions. Go at once before it is too late." He stood quickly, abruptly realizing the import of his instructions. "It is vital that we locate this woman before the Americans do."

CHAPTER 29

FAMILY VALUES

Hyatt Regency Washington on Capitol Hill, Washington, DC, USA
38° 53′43″N latitude, 77° 00′41″W longitude
Wednesday, 3:15 PM, August 5, 2009

Samantha Thurston took a deep hit from her cigarette, stole a glance to her left, and considered the disposition of her lover of the moment, Clifton MacDonald. He seemed equally sated from their afternoon's tryst, followed by an afternoon snooze. His lovemaking had been adequate but hardly exceptional, even after cutting him some slack for his age. She'd score him maybe a five for technical merit but barely a three for artistic presentation. She'd had better, much better, the day before. This brought her thoughts back to Jamieson and her real concerns: the woman who possessed the prophecy gene and his upcoming attempt to capture her.

Little did MacDonald know that, as of yesterday, Jamieson had switched employers, at least to the extent that the anticipated result would benefit Thurston, not MacDonald. Until then, it was important that MacDonald continue to think he remained in control.

She looked over at the requisite red-numbered clock typical of hotel rooms and subtracted three hours. Jamieson was probably approaching Silverstein and issuing his request about now. Jamieson wouldn't say what he meant by a "little surprise for Silverstein," other than that Silverstein's assistant, a woman named Kipling, would be particularly impressed.

*   *   *   *

MacDonald looked to his right, admiring the fine female form whose leg still entwined his. *One fine lay!* With an inward grin that gradually spread to his facial features, he had to admit to himself, modesty aside, that his own performance had been nothing short of outstanding—probably an eleven on a scale of ten. Despite her physical attributes, however, Thurston was becoming a pain in the ass and would have to be dealt with. How he would go about doing so was a temporary mystery, but one that would resolve itself in due course.

Aside from Rafferty's news about Silverstein's discovery, one other aspect of this operation had fallen into place. The five participants who had the unique opportunity to be a part of this operation had contributed their share. MacDonald had the resources he would need to fund development of the prophecy gene. It was a no-brainer that Rafferty could not use his own facilities at the Naval Research Laboratory—that a remote, secure location would be a requirement for the upcoming genetic testing and development. And all that would cost dollars. MacDonald had set aside Thurston's idea of shortchanging his investors. Such a tactic could easily backfire.

Words from his alluring companion interrupted his thought process. "When are you planning to send Jamieson after Silverstein?"

*   *   *   *

MacDonald stumbled in his reply. "I'm sorry, what did you say?"

Thurston caught MacDonald's eye. "I said, when are you planning to send Jamieson after Silverstein? How long do you plan to wait?"

"When Rafferty called Silverstein this morning, he gave him forty-eight hours, said he'd expect a reply by then."

Uh-oh! She hadn't considered that MacDonald might deliver an ultimatum before approaching Silverstein. *Shit!* It didn't matter to her or Jamieson when they contacted Silverstein—as long as they were the first to do so. But Silverstein might find it suspicious if Jamieson arrived before the deadline.

Thurston sighed. Well, so be it. Acquiring the female with the unusual DNA was all that mattered.

*   *   *   *

"What was that all about?" MacDonald retorted; her reaction to his reply had been odd.

"What was what all about?" She glanced over, acting oblivious.

"You reacted when I mentioned Rafferty's ultimatum. Would you have given Silverstein more time? I thought his offer was generous."

*   *   *   *

Thurston had to think fast. Maybe she had given MacDonald's intellect short shrift. "Rafferty probably did the right thing. I guess I'm too impetuous."

MacDonald leaned toward her, balancing his head on his right palm. "I like spontaneity in a woman."

I bet you do, you son of a bitch! Thurston grinned and turned quickly onto her right side to keep her face from exposing less complimentary thoughts. She wouldn't make that mistake again. As history books could attest about her namesake, Cleopatra was not a stupid woman.

Thurston reflected on the years of preparation to get to this stage in her life. Fate be damned, she thought; random happenstance controlled much of life's journey. Her arrival into this world had come earlier than expected, during a visit by her French mother and Egyptian father to America. As a result, she maintained dual American and French citizenships. In the early 1970s, as decided by her mother, she emigrated from France to the States as a two-year-old following her parents' divorce in

1969. Summers with her wealthy father in Cairo until the age of thirteen when he passed away suddenly were memories she treasured and shared with no one. Her own mother's death just five years later had less impact but, nonetheless, left her an orphan at the age of eighteen. The money left to her, first from her father and then her mother, was sufficient to maintain the standard of living she had come to appreciate through her teenage years.

Concluding early on that her genetic lineage would not translate into longevity, her decision to live life to the fullest led to a lifestyle that many would consider immoral, or at best, loathsome—not that such thoughts had any influence on her choices. Relying on her considerable intellect, she had hidden most of the unpleasant parts of her life from prying eyes. How else could she have parlayed her position in life from a sophisticated, high-class slut to a member of the highest legislative chamber of the United States?

Along the way—during her early thirties—she had a meeting, one that would change her life and give her purpose. A friend of her father's, affectionately known as Uncle Mohammed (although there was no blood relation), with whom she had kept in contact since her beloved father's death, had approached her and suggested that she might be of use to the organization her father had founded, the Blade of the Sinai. Since her love for her father exceeded any other she had, or expected to have, the thought of carrying forward in his footsteps appealed to her.

It had been quite a shock when Uncle Mohammed revealed new details concerning her father's life. She had naively assumed, as a young girl might, that his position with Sphinx Petroleum represented the full extent of his professional life. Although he had remarried following the divorce from her mother, Thurston considered that event a natural progression and one she hardly held against him. That he had three sons with this new woman had not bothered her. She was his only daughter and his favorite of the four. She knew that because he had told her so.

With her life having found new meaning, she developed a plan to place herself in as advantageous a position as possible in pursuit of the Blade's interests. When the opportunity arose during her social dalliances with the upper crust of American society to attach herself to an up-and-coming politician named Maxwell Thurston, she took full advantage of it. With her natural charms and physical endowments, her conquest of him had been easy. Also easy, and vital to attaining a position of power, had been her qualities as a partner in his political ambitions. It was only four years into their marriage when Maxwell sought and won the seat of U.S. senator from Kansas, with much of the credit belonging to her, many would agree. That she had had to sleep with a few core constituents to seal the deal had been a small price to pay.

With broad acceptance as her husband's confidante and intellectual equal, she had arrived near the top of the political establishment. Aside from her penchant for occasional naughty behavior, none of her past was hidden from public view. In fact, her fluent French and passable Arabic proved quite useful on occasion, and alluring to the press. Her sophisticated upbringing in France and the Middle East, together with a personality that the public found engaging, worked to her benefit. Interestingly, her appeal extended not only to the male of the species but also to the female, giving her a charisma that South African-born Teresa Heinz Kerry would have found helpful in the 2004 presidential election. True, there was the occasional wife who had suspicions regarding her husband's indiscretions, but they were few. Samantha Thurston had been very careful. When her husband passed away, there had been little opposition to her being named his replacement in the Senate.

Until now, Thurston's role as a mole within the U.S. government had lain dormant, waiting to be exploited, to be called upon as needed. Her first assignment had appeared unexpectedly. Last month's report to Uncle Mohammed triggered an avalanche of communiqués from the Blade. She had obviously stumbled upon something of extreme interest to them.

Then there was this Silverstein fellow. Uncle Mohammed had told her that, remarkably, he had thwarted a Blade operation two years earlier. He gave no details. How could an ordinary government scientist's name come up twice in recent Blade activities? Could he be CIA? Coincidentally, Uncle Mohammed had given her the news that in that operation, two of her three half brothers, the Ishmael twins, had been killed. They were family. As she thought about them, Thurston sensed her blood pressure rising and felt the pain of their loss. She stared down at her left hand and consciously released her grip; her fingernails had nearly punctured the skin. She took shallow breaths to slow her thrashing heart. Pure hatred, she knew, could mimic adrenaline as a stimulant.

"Could you ever have imagined you'd end up in Washington in one of the most powerful positions in the country?" Thurston flinched at MacDonald's unexpected query. "I liked your husband. He was a man who commanded respect. Who'd ever think that someone as young and robust as he would pass away so suddenly?"

Thurston's emotions seesawed. Within seconds, sadness replaced hatred. She continued to face away from MacDonald, lest he see through the betrayal that lay hidden inside the tear that rolled down her cheek.

It had been a regrettable but nonetheless necessary part of Thurston's plan to serve her father's memory. Her husband's death had not been a natural one, but no one would ever know that—not even Uncle Mohammed.

CHAPTER 30

REASONABLE FACSIMILE

Chef Lee's Mandarin House, Monterey, California, USA
36°35'45"N latitude, 121°51'57"W longitude
Wednesday, 12:20 PM, August 5, 2009

Silverstein and Kipling had been shaken by the unexpected appearance of Dickey and My's sister minutes earlier. They drove to lunch in Silverstein's Porsche. Neither said a word on the five-minute drive. Silverstein couldn't help but wonder what Kipling was thinking but knew better than to be the first to speak. Upon arriving at the restaurant, Silverstein came to a further conclusion, one that complemented his thoughts minutes earlier. Not only must no one else know that Kipling possessed the prophecy gene, *neither must she.*

This revelation occurred as Silverstein sought guidance from incidents in his past. In science, they called this technique analog pattern recognition: looking for historical situations that matched the present in order to predict the future. The technique had had its successes and failures—more of the latter, unfortunately, in meteorology, because activity in the earth's atmosphere was damn *nonlinear:* a fancy scientific term that simply meant that what happens next is the result of several factors, not just one—and therefore not as predictable using analogy as one might hope. In terms of human interaction, however, the technique fared better. What was it someone once said? *Those who failed to remember the past were doomed to repeat it.*

The situation that Silverstein recalled in crushing detail had occurred in college, during his sophomore year at Penn State. It involved his room-mate, Timothy Johnson. Johnson had known from an early age that he had been adopted, and he stressed that he couldn't have asked for better parents. All was well until the day when, as one of the first of a wave of adoptees who thought it best that they ferret out their roots, Johnson sought out his biological mother and father. Their identities would best have remained buried forever. Timothy had been born in prison to a mother serving a life sentence for the murder of a business executive and his family. His father, her partner in the failed robbery attempt, initially avoided capture but died later in a police shootout. With that information, Timothy concluded that his fate was sealed, that he was a *bad seed.* No amount of Silverstein's logic could persuade him otherwise. Johnson dropped out of school, and Silverstein never heard from him again.

From that brief lesson, Silverstein learned that knowledge concerning *who we think we are*—whether factual or imagined—may be more impor-tant than reality. If Kipling knew that she had inherited a characteristic that made her unique among humankind, would she consider herself a freak? Would her life, until now normal and fulfilling, change for the worse? Silverstein concluded that he wanted no part of such an experi-ment.

Easier said than done. As the waiter led them to a booth by a window, Silverstein knew that he would need all his wits to deflect Kipling's ques-tions. How much Kipling might suspect based on her possession of the prophecy gene—or how much she had inferred from Silverstein's conver-sation with Dickey—he had no way of knowing.

It didn't take long before the interrogation began. Silverstein did his best to keep his face neutral and not give away the stress manifesting itself in his ever-tightening chest and stomach.

"What did you mean by 'What would you do with that information?'"

"What?" *Think, Silverstein, think!* Silverstein flinched, pretending to realize that he just remembered his earlier statement. Barely in time, he realized he had a way out. "Oh! Sorry. There's something I haven't told you yet, about who I spoke to before Travers."

"Who was that?"

Silverstein waved his hands and nodded his head to suggest that he now knew why she was confused. "Rafferty called earlier this morning. He gave me forty-eight hours to reveal the source of the DNA." Silverstein knew he had to construct his next sentence carefully. "He said that time was of the essence, that once they completed the DNA analysis, he wanted to move forward with psychological testing of the individual. He wants to know now where the sample came from. I put him off, saying that I didn't know." Silverstein paused for effect and shook his head. "I'm surprised he's already convinced that I gave him the real thing. But from our perspective, we need more time, not less, because Weaverman's life is at stake. Once they discover your sample is bogus, we have nothing to hold over them." *Think, Silverstein, think.* Silverstein made his words sound routine, adding some embellishment. "He said it would take a week to complete the analysis, but they already knew that the sample came from a woman who was alive."

Silverstein poured tea into the small cups on the table, willing his hands to remain steady. He stared casually at the menu, hoping that he had successfully deflected Kipling's concern. He glanced up and caught Kipling's eye, praying that his words had rung true. His heart hammered.

Kipling's anxiety seemed to abate as she digested the words, but then her flawless logic took hold. "You said, 'I think I know, but I'm not sure.'"

You're doing fine. Steady as she goes. "Dickey assumed I knew where the sample came from, that I could point him in the right direction. You heard me." Silverstein paused and realized that he could add a measure of innocence to his rebuttal. "Why are you grilling me? I told him I never knew where the sample came from, that we were flying to Pennsylvania to locate the source." Time to shift the conversation. "We've diverted Dickey's attention. I say we fly to Johnstown as planned. What do you think?"

Instead of responding to his question, Kipling opened her menu. "Let's eat first."

The meal passed in silence, with Silverstein wondering what was percolating inside Kipling's head. He ate his usual Chef Lee's Noodles, a huge bowl of broth and noodles intermixed with meat and seafood. Kipling ordered the lunch plate of almond chicken, which included soup, a huge mound of white rice, two deep-fried wontons (with an accompanying sweet and sour sauce and a squirt of hot mustard), and a slice of navel orange. Fortune cookies followed with the bill.

Kipling took a final sip of tea and leaned back. "I'm sorry. This whole thing with Dickey, My ... Vi ... has me on edge. I'll be better, I promise."

Suddenly, Kipling looked around the restaurant. Silverstein had seen that same expression last Friday, at the Branding Iron Restaurant. "What is it, Linda?"

Kipling shook her head. "Oh, nothing. Sometimes it's like I get these premonitions."

Damn! Silverstein hoped that he hadn't reacted visibly to the p-word.

Kipling removed some bills from her pocket and placed them in the tray. "Unfortunately, I don't think Dickey can afford to lose track of us. I wouldn't be surprised if he follows us all the way back east. That's not something that makes me feel warm and fuzzy inside."

Silverstein scanned the parking lot for the white Nissan Maxima they had watched drive away from NRL.

Kipling continued. "Assuming we make it to Pennsylvania, what then? There are two outcomes to our meeting with Houston. One is that she is involved in the deception, and Travers is correct. That's a problem, because then we have nothing for Dickey. The second possibility is that we believe her. Then what? How can we use that information to defuse Dickey and Rafferty? Particularly since we know any Johnstown DNA comes from a dead person. And a male, at that. I'm not seeing any outcomes that are particularly desirable—"

Silverstein didn't catch Kipling's last words because his attention strayed. He motioned Kipling to look outside. They watched as Dickey walked to the car that was pulling up on the street. He replaced Vi at the wheel and then turned left down a residential street away from their view. "You're right, Linda. He intends to follow us."

Unexpectedly, Silverstein's attention was drawn to the waiter who had already delivered the check. "Sir," he addressed Silverstein, "someone named Dick asked that I deliver this envelope to you."

Silverstein opened the sealed nine-by-twelve and withdrew two sheets of paper. On the first, handwritten on a FedEx Kinko's letterhead, there were only a few words:

> *One more thing, Dr. Silverstein. In case you think I might be bluffing about Weaverman, take a look at the enclosed picture.*

Silverstein slid away the first page to reveal a second sheet, a higher quality stock used for printing photographs. He stared at a close-up of Weaverman holding a copy of the *Washington Post*. From the headlines, Silverstein recognized it as today's paper. Seated in a nondescript room lit by light from a side window, Weaverman appeared haggard but alive.

Silverstein pondered the message and photograph for a moment, lined up the bottoms of the two sheets of paper, held them up to the light, noticed that one was slightly shorter than the other, and smiled. "Guess what, Linda? Our friend, Dickey?"

"Yeah?"

"There's a good chance he just made his first mistake."

CHAPTER 31

ERRANT RICOCHET

Airport Road, outside the Naval Research Laboratory, Monterey, California, USA
36°35'37"N latitude, 121°51'16"W longitude
Wednesday, 1:40 PM, August 5, 2009

Silverstein fidgeted in his seat outside the gate of the Naval Research Laboratory, his hands gripped tightly to the steering wheel, but with the engine off. He glanced yet again into the rearview mirror and then at his watch. It had been forty minutes since he and Kipling had parted at the restaurant.

"Where is she, goddamn it? She should have returned by now," Silverstein spoke loudly in frustration. He considered calling her. No reason. She'd be here soon enough.

To shake Dickey and Vi from their trail and to achieve their agreed-upon goal, Silverstein and Kipling had agreed to split up after their lunch at Chef Lee's; she remained behind while Silverstein drove back to NRL. Dickey followed for a short distance but then turned away. Before they separated, Silverstein and Kipling exchanged cell phones, the logic being that if Dickey tried to call, it was Silverstein he wanted to reach. Dickey was probably wondering why Kipling hadn't returned with him.

Silverstein knew that Kipling's taxi would return soon from New Monterey, the west side of the town of Monterey. Earlier, when she had examined the sheets of paper, she cracked the logic behind Silverstein's smile. The photographic sheet was about a quarter of an inch shorter than the eight-and-a-half-by-eleven on which Dickey had written his note. This observation, together with the photograph of Weaverman sitting in a sun-lit room holding a copy of today's *Washington Post*, produced the obvious conclusion: that unless Scotty had beamed Dickey and Vi across the North American continent, Dickey could not have hand-carried the photograph from Washington, DC. It would have been either yesterday or very early in the morning today when he and Vi departed the East Coast. That deduction implied that someone had sent the photograph to the West Coast electronically. Anyone who has received a fax knows that the top of the page carries information concerning the sender, often a name and phone number. Silverstein concluded that Dickey had cut that strip of paper from the sheet.

The cover letter meant that Dickey had used Kinko's to receive the fax. Because Kinko's had only one Peninsula location, Kipling had hopped a taxi to New Monterey. The only remaining obstacle to Kipling's analysis was how, if Dickey had removed the offending information from the fax, they would retrieve it. Silverstein reminded her that facsimile machines usually store their information electronically because the printers often cannot keep up with input, particularly in such a busy store as Kinko's. Silverstein was hoping that the file was still available from the fax machine's memory.

Silverstein stared at his watch yet again. Suddenly, he noticed in his rearview mirror the white Nissan Maxima. It pulled off the road, several hundred feet back. *Thank goodness!* Dickey and Vi represented Silverstein's only concern. Kipling's yellow taxi would appear soon.

Silverstein's head snapped to attention as Kipling's cell rang inside his jacket. *Probably Kipling calling to say she was on her way.*

"Silverstein."

Dickey's voice sounded all too familiar. "Dr. Silverstein, I was hoping that you hadn't gone too far. I would have stayed and kept you company, but I had bigger fish to fry. You'll forgive me."

Silverstein sighed. "It's you, Dickey. How nice. I thought our business was over. I told you I would get back to you from Pennsylvania."

Dickey seemed to ignore Silverstein's statement. "I must say that you are every bit as clever as your reputation suggests. Why just this morning, I was telling Vi there was no way you would notice that I had cut a strip from the photograph. And even if you did see it, that you wouldn't make anything of it. But, by God, you figured it out!"

Silverstein ignored the implication in Dickey's words. He squinted into the rearview mirror.

Dickey's voice registered mock concern. "You're still there, aren't you? I think I can hear your breathing."

"I'm here."

"As clever as you are, Dr. Silverstein, you mustn't belittle my capabilities either. I didn't graduate summa cum laude in college because I was stupid."

"What's the point of all this, Dickey? I never called you stupid." *At least not in words to your face.*

"You see, it's most important to Dr. Rafferty that he acquire the individual who possesses the DNA."

What the hell's he talking about? "Tell me something I don't know. I told you that we're traveling east tomorrow to locate her. Don't you believe me?"

"You placed me in an untenable position, Dr. Silverstein. It would be far too easy for you to elude us. Then I'd have lost control. You might say to yourself that Weaverman just isn't worth all this hassle ... and that wouldn't do. That's why I dreamed up the little bit with the shorter paper. I can't believe it actually worked and that you two then split up to throw me off. Wasn't it a nice touch when I followed you briefly from the restaurant?"

"What do you mean?" Silverstein cringed because he knew the answer.

Dickey delayed stating the obvious. "Even if you had gotten your hands on the original fax, which, by the way, I picked up from my hotel and not Kinko's, you wouldn't have learned much. Dr. Rafferty sent it from his NRL office."

As Silverstein watched the Maxima pull away from the curb, he felt a cold shudder inch down his spine.

Dickey continued. "Your brilliance has helped me, Dr. Silverstein, and I thank you. But I owe as much to your gullibility."

Silverstein's eyes strained to his left as the Maxima passed. His face turned ashen as Kipling's face appeared in the right rear window.

CHAPTER 32

RELEVANT RELATIVE

George Bush Center for Intelligence, McLean, Virginia, USA
38° 56'06"N latitude, 77° 08'46"W longitude
Wednesday, 4:45 PM, August 5, 2009

Lopez and Miller plodded into Lopez's office, having just returned from Romguard Control. It had been a long and tense afternoon. "What was I to do?" Lopez looked up to catch Miller's eye. "I sensed from your reaction you would have done differently."

Miller nodded and curled up his forefingers, rubbing his eyes. They were both exhausted. "It's not my place to question your judgment. You made a split-second decision. Let's leave it at that."

Lopez fell backward into his chair. When they had left Winston at the controls moments earlier, the Romguard was riding the back of Mac-Donald's paramour, who had departed the hotel ahead of her lover. Watching the lunchtime meeting earlier, as the Romguard stuck safely to the wall alongside the table, Miller had been the one to identify the mystery woman as Senator Samantha Thurston. When the two politicians chose to bed each other, Lopez concluded there might be more to Mac-Donald's relationship with Thurston than senatorial banter. Nonetheless, it was possible that Senator Thurston had nothing to do with the prophecy gene and that her surveillance would prove a wasted effort.

Lopez's hackles were rising, and he couldn't just leave it at that, although he suspected Miller's concern. "Why would you have stayed with MacDonald? We already know he's involved."

"That's right. He's involved. Isn't that enough?"

"What do you mean?"

Miller stared back, incredulous. "Have you forgotten already how this all started? Does the name Weaverman ring a bell? Do you remember Victor's request, that you try to save the life of his friend? Did it never occur to you that MacDonald might lead you to him?"

Lopez acquiesced. "I can see you think I've lost my mind. But from what we're piecing together, what's going on here is far bigger than Weaverman. Just give me a few hours with Thurston." He waited a moment to make sure he had Miller's attention. "Okay? If nothing turns up, we'll return the Romguard to MacDonald tomorrow. We'll catch him when he leaves his apartment in the morning."

Miller seemed to accept Lopez's argument, and his demeanor softened. "Sanfold did a good job, I thought. We now know MacDonald knows about the prophecy gene. It's a damn shame we lost our audio." He blinked. "If nothing shows up with Thurston, do you think Peter could do a quick repair before we tail MacDonald again?"

"Good point. Video is good, but the audio's really the payoff."

Miller changed tack. "What did you make of MacDonald's phone call where he mentions Silverstein? By the way, was that all Sanfold could give you?"

Lopez swiveled back and forth in his chair. "That's it. The angle was bad. Regarding Silverstein, it does rather make sense, doesn't it? We know that Rafferty's goon—Kipling said he called himself Dick, right?—tried to shake him down for the hair sample. Kipling told us that much last Friday." Lopez looked up at Miller and snapped his fingers. "Maybe I've been wrong in assuming he works for Rafferty. It makes more sense that he takes orders from MacDonald."

Miller completed that thought. "A senator has more wherewithal than an NRL scientist."

Lopez leaned forward and started fresh. "Follow me, okay? We've been getting chatter for months now out of Russia and the Middle East about some new scientific breakthrough involving what we first thought was ESP, or something like that. It's likely that that's what we're now calling the prophecy gene. No sooner than we think there's nothing to it, we get a call from Kipling telling us that an NRL scientist has discovered the same thing. Weaverman turns up missing after he contacts Victor for help. Trying to stay in the loop to locate Weaverman, Silverstein turns up the heat by saying he has a DNA sample from someone possessing the prophecy gene." Lopez hesitated. "Incidentally, Dick's attitude toward Silverstein won't be all that favorable when he discovers the hair sample is bogus."

"They'll think Silverstein is holding out on them. They'd never suspect that he lied to them as a ruse." Miller sat up straight. "Damn!"

"What?"

"Let's say Rafferty had just processed the hair sample, and he already knew it was bogus. That could have been the reason for Rafferty's visit."

Lopez's eyebrows arched. "You need some sleep. You're forgetting something."

"What?"

Lopez reached down for a sheet of paper. "Remember, we did have audio back in Rafferty's laboratory. Here's what he said. *It's me. I've got news, some of it you're expecting to hear, and some of it that'll surprise you, that'll knock your socks off. Can I come over? … I'm on my way.*"

Miller replied, "Sorry, I'm slipping. I'd forgotten that. You're right. Rafferty hardly sounds disappointed. Maybe the news had nothing to do with the hair sample."

"Come on, Marc. We saw him remove and manipulate the sample. Then he spent all afternoon scurrying about the laboratory. Whatever he called MacDonald about had to do with what he discovered right then and there." Lopez shook his head. "There is one other possibility, you know."

Miller looked up, having sensed Lopez's implication. "That's impossible, Hector. Kipling told you that she gave Dick her own hair." He thought for a moment. "Can I see Sanfold's analysis again?"

Lopez opened a manila folder. "Don't forget, we came in late on Rafferty. We missed the first part of his story while Winston was fighting to control the Romguard." He handed the single-page sheet to Miller. "Note my penciled additions in parentheses."

Lopez watched as Miller scanned Sanfold's translation. Miller counted on his fingers between bursts of his trademark sign of concentration, closed eyes. "What do you see, Marc?"

Miller blinked. "Relevant words are there, obviously, like *DNA* and *clairvoyant*. What I look for is repetition. I'm a big believer that if something's important, it tends to get repeated. Notice that the word *she* appears three times and *her* once?"

Lopez pursed his lips. "What you're saying is that they're talking about Kipling's DNA."

"Just a suggestion."

"Makes sense, but what are the chan—" The ring from Lopez's phone cut him off. The internal CIA caller ID said *Communications*. "Yeah, Jeff. What's up?" Lopez listened and nodded his head at the explanation. "New York, huh? Interesting. Keep an eye on him, will ya? Thanks."

Lopez hung up the headset and addressed Miller. "Guess who just turned up at JFK airport?"

Miller responded immediately. "Sidki."

"How did you know *that?*"

"You keep forgetting that I believe in correlations. The last time that Silverstein was involved, Sidki was on the scene. Q.E.D., *quod erat demonstrandum.*"

"That correlation is about as tenuous as they come." Lest he forget, Lopez reminded himself that they had been tailing Ali Sidki, a Saudi national, for years. They knew he freelanced for several worldwide terrorist organizations, mostly coordinating arms deals.

Ghali, the Middle Eastern terrorist who had played a key role in the hurricane debacle in 2007, had been the Agency's second success story using the Delta chip, developed by the CIA's Mensa team. Sidki had represented the first. Mensa had come up with the idea that it was technically feasible to track an individual worldwide, at least while he or she remained outdoors, using National Assets—an ambiguous reference to the nation's global satellite network used for spying. It was simply a matter of implanting the Delta chip, a microchip powered by a tiny lithium battery (good for ten years), on the body of the intended. In the case of Sidki, the Agency had decided that, as a low-level gofer, he could prove more valuable alive, provided they could track his movements. For that reason, he was the perfect candidate for a trial.

The chip's innovation lay in its unique transmission pattern involving thousands of broadcast frequencies. Any single-frequency transmission lasted no more than a fraction of a second and took place microseconds before the subsequent, alternate-frequency broadcast of electromagnetic energy. Unless you knew the sequential order of the firing frequencies, the microchip proved undetectable.

The Mensa team had concluded that the ideal location for the chip lay beneath the skin directly on top of the head. *For two reasons.* First, when outdoors, this location permitted unimpeded transmission to a satellite, with no intervening body mass to weaken the faint signal. The chip had to be inserted surgically—and therein lay the second advantage. Assuming that the victim had no knowledge of the surgery, the tiny incision would produce only minimal soreness for a day or two afterward. The top of the head is one of several places on the human body that cannot be examined (by oneself) without a mirror. Because of the brief duration of any discomfort, and the fact that the chip lay beneath hair (hopefully), by the time the victim got around to thinking about it a second time, any pain would have disappeared. The dissolving sutures would leave no trace.

Of course, as in all things ostensibly simple, the difficulty lay in the execution—implanting the chip without the victim's knowledge. In the case of Sidki, pure serendipity intervened. While being tailed by an agent, Sidki suddenly fell victim to appendicitis and required surgery. The speed with which the Agency responded to this fortuitous occurrence became an in-house legend. An Agency surgeon arrived on the scene within eight hours. The fact that the hospital happened to be located in a less-than-affluent country, where corruption and payoffs proved routine, facilitated matters. Money changed hands. The agent required only fifteen minutes alone in the operating room.

Now, two years later, the Delta chip was performing as advertised and had pinpointed Sidki in New York, following a flight from London's Gatwick Airport. This was the first time he had returned to the United States following his assignment to investigate the incineration of the two goons who had tried to snuff Silverstein. Lopez continued. "So do you think Sidki is here because of Silverstein?"

"Could be."

"We're tying loose ends together with spider webs! There's nothing concrete and so—" Again, the phone. "Goddamn it, what is it now?"

"Lopez." He listened for a full sixty seconds before hanging up. He sat speechless, a stunned expression on his face.

Lopez reviewed the sequence of events that had led to this impossibility. The Sidki reference reminded him that, at about that same time, the Agency had a fledgling program to create a DNA database for all known terrorists, to which they added Sidki's name following the implant of his tracking device. After the incident in California when Silverstein had nearly lost his life in a car chase through his own housing development, Agency personnel could salvage no DNA from the two bodies charred from the inferno of their car crash. Months later, with new technology, their DNA *was* retrieved, providing an interesting fact: the two assassins were twins. Subsequent ground intelligence provided additional details. They had been born in Egypt, and their family name was Ishmael.

"What is it, Hector?" Miller was patiently waiting for the other shoe to drop.

Lopez focused on a crack on the ceiling. "I didn't tell you that when I came back to my office before the hotel romp, I ran Thurston's and Mac-Donald's names through the Agency's database, to see if anything would turn up. The only thing of interest was that Thurston's father was Egyptian."

"Really?"

"Remember when we had to record our DNA for the Agency last year?"

Miller stood and put his hands in his pockets. "Yeah, I remember. I wasn't any too happy about it. A requirement of the Patriot Act for anyone possessing a Secret or above clearance in the federal government."

Lopez continued. "Do you also remember that we lowly civil servants weren't the only ones? Our honorable members of the House and Senate did the same."

"Go on."

"When I saw Thurston's Egyptian reference, on a lark I asked Statistics to run her DNA through our in-house DNA database." He didn't have to remind Miller that the CIA's database included, in addition to the Agency's special additions, all available state and federal, criminal and noncriminal sources of DNA, including the new additions resulting from the Patriot Act. In the case of Sidki, because of the Agency's investment in the Delta chip, they had tried their best to keep his name off other government terrorist lists (a goal not easily achieved); because they intended to maintain tight control of his actions while inside the country, Lopez had convinced his bosses of the soundness of that request.

Lopez looked straight at Miller. "Guess who Thurston shares her DNA with?"

Miller turned his palms face up. "I give up."

"Do you remember the Ishmael twins?"

Miller's face contorted, his head snapped back, and he sat down. He thought for a moment and then replied. "In Monterey? The guys who broke into Silverstein's house and then chased him around the block?"

Lopez turned his back to Miller and stared out the window. "The same. They share a parent."

Miller's comment mirrored Lopez's sense of the matter. "You're kidding, right? That's un-fucking-believable!"

CHAPTER 33

CODE

Russell Senate Office Building, Washington, DC, USA
38°53'32"N latitude, 77°00'28"W longitude
Wednesday, 4:55 PM, August 5, 2009

Thurston shook her head in disgust; her tryst had eaten up the afternoon. She massaged her temples and barked out an order to Grafton over the intercom, "No more calls, please. I'm busy." Grafton would stay until Thurston departed, which was usually six o'clock. Although five o'clock was normal quitting time both in Washington and in Kansas, her constituents back home expected her to adhere to central daylight time, one hour earlier

Things were progressing rapidly, perhaps too rapidly. Upon Thurston's return from the Hyatt, Jamieson had called her cell to say that Silverstein's assistant, Linda Kipling, was under his control and being used as leverage against Silverstein. However, there was a problem. Silverstein said that he did not know who the female was and that he and Kipling were heading back to Pennsylvania to determine the source of the DNA. To ensure that Silverstein followed through, Jamieson had taken drastic measures, snatching Kipling.

Jamieson's call rammed home the obvious to Thurston: she had passed the point of no return. Future actions and outcomes could endanger her position. Although worrisome, this thought excited her because she had just received confirmation that she was doing the right thing.

Uncle Mohammed had signaled this morning that her half brother Caliph was on his way to the United States to locate this same woman. What had started out as a personal venture having monetary implications had metamorphosed into something more serious. Thurston would help in any way possible to ensure that the Blade would be the first to acquire this female with the unusual DNA. Her efforts to infiltrate the highest levels of the government were paying off. It was up to her to do everything necessary but at the same time to escape unscathed. She had come too far to blow it all on one assignment.

How could she help her cause? She would lead Caliph to Silverstein and thus to the female they were searching for. But meanwhile, Jamieson could do the heavy lifting, following Silverstein to Pennsylvania. That would occur tomorrow. Until Jamieson struck pay dirt, his assistant would play nursemaid to Kipling in the Monterey Peninsula town of Carmel.

For the time being, there was nothing to do but wait. She would continue her association with MacDonald, to ensure that the information she obtained through Jamieson proved reliable. Although Thurston hoped she could trust the latter's allegiance, there was no sense in being overconfident.

Thurston's computer beeped. *You've got mail!* She tapped the return key to awaken the hibernating screen. At the same time, she heard a housefly flutter over her head. The sound was annoying. "How did you get in here?" she said aloud as her eyes followed its path to the rear wall.

Thurston glanced at the e-mail, which was different from most. Clandestine communications arrived in a variety of ways: text messages on her cell phone, by fax at home, by U.S. mail, once by courier, and occasionally by e-mail. The Blade encrypted these communiqués using a simple method of transfer that Uncle Mohammed had taught her. A casual observer would see only a string of meaningless numbers separated by spaces. She looked down at this sequence, relieved to see it wasn't too long:

*6 122 2 21 3 15 4 22 67 7 6 23 39 15 2 46 17 0 0 27 9126 3281 2856
9126 6468 6628 8379 4127 7532 5772 8 59 12 9*

Thurston noted the first digit in the series and walked to the opposite wall. There she scanned the volumes that one might expect to find in the library of a U.S. senator, but among which were interspersed a few personal favorites, including the complete sequence of Tom Clancy's thrillers. She removed number six, *The Sum of All Fears*, and returned to her desk.

She opened the novel to page 122, the second of the numbers in the sequence, and proceeded to make the translation. Starting on that page, and using the third number in the sequence, she went to the second word on that page. That word, *President*, provided the first letter for the translation, *P*. It was always the first letter of the word so defined, including articles and the letter *a* by itself, and only one letter per page. The second letter came on page 123 on the 21st word, the word *and*. Continuing, she painstakingly translated the rest of the numerals.

There were only four other rules. Chapter titles were ignored. Hyphenated words counted only as one word, as did abbreviations. If a zero appeared in the code sequence, you skipped that page and went to the next. Because of two sequential zeroes in this message, she passed over two sequential pages. The remaining rule concerned numerals. If a four-digit number appeared, it represented a number. Again, the code was simple. Starting with the first four-digit number, you used the first digit of that number and subtracted one. Thus, the sequence 9126 translated to eight. For the second four-digit number, you used the second number of the four and did the same, again subtracting one. Thus, 3281 translated to the digit one. After you sequenced to four, the maximum number of digits, you reverted to the first of the four digits—but always subtracting one.

In minutes, Thurston translated the numeric sequence into the following: PACKAGEINNEWYORK8145556666SOON. Her brother had arrived in New York. She had a phone number, probably a cell, with which to reach him, and she was supposed to get in touch soon. Uncle Mohammed had given her details earlier. Caliph would arrive by private aircraft with three other Blade members, one of them a principal named

Sidki, and the other two the pilots of the aircraft. In a pinch, Caliph could use the pilots for other duties.

The buzzing of the fly was becoming more irritating. She looked up. "Get the hell out of here if you know what's good for you."

Thurston memorized the phone number, shredded her decoding page, and deleted the e-mail on her machine. That e-mail existed on a separate hard drive that was not duplicated on a central server—a measure of security unique to members of Congress. To prevent anyone from discovering the message even after it had been deleted, she initiated a disk erasure program that made it impossible to retrieve information from that drive.

It was time to leave the office. Uncle Mohammed would expect her to call Caliph immediately. She would use a pay phone on the street.

As she stood to leave, she heard the overhead flight of the housefly and followed its path to the wall next to the door into Grafton's office. She grabbed her copy of the *Post*, folded it into thirds, lowered it to her right side, walked steadily toward the door, and while looking out the corner of her eye, raised the folded newspaper. The fly appeared to be taking off. She would have to be quick.

Her aim was on the mark. "Take that, you son of a bitch."

Thurston recoiled at the sound of her newspaper hitting the wall. *That was loud.* She examined the back side of the newspaper, surprised to see a stain the size of a quarter. This one had more than its share of guts, she thought.

CHAPTER 34

SPIT

Delta Airlines flight, Atlanta to Pittsburgh, somewhere over West Virginia, USA
Thursday, 4:40 PM, August 6, 2009

The Navy's preeminent, but weary, meteorologist stared out the starboard window of the MD-88 at the countryside below; seasoned air travelers knew to request a seat away from the sun. He felt pleased with himself—Dickey would have a surprise waiting for him at the airport. The evening before, waiting for this morning's flight, had given Silverstein plenty of time to think—and plan.

Silverstein nearly always flew first class, paying the extra cost himself above the coach fare the government allowed. Money was not an issue for Victor Mark Silverstein. For this Thursday's flight to Pittsburgh, besides paying for the entire fare because this trip was not government business, he had settled for coach accommodations. Why? He wanted to sit as far back in the plane as possible. Dickey had asked for Silverstein's flight itinerary and said that he would be flying to Pennsylvania on the same planes—but with Kipling and Vi (presumably short for Violet) left behind.

Flying out of Monterey made the trip to Pittsburgh a three-plane ordeal: Monterey, San Francisco, Atlanta, and then on to Pittsburgh. It seemed to Silverstein that doubling back to get anywhere, whether in life or in a series of aircraft bound for the home city of the Steelers, made little sense. Nonetheless, the airlines' hub system produced such itineraries.

For this trip, Silverstein had made two additions to his person before he left the house. Contrary to his usual practice of relying on credit cards, he crammed a stack of fifty-dollar bills into his wallet. This was a mission different from most, and they might come in handy. The second item would not leave the airport proper, back in Monterey. Accordingly, Silverstein arrived at the airport well before his departure on Thursday morning, far earlier than anyone, especially Dickey, would consider arriving for a flight. It allowed him the time he needed. For no matter what happened on his trip east, the Monterey Peninsula was where Kipling sat helpless and where Silverstein intended to return.

Dickey arrived as promised, and they flew to San Francisco. More than once, Silverstein considered losing him and hopping another airline. He discarded this thought. It would solve nothing and serve only to piss off his flying companion.

The idea of Dickey sitting behind him was not a thought Silverstein relished—thus the coach seat in the back of the plane. He remained within eyesight at both the San Francisco and Atlanta airports. During boarding of the plane to Pittsburgh from Atlanta, after Silverstein had taken his seat, Dickey caught his eye in a peculiar way. Standing in the aisle, ten or so seats to the front, he had pointed his right hand at Silverstein and pretended to fire a weapon, at the same time revealing a knowing smile. He then disappeared to the front of the plane, probably to first class.

Silverstein cringed at the memory of yesterday's events. As furious as he was at Dickey, he was angrier with himself. After having analyzed Dickey's deception involving the fax for the umpteenth time, he acknowledged that Dickey's trick had been damn clever.

Silverstein noted the time. It had been a day since he had stared helplessly at Kipling as she rode by. Outside NRL, he had briefly considered giving chase and having it out with Dickey. Dickey had anticipated as much and made it clear in a cell phone conversation that such a plan was ill advised, that Kipling would be the loser. He promised that no harm would come to her if Silverstein cooperated.

As troubling as the thought of Kipling being held hostage was, it felt ironically comforting that she remained out of the fray. The notion of her possessing the prophecy gene was still incomprehensible to Silverstein. What were the odds? With her sitting out the action back home, at least he didn't have to worry about her. Yet.

All of which led to an obvious dilemma for Silverstein. What to do next? He had made three telephone calls upon arriving home Wednesday evening. First, he called Peggy Houston, the curator of the Johnstown Flood National Memorial, getting her out of bed to confirm his late arrival on Thursday. They agreed to an early morning meeting at her workplace on Friday. In Silverstein's mind, whether this meeting occurred would be determined by the result of his second call, to Jimmy Travers at the Smithsonian.

Travers already knew that he would receive the envelope back on Thursday. Silverstein was relieved when Travers assured him that the "gibberish" (Silverstein's word) in Weaverman's e-mail was, in fact, not gibberish at all, and was all that he needed to make the comparison. Silverstein begged him to perform the DNA testing on the envelope's saliva as quickly as possible, comparing it to Weaverman's genetic code, and to overnight the envelope back to Peggy Houston. If the comparison came back positive, that envelope might prove to be the bargaining chip to set both Weaverman and Kipling free. Silverstein had been evasive when Travers asked what a positive comparison would mean. He agreed to call Silverstein on his cell with a yea or a nay.

Travers's response was crucial. If Augusta Schmidt's DNA didn't test positive for the prophecy gene, what point would there be in continuing to Johnstown? And if so, Silverstein's third call last night would be insurance indeed. Strictly speaking, a negative response from Travers wouldn't prove fraud but, from Silverstein's viewpoint, it would produce a sufficient roadblock to continuing. Contrarily, a positive result made a decision clear-cut. A match meant that Houston's story was not fiction, that the girl, Augusta Schmidt, was special indeed and that Silverstein needed to keep his appointment in Johnstown. Notwithstanding the argument made by the defense team in the OJ trial that a DNA result could prove erroneous, anyone with a smattering of statistical sense would conclude that a positive match implied something of consequence. Of course, one had to temporarily sidestep Travers's determination that the author of the letter had been male. That fact made no sense either. *If the genes don't fit …*

Silverstein shook his head in frustration. *Simplify things, Silverstein! You'll go nuts with minutia! If the test proves negative, forget Johnstown and Peggy Houston. If positive, continue and worry about the inconsistencies later.* Still, Silverstein had to face the follow-up question. Even if Augusta Schmidt possessed the gene, what good was it for his present predicament? She had been dead for more than a century. Weaverman's fate and Rafferty's interest stemmed from a belief that the donor was alive.

Silverstein's mind jolted to the present as the landing gear touched terra firma, Pennsylvania. As they taxied to the gate, Silverstein took advantage of the rule that allowed cell phone use following touchdown. After the usual thirty-second boot-up, Silverstein waited for his phone to query AT&T's national cell phone system. Sure enough, within seconds, the phone chirped to indicate he had voice mail. Travers has called, thought Silverstein. He pressed the automatic dial-up for voice mail and listened to two messages in sequence. His heart hammered.

The first message was indeed from Travers. He had the envelope and would have the DNA results by that evening. The second message provided some relief to Silverstein's mind. It confirmed what the third phone call of the previous evening had set in motion. That call had included a plea to Hector Rodriguez Lopez, Jr. He would be waiting at the airport when their flight arrived. The cavalry were galloping to the rescue. Silverstein's description was specific enough that Lopez would have no trouble identifying Dickey and removing him from action.

Silverstein exited the Jetway, entered the central pathway, and leaned against the wall to take in the scene. Dickey would have left first. Perhaps Lopez and his team had already apprehended him and left the area. If so, Lopez would call soon and give him an update. Rather than leave the gate, Silverstein chose to take advantage of the adjacent men's restroom. He did so and returned to the walkway. Still nothing. He removed his cell phone from his pocket, switched the ringer to vibrate, and held it in his hand, expecting the call anytime.

The vibration came soon. Silverstein flipped open the phone and, without checking the caller ID, answered abruptly. "What took you so long?"

The answer at the other end was hardly the one he had expected. "It's occurred to me that you've been holding out on me."

Silverstein caught his breath. It was Dickey. *Think fast!* "Dickey? I've been waiting at the gate. Figured we might as well share a car. Where are you?" *How could he have gotten off the plane and bypassed Lopez? Had he recognized the trap and slipped by? Hadn't Hector come? Something was wrong!*

"I missed your plane, but I'm on another flight right now. I might have to hang up. They're closing the doors."

"How could you have missed the flight? I saw you." Suddenly, Silverstein remembered the expression on Dickey's face. "What the hell are you talking about? I told you I'm on my way to Johnstown, and I am."

"The flight to San Francisco this morning gave me time to think. Some of the details you've fed me don't quite add up."

Silverstein was getting worried. He scanned the gate area, half-expecting Dickey to appear within eyesight. "What details?"

"Little things, Dr. Silverstein. Your reaction in your stairwell when Kipling wanted to give me the hair samples. This nonsense about going to Johnstown. But one other thing of more consequence occurred to me. I can't believe that I didn't think about it until we arrived in San Francisco this morning. When I left your house that night with the hair samples, I opened the sealed envelope to make sure there was something inside. Later, at the hospital, while I waited for Myra, I took out the hairs and laid them on a white sheet. Nothing unusual, I thought. Blond hairs. Then, in San Francisco this morning, I got to thinking. I had seen hair of that color only hours earlier. Back in Monterey. I don't suppose you can guess where."

Silverstein's body reacted with an electrifying chill.

Dickey continued. "Before we left San Francisco, I made a call back to Dr. Rafferty. On a hunch, I asked him to check the DNA in the saliva on the envelope that Kipling gave me. They can do that sort of thing now.

Did you know that?" He paused. "What are the chances that the person who retrieved the hair samples would have asked the donor to lick the envelope? Slim to none, I figured. Do you see my way of thinking? You can imagine my surprise, then, in Atlanta, when Rafferty told me that the two were similar. He hadn't had time to do a lot of testing, but he did say he had enough markers to confirm that the same person provided both sets of DNA."

Silverstein shook his head, still listening.

"Are you still there? I suppose you are." Dickey hesitated. "I'm sorry, Dr. Silverstein, but I've got to hang up. The flight attendant just gave me a naughty look. I'll be back in San Francisco in about five hours. Have fun in Johnstown."

CHAPTER 35

DEAD RUN

Concourse D, Gate 79, Pittsburgh International Airport,
Pittsburgh, Pennsylvania, USA
40°29'48"N latitude, 80°14'50"W longitude
Thursday, 5:15 PM, August 6, 2009

Lopez and Miller stood on opposite sides of the central walkway. Lopez
had the more direct view. He, Miller, and three field agents trained in the
use of Crimson had flown up this afternoon. Lopez knew that Miller
would say that they were finally doing the right thing. Silverstein had
called the previous evening and asked for help. Dick had kidnapped
Kipling, according to Silverstein, and was holding her hostage while Silverstein went searching for some mystery woman in Johnstown, Pennsylvania. Lopez didn't understand that part and Silverstein, clearly upset,
didn't explain.

Silverstein's call had come following a particularly somber moment.
Considering the Romguard's short lifetime, its demise was a surprisingly
sentimental loss for the team members, particularly Winston. Their affec-
tion had evolved to the point where they considered the mechanical insect
a bona fide member of the team. Winston offered an unnecessary apology.
He had caught the movement of the newspaper but had reacted too
slowly. Lopez hoped that the bug's self-destruction system had worked as
designed.

Once the emotion died down, everyone raised mugs to the Romguard and its ultimate sacrifice. Their little friend's final hour had been heroic indeed. It had been clear from the start that Senator Thurston had noticed the mechanical fly in her office. In hindsight, Winston remembered that she had reacted to the Romguard back at the Hyatt. Winston concluded that her hearing was significantly more acute than average.

Consequently, those final minutes in Thurston's office were challenging ones, with everyone in the room on edge, knowing that their bug was under surveillance. But all had worked out; they had witnessed the decoding of the e-mail message. Despite Miller's proclamation that he himself could crack Thurston's code, the Agency's cryptography section was working overtime to decipher which rules Thurston had used. (They had already figured out that the first number in the series referred to Tom Clancy's sixth novel.) If Thurston should receive another coded transmission, they would be ready—the Patriot Act gave them considerable latitude in monitoring Thurston's communications, whether landline telephone, cell phone, or e-mail.

Without the Romguard's video trail of Senator Thurston turning pages, they would have had nothing. This was one instance when the loss of audio had no impact. The decoded communiqué, PACKAGEINNEWYORK8145556666SOON—read directly from Thurston's notepad as the Romguard clung desperately from the ceiling above—had been an intelligence windfall. They traced the telephone number to a Pennsylvania-based cell phone whose location corresponded to that of Sidki. They might have missed that coincidence had it not been for Miller's uncanny ability to link together disparate bits of information.

Lopez glanced around the terminal. All of his team had come disguised, which was standard operating procedure for them. For Lopez and Miller, hair (beards and mustaches) also hid facial features. Even their own mothers would have had difficulty recognizing them. All were wearing the casual business attire option of the Cooper, invented by Chris Cooper, an Agency ITE (image transformation expert—in vernacular terms, a makeup artist). Cooper had attended to the body hair embellishments of Lopez and Miller before they left Dulles Airport.

Cooper hailed from the Mensa team. The Cooper was Chris's most popular invention, outerwear that, given fifteen seconds and a few zips and pulls, changed the complete external appearance of an agent. The ingenious outerwear permitted the user to have three different changes of clothing (from the viewpoint of an observer) available nearly instantaneously, and to change back and forth at will. Cooper had been a professional magician prior to joining the Agency. Knowledge from this line of work no doubt played a part in his cunning design.

Although Lopez and Miller didn't always choose to hide their identities, a layperson might question why they would do so at all. After all, their mark, identified by Silverstein, had never met them. Further, Silverstein, a friend, had been the one to call on their services. Other than the fact that most agents wanted to keep their identities hidden (a good enough reason by itself), the advantages of a disguise came from years of experience. Having the ability to change looks almost made an agent invisible and allowed for considerable flexibility in conducting a field operation—not the least of which was the ability to escape threatening situations. In the case of Silverstein, who knew both Lopez and Miller, they had learned from experience that it wasn't always to their advantage to have a cooperating civilian recognize them. Civilians had a nasty habit of zigging when they should be zagging.

Lopez held a briefcase and spoke into what looked like a cell phone. In fact, he was talking on a special encrypted frequency to the other members of his team, who were all within a small perimeter surrounding the gate. "It shouldn't be long now. Early thirties, blond hair, athletic build. Get ready to activate Crimson."

If he had spent more time with Sanfold, Lopez thought, he could have lip-read Miller's response across the aisle. "Roger. Crimson a go." Three successive key clicks served as acknowledgments from the other agents.

Crimson, invented by legendary agent Joseph P. Crimson in the early 1990s, referred to a now-standard Agency procedure for apprehending a solo individual. As long as the target remained unsuspecting, Crimson's success rate was over 95 percent, according to Agency statistics. Minimal commotion and recognition by the surrounding public defined success.

Although the technique required weeks of training to account for variations in execution (and bimonthly practice thereafter), to an outsider the process would seem straightforward. Two of three agents approached the mark from the front, one on the left and one on the right. Each agent grabbed the mark's wrist on his side and pivoted it inward to block their actions from view. Simultaneously, the third agent would advance from the rear and stab the victim in the buttocks with a syringe containing chemicals that, within seconds, created a mental paralysis that had little effect on the individual's physical abilities. Once administered, the mark followed verbal instructions without objection.

Lopez scanned the travelers exiting the Jetway. Most had deplaned, and no one matching Dick's description had come by. *Did they have the wrong gate?* He checked his notes. "Where is he?"

Miller's reply was immediate. "Here comes Silverstein. He's acting normally, looking around, probably for us. He's stopped and is waiting. Maybe Dick's still on the plane?"

Lopez was getting worried. "Something's wrong here. And it looks to me like Silverstein's confused, too. Maintain position."

Lopez watched as Silverstein disappeared into the bathroom and then returned to the central walkway. It wasn't long before he opened his cell phone, obviously receiving a call. From his angle, Lopez had a clear view of Silverstein's face and watched as two emotions evolved in rapid sequence, disappointment followed by anger. Before Silverstein completed the call, he began to pace back and forth within the walkway, oblivious to pedestrians trying to avoid him.

"What's going on, Hector? From my angle, he's spooked." Miller had also spotted Silverstein's agitated behavior. "I think it's time we had a talk. Dick's obviously not here and something's upsetting him."

Lopez decided to act on Miller's suggestion, but it was too late. Silverstein calmly folded his telephone, shoved it into his right pants pocket, looked up and down the pathway one more time—and then took off at a dead run toward the terminal!

Lopez was hyperventilating. "What the hell? Does anyone see anything, any threats?" Four negatives came back in sequence. "I'll call him on his cell." Lopez whipped out his cell phone and pressed the speed-dial digit he had programmed and used to leave Silverstein a message just hours earlier. "Answer the phone, goddamn it!" Five rings passed before Silverstein's voice mail kicked in.

Lopez issued a command to the three accompanying agents. "You can stand down." He stepped into the pathway and scanned the hundreds of feet worth of exiting passengers. Silverstein was long gone.

Lopez regretted the order, but all members of his team realized he had no choice. He would much rather have chased after his friend, Victor. But the last thing he needed was to explain to airport security who they were and why they were chasing an innocent civilian. In an emergency he could have pulled rank over local authorities, but there were risks in doing so.

Miller walked over and was the first to say it. "What happened? Something in that phone call scared him."

"Looked like it to me, too."

Lopez and Miller walked briskly in Silverstein's direction. Silverstein would obviously have taken the short train ride to baggage claim and transportation. The Pittsburgh International Airport wasn't all that big. They still might catch him.

If so, Lopez had two questions he wanted to ask. The first was one he had been dying to raise the previous evening. *What the hell was so important in Johnstown?* With his second question, however, Lopez would make it a point to look Silverstein directly in the eye. *Is there something I should know about Linda Kipling?*

CHAPTER 36

DOWNLINK

Russell Senate Office Building, Washington, DC, USA
38°53'32"N latitude, 77°00'28"W longitude
Thursday, 5:20 PM, August 6, 2009

Thurston rechecked her sequence of coded numbers:

> 6 49 1 8 3 3 0 15 32 29 1 46 56 0 45 0 0 39 0 9 24 0 61 3 28 56 12 23
> 0 0 0 25 19 0 41 5 30.

Although she had all of his novels lining her shelves, field operatives for the Blade carried only three miniaturized copies of Clancy's thrillers, numbers one, five, and six: *The Hunt for Red October, Clear and Present Danger,* and *The Sum of All Fears.* In an emergency or when speed was paramount, either side could use a pay phone; if that was unavailable, a one-use, throwaway cell phone was allowed. Otherwise, the slow, tedious code-and-count method represented the Blade's preferred method of covert communication. As far as Thurston was concerned, they could have used only one book for their transmissions. Her favorite was number six. No one could ever break this code.

Thurston rested her finger on the send button of her cell phone but then withdrew it. Much hinged on her decision. She paced the office, mentally walking herself through the potential outcomes that this message would set in motion. They all stemmed from the telephone call she had received from Jamieson an hour earlier.

Jamieson said he had identified the mystery woman with the special DNA and was on his way to retrieve her. In fact, she was Linda Kipling, Silverstein's assistant. He didn't have time to go into detail, other than to say he had finally seen through Silverstein's ploy. Silverstein had wanted to draw Jamieson as far away as possible from the very woman they were searching for. The hostage they had been holding as an inducement for Silverstein to cough up the real woman turned out to be the prize herself. Thurston hadn't had time to ask him how he knew that. He also said he had immediately informed his partner babysitting the woman in Carmel, California. They were to stay put and await his arrival. By Jamieson's estimate, he would arrive back in Monterey on the last flight of the day from San Francisco, around 9:30, West Coast time. He promised to call Thurston again from San Francisco.

Earlier in the day, hours before she had this new information, Thurston had sent her first text message to her brother's cell phone in New York. She told Caliph to stay put and await further instructions. Based on Jamieson's new information, she knew what needed to be done. Uncle Mohammed had made it clear to her brother that once he and Sidki reached American soil, Cleopatra would control the operation. Interestingly, her brother Caliph had no idea who Cleopatra was. Uncle Mohammed knew as well as she that her cover was so deep that not even blood relatives could be trusted with such information.

Thurston was reasonably confident she could trust Jamieson—with the emphasis on the word *reasonably*. He would obey her orders and do with this Kipling woman as Thurston requested. The obvious course of action would be to deliver Kipling to New York, where Caliph would take possession and fly her back to Egypt. Why do something yourself when someone can do it for you?

Two considerations made this plan less palatable than would first appear. She had to trust that Jamieson would follow through. If he did not and delivered Kipling to MacDonald's henchmen instead, retrieving the woman would become next to impossible. That was her first concern. The second was just as troublesome. Any number of things could go wrong transporting Kipling back to New York on a commercial aircraft. A fan of American football, Thurston remembered the quote from former University of Texas coach Darrell Royal (no fan of the forward pass): "Three things can happen when you put the ball in the air, and two of 'em are bad."

If Kipling should try to escape, a simple plan could evolve into chaos. Jamieson was intelligent and capable but might not be up to the task. Besides, Caliph possessed an aircraft that would facilitate Kipling's abduction. And in addition to Sidki, Caliph could count on the skills of his two pilots, who were trained agents in their own right.

The importance of this assignment, her first from Uncle Mohammed, dictated that she take no chances. Too much lay at stake to trust both loyalty and chance at the same time. And because she could not depend on Jamieson's reaction to her decision, it would be necessary to keep him in the dark. She would call him, obtain the necessary details, and pass them on to Caliph once his plane landed.

Thurston pressed the send button. Caliph and Sidki should fly to Monterey, California, immediately—on the same private aircraft that had brought them to New York in the first place.

CHAPTER 37

WIND-DRIVEN MATTER

Carmel Bay Motor Lodge, Cottage 14, Carmel, California, USA
36°33'39"N latitude, 121°55'15"W longitude
Thursday, 2:45 PM, August 6, 2009

The dream world from which Linda Kipling awoke was not a threatening one. By contrast, a tug on her right leg reminded her that not all was well in the present world. Without giving away that she had awakened, Kipling glanced sideways at the bedside clock. Two forty-five. *PM?* She blinked and looked again. The filtered light penetrating the closed motel window confirmed that it was indeed afternoon.

Kipling had slept since midnight, over fourteen hours. Dickey had kept her up late, probably to ensure she slept as late as possible into the following day. Ironically, this had been the best night's sleep she'd had in years. For that, there was good reason.

As her thoughts returned to focus, Kipling recalled the oft-quoted statement that hindsight is 20–20. She reflected on that as she surreptitiously eyed her captor, Violet, last name unknown, who worked for Dickey. Perhaps she should have turned him over to the police that night at Silverstein's. Dickey had informed her the previous evening that he would be traveling east with Victor this morning. He told her not to worry, that Violet would only hold her as collateral until Silverstein turned over the woman whose DNA matched the hair in the envelope. The second half of that statement came as no surprise to Kipling.

Kipling should have been more wary during her taxi ride to the Kinko's store in Monterey. But Silverstein's exuberance at thinking that Dickey had made a critical mistake, one that could be used to their advantage, had tempered any sense of danger.

Kipling had exited the taxi across the street from the store. Dickey snatched her before she even had time to check out Silverstein's theory. Violet had been driving. She simply drove up alongside Kipling, where-upon Dickey opened the right rear door and jerked Kipling inside. She acquiesced—there wasn't much room to fight in the backseat of a four-door automobile. Ten minutes later, the sight of poor Victor—knowing that he would feel completely responsible for her sorry situation—had been almost too much to bear.

They checked into a motel in Carmel, Monterey Peninsula's famous seaside village just over the hill from Monterey proper. No doubt inspired by Myra's woeful tale, the procedures taken to ensure no further display of Kipling's anger were impressive, yet remarkably humane. Using a rope-like contraption that simultaneously controlled three of her four limbs, Kipling could choose which of her two arms remained free. With her right arm loose, she could eat and go to the bathroom without much difficulty. At night, following Chinese dinner in takeout containers, she was led to bed and given the luxury of having two arms and one leg free (the other attached to the bed frame) for sleeping—under *one* condition, low-tech, but effective nonetheless. They asked her to take *two* Ambien tablets. Still anticipating Violet's revenge for the damage inflicted on her sister, Kipling agreed. Kipling was familiar with the prescription sleeping aid and knew that although one tablet was the usual dose, a second wouldn't kill her. Under the circumstances and given the surprising benevolence of her captors, she concluded it was best not to complain.

Kipling slowly turned her head, scanned the motel room, and focused on Violet. Rather than reading a magazine or watching television as you might expect from low-life kidnappers, she was typing on a laptop. *Inter-*

esting. Kipling shuffled on the bed so that Violet knew she had awakened. Violet glanced over.

"What are you writing, may I ask?" Kipling decided to try some dialogue. Conversation had been minimal the previous night.

Violet answered softly. "It's an essay."

"Essay?"

"I'm working on a master's in psychology. I specialize in troubled children. I need ten more credits to complete my course requirements."

You've got to be kidding me! Kipling couldn't believe it. An educated kidnapper?

For the next ten minutes, they exchanged banter. When Dickey needed help for this assignment, Myra had suggested that her sister fill in. Violet explained that since money is always in short supply for graduate students, she had agreed. Kipling considered it prudent not to mention that a felony kidnapping conviction could delay Violet's education plans.

Kipling decided to bring into the open one obvious sticky issue. "For what it's worth, I didn't mean to hurt your sister. It just sort of worked out that way."

"That's all right."

Kipling's jaw dropped. "Help me out here. Isn't Myra your twin sister? I expected you to be pissed as hell."

Violet sighed. "My and I have never gotten along. In some respects, she deserved it." She hesitated before making her second point. "That's all I'm going to say. So don't worry. I'm not going to take it out on you. I'm not the violent type. Besides, I'm a lot smarter than she is."

Kipling wondered to herself how one identical twin could be smarter than the other.

With Violet's last comment, she pointed her finger at Kipling. "Please keep that in mind. You're probably ready for breakfast. You know the drill."

Violet tossed to Kipling the halter that would immobilize three of her four limbs. First, Kipling sat up in bed and fastened her two ankles together with handcuff-like manacles. She then hitched a rope to the ankle restraints, hooked the other end and remaining shackle to her left wrist, and pulled the rope connection taut using a small winch-like device. Not until that was accomplished did Violet walk over to loosen the restraint that kept Kipling tied to the foot of the bed. Violet backed away.

With both legs shackled and her left arm secure, Kipling could nonetheless shuffle and hop her way to the bathroom. Afterward, her free right hand permitted her to enjoy the bagel and orange juice Violet had saved from breakfast. Watching Violet concentrate mightily on the words she composed on the screen added to the absurdity of the situation.

As Kipling took her first munch on the bagel, an image wafted into her consciousness. She paused in mid-chew. Such visions occurred randomly. Sometimes they came in waves. Sometimes weeks or months would separate them. At one point in her life, nearly a year passed in between. The episodes usually took the form of mental images; rarely, words. This image was quite clear. Violet's cell phone would ring, and her face would register surprise at the message.

The first time Kipling recognized that she had this special gift was during her seventh birthday party. She had just blown out the candles on her cake when into her head popped the image of her friend Billy, her next-door neighbor, falling. Forty-five minutes later, Kipling watched as Billy tripped down the steps that separated their family room from the kitchen. He broke his arm. Foreseeing such an event—and then watching it happen—proved disconcerting to a little girl.

She mentioned the incident to her father, who promptly taught his daughter a new word, *coincidence*. Things like that happen all the time, he said. By the time her twelfth birthday had passed, Kipling fully understood the meaning of coincidence and knew that what she experienced was not part of that definition. She was also intelligent enough to realize that it was unlikely anyone else she knew possessed this unusual trait. From then on, Kipling accepted her mental gift as routine—no different than if she had recognized a musical or athletic talent. She mentioned this ability to no one and on more than one occasion had forgotten about it completely until it inexplicably exposed itself again.

Rarely did Kipling's visions prove useful in any practical sense. If only once she could foresee tomorrow's lottery numbers, she thought. Worse, there were times when she subconsciously augmented her thoughts to produce images beneficial to herself. Those never came true. As an adult, she came to final terms with her ability and accepted the occasional advantage that a vision might provide.

Ironically, when Silverstein first brought up Weaverman's research and the likelihood of a genetic explanation for the Russian rat's ability to traverse the mazes, Kipling hadn't even considered the possibility that her own talent related to Weaverman's unusual gene sequence. That didn't happen until days later—the evening at the Branding Iron restaurant—when she flinched following the vision of a black woman and a blond-haired man arriving at the restaurant. She then remembered that they had also been standing outside the gate at NRL. Only then did she make the correlation.

On her motorcycle ride to Silverstein's house that night, Kipling hatched a plan. Dickey had obviously come for the DNA evidence that Silverstein told Rafferty he had. If given the opportunity, she would provide her own hair in the envelope she had asked for at the Branding Iron. This course of action served two purposes. First and foremost, it would satisfy Dickey and remove him from their lives. Beyond that immediate threat, the plan provided a clandestine way for her to determine if she did in fact carry Weaverman's gene sequence. The last thing she wanted was to suggest to Silverstein anything of the sort.

To Kipling's way of thinking, the outcomes were win-win. More likely than not, the comparison would prove negative. Although Dickey and his handler would be pissed as hell, they would be long gone. Conversely, a positive result would provide Kipling with a logical explanation for her unusual ability. She had spent her professional life engaged in scientific study founded upon data, logic, and experimentation. In terms of what a positive outcome might portend for Kipling's future, she would worry about that later.

Kipling was well aware that her occasional episodes of foresight amazed Silverstein. Worse, at the bottom of the NRL steps, when Silverstein was on the phone with Dickey, there was an instant when Silverstein's eyes betrayed him. It was clear that Dickey was requesting the identity of the person whose hair he had sent forward for testing. And that meant that the genetic match had been *positive*. Poor Victor. She could imagine his mental wheels spinning furiously.

Once Kipling deduced that Silverstein knew, she planned her reaction carefully. She play-acted her reaction to be the one she would have taken had she known nothing. In her mind, she had to keep up this pretense because she had promised herself long ago never to tell anyone about her gift. It would take a monumental override to violate that oath. Also, she knew Victor all too well. He would assume, not illogically, that Kipling had no realization of her gift. In keeping with his idea of protecting the weaker female—a concept that infuriated Kipling—he would hide his discovery, considering the implications.

Kipling had taken her last swallow of juice when the cute jingle on Violet's cell phone disturbed the quiet. The expression on Violet's face replicated what Kipling had seen on Silverstein's face just twenty-four hours earlier.

Oh, shit! It's hit the fan now.

CHAPTER 38

INHERITED SALVATION

Airborne, 450 miles west of Pittsburgh, Pennsylvania, USA
Thursday, 8:15 PM EDT, August 6, 2009

Silverstein checked his pulse. It had slowed some. The stress and resultant adrenaline rush of the past three hours had begun to ebb. Time to consider the boxed dinner offered earlier. He glanced at his watch. They had been in the air a little over an hour. It was 8:15 eastern time, which meant it was just after five in the afternoon in Monterey. Barring the unexpected, he would make it in time.

Most of the people who lived within the orbit of Victor Mark Silverstein knew of his unusual upbringing, that his unmarried, biological mother had been a domestic servant of the Silverstein family in the late 1950s. They also knew that she inexplicably walked into the path of a city bus in Atlanta, Georgia, on the 30th of April in 1962, and died. Because the Silversteins knew of no other family members, and couldn't find any even after a thorough search that included a private investigator, the childless couple, already in their forties, adopted three-year-old Victor. To this day, Silverstein still marveled over the selflessness of his adoptive parents. They had taken him in as their own. He had memories of the complete, unmitigated love of a mother who would chastise anyone foolish enough to question that Victor was her son, despite their difference in skin color.

When both his adoptive mother and father passed away in 1997, leaving a sizable sum to charity, Silverstein inherited the remainder. The estate included their modest home in Atlanta, stock, cash, and a bungalow on the Big Island of Hawaii. He sold the Atlanta house. Together with the stock and cash, the sum came to a little more than three million dollars. This was on top of the one-million-dollar trust his parents had set up for him when he reached the age of twenty-five, two years after graduating from Penn State and moving to California. That initial sum had increased handsomely during the stock market boom of the 1990s. Because Silverstein's former wife had come from a moneyed family as well, their split nine years earlier had been financially neutral.

Except for his father's prized 1955 Buick Roadmaster automobile, the only memento of value of his parents that he chose to keep was their Hawaiian cottage. When he visited there, memories came alive. His father had bought the nondescript residence after his World War II stint in the Navy, where his last assignment found him serving as a physician in Honolulu in the years following Pearl Harbor. The Silverstein family spent many a vacation there throughout Victor's childhood and teenage years. Even as an adult, he would occasionally meet up with them there. Only a handful of people at NRL knew that he owned this property, and none knew the address.

Except for his indulgence in expensive cars, Silverstein was hardly a spendthrift. His parents had taught him that waste was a sin, whether it be with food, natural resources, or money itself. For that reason, Silverstein always ate everything on his plate, not wanting to tempt his mother to rise from the grave and embarrass him in front of anyone within earshot.

All of this meant that Victor Mark Silverstein was not without assets and, in an emergency, could call upon resources that a person of ordinary means could not. In Silverstein's mind, this was just such an emergency. Accordingly, he found himself looking out the starboard window of a private aircraft flying directly to Monterey, California.

Because time constraints required him to fly the distance without refueling, he'd had to charter a larger Gulfstream. And if that wasn't enough to challenge his checkbook, the one-hour deadline for their departure he had mandated to the owner of Blair Aviation at Pittsburgh International came with a high price—150 percent of the usual hourly rate for the planned one-way flight.

Earlier, in front of the gate from which he'd arrived from Atlanta, he had made the split-second decision to rush back home. Silverstein knew that Dickey was returning to San Francisco from Atlanta, a flight that took around five hours. Dickey had made a critical mistake in telling him so. Silverstein knew that he had misjudged Dickey's intellect, but the reverse held true as well.

Leaving Atlanta at five o'clock East Coast time would put Dickey into San Francisco around seven or so. If he had a perfect connection, Dickey could land in Monterey an hour later. Fortunately, that connection did not exist. Silverstein had spent the last ten minutes on the Gulfstream's onboard telephone confirming that fact with his Monterey travel agent. She told him that the earliest flight that Dickey could take would place him in Monterey no earlier than 9:25. Even if he chose to drive, the two-hour trip wouldn't buy him any time.

Silverstein's pilot, Max Shafer, a pleasant, tall, graying man with a smile that came from one side of his mouth, estimated a 9:15 arrival time, ten minutes ahead of Dickey. Silverstein would be waiting when Dickey stepped off the plane.

The only thing that mattered since his phone conversation with Dickey was to rush back to Monterey to rescue Kipling. Now with the Gulfstream jetting its way across the continent, Silverstein had done all he could. He thought about his friend Hector Lopez standing at the altar with no bride in sight. Worse, his best man had gone running from the church. Back at the airport, Silverstein had a moment's empathy with Hector's dilemma. But then he shut off his cell phone. He hadn't been in the mood to talk to anyone.

Should he call Lopez? He owed him an explanation. On the other hand, what could Hector do now, and further, would he get in the way and make things worse? Silverstein might have to tell Lopez the truth, that Dickey had determined that Kipling possessed the prophecy gene. Just twenty-four hours earlier, Silverstein had vowed that no one should have that information.

What to do now? Silverstein's plan extended no further than forcing Kipling's whereabouts from Dickey and then storming the fort. That wasn't much of a plan. Once he rescued Kipling, what then? It wouldn't be long before Dickey's bosses in Washington knew what he knew. Would they send reinforcements? Would Silverstein be forced to let Kipling in on the secret that he had vowed never to divulge?

Silverstein shook his head. *No!* For the time being, as much as he could probably use Lopez's help, it was best to keep him out of it. He needed to protect Kipling. Until this crisis blew over, he had no choice but to take Kipling far away, someplace where not even Dickey could find her.

Silverstein unbuckled his seat belt and made his way to the cockpit. He informed Max and his copilot that once they landed, they should refuel and stay close to the aircraft. Within a very short time, they would continue their flight westward.

CHAPTER 39

LUMINARY

Pittsburgh International Airport, Pittsburgh, Pennsylvania, USA
40° 29'47"N latitude, 80° 15'25"W longitude
Thursday, 9:20 PM, August 6, 2009

Lopez questioned his decision. Should he have ordered Miller to stop Silverstein? Well, it was too late for that. Should they have followed immediately? No. Until they had a grasp of the situation, they couldn't go flying off willy-nilly.

Lopez took a sip from his cappuccino grande and glanced across at Miller. They were enjoying some fresh air in a parking lot outside the terminal. The other agents were grabbing a bite inside. "I screwed up. We should have nabbed Silverstein when we had the chance."

Miller responded. "Who would have thought he'd rent a private jet?"

It had been four hours since Lopez had watched Silverstein take off like a house afire. He had waited for Silverstein to call, to explain himself. But there had been no call.

Yet again, Lopez had come up short. Silverstein had requested his assistance. Lopez had agreed and had nothing to show for it. Just as in the 2007 escapade, when Lopez had twice come late to Silverstein's rescue, it was happening again.

After Silverstein had inexplicably run away, Lopez and his team had tried to find him. Something in Silverstein's phone call had set him off. Would he leave on another flight or travel by car?

Their only certainty was that Kipling's kidnapper had not accompanied Silverstein on the flight from Atlanta. Silverstein's reaction once he deplaned clearly reflected that confusion. After all, that had been the plan, for Lopez's team to bag Dick in Pittsburgh. Lopez figured this puzzle was central to Silverstein's quick departure. In fact, it wasn't much of a stretch to assume that Silverstein's phone call had come from Dick. Not irrelevant to Lopez's analysis of Silverstein's mental state was his facial expression, of which Lopez had the best view when he sped by. Lopez had witnessed panic in his face. Only one reason made any sense. Kipling's status as a hostage had deteriorated.

Lopez had ordered his underlings to fan out. It was a fluke that they had intersected Silverstein's trail—though perhaps not obviously so to someone who operated under a different form of logic. Miller, instead of hustling to cover airline departures and rental car agencies, had rushed to baggage claim and out onto the sidewalk. In a photographer's instant, Miller spotted the six-foot-three silhouette of a man with a dark complexion scooting into the back of a taxicab. Another cab allowed Miller to shadow Silverstein to a section of the airport where private aircraft parked.

By cell phone, Miller asked Lopez for orders. Lopez told him to reconnoiter but not make contact. That had been a tough decision. Obviously, Silverstein wanted to be left alone, or he would have sought Lopez out at the gate. Lopez realized he had made the wrong decision when, at 7:15, Miller watched as Silverstein's Gulfstream taxied away from the hangar. Who would have thought that Silverstein would rent a private jet—and so quickly? A quick display of his credentials to the office staff gave Miller the information he needed, confirming that Silverstein's departure likely had to do with Kipling. Why else would the pilot file a flight plan straight to Monterey, California?

In a quandary following Silverstein's departure, Lopez chose to remain in Pittsburgh instead of flying back to Washington. Their Agency aircraft sat poised to fly across the continent if necessary. But what would they do when they got there? Although he had the seniority to take initiative, Lopez's bosses could come down unpleasantly hard if his whims burned up thousands of dollars in aircraft fuel for no good reason. Worse, even though Lopez would do anything within his power to help his old friend, that obligation had limits within a government agency that had no authority to operate inside national perimeters.

Lopez downed the last of his coffee and chose to make his case to Miller. "I'm convinced Kipling has the prophecy gene, and Dick figured it out. Why else would he not have been on the flight? Silverstein had convinced him they were flying here to find that very person." He paused. "And then, for Silverstein to suddenly turn around and head back to California. On a private jet, for crissake!"

Miller shook his head. "Makes sense, but where does that leave us? We have no authority to pursue a kidnapping. And Silverstein has made it clear he doesn't want our help."

Lopez scowled. "Yeah, but think about it. If Kipling has what we think she has, that makes her a very special woman indeed. Remember that the first notion of a prophecy gene didn't come from here. It came from the Middle East. And on top of that, remember what we just found out about our illustrious senator from Kansas, who we now know is communicating with Sidki. If Senator Thurston is related to the Ishmael twins, there's trouble to be had, and it's starting right here in Three Rivers."

Lopez observed Miller flinch and step aside. He was undoubtedly reacting to his standard-issue Agency phone vibrator, attached to the earpiece in his ear.

Lopez wanted to head inside and go to the bathroom, but instead he watched Miller's reaction to the call. Miller paced back and forth in short deliberate steps. Then he wrote something on a pad.

"What?"

"That was Winston. They tracked Sidki back to his aircraft. His signal disappeared two hours ago, which suggests he's back in the air. The reason Winston didn't call right away is that he's been with the code crackers. They've just deciphered Thurston's code. And guess what? Four hours ago she sent a message from her cell." Miller handed his pad to Lopez.

Lopez read the words: *ASAP MONTEREY CA CALL ENROUTE.*

Miller stated the obvious. "It seems to me we now have a good enough reason to expend Agency resources on Silverstein."

Lopez pulled the sleeve back from his wristwatch, did the flight comparisons in his head, and stared at Miller. "Sidki will arrive at about the same time as Silverstein. You know what this proves?"

Miller nodded. "Yeah. It's looking more and more like Kipling is the new bright star in our universe."

CHAPTER 40

COLLISION

On approach to Runway 10R, Monterey Peninsula Airport,
Monterey, California, USA
Thursday, 9:05 PM, August 6, 2009

Silverstein strained to see through the window, peering into the gray of an oncoming night as the Gulfstream tracked the electronic signal from the ocean to runway one zero. Although the last vestiges of daylight provided some illumination, clouds hid the ground from view.

Max had informed him that they were second in the landing pattern, two miles behind another private jet that had beaten them to the outer marker. There was nothing unusual about private aircraft at the Monterey airport. During the yearly AT&T golf tournament, the airport had scarcely enough space to park them all. People with considerable wealth resided on or visited the Monterey Peninsula. Silverstein asked Max to radio ahead to have the fuel truck standing by.

Should he do anything more before landing? Silverstein stared at his cell. He had delayed long enough. He turned it on. Three voice mail messages were waiting.

Not surprisingly, the first two came from Lopez. Knowing that he would be angry and confused, Silverstein chose to skip them but promised to call him the moment Kipling was free. He waited for the third message. Good! It was Jimmy Travers from the Smithsonian.

Silverstein listened and switched off the phone. "Mother of God!" *Klinefelter's syndrome?*

Carmel Bay Motor Lodge, Cottage 14, Carmel, California, USA
36°33'39"N latitude, 121°55'15"W longitude
Thursday, 9:10 PM, August 6, 2009

"It's time we get going. Dick will be here soon." Violet's mood had changed following call number one earlier in the afternoon, and it was no different after number two. No more idle chitchat to pass the time.

"There's been a change of plans. We're leaving." That had been Violet's pronouncement two hours earlier following that second call. Dickey had landed in San Francisco and would arrive in Monterey by 9:30 that night. He would drive straight to their motel. Why Violet would choose to share this information puzzled Kipling. Maybe it was a psychological ploy, something about endearing the captor to the captured by sharing privileged information. If anyone should know this sort of thing, it would be a psych major. On the other hand, thought Kipling, maybe Violet wasn't as smart as she thought.

In any event, Kipling knew the reason for the sudden change of plans. The vision she received just moments before the first call had been unambiguous. Dickey knew that she possessed the prophecy gene. He was coming to get her. If only her sixth sense could give her an idea of what to expect next.

Comstock Aviation tarmac, Monterey Peninsula Airport,
Monterey, California, USA
36°35'19"N latitude, 121°51'26"W longitude
Thursday, 9:20 PM, August 6, 2009

After conferring with the pilot, making sure he understood the likely sequence of events, Silverstein hopped from the plane onto the tarmac just a few hundred feet from where he had boarded that morning. The worker from the refueling truck was already going about his business. Silverstein willed his legs to move against the stiffness that had accumulated during five hours of flight. Altogether, he had spent twelve of the past fourteen hours in metal tubes crisscrossing the United States. As he glanced back at the commercial terminal, he noted in his peripheral vision the aircraft that had landed ahead of theirs. Four men stood outside the aircraft, two of them with cigarettes in their hands, one with a telephone to his ear. That's odd, thought Silverstein. It was rare to see anyone smoking on a tarmac these days.

50 miles east of Denver, Colorado, USA
Thursday, 10:25 PM MDT, August 6, 2009

Lopez turned and glanced to the rear of the Lear, Model 60. He knew this aircraft well because he had used it before. He unconsciously thanked the drug runners from whom they had confiscated it. They had augmented the fuel tanks to accommodate a 3,500-mile range.

If he didn't go to the head soon, he would burst. Lopez glanced over at Miller, reclining, semiconscious to the world after he and Lopez had received the latest from Winston. The other three agents snored loudly. Lopez walked aft. Inside the tiny lavatory, he straightened his arms in a stretch, rested them on the tiny sink, and let his head sag to his chest. He thought of Barbara, his wife, who would give him reassurance. He could use some of that about now. He and his team weren't where they should be and wouldn't be for another two-plus hours.

Winston had just informed them that Sidki had landed in Monterey. Tracking satellites had confirmed Sidki's signal once he exited the airplane. Based on the flight plan Miller had coerced from the Pittsburgh staff, Silverstein was likely to be on the ground there as well. If only he would answer his phone. On the off chance he'd check for messages, Lopez had left two. Because Silverstein would know nothing about Sidki, Lopez left a detailed message explaining that he had more to be concerned about in Monterey than Dick's accomplice. And on top of these considerations, where was Dick?

Russell Senate Office Building, Washington, DC, USA
38°53'32"N latitude, 77°00'28"W longitude
Friday, 12:30 AM, August 7, 2009

Samantha Thurston terminated her call. It was one of those times when secure communication channels had to be bypassed. Little risk, of course. Bought anonymously, one-use cell phones had no owner and no associated address. That's why terrorists used them so frequently. Although modern tracking equipment could identify the general location of a cell phone transmission, the odds were tiny that a single communication between two one-use phones would be listened to, and even smaller that their location would be determined.

Although it was late and she felt the strain, Thurston nonetheless felt satisfied that all components were in place, that she had thought this out as well as she could, and that this mission would prove successful. Earlier, she had talked to Caliph on his cross-continent flight. Just now, he brought her up to date. He and Sidki had arrived in Monterey. Their plane would refuel shortly. There would be little to interfere with their capture of Kipling and her transport back to Egypt.

Two hours earlier, on a pay phone minutes from her office, Thurston had spoken to Jamieson one last time, to provide him with the details he required. He had flown into San Francisco and was awaiting his flight to Monterey. She informed him that MacDonald wanted to take no chances and had leased a private jet in Monterey to transport Jamieson, his assistant, and Kipling back to Washington. It made no sense to risk commercial aircraft in a situation like this, she told him. He should round up Kipling and return to the airport as quickly as possible. In her discussion with Caliph, Thurston provided a description of Jamieson and informed him of the acting role he and Sidki would play in Monterey.

Thurston had withheld two aspects of her plan from Jamieson. If Caliph and Sidki arrived in Monterey ahead of Jamieson, they would follow him. It was possible, though unlikely, that Jamieson would call MacDonald to confirm his decision to use a private aircraft. If that happened, it might be necessary for Caliph to switch to Plan B and for him to play a more active role in Kipling's apprehension.

Even assuming that Plan B proved unnecessary, Thurston had withheld one other significant detail from Jamieson. Although he and his assistant would have the pleasure of accompanying Kipling to her destination, only one of the three would be alive when they landed.

Commercial Passenger Terminal, Monterey Peninsula Airport, Monterey, California, USA
36°35'14"N latitude, 121°51'01"W longitude
Thursday, 9:35 PM, August 6, 2009

At the Monterey airport, commercial passengers entered the terminal from the tarmac from either side of the baggage claim area. Typically, they looked ahead for waiting friends or relatives, or to the street in front of the terminal. Rarely would their eyes trail upward to the staircase in front of them. The top of those stairs provided an excellent overview.

After arriving at Comstock Aviation and noting no planes at the commercial terminal, Silverstein walked back to the terminal. There was no rush. On the way, he stopped to locate the .38 Special he had placed inside a plastic bag—and had hidden in the brush along the short road that connected the front of the terminal to the airport tower situated above the airport proper. With the comforting feel of his father's handgun under his jacket, Silverstein waited.

*   *   *   *

Silverstein noted the wall clock below him. Right on time. Passengers from the San Francisco flight were arriving through the curved gateway below. A family with two children, a single couple, and two separate women stood waiting for the arrivals. As Silverstein watched, two men in leather jackets joined the group but stood off to the side. The two children in the family held a hand-drawn welcome sign. The parents stood back slightly, with a camera ready for the upcoming moment. An older woman, a grandmother perhaps, was the first to arrive. The ensuing laughter, kisses, and flashes from the cameras temporarily stole the scene.

Right behind the grandmother walked Dickey, arriving back in Monterey as he had so foolishly announced earlier. He looked to his left, then right, and then walked left. When Silverstein had arrived earlier than Dickey the previous morning, Silverstein had had the good sense to stand outside and wait for Dickey's arrival. The information that had resulted proved quite useful now. Dickey had walked from the long-term parking lot. He had not turned in his rental car. He was returning to the automobile he had left in airport parking.

Silverstein had predicted that Dickey would turn left. He would walk past the airline counters, out the door, and up the sidewalk toward long-term parking. Silverstein stepped down the stairs to observe Dickey's departing form. He ambled past the two single women and the couple, who were still waiting for their arrivals. Picking up his pace, Silverstein walked past the two men in leather jackets who no longer seemed concerned with the arriving passengers.

There would be no reason for Dickey to be suspicious. Silverstein fell into stride about seventy-five feet to the rear as they ascended the slight grade outside the terminal. He would close the gap as they got closer to parking. Even if Dickey chose to look back, the minimal lighting would prevent him from recognizing his follower as a black man, let alone a specific individual. Besides, nowhere in Dickey's deepest thoughts could he imagine Silverstein in Monterey, California, at this moment. Silverstein was damn sure of that fact.

As his consciousness dismissed anything other than his goal of freeing Kipling, Silverstein reviewed his plan one more time. He had mentally rehearsed the next few minutes numerous times. The plan was simple enough. He would catch Dickey off guard, beat him to within an inch of his life if necessary, and find out where he was hiding Kipling. He would then force Dickey to drive him to her. He would rescue her, leaving Dickey and Vi behind.

They would drive immediately to the airport in Dickey's car, jump in Silverstein's waiting plane, and hightail it to Hawaii. Only then would he turn on his telephone and call Lopez. Beyond those actions, Silverstein had given no thought. He and Kipling would worry about what to do next when they were safely out of the area.

Silverstein cut the separation to fifty feet. He slowed and watched as Dickey searched for his car in the dim parking lot. With luck, Dickey wouldn't look back until it was too late. As luck would have it, another aircraft was landing on the adjacent runway, providing background noise to cover Silverstein's footsteps. Dickey spotted his vehicle. Twenty-five feet. Then ten feet separated them. Dickey opened the trunk and placed his bag inside. As Dickey lowered the lid, Silverstein sprinted across the remaining gap, rage surging through his body.

Silverstein grabbed Dickey's shoulders, pinned Dickey's legs against his own, and thrust him forward hard onto the trunk lid, producing a satisfying thud as Dickey's head reverberated against the yellowish cast of the white sheet metal.

"What the hell! Take my wallet. It's yours." Dickey gasped.

Silverstein relished the upcoming moment, at seeing Dickey's astonished face. While simultaneously reaching inside his waistband with his right hand to retrieve his weapon, Silverstein grabbed Dickey's right shoulder with his left hand and turned him right side up, still flat on the car's trunk. Silverstein then leaned forward across Dickey's pelvis, keeping him in place. At the same time, he thrust the barrel of his gun into Dickey's chest.

The first words from Dickey's mouth mirrored precisely the look on his face. "How the hell—"

"Caught you by surprise, didn't I?" Silverstein relished the moment. "But that's enough for pleasantries. I'll give you two chances to tell me where you're hiding Linda. I advise you to take me up on the first, because you'll be gushing blood when you're offered the second."

Silverstein could sense the wheels in Dickey's head turning, going over the options. He grew impatient. "I'm waiting."

"Listen to me first. Something …"

Silverstein cut him off and pushed the barrel of his gun hard into Dickey's lower abdomen. "Answer my question, goddamn it!"

"She's in Carmel. Violet's babysitting."

"Where in Carmel?"

"Carmel Bay Motor Lodge, Cottage 14."

"I appreciate your honesty, but I doubt you'd believe me either if you were in my position. I want you to call Violet and ask her to tell you where she is. Before she responds, hand me the phone."

Silverstein's concentration on his task was such that he reacted to the smell of leather on the light westerly wind a second too late. He saw stars as something struck him from behind, and he crumpled to the ground at Dickey's feet.

Washington Circle on Pennsylvania Avenue, northwest bound, Washington, DC, USA
38° 54' 09" N latitude, 77° 02' 58" W longitude
Friday, 12:55 AM, August 7, 2009

Damn circles! Thurston's car almost wandered into the traffic to her left as she listened. Her facial features tightened. The second of three cell phones she had purchased had rung only seconds earlier. She had already discarded the first. Caliph was asking for guidance.

Apparently, this Silverstein fellow had accosted Jamieson in the parking lot outside the Monterey airport terminal. Somehow Silverstein had made his way back to California and had ambushed him. Jamieson told her earlier that he had left Silverstein in Pittsburgh. How he had returned to California ahead of Jamieson baffled Thurston.

Thurston complimented herself. Her order for Caliph to follow Jamieson had turned out to be wise indeed, but for a reason completely unanticipated.

Thurston let out her breath slowly and willed herself to calm down. Aside from this surprise, things were going quite nicely, thank you very much. In fact, this unexpected event could be used to their advantage. Uncle Mohammed would be pleased indeed with her logic. With that thought came an obvious resolution to Caliph's question, a solution that would permit Jamieson one final contribution before his own demise. He and Silverstein had been at odds for some time, hadn't they?

"Caliph. Tell Jamieson that MacDonald says for him to kill Silverstein. And if he won't, you do it. Just make sure he's to blame."

CHAPTER 41

GENDER EQUALITY

Route 1 southbound, Monterey Peninsula, California, USA
36°34'57"N latitude, 121°53'45"W longitude
Thursday, 10:05 PM, August 6, 2009

Silverstein opened his eyes but saw nothing. Lying on his side with knees bent, he reached out into the blackness and banged his left hand into something not far from his face. Almost at the same time, his right hand shot to his face to mitigate the pain that now enveloped his whole head. He rubbed and probed cautiously, feeling what seemed like liquid, no doubt blood.

His thoughts returned to those seconds before he lost consciousness: Dickey splayed on the trunk in front of him, the whiff of leather. Someone had hit him from behind. But who? This made no sense because Dickey had returned to Monterey alone. A cop would have shouted a warning.

After feeling around to determine the perimeters of his environment, Silverstein deduced his situation. The clincher was the noise and movement of a car in motion. They had put him inside the trunk of a car, probably Dickey's. Luckily, among his fears, claustrophobia did not make the list.

Silverstein took stock. His hands and legs were free. He felt inside his coat and pants pockets. They had taken his cell phone but had left his wallet and key chain, on which resided his tiny LED flashlight. Since he was a child, he had always thought that the coolest thing you could carry was a flashlight, useful in desperate situations. LED technology had made the concept practical.

His deduction had been correct. He explored the trunk's interior, aware that his weapon would not be among its contents. To fit him into the trunk, Dickey had removed his overnight bag. With difficulty, considering the minimal space available for movement, Silverstein explored the tire-changing tools accessible beneath the floor. He removed the lug nut wrench, a weapon of sorts.

Although what had just happened might have changed the situation, Silverstein hoped that they were headed to Cottage 14 of the Carmel Bay Motor Lodge. He would plan his strategy based on that assumption. Silverstein marveled to himself that he still remembered Dickey's reply to his forceful question, despite the blow to his head.

There wasn't much time to think. The drive to Carmel would take fifteen minutes at the most. Would Dickey leave him in the trunk? Silverstein beamed the LED at the trunk-locking mechanism and saw that he could open it if need be.

This discovery gave him three options. At the next stop, he could pop the trunk, jump out, and run. With any luck, that would occur at a red light or some other busy location to provide cover. Unfortunately, this choice had a serious shortcoming. He might find himself nowhere near Kipling and by the time he got to her, assuming that Dickey had not lied about the address, she and Dickey would be long gone. Scratch option one.

Another possibility was to wait until Dickey opened the trunk, which would likely occur at the motel. Silverstein could pretend to be unconscious. Ideally, Dickey would close the trunk and go to retrieve Kipling, leaving Silverstein in a commanding position once he escaped from it …

Silverstein stopped in mid-thought. He had assumed that Dickey was alone up front. But he could hear sounds inside the car. He edged himself forward and rested his ear flush to the back side of the rear seat. He could make out voices, too muffled to decipher words. Would someone who had just saved Dickey from an attack in an airport parking lot be hitching a ride? *What the hell?*

On the other hand, Silverstein realized that a clue he had earlier ignored now had significance. Only minutes before being cold-cocked, he had walked by a reasonable source for the smell of leather.

Carmel Bay Motor Lodge, Cottage 14, Carmel, California, USA
36°33'39"N latitude, 121°55'15"W longitude
Thursday, 10:10 PM, August 6, 2009

Kipling had adapted to the bondage procedure and sat quietly with her ankles shackled together as usual, but now with *both* hands tied together. Although Vi wanted to take no chances with her transport, she had offered Kipling one final courtesy, a trip to the bathroom. Vi scurried about the room, packing bags and readying herself for the next step in this strange odyssey.

Kipling had spent the last few hours trying to predict the future, not by using her unique gift but by applying old-fashioned logic. The fact that Dickey was returning so quickly meant that either he had never left California or had left the state and come back. Which led to the $64,000 question: where was Victor? He had flown with Dickey this morning, on their way to Johnstown. She could imagine Silverstein trying to draw Dickey away and, in the process, losing him, then returning to rescue her. But the fates had intervened. Somehow Dickey had determined the truth about Kipling. This begged the question of whether Silverstein knew this. For all she knew, he was twiddling his thumbs in Pennsylvania.

Kipling concluded she had no one but herself to rely on. Still, because she was valuable property, it was unlikely that her life was in danger. What would they do to her? Probably take her to some secret facility for testing. They'd recheck her DNA, run psychological tests, and most importantly, set out to determine when and how her unique ability manifested itself. She could save them a lot of trouble. If there were any patterns to her ability to see into the future, Kipling would have figured them out long ago.

*   *   *   *

Silverstein chose option three. When they opened the trunk, he would appear awake and ask for an explanation. To know how these strangers fit into this puzzle was worth the price of admission alone.

The automobile came to a stop. Silverstein counted two doors opening and closing. But wait! He had seen two men in leather jackets at the airport. Had one of them remained behind? His fingers tightened on the handle of the wrench, keeping it hidden behind his body. In an instant, the discrepancy had an answer. The car sped away. He relaxed his grip on the wrench.

*   *   *   *

Suddenly Violet's demeanor changed. Dickey had called minutes earlier and something was up. She wouldn't provide any details except to say that they would be having company.

It wasn't long before they heard a knock.

Violet answered the door and two men in leather jackets walked in, neither of whom was Dickey.

"Hello. My name's Nicholas, and this is Francis. I guess Dick told you we've been sent to give you folks a ride."

"I'm Vi."

"Nice to meet you." The one called Nicholas gestured with his hands. "Dick'll be back in a few minutes. He's running an errand."

This exchange took place in front of the door. Nicholas took note of Kipling and walked toward the bed.

Kipling kept her cool, sitting up straight and maintaining eye contact. She concluded that Nicholas worked for the same people as Dickey and Violet. Their boss had sent reinforcements.

Kipling assessed the details of Nicholas and his partner, Francis, who was still standing by the door. Leather jackets were common enough and so was their cut of clothing. It was another product made from leather that stood out to the discerning eye. Their shoes. Kipling considered it unlikely that either Nicholas or Francis had bought them in this country. And further, neither one looked like a Nicholas or a Francis.

*   *   *   *

Silverstein concluded that he now shared the automobile with only one man, probably Dickey. Did that mean he had dropped off his passengers somewhere other than Kipling's motel? Not likely. Silverstein had regained consciousness not long after they departed the airport. He remembered the long drive uphill, undoubtedly Route 1 south from the airport, and then the slow descent into Carmel. Considering the multiple towns that made up the Monterey Peninsula, what were the chances that someone needed a lift to Carmel, the same location where Dickey was holding Kipling?

Silverstein shone his light on his watch: 10:19. It was 1:19 back in Pittsburgh. Had Lopez returned to Washington, cursing Silverstein's existence?

The car slowed and stopped. Its speed had remained low, and only a few minutes had expired since they had dropped off their passengers. Silverstein heard the driver's door open and then close. His heartbeat accelerated. Wielding his wrench against someone with a gun, from a position of weakness, was not an ideal situation.

This was it! He sensed movement, heard the key in the lock, wrapped his hand tightly around the shaft of the wrench, and looked upward as the trunk lid rose quickly.

"Get out." It was the familiar voice of Dickey, ironically comforting. With Silverstein's .38 in his right hand, Dickey motioned for him to climb from the trunk.

Considering his predicament, Silverstein realized that his weapon was useless and released it from his grip. He placed his hands on the trunk's edge and maneuvered his feet over the lip and onto the ground. Dickey backed up. Silverstein forced himself to stand straight, not an easy process, he discovered. He instinctively raised his hand to protect the right side of his head from the pain. He staggered and sat down on the bumper to regain his equilibrium.

Because his eyes had adapted to the blackness of the trunk, he could see rather well in the partial darkness. Dickey had parked on the right side of Scenic Road in Carmel, facing south. The sound of ocean waves to the right supported his deduction. Concerned that Dickey might still have company, Silverstein snapped his head toward the front of the car, inducing a wave of dizziness in the process. They were alone.

Now what? Dickey wasn't speaking, and Silverstein needed answers.

"Okay! I bite. Who are your friends?" He watched Dickey lower his right arm to his side, Silverstein's firearm pointed downward.

"Before I give you back your revolver, I want your word that you won't fight me."

Dickey's reply was hardly what Silverstein had expected. For Dickey to say something like this suggested that he was as confused as Silverstein.

"You have my word."

Dickey rotated the firearm in his hand and extended it to Silverstein. He reached into his jacket pocket and followed up with Silverstein's cell phone.

"Okay, Dickey, what the hell's going on here?"

*   *   *   *

Dickey drove to within a block of Kipling's motel and parked on a side street. There was a moment of silence while Silverstein reflected on the new information. Silverstein looked left to assess Dickey's demeanor. For the first time since they had met less than a week earlier, it appeared, at least on the surface, that they were on the same side.

Dickey had told him he had no idea who the two men were and had not expected them. Silverstein believed him. In fact, Dickey's statement just seconds before Silverstein lost consciousness had implied something was amiss. *Listen to me first. Something ...*

Except for naming names, Dickey came clean. From what Silverstein could glean, Dickey owed his allegiance to two bosses. He called them numbers one and two. Boss number one paid his salary. Somehow—Dickey offered no details—boss number two had recently entered the picture. While in San Francisco, on his return from Atlanta, number two called to tell him that number one had ordered up a private jet to transport the three of them back to Washington. Silverstein wondered if the jet on the tarmac next to his might have been that one.

Dickey said that he was suspicious. Because he knew that number one would have informed him about any change in plans, Dickey telephoned number one. Interestingly, from the way Dickey discussed his two bosses, it almost sounded as if he was playing one off the other. This conclusion stemmed from Dickey's statement that he did not ask number one outright about the plane.

Instead, he informed number one that he had located the person they were looking for and that she was Silverstein's assistant. Dickey said he would deliver her back to Washington. Number one said he was thrilled and left it up to Dickey to determine the best way to return her to DC. There was no mention of a private jet. All of this meant that boss number two was up to some hanky-panky—which could leave Dickey in the lurch.

Dickey explained that when the two strangers had arrived in the parking lot and rescued him from Silverstein's assault, confusion compounded his bewilderment. They introduced themselves as Nicholas and Francis, and said number one had hired them. Knowing this to be a lie, Dickey played along. At the least, they worked for number two, Dickey figured. Nicholas informed Dickey that number one had ordered Dickey to kill Silverstein. It was then that Dickey knew he had trouble. Number one had never asked him to seriously harm anyone. Realizing that his own well-being was at stake, Dickey agreed. Nicholas told Dickey to do in Silverstein using his own weapon and return with the body.

Dickey killed the engine and Silverstein renewed the conversation. "Let's say I buy your story. Now I need to know your intentions. Are you still planning to take Linda back to Washington?"

Before he could answer, Dickey's cell phone rang.

"Yes."

Silverstein computed the odds. Number one, number two, or Nicholas? Number two or Nicholas, probably.

Dickey listened and replied. "Yes. They saved my butt."

Probably number two.

Again, silence for some seconds and then Dickey's response. "It's done … I understand."

Dickey closed his phone and looked across at Silverstein. "I just told them that you were dead."

"Who was it that wanted to know?" Silverstein asked matter-of-factly.

"Does it really matter?"

Dickey's tight-lipped response meant that Silverstein had learned as much as he was going to about Rafferty's chain of command. Nonetheless, one slipup earlier had proved interesting. Silverstein wondered if Dickey had even noticed when he said it. Repeatedly, boss number one came across as a *he*. Likewise for boss number two. Except for once. A coincidence? Unlikely, thought Silverstein.

CHAPTER 42

HASTA LA VISTA

Outside the Carmel Bay Motor Lodge, Carmel, California, USA
36°33'39"N latitude, 121°55'15"W longitude
Thursday, 10:40 PM, August 6, 2009

They sat in the front seat and nodded agreement. Their strategy hardly reeked of sophistication, but it was the best they could come up with under the circumstances. The question of what Dickey planned to do with Kipling afterward remained unanswered. Silverstein chose not to press the issue. The situation concerning Nicholas and Francis loomed more urgently. Indeed, if Dickey had followed orders, Silverstein would have been dead by now. He had to concede that much to Dickey.

Between them, Silverstein's firearm represented their only persuasive piece of hardware. They had to assume that the strangers who had arrived by private aircraft possessed their own firepower—not a comforting thought. With their plan in mind, Silverstein relinquished his .38 to Dickey. In exchange, Dickey handed Silverstein the car keys. Silverstein would be the designated driver because he knew the area and the quickest route back to the airport. Silverstein explained how he had returned to Monterey ahead of Dickey and that his aircraft and pilots were waiting for his return. Dickey seemed impressed.

Its exorbitant cost notwithstanding, Silverstein's private mode of transportation would enable a satisfying conclusion to their immediate dilemma. They needed to get the hell out—way out—of Dodge.

They slammed the car doors and made their way toward number fourteen.

*   *   *   *

Everyone was sitting waiting for Dickey to return. Kipling remained on the side of the bed facing the door, headboard to her right. Nicholas and Francis sat to her rear, near the opposite side of the bed, in the two chairs adjacent to the table on which Violet had rested her laptop hours earlier. Violet sat at the foot of the bed. The earlier pleasantries had dissolved into silence.

*   *   *   *

The rooms at the Carmel Bay Motor Lodge took the form of cottages scattered throughout a wooded area not far from the town's center. For their purpose, keeping a hostage under control, Silverstein reasoned that Dickey had wanted as private a setting as possible. They crept forward along an asphalt-covered pathway through a darkened area lit only by walkway lights. The residents of Carmel did not believe in superfluous exterior lighting. For the situation at hand, darkness suited the two men nicely.

Large wooden numbers on stakes, lit dimly by a light below, identified each cottage. They arrived and took the positions they had agreed to back at the car. Dickey caught Silverstein's eye, nodded, raised his right hand to the door, and knocked. Silverstein was to wait outside until Dickey had the situation under control and Violet came out to retrieve him. The four of them would then make their getaway in Dickey's car, leaving Nicholas and Francis bound and gagged, with time to ponder their errors until the hotel staff arrived the following morning.

*   *   *   *

Nicholas motioned to Violet that she should remain seated, that he would answer the door. For the first time since they arrived, he opened his jacket and removed a weapon from under his left armpit, a Beretta nine-millimeter, Kipling recognized; knowledge from her Park Service training occasionally came in handy. He placed his right arm behind his back and opened the door. Dickey walked in. Kipling followed Dickey's eyes as he scanned the room, catching, in turn, Kipling, Violet, Francis, who was now standing, and finally Nicholas. After closing the door, Nicholas dropped his hand and weapon to his side.

Nicholas spoke first. "As we discussed earlier, is the situation under control?"

"You didn't think I'd question orders from MacDonald, did you?" Dickey answered quickly.

Nicholas raised his weapon and made small circles in the air with the barrel, seemingly preparing himself for a point he wished to make. "Tell me, I've been wondering, how did this Silverstein fellow manage to arrive in Monterey when you did? I understood that you left him behind."

If there hadn't been enough excitement to maintain Kipling's interest, his mention of Silverstein's name got her attention. *Victor's in Monterey?*

Dickey answered matter-of-factly. "He's a resourceful fellow. He rented a private jet in Pittsburgh and flew here ahead of me. If you hadn't saved my ass at the airport, he and Kipling would be long gone. His aircraft's sitting there waiting for him, you know. He had planned to leave the same way he came."

Nicholas did a double take before his next comment, appearing to find this last statement of interest. "And how is it you know so much about his intentions?"

"Before you arrived on the scene, he told me as much. Sort of bragging about it, you know." Dickey paused. "You sure have a lot of questions. I've one for you. How come in the two years I've worked for MacDonald I've never heard of a Nicholas or Francis?"

Nicholas grew impatient. "Never mind that. Back to Silverstein. Convince me that you finished the job."

Kipling almost bit her tongue. *What is he talking about?* She was afraid she knew.

"I told you, it's done. His body's in the trunk."

Oh, my God! Kipling felt herself go light-headed and fall briefly backward.

"If that's the case, you won't mind if I take a look at your weapon?"

Dickey appeared to hesitate but then removed a firearm from the waistband of his pants. He handed it to Nicholas. Nicholas in turn took a quick look and in one motion tossed it to Francis.

Kipling rotated her body in time to see Francis rest the barrel against his nose. He shook his head.

At this signal, Nicholas backed up several feet, pointed his weapon at Dickey, and told him to kneel. Simultaneously, he snapped the fingers on his left hand and pointed, suggesting that Francis check outside. Francis drew his own weapon, slipped out the door, and closed it behind him, having handed Dickey's gun to Nicholas who shoved it into his jacket.

Nicholas's words gave away that his mood had changed. "Tell me the truth immediately, or you are a dead man."

For all the intensity in the room, Dickey appeared unruffled, consistent with Silverstein's description of him the previous week at the Branding Iron. "I assume you're concerned that I didn't fire my weapon." Dickey shook his head in seeming disbelief. "What the fuck's wrong with you? We're on the same side here. Do you think I'm an idiot? The last thing we need is someone investigating a gunshot in this congested area. When I opened the trunk, he was still unconscious. I finished off the job with a plastic bag around his head. That was fifteen minutes ago. He's dead by now and in the trunk, just like you asked. Go take a look."

Nicholas seemed unconvinced. "And where would you find a plastic bag?"

"Goddamn it! In my carry-on. Where else? It's a Wal-Mart bag, if you need to know. You haven't been in this business very long, have you?"

Dickey held his hands to the side, in a manner of conciliation. "Would you put away the goddamn gun?"

*   *   *   *

Although the area surrounding the cottage lay in shadows, the small yellow porch light provided illumination close by. Silverstein had chosen to remain out of sight, around the corner of the cottage, in case something like this happened. Shortly after Dickey had disappeared inside, Silverstein heard the door open and someone walk out onto the porch. It couldn't be Dickey. Violet? Silverstein remained motionless. He pressed himself tightly against the wood siding of the cottage and held his breath. At this time of the evening, Carmel turned into Quietland, including the cabins that comprised this motel. Quiet was good, and bad.

Uh-oh! Whoever it was that had exited the door was coming his way. The creak of the old wooden flooring grew closer. Silverstein stood mere inches around the corner. If whoever it was made it even close to the edge of the porch, he would see Silverstein. If that happened, Silverstein would have no choice but to attack. He could turn around and run into the woods behind the cottage, but that would leave Dickey holding the bag with no backup. From nowhere, a lightning bolt of a thought occurred, along with a tightening sensation in his chest—Silverstein had to consider the possibility that these two strangers had also come for Kipling.

Oh, shit! Silverstein's eyes trailed down to his left, and there it was, a wrist and an extended firearm probing the air in front. He had no choice. Only a fraction of a second remained before his element of surprise lapsed.

The motions happened fast. The martial arts training his parents had insisted upon back in Atlanta, combined with his boxing in college, gave him an edge. Silverstein extended his left hand to grab the wrist and twist it away to the attacker's left. Simultaneously, with his right hand contributing, he pulled forward with all his strength, the intent being to drag his assailant off balance from the porch that rose about a foot from the ground proper. It worked. The next step was more important. As the attacker tried to regain his footing, he instead fell forward at a 45-degree angle to the ground below. It was during this descent that Silverstein struck with a full right fist to the assailant's right temple. With luck, he would be unconscious before hitting the ground.

In case the first blow did not achieve the desired effect, Silverstein leaped to the side to try again. It proved unnecessary. One of the two leather-jacketed men whom Silverstein had seen in the airport now lay sprawled on the ground. Silverstein stared at the unconscious body and did a double take. A short, scrawny, wimp of a man—hardly what he had expected.

Responding to a sudden stab of pain from his own head wound, Silverstein's fingers gingerly traced the area. The odds were fifty-fifty that he had exacted his revenge on the appropriate man.

His body tense, Silverstein craned his head to assess the outcome. All was well. Very little sound had resulted from the short-lived violence. Amazingly, the assailant had not discharged his firearm during the three-second struggle. Silverstein reached down, retrieved the weapon, and inspected it. *Unbelievable!* He blinked. The idiot hadn't disengaged the safety. This explained why there had been no accidental discharge when Silverstein grabbed the man's wrist.

This discovery could mean only one thing. At least one of the leathered intruders wasn't very well trained. Hopefully, Dickey would have an equally easy time with the second one.

*   *   *   *

Nearly beside herself from Dickey's statement that her boss was dead, Kipling watched as Nicholas motioned Dickey to his feet. The tension in the room had subsided. Nicholas pushed Dickey aside, walked to the door, opened it with his left hand, and peered outside, leaning on the doorjamb with his weapon flat against the woodwork. He apparently saw nothing and turned to come back inside.

Kipling did not see it coming. If there was any uncertainty in her mind concerning the relationship between Dickey and Nicholas, that doubt evaporated at once. As Nicholas turned back into the room and closed the door, Dickey leaped toward him, both hands targeting the weapon in Nicholas's right hand.

Dickey's concentration held. With both hands, he grabbed Nicholas's right forearm. He forced Nicholas's arm back over his head, and in the process, brought him stumbling backward. Violet's scream punctuated the ongoing violence only feet in front of the bed. Nicholas's weapon pointed in her direction as the two slammed onto the old wooden flooring. She immediately climbed onto the bed next to Kipling to escape the line of fire.

Kipling shuddered as the struggle ensued. Whoever ended up in possession of the weapon would be the victor. Dickey readied a blow to Nicholas's head. Unfortunately, Nicholas had the same idea and struck Dickey first. Dickey reacted to the blow but maintained his grip on Nicholas's gun hand. In the resulting scuffle, Nicholas rolled Dickey to his left, giving Nicholas the superior position on top.

The struggle continued, so fierce and fast-paced that it was impossible to determine who would prevail. Then a gunshot shattered the air in the small cabin. Both Kipling and Violet jumped—maybe a foot.

*   *   *   *

Silverstein had dragged his assailant to the back of the cottage. He used the victim's belt to tie his ankles together and his two sets of shoelaces to secure his hands behind him. He withdrew his handkerchief, wiped the weapon clean, and without thinking, tossed it into the brush. As a final touch, he removed one of the victim's socks, rolled it into a ball, and stuffed it into his mouth.

A scream and then a muffled explosion came from within the cabin. *Linda!* Silverstein sprang to his feet and rushed to the porch.

*   *   *   *

Kipling opened her eyes and stared at the floor to her side. *Which one was shot?* She drew a breath and whispered. "Please God, help us here."

*   *   *   *

Silverstein stood in front of the door to the cottage and realized it was too late to go back. He had foolishly assumed he wouldn't need his assailant's firearm. Dickey needed help, and there wasn't even time to check the door handle. He dropped back to the edge of the deck, took several short steps to build momentum, raised his right foot, and concentrated the strength of his leg into the flimsy old lock. The door blasted open.

Silverstein took in the situation in a nanosecond. Kipling and Violet were hunched together on the left side of a bed. Perpendicular to the bed, two men lay on the floor, one on top of the other. The head of the one on top jerked around, reacting to the sudden noise behind him. *It wasn't Dickey.*

In reaction to Silverstein's appearance, the one on top rolled to Silverstein's left, off the body below him. His right hand, gripping a pistol, rose to aim at the intruder. Silverstein had nowhere to go. The best he could do was leap toward the man and hope that he'd arrive in time to divert the man's aim. Silverstein jumped. What he witnessed then frightened him nearly as much as the firearm he was facing.

Kipling had stood up from the bed and appeared to be *hopping* toward the action. Because the man on top of Dickey had rolled onto his back toward Kipling, he did not see the threat coming from his right. After two or three hops, Kipling leaped forward, landing on the man's arm before it rose high enough to aim at Silverstein. The force of her fall caused the man's shot to sail just below the lunging Silverstein.

Silverstein and Kipling nearly collided. She rolled to the side. He was in a rage. Too many people in the past week had taken advantage of him. It was time for revenge. He forced his left knee upward to pin the forearm holding the gun. Simultaneously, he whacked the right side of the man's skull twice with his fist. The action was over almost before it started. The body lying underneath Silverstein went limp.

Silverstein struggled to his feet. With his assailant unconscious, the immediate crisis was over. Silverstein kicked the firearm away from the body and looked to his left at Kipling. For the first time, he noticed that her hands and feet were tied. "Are you okay?"

She nodded.

Their attention shifted to Dickey. Violet was already kneeling by his head. Silverstein grabbed the unconscious assailant by the legs and pulled him to the side. He knelt down over Dickey and realized at once that it was too late. Silverstein felt for a pulse but shook his head. Dickey had taken a bullet to the center of the chest. Violet, probably a Catholic, crossed herself.

Silverstein closed his eyes and recited to himself the Kaddish prayer, repeated by Jewish mourners following the death of a loved one. Dickey's occupation and previous deeds notwithstanding, Silverstein knew that when push came to shove, Dickey had acted honorably.

Silverstein stood, closed the door, and gathered his wits. "Do either of you know who these guys are?"

Kipling shrugged her shoulders.

Violet, about whom Silverstein knew even less than he did about Dickey, spoke. "Dick told me on the phone that we would have company, but I have no idea who they are. This one's called Nicholas. The other's Francis." With her next words, she practically shouted. "Where is he?"

Silverstein gestured. "I caught him off guard. He's tied up out back." He thought quickly. "I know this is the last thing we're supposed to do, but I say we get the hell out of here. Police are probably coming even as we speak. If not, we'll call them on our way to the airport." As he spoke, Violet undid a strange-looking harness that tied Kipling. "Let's go."

Silverstein cracked open the door and peered outside. No sign of anyone yet. Maybe neighbors thought the muffled shots were firecrackers. He surveyed the room. One firearm on the floor. Where was his .38?

Silverstein looked to Kipling for an answer. "What happened to Dickey's gun? It's mine."

Kipling thought for a moment and replied. "Francis told Nicholas it had not been fired." She snapped her fingers. "Look inside his jacket.

Silverstein patted Nicholas's leather jacket. Sure enough. He withdrew the weapon.

He surveyed the room. "Violet, Linda, get your things." He thought through what the police would see. One man tied up behind the cottage, his firearm off to the side. Inside, a dead man and another beat up. He noted the gun lying on the floor. Silverstein hadn't touched it. Good! The only fingerprints on the firearm would be those from the two men left in the room.

A siren wailed in the distance. Silverstein tried to assess everything sensibly but couldn't. Getting knocked unconscious an hour earlier had scrambled his brain. "Let's get out of here. There's no more time."

They walked to the door, with Violet bringing up the rear. She gasped. "He's coming to. We should tie him up."

Silverstein spun around, saw Nicholas stirring, his head weaving from side to side, and shook his head. "Goddamn it! We don't have time for this." He walked back to Nicholas and, with the butt of his own .38, landed a third strike to the temple. In the back of his mind, he also realized that if the police found Nicholas tied up, a shrewd defense attorney might have grounds to claim that he had nothing to do with Dickey's death.

Silverstein could still hear the siren. "Let's go!"

✳   ✳   ✳   ✳

Trying not to run, the three of them walked as fast as they could from the cottage. They drove to the airport without incident. But two blocks from the motel, Silverstein stopped at a service station with a pay phone and asked Violet to call 911 anonymously—impossible using a cell phone—to report gunshots at the Carmel Bay Motor Lodge. The siren they heard must have had nothing to do with them. Hopefully, the police would arrive in time. This worried Silverstein. If Nicholas and Francis escaped, Dickey's murderer might never face justice. Although he had hardly acted within the law during the past week, Dickey didn't deserve the fate that had awaited him in Carmel, California.

Silverstein returned Dickey's Maxima to the same long-term parking spot from which they had driven earlier.

For a moment they sat quietly in the car, each not quite sure what to say. Silverstein spoke to Violet in the rearview mirror. "Violet, what do you want to do? I'd offer to take you with us, but I don't see the point. Do you have money to go home?"

Violet's reply was thoughtful and measured. "I have my ticket. I think I'd better go. I'll get a room somewhere and leave tomorrow. Oh! Here's your cell phone."

Kipling turned in her seat, took the phone, and offered her hand. "I don't understand half of what happened today, but I thank you for your kindness. Good luck in your studies."

Silverstein observed a nod. Violet removed her bag from the backseat, got out, and started walking to the terminal.

Kipling turned to Silverstein. "If we get tied in to what happened here, we might need her to corroborate what happened. Do you think it's a good idea to just let her go?"

Silverstein reached for the door handle. "I hear you. But not only do we have her cell phone number, I memorized her last name and address from her suitcase tag." He took stock and gestured. "If there's any more luck waiting for us this evening, it's bound to be bad. Nicholas's plane is sitting next to mine. If they escaped and found a car, they're on their way to the airport. Let's get the hell out of here."

*   *   *   *

When they arrived at their plane, Max was waiting, standing just outside the cockpit. His pleasant demeanor had vanished. Being asked to fly a quarter of the distance around the globe probably had something to do with that. Silverstein noted a sort of collar that encircled his neck, but decided this was not the time to question Max's fashion statements.

They boarded. Silverstein pulled up the steps, latching the door as Max had shown him back in Pittsburgh. They took their seats and before long felt the plane's wheels bid goodbye to mother earth. Silverstein sat on the port and Kipling the starboard side of the Gulfstream. He explained that they were flying to Hawaii. She didn't object.

They had flown for about a half hour when Silverstein realized his energy was spent. It had been one hell of a day. He stared out the window, the hypnotic whine of the engines lulling him to sleep. The midnight skies were black, stars visible, the air clean. The lights along the coastline appeared ever so clear, even at this altitude.

Lights?

Silverstein jerked against his seat belt, unfastened it, rushed to the cockpit door, and knocked. It was locked. The door opened, and the words left his mouth before the visual caught hold of his brain. "What's going on, Max?"

An unfamiliar face and a strange-looking weapon greeted him. "You were expecting Hawaii, Dr. Silverstein? I'm afraid there's been a change of plans. Mexico City is a better choice for me." A hesitation. "My name is Aziz. And by the way, Nicholas sends his regards. He told me to tell you that you should have taken the time to tie him up."

CHAPTER 43

A DARKER SHADE OF RED

Comstock Aviation tarmac, Monterey Peninsula Airport,
Monterey, California, USA
36°35'19"N latitude, 121°51'26"W longitude
Friday, 12:15 AM, August 7, 2009

Lopez looked over his shoulder at his own aircraft. The ground crew was just beginning to refuel. "Are you sure?"

"That's what they're telling me," Marc Miller replied.

Lopez shook his head. "You're telling me *Sidki's* on his way to the airport right now?"

"Yup. The fact they keep losing his signal probably means he's in a car." Miller listened further on his cell phone. "He's on Highway 1, about two miles to the west."

"Then that's his aircraft right there." Lopez nodded toward a second civilian jet sitting nearby. "But where the hell is Silverstein's plane? I was hoping that was it."

Byron Strauss, the Crimson team lead, bounded down the aircraft steps. "Boss, the tower tells me a Gulfstream took off some thirty minutes ago. The tail number's the same as the one we followed from Pittsburgh."

The wrinkles in Lopez's forehead furrowed. "Going where?"

"Mexico City."

Lopez's mind did a double take. "Thanks."

He turned to Miller. "Mexico City? Why would Silverstein go to Mexico City? That's the last place I'd expect him to go. Goddamn it! We just missed them."

Too little time to think. Just fifteen minutes earlier, they had landed in Monterey. Now here they were, with new information that made no sense. Silverstein had been here and, inexplicably, had vanished, allegedly on his way to Mexico.

Miller shook his head. "If Sidki's coming to the airport, he's undoubtedly going to fly away on that plane sitting right there."

Lopez nodded. "Well, if he's captured Silverstein and Kipling, we'll see that firsthand. We have a pretty good viewpoint."

"Never happen. I'll bet you a dinner. Why would Silverstein's plane have already departed? People don't steal airplanes, at least not that often. If his plane's gone, he's on it, and Kipling's with him."

"Can't I hope that Silverstein outfoxed Sidki, and Sidki's playing catch-up?"

"Right. If so, why would he file a flight plan to Mexico?" Miller glanced at his watch. "We don't have much time. Do we let Sidki go on his way? He certainly knows more than we do."

Lopez sighed. "We have to, Marc. Unless Sidki pulls up to the plane here with Silverstein and Kipling, we have no choice. He's too valuable a resource to relinquish. Besides, I'd like to think Silverstein skipped town without even running into Sidki."

Lopez knew that Miller was letting his frustration get in the way of logic. Sidki's tale was legendary within the Agency. Implanting that transmitter in the top of his head had taken extraordinary timing, and luck. That tiny piece of electronic wizardry gave the Agency frequent tabs on someone known to have connections to Middle Eastern terrorists. The fact that he might soon be walking mere yards away from CIA personnel meant zip.

"Okay, Marc. Let's think this through. What are the possibil—" Lopez stopped in mid-sentence and looked back toward Strauss. He snapped his fingers. "Byron, set up video surveillance from inside the plane. Include infrared. We're in good position. I want pictures of anyone entering that aircraft." Lopez watched Strauss running back to the plane and then turned his attention back to Miller. "What's your take?"

Miller obliged. "One possibility is that Silverstein and Kipling are winging their way to safety."

"And why would they be going to Mexico?"

"I'll get to that."

"What else?"

"Option two is that someone stole Silverstein's plane. Maybe Sidki's friends."

Lopez shook his head. "You're the one who thinks that's impossible. Option three?"

"You don't want to hear three."

"Try me."

"Option three is that options one and two are both correct. Silverstein and Kipling are on the plane, but they've been hijacked by Sidki's goons."

"But why? Sidki's own plane sits right there."

"I don't know. You asked me for my thoughts." Miller paused. "But you've got to admit Mexico City gives credence to that option."

Lopez wiggled his toes in his shoes to stimulate circulation. The cool night air was taking its toll. "That would mean Sidki's team has been split up."

"If that's true, I'd wager the plane sitting next to us will be headed to Mexico City very soon."

"Maybe, maybe not. If they've got what they want, why send two planes?"

Miller thought for a moment. "To transfer Kipling back to their own plane. There's risk in doing a hijacking, even if no one knows about it."

"Good point."

"So where does that leave us?"

Lopez shivered, wrapped his upper torso with his arms, and rocked back on his heels. "We don't really care about Sidki and company. Right? Only as they concern Silverstein and Kipling. The reason we're here in the first place is to make sure Kipling doesn't end up in foreign hands."

"You know as well as I do we may be too late for that. By the time we get out of here, they'll have more than an hour's jump on us. Besides, I'm sure all they intend to do, wherever they're going, is refuel. Even if we got there before they left, it'd be a nightmare to find them. We have no jurisdiction in Mexico." Miller shook his head. "Besides, the worst-case scenario? I bet Mexico City isn't even their destination. If they've gone to this much trouble to kidnap Kipling, you can be sure they'll pull out all the stops. We need information. We've got nothing."

Lopez cupped his face in his hands and then reacted. "Marc! I just thought of something. You know it's unlikely Sidki's in charge of what's going on here. He normally doesn't do this sort of thing."

Miller responded slowly. "Are you saying that Sidki's with someone? Whoever's in charge could be on the plane that just left, you know." He blinked. "But assuming you're right, are you suggesting we bag him?"

"That's exactly what I'm saying. We need something, anything. We're in pitch-darkness here."

Lopez's mind raced at warp speed. They were down to the wire. "This'll only work if there's two of them. More than that and too much can go wrong. And if Sidki's alone, we back off. Okay? But I'm betting he's with someone." He paused. "Even so, the only way we can even consider this is to make sure Sidki gets away."

"That can be arranged. He'll escape and fly away."

"Are we agreed?"

"Agreed."

Lopez spun in place, sprinted back to the steps of his plane, and barked his order up the steps. "Byron! We need to activate Crimson! Now!"

CHAPTER 44

RETRIBUTION

1453 30th Street NW, Washington, DC, USA
38° 54'33"N latitude, 77° 03'33"W longitude
Friday, 3:20 AM, August 7, 2009

The junior senator from Kansas exhaled forcibly, tossed the throwaway cell on the sofa, and pumped her fist in the air. "Yes!" Samantha Thurston dragged herself to the bedroom and fell backward on the bed, exhausted.

It had been after midnight when she pulled into her Georgetown garage, and more than three hours since her last conversation with Caliph. She felt twinges of pain in her chest when the phone rang a little after one in the morning, and she recognized MacDonald's voice. He was excited and gave her an update on Jamieson's progress. He said that Jamieson had called from his plane after landing in Monterey. MacDonald thought she should know.

MacDonald's call meant that what she had been afraid would happen, had happened. MacDonald didn't say anything was amiss, only that Jamieson had located the mystery woman and that they would return her to Washington. Jamieson had obviously not questioned him to confirm the existence of the private aircraft Thurston told Jamieson that Mac-Donald had sent. Jamieson now knew that Thurston was working on her own. Although he might have suspected as much, how he would react to this new information was unknown.

MacDonald's call escalated Thurston's adrenaline to a level one might expect when fleeing a starving African lion. Everything could have turned to shit. But then, minutes ago, on his way to the airport, Caliph called with good news. It was a sad loss, but one well within a short list of acceptable outcomes. Jamieson was dead. He had obviously teamed up with Silverstein—that in itself made little sense to Thurston—and had tried to steal Kipling away. Jamieson had failed in his attempt, and Caliph shot him to death. Caliph offered no details, except to say that he and Sidki had taken time to dispose of the body.

After Jamieson's demise, Silverstein somehow got the upper hand at the motel. The three of them, Jamieson's partner, Silverstein, and Kipling, left Caliph and Sidki behind. What they hadn't counted on was for Caliph to have time to call his pilots who waited at the airport. Both skilled agents of the Blade in their own right, they overpowered the pilots of Silverstein's aircraft and waited for his return. They had reasoned that there was less chance for something to go wrong if they apprehended Silverstein inside his own aircraft.

Once Silverstein's aircraft was under Blade control, Caliph's chief pilot, Aziz Riad, replaced Silverstein's copilot in Silverstein's aircraft. Thurston remembered Riad, a cousin, from her teenage visits to Cairo. Riad's copilot then escorted Silverstein's copilot back to Caliph's aircraft. It was a simple matter of waiting for Silverstein and Kipling to return.

Caliph had ordered Riad to take off immediately once they apprehended Silverstein and Kipling, and not to wait for him. When Caliph called Thurston, he said that Silverstein had been in the air for some thirty-five minutes. Under Uncle Mohammed's instructions to take no chances in returning to Cairo, Riad exited U.S. airspace as quickly as possible. Hence the decision to fly to Mexico City. Caliph and Sidki planned to rendezvous with Riad there. Caliph seemed especially interested in meeting the plane.

Once Caliph caught up with Riad, they planned to transfer Silverstein and Kipling back to Caliph's aircraft, release Silverstein's copilot back to his original airplane, and make their way to Cairo.

Thurston closed her eyes to sleep, but the implications of all that had happened kept her mind on edge. Significant dangers remained. It wouldn't be long, probably later in the day, until MacDonald called. He'd be worried that he hadn't heard from Jamieson. She decided that wasn't necessarily a bad thing. With Jamieson gone, there was no one to report to MacDonald what had occurred in Monterey. Word would eventually reach him regarding Jamieson's death—if they found the body. Concerning Jamieson's assistant, she was hired help. Jamieson would have told her very little about the operation. That loose strand should be self-healing. MacDonald would lose his connection to Kipling, a desirable outcome.

If only it was that simple, she thought. What about this man Silverstein? Other than his being a famous Navy scientist who had interacted with both Rafferty and Jamieson, she knew nothing about him. Either on the way to Cairo or shortly afterward, Silverstein would vanish. If so, could he be traced back to Thurston? MacDonald might search for Jamieson or Kipling through him. Could that bring trouble? Not if Silverstein turned up missing. Again, in Thurston's mind, the problem appeared to be self-limited.

With these immediate threats seemingly discounted, Thurston was about to drift off to sleep when one of Caliph's comments replayed itself in her mind. It was something he said right at the end of their conversation. It didn't make any sense at the time, and now she wondered if it related to his earlier disquiet about not being on the aircraft personally with Silverstein. He said there was some unfinished business that needed attention, unrelated to Kipling. It had something to do with her boss. Thurston blinked fully awake. Again, the name Victor Mark Silverstein. Why would Caliph care anything about him?

CHAPTER 45

DROPPED CALL

Comstock Aviation, Monterey Peninsula Airport, Monterey,
California, USA
36°35'18"N latitude, 121°51'24"W longitude
Friday, 12:25 AM, August 7, 2009

Even after years of participating in operations like this, Lopez reacted to the pressure. Moisture beaded on his skin, and his heart hammered. He stood out of sight next to the administrative offices of Comstock Aviation, watching the Crimson team prepare to execute the sequence they practiced often. Only this time, the situation was dead serious. Realism would replace the laughter and shenanigans that accompanied rehearsals. Although the three-person Crimson team usually operated on its own, this time was different. Lopez would likely provide a necessary cog to the success of an operation conceived only minutes earlier.

Miller had rushed to the street to provide surveillance for Sidki's arrival. Using a nearly invisible headset attached to a secure cell phone frequency, CIA personnel in Washington informed Miller of Sidki's movement as he approached the airport. In position, Lopez and the Crimson team listened as well.

Sidki and his companions—if there were any—would proceed to their aircraft. They could go by way of two routes. They could walk there directly across the tarmac and bypass the terminal for Comstock Aviation, one of several fixed base operators for private aircraft at the Monterey Peninsula Airport. Lopez considered it more likely they would enter the terminal from the street, go inside, and exit the building on the aircraft side. The building remained open all night for private flyers, in contrast to the commercial terminal next door that locked its doors at midnight. Although their aircraft undoubtedly included a bathroom, it made sense that they would use ground facilities, particularly if they anticipated an extended flight out of Monterey. Because Lopez had only one Crimson team, his assumption that the arrivals would make their way to the aircraft by way of the bathroom was crucial.

Joaquin Ramos, the agent whose job it was to advance from the rear to inject the tranquilizer, waited outside the building not far from Miller. Byron Strauss and Billy Anchor, the two who would approach the victim from his front, stood within view of Lopez. As in Pittsburgh, they wore the Cooper's casual business attire.

"There's a taxi pulling up," Miller whispered. Three separate tones followed on Lopez's earphone speaker, one from each member of the Crimson team, to signal they had received Miller's transmission. Lopez's tone followed.

Miller's next transmission would be crucial. Was Sidki alone? If only Sidki arrived at the airport, all bets were off, and the Crimson team would stand down. As Lopez and Miller had discussed earlier, it wasn't in the cards that they apprehend him. And if three or more men exited the taxi, the situation could get sticky, and Lopez might choose to call off the operation. The ideal number was two, Sidki and one other. Miller would recognize him immediately. He was a short man, scarcely five-foot-five in height.

Lopez smiled inwardly at Miller's next comment. "Two men, one carrying his jacket and the other wearing his. I recognize Sidki. He's the one wearing a jacket."

Lopez held his breath. Would they come inside the building?

"They're talking and … they're heading inside." Miller voice exuded calm.

Lopez's heart skipped a beat. So far, everything had gone according to plan. Timing and luck would now come into play. Even a two-man situation harbored considerable risk. Lopez would necessarily play a role. He would distract Sidki while the Crimson team performed their magic on the second man.

Lopez walked into the open and waited. He had memorized the well-lit interior of the building. He stood in a corridor that represented the bottom of a backward *L*, with Lopez standing at the tip. Ahead, the vertical portion of the L turned to his left. At the intersection stood Strauss and Anchor, engaged in conversation at a coffee bar that had closed for the night. They faced the door to the facility that ran along a wider corridor that represented the vertical portion of the *L*. Sidki and his partner would be approaching from that door. The restrooms lay along the wall behind Lopez.

Lopez walked slowly. He wanted to time his movement to intercept Sidki and his partner at the juncture.

Unexpectedly, Miller's voice interceded. "Stop! Only Sidki's coming inside. His partner is holding back."

Shit! This was exactly what Lopez didn't want to happen—the man they really wanted going directly to the plane.

Lopez kept moving. At the least, he intended to get a close-up view of Sidki. He looked ahead and stopped after passing Strauss and Anchor. He saw the diminutive male coming through the door. He removed his lighter and a cigarette from his coat pocket, stopping in mid-step to light the cigarette. In reality, a miniature digital camera was snapping twenty frames a second as Sidki walked by. Lopez could present to Archives an updated photograph of their walking transmitter.

Lopez glanced to his left, nodded hello to the passing stranger, and watched Sidki stroll toward the restroom. Miller's voice interrupted his momentary disappointment. "Good news! He's still out front, making a cell call."

Hot damn! Lopez couldn't believe it. The situation couldn't have evolved better. "Crimson team! Now!"

Lopez watched as Strauss and Anchor accelerated by on his right. He proceeded slowly behind them. With this turn of events, he would have no role to play and could just watch the outcome. Assuming Sidki's partner stayed put for at least a few more seconds, his apprehension would be textbook. Lopez had observed such a capture only once and was anxious to watch this team in action.

By the time Lopez opened the double doors to exit to the street, the Crimson sequence had begun. The man, whom Lopez did not recognize in the dim streetlights, was looking at the ground and talking into his cell when Strauss and Anchor approached from the front and, simultaneously, Ramos from the rear. The stranger sensed that something was amiss but too late. Seconds later, with four strong arms now inhibiting his upper limbs from any controlled motion, his will to resist vanished.

Lopez drew up short. He realized at once that in addition to the obvious treasure of potential information he now had in his possession, he had one more. The cell phone had fallen during the brief scuffle. Lopez rushed over, picked it up, placed it to his ear, and listened to a single word repeated several times before the line cut off. Lopez scrolled through the phone's options and located both the number for the phone in his hand and the one that had just disconnected. He immediately called Langley from his own phone and asked them to trace the second number. New 911 emergency requirements, combined with updated technology, allowed cell phone companies to determine the geographic location of a cell call.

Lopez wrote down what he had heard on the phone, probably a name. It meant nothing to him. But one other tidbit brought back conversations he had had only recently with Miller. It was probably a coincidence. On the other hand, it was worth noting. The speaker had been female.

CHAPTER 46

MORTAL CONFLICT

Blade of the Sinai safe house, Cairo, Egypt
30°07'56"N latitude, 31°25'45"E longitude
Saturday, 2:02 PM, August 8, 2009

Silverstein recoiled as someone removed the hood from his head and cut the plastic band that bound his wrists. His handlers had controlled his movement since he stepped off the airplane.

Silverstein squinted into the light from the single bulb that lit the tiny room. He focused on the person standing in front of him, a dark, beefy man with an excellent mustache. The large man said nothing but gestured appropriately, with no obvious animosity. He turned, walked away, and closed the metal door behind him. Silverstein listened to a lock clicking shut, walked to the door, and peered through a small, wired window that fronted a hallway.

Silverstein glanced about his new home. Famished, he eyed a plate of fruit and meats, together with a pot of tea, sitting on a table in front of a small bed. Not bad as cells go, if that was what this was, he thought. It was more than a cell, though, with a privacy curtain for the toilet, a small washbasin, and a tiny enclosed shower. On a shelf next to the basin lay towels and toiletries. A barred window, high on the wall, faced the toilet. He stood on his tiptoes to look outside. There was light, but he saw only the walls of another building.

Silverstein stared at his watch, blinked several times, and realized how completely exhausted he was. Although he had caught some shuteye on the plane, his sleep had been tortured. Too much had happened; too much to worry about.

He looked again, and the digits came into focus. It was a little after four in the morning, Pacific daylight time. He had to stop and think. It was now Saturday, two calendar days after their wheels had left the ground before midnight on Thursday in Monterey. That would make it two in the afternoon, Cairo time, assuming Egypt used daylight saving time. Cairo was ten hours ahead of Monterey, Silverstein knew.

Long before he had overheard the pilot on his radio mention Cairo, Silverstein had determined their intermediate stops. They had landed twice to refuel after Mexico City, first in Bermuda and then again somewhere in Spain, before touching down in Cairo. Silverstein had kept track of the time they had spent in the air since Monterey. A ball-busting twenty hours, not counting three hours on the ground in Mexico City and two hours each on the latter stops. Aziz traded duties with his copilot who had met them in Mexico City. Both took turns with Francis babysitting their guests.

The Cairo airport was the last place he had seen Kipling. They sat in the plane for some time before being escorted off. He went first. His captors, replacements for the ones on the plane, hooded him prior to a short drive in a vehicle driven by someone who needed lessons in manual shifting. He hoped Kipling was nearby, but this was uncertain. He didn't think she had shared the same vehicle from the airport.

Silverstein decided he might as well get some sleep. If they had wanted to kill him, they wouldn't have offered him room and board, he assured himself. He lay on top of the bed without taking off his clothes. He closed his eyes but couldn't make the day's events disappear from his thoughts.

If Silverstein could scribble down on paper a list of things he wished he could go back and change, not tying up the stranger on the floor in Carmel would rise to the top two, and probably to one. He should have listened to Violet. And then, getting hijacked in his own goddamn aircraft had to take the cake.

Back in Monterey, Silverstein had considered for a millisecond trying to overpower Aziz but had recognized his weapon as a stun gun, probably a Taser. Although its yellow stripes designated it as a nonlethal weapon, it was still capable of leaving its victim convulsing on the floor.

The Taser, together with the remote control that Aziz held in his other hand in prominent view, made it clear that he was a professional. Aziz explained that the signal from his remote would activate a mechanical injector housed inside a neck collar. And Max was the one wearing that collar. Silverstein remembered the odd neckwear. Aziz seemed proud of the device. One press on the remote would release a chemical that would not kill Max but would render him paralyzed for upward of a minute. He explained that a technical description of the device to Max had had the intended effect.

Before he locked the cockpit door and suggested they enjoy the rest of the flight, Aziz asked that Silverstein relinquish his weapon and cell phone; Kipling's cell, too. He also explained that, lest they be concerned for their safety, he was a licensed pilot and could fly the plane if needed.

Kipling's reaction to all this caught Silverstein by surprise. Still determined not to let on that he suspected Kipling of possessing the prophecy gene, Silverstein ranted over their bad luck. "Boy, are they in for a surprise when they realize you're not who they want." She just nodded and seemed resigned to their fate.

Silverstein wondered who these guys were. Dickey hadn't known them. Now that they had landed on foreign soil, all bets were off. Kipling's fame had spread far beyond Washington, DC, and an NRL employee named Rafferty.

Silverstein's mind clicked. Back in Mexico City, something interesting had occurred. On the way there, he had concluded that a hijacked airplane wasn't in Aziz's best interest. True to Silverstein's prediction, Aziz waited for his own aircraft to arrive from Monterey. When it did, considerable conversation took place between Aziz and the smaller of Silverstein's two assailants back in Carmel—a man called Francis, Kipling said—the one whom Silverstein had overcome by the front porch. Nicholas was nowhere in sight.

From the moment Francis had arrived, Silverstein sensed something was wrong. From occasionally listening to Al Jazeera, the Middle Eastern television network that had risen to prominence in the 1990s, Silverstein recognized the language his captors used as Arabic. He couldn't understand the conversation but listened for words he might recognize. Although he never heard the name Nicholas, the name *Caliph* came up several times. Was Nicholas in fact Caliph, and why would he have stayed in Monterey?

As Silverstein had anticipated, Aziz and Francis transferred him and Kipling to their own plane, a larger jet aircraft. On the ground in Mexico City, Aziz offered them food and drinks. They then took off again.

Silverstein repeatedly attempted conversation with Kipling. They had been in tight spots before and had discussed their way out together. Not so, this time. No convivial banter with Silverstein's wisecracking put-downs. Kipling didn't want to talk.

*   *   *   *

Kipling lay back on her bed and wondered what Silverstein was thinking. He probably wasn't far away. Several armed men had met their aircraft at the airport. After Silverstein descended the steps, Kipling asked to speak to the one called Francis. She told him she understood why she was there and that she would cooperate completely—but *only* if they provided frequent feedback that Silverstein was well and being fairly treated. If anything happened to her colleague, she told him, they might as well shoot her. Once they exited their cars at their destination, her handler removed Kipling's hood. Down the pathway, she watched the still-hooded Silverstein walk away. Francis assured her he was safe and would reside nearby.

Although clearly a holding cell, with no windows and a single locked door, Kipling's accommodations were impressive, with multiple rooms, a stocked kitchen, and expensive appointments. As nice as a suite in a luxury hotel in the States. Her captors obviously recognized her importance and chose to treat her accordingly.

She felt sorry for her boss. He had been confused over her disposition during the flight. Her behavior had been partly on purpose. She felt resigned to her destiny. The blessing, or curse—depending on your viewpoint—that she had possessed since birth had come to the fore. Whether Kipling had ended up in Washington, DC, or elsewhere, she recognized that the world would change forever for Linda Ann Kipling. She resigned herself to her plight and tuned out. Silverstein suffered the effect.

Besides, although Kipling thought she understood everything, she had no idea how much Silverstein knew. He still believed—or that's what he said—that Kipling had been caught up in this affair innocently.

But there was a third reason Kipling chose to remain coy with Silverstein. In quick succession after her clairvoyance manifested itself back at the Carmel motel, another visualization came upon her at the Monterey airport, after they had boarded the aircraft. Most of the time when these visions came to her, their meaning was clear. But not this time. The implication was troubling. There was no point in worrying Victor.

In the mental picture that had flashed before her eyes, Silverstein and Nicholas were together again. How could that be? Nicholas hadn't even boarded the plane in Mexico City. If Francis had managed to escape, wouldn't Nicholas have come along as well? Aziz's comment to Silverstein when they boarded the plane made it clear that Nicholas had been the one to sound the alarm.

Perhaps Nicholas had remained behind in Monterey for a reason. Why else would Kipling's vision depict the two of them in a life-and-death struggle inside Silverstein's house?

CHAPTER 47

LONG DISTANCE

Russell Senate Office Building, Washington, DC, USA
38° 53'32"N latitude, 77° 00'28"W longitude
Saturday, 10:15 AM, August 8, 2009

A long encrypted message had come through on Thurston's permanent cell phone, and she had chosen to translate it in the quiet of her office. She had decided yesterday that there would be no flight back to Kansas this weekend.

Friday had been hell. Having had Caliph's voice suddenly drop from his call, to be replaced by another, had been stressful. Fortunately, the cell phone Caliph had called had been the last of her throwaway versions. The instant she realized that security was compromised, she switched off the phone, removed the battery and, for good measure, mangled the plastic device using two pairs of pliers. The mere seconds it took before Thurston switched off the phone prevented anyone from tracing her location. She understood the technology that allowed 911 services to locate subscribers.

What had happened in Monterey? Thurston hadn't expected Caliph to call back so soon. She was already in bed after a grueling but satisfying day. Ten minutes earlier, Caliph had detailed the evening's events. She already knew that Silverstein and Kipling were safely on their way to Mexico City. Mission accomplished. Caliph was in a rush to leave for Mexico City. He called a second time to ask her to send a secure summary to Cairo. Uncle

Mohammed would relish their success, he said. They were about to conclude the call when she heard a sharp clatter, followed by a strange man's voice.

Thurston had panicked. She wanted answers fast. Her cousin, Aziz, was Caliph's pilot. She had his satellite phone number and considered violating procedure to reach him. Thurston recognized how upset she was when she realized he could add nothing—he had departed Monterey before she talked to Caliph.

Logical thinking replaced alarm. By powering down her phone she had not compromised her location. More importantly, their primary undertaking had succeeded. As Caliph had requested, she would inform Uncle Mohammed of their triumph, but she didn't know whether to complicate the message by telling him what had occurred during Caliph's phone call.

Could there be a rational explanation for what happened? If Caliph had accidentally dropped the phone, someone could have picked it up. But wouldn't he have handed it back to its owner? She could think of no innocent explanation to explain that strange sequence of events. Her heart skipped a beat as another thought came to mind. Had Sidki disappeared as well?

Thurston chose to relay exactly what she knew. Her coded message read: targets apprehended, flying Cairo. Caliph missing.

Following completion of Caliph's request, Thurston waited patiently for word—from anyone. Caliph preferably, but Sidki or Uncle Mohammed would do. Friday passed and merged into Saturday. The message that arrived Saturday morning would provide an answer, she hoped.

She completed the translation, a memo from Uncle Mohammed. As all such messages were, it was curt, and she read between the lines. What she feared was true. Caliph had disappeared at the Monterey airport, and Sidki flew to Mexico City without him. Silverstein and Kipling were under Blade control in Cairo and had been cooperative. Thurston wondered why Silverstein was still alive. Mohammed's final line took the form of a question. Could Thurston locate Caliph?

Thurston equivocated. Could she do anything to find Caliph? She had no intelligence connections, and even if she did, how could she use them? Other than hiring a private detective, no options came to mind.

Even if Caliph had been assaulted, he would have made contact later. The only explanation for Caliph's complete disappearance was kidnapping—or worse. A random attack at a small-town airport at night by hoodlums? Not likely. But who, then? Had government intelligence spotted Caliph when he entered the country? Were they on to him? That didn't make sense either. Linda Kipling had been the object of everyone's attention. Jamieson and Caliph had been the hunters, not the hunted. But what other explanation could there be?

If Thurston was going to be of any help to Uncle Mohammed, she needed more information. She looked at her watch and added seven hours. Late afternoon in Cairo.

Thurston removed her cell phone from her purse, composed an e-mail message consisting of two digits, and sent it on its way to an anonymous server that would forward the numbers to the proper party. These digits referenced a specific pay phone in the Washington area. When she had first arrived in Washington with her senator husband, she had spent days choosing locations to which she annotated, on a list, a two-digit number, an address, and a phone number. She stopped adding digits when the list topped twenty. She had mailed a copy of that directory to Uncle Mohammed. When she needed to talk, she would e-mail him with the numbered location, and he would reply with the day and time. If vice versa, he would code the day and time, and she would return a two-digit location.

As cell phones became prolific, several pay phones had dropped from her list. Days ago, Thurston had verified that location sixteen was still operational, underground on the platform between trains at the Union Station Metro. It was a convenient spot within easy walking distance of the Russell Senate Office Building. It was time to talk to Uncle Mohammed.

CHAPTER 48

RECOMPENSE

George Bush Center for Intelligence, McLean, Virginia, USA
38° 56'06"N latitude, 77° 08'46"W longitude
Saturday, 9:40 PM, August 8, 2009

Lopez drummed his pencil on the desk and glanced up at Miller.

"What do you think the chances are, the Mensa team?" Miller's voice was low and his eyes bloodshot from lack of sleep.

"We'll know soon." Lopez tried to focus on the numerals of his watch. Neither of them had had much sleep since Friday. "He'll be out of surgery within the hour. Dr. Sampson tells me they'll begin hypnosis tomorrow morning."

Miller switched to another subject. "That was one smooth operation in Monterey. I had never seen the Crimson team in an actual operation before."

Lopez nodded. The Crimson procedure had been flawless. By the time Lopez had picked up the cell phone, their target stood placid and responsive to command. Still, there had been time for the situation to turn nasty. Because Sidki would return to search for his partner, Lopez knew they had to act fast.

With no taxicab in sight and no other transportation available, Lopez ordered everyone, except Miller, to walk back toward the commercial terminal and the adjacent parking lot. They would have preferred to march their mark directly to their own aircraft that sat adjacent to Sidki's, but couldn't take the chance. It was better to remain behind until Sidki departed. Lopez remembered an airport hotel a short distance away. They walked there as fast as their charge's legs would move, rented a room, and waited for Miller to report that Sidki's plane had departed. Miller waited inside the aircraft.

Sidki had no idea what had happened to his partner. Miller reported him traipsing back and forth between the private terminal and his aircraft. Ramos, after completing the escort, returned to the airport to report on Sidki's actions outside the terminal. Ramos used the second of the Cooper's three fashion statements. He took on the appearance of a security guard, complete with a realistic-looking hat stored in a pouch that was part of the Cooper. Playing his role to the hilt, Ramos walked up to Sidki and asked if he could be of assistance. Sidki declined and appeared agitated. Under Ramos's watchful eye, Sidki explored the entire airport available to a pedestrian, as well as the surrounding streets, going so far as the motel where the Crimson team waited with his partner.

At 1:55 AM Miller reported Sidki's aircraft taxiing away into the night. Not long afterward, Lopez, his team, and their new prized possession departed Monterey. En route (and previously at the motel) they administered more drugs to maintain their captive's compliant disposition. Six hours later, they arrived at CIA headquarters.

Lopez heard a knock on his door and looked up. "Yeah!"

Dr. Philip Sampson, Mensa surgeon and the brains behind this new technique, strolled in, still clothed in his scrubs.

Miller rose quickly, offering his chair.

"No, thanks. Just wanted to give you a heads-up." Dr. Sampson stood tall, about six-five, with long, bushy hair. Even apart from his status as a research scientist and surgeon, his physique commanded attention.

Lopez stood as well. "How'd it go? Tell me this is going to work."

"We won't know until we try the hypnosis, but I'm marginally confident."

Lopez pondered what it was he should be asking. On the return flight yesterday, he had recalled Dr. Sampson's lecture from weeks earlier.

Miller, who hadn't attended that part of the seminar, had listened to Lopez's summary of what he remembered. The Mensa team had come up with a revolutionary method for interrogating uncooperative individuals in order to extract needed information. From the plane, Lopez had called Sampson and explained their situation. This would be the first test of Sampson's hypothesis. Experimentation on animals could go only so far, Sampson had emphasized at the seminar. He had been waiting for a suitable subject.

Lopez, exhausted, chose to admit his ignorance. "Doc, we're dead tired, and our minds are mush." He gestured toward Miller. "Marc missed your seminar. Tell us again, please, what you did in the operating room and why it might work."

Sampson accepted Miller's offer of a chair but soon took to his feet again. He was being asked to talk about his *baby*, and his excitement permeated the room. Any scientist would talk at length about his own research.

Sampson spoke deliberately, his hands constantly in motion and an indispensable part of his presentation. "In layman's terms, we've created an artificial amnesia in the subject. We estimate the amnesia will last about twenty-four hours or so, with no aftereffects."

Miller listened intently. Lopez's abbreviated explanation hadn't covered everything. "How do you do that?"

"You've heard of people having amnesia after getting hit on the head." Sampson became even more animated. Curious people, these scientists. "There are several forms of amnesia. For discussion purposes, let's limit ourselves to the most common types. There's retrograde and anterograde amnesia. It's simple. If you have retrograde amnesia, you can't remember things that happened before the amnesia. With anterograde amnesia, you can't remember what happens afterward. Retrograde amnesia is the stuff you see in books and movies. Think of Robert Ludlum's Jason Bourne.

"In the 1990s, for the first time, scientists performed animal studies on this sort of thing, using surgery. Rabbits, cats, monkeys, rats. By manipulating parts of the brain, they found you could create retrograde amnesia. I concluded we could do the same thing in a human."

Sampson's excitement rubbed off on Miller. "Back to the animals. How's it possible to know whether an animal can remember something? You can't go interviewing them."

Sampson took a long look at Miller before apparently realizing that naive questions often came from people outside the field. "Easy. You train two groups of animals to do the same task. For example, eye-blink conditioning, object discrimination, learning mazes. Then you separate them, induce amnesia in half the group, and look at the results."

Miller seemed to realize that Sampson had done his best not to make him look like a fool. "Let me try again." He shook his head and closed his eyes tight. "I thought the whole point of this exercise was to have the subject recall memories, not forget them."

Lopez decided to interject. "I did go to your seminar, Dr. Sampson. Let me see if my recollection is accurate."

Sampson nodded.

Lopez cleared his throat. "Dr. Sampson's objective is to extract information from someone who is uncooperative. Under normal circumstances, you'd use hypnosis. But that requires a willing subject." Lopez, who had been addressing Miller, glanced up at Sampson. "By the way, in your seminar, you stressed that stored information in the brain is nothing more than memories." He hesitated. "How am I doing?"

Sampson nodded again.

"By wiping out past memories, all that you have left are memories you create now. And correct me if I'm wrong, Doc, that's what you hope to have left after the surgery you just finished."

"That's right. Classical amnesia like in the movies."

Miller decided to redeem himself. "Okay, I get it. If all past memories are gone, then what's left is a cooperative, compliant person." Miller smiled. "You can then hypnotize the subject willingly, telling them you are there to help them regain their mem—" He stopped in mid-word. "But if the memories are gone, what good does it do you?"

Sampson stuffed his hands in his pockets, making Lopez wonder how he could talk without them. "Good question. There's one more piece to the amnesia puzzle that makes all of this work. The specific form of retrograde amnesia we're creating is called temporally graded retrograde amnesia. To create that condition, we induce changes to the medial temporal lobe in the brain, in particular the hippocampus proper." Lopez knew it couldn't last. Sampson's hands flew back into action, delivering the signal that a forward pass was incomplete. "Those are scientific details. Don't worry about them. The point is that with temporally graded retrograde amnesia you tend to remember older memories better and first, and with time, more recent memories. That's quite common in amnesia, by the way."

Lopez could sense Miller's logical extrapolation to Sampson's explanation. Even when operating on fewer than all mental cylinders, Miller was one of the smartest members of his team.

"I get it. As the memories come back to the subject, they return from the past forward. By the time they return to the present, it's too late. The subject has already spilled his guts." Miller shook his head and smiled. "Damn, is that clever or what?"

Sampson stood tall—which wasn't hard in his case—and basked in the glow of Miller's praise. "Suffice it to say, we don't know at what point in the process he'll clam up. But before that happens, we should have plenty of information. And if this works, it'll eliminate the need for torture, although most psychologists have concluded that torture doesn't get you much information anyway. People will do and say anything if you threaten them enough." Sampson's hands took off again, almost flailing. "Remember back in 2005, during George W's second term, when his administration was accused of torturing al-Qaeda enemy combatants? As you know, we were involved in some of that. Ever since, we've been working on a better way. This may be it."

Miller squirmed in his seat and grimaced. "There are some who might suggest that brain surgery is a form of torture."

Sampson's head bobbed up and down. "That's a good point. In the long term, we'd like to use chemicals to achieve the same thing. Some of those animal studies I mentioned have used excitotoxins, but there is evidence that the effects may extend outside the hippocampus, and that complicates things. For the moment, surgery seems to be the way to go. And remember, except for a hole in the head, which we can patch up, there's no permanent damage."

Sampson paused. "I guess I didn't mention that with our microsurgical methods, the hole is rather small and leaves no noticeable pain. And without a mirror, the patient can't even see the area ... we shave the head only in that location." Sampson seemed satisfied with his response to Miller's qualms.

Lopez nodded. He was still thinking the process through. "Okay. I understand the progression, and you say you'll start the hypnosis tomorrow."

"Correct. First thing."

"Can we sit in?"

"Absolutely. You'll be there to guide the interrogator, Dr. Craig Leopold, our hypnosis expert. He's Mensa, of course." Lopez did everything he could to keep from rolling his eyes. Every single member of the Mensa team thought they were God's gift to the CIA. "Before Craig starts, he'll need guidance from you, telling him what you're after. You'll play no direct role in the hypnosis, but during the process, you can pass him information by way of a keyboard, guiding him in the directions you wish.

"Be aware that there will likely be several sessions as the memories return from the distant past forward. We'll continue until you tell us to quit. At some point, we predict that the subject will become uncooperative, and that'll be it." Sampson paused for a moment. "One more thing, and this is important from your point of view. We fully expect that the subject will not remember that he's told us anything."

Lopez remembered. "You didn't forget my special request, did you?" Although the future of their boarder remained uncertain, it would have been foolish not to insert the tracking transmitter that had been so successful with Sidki.

"Not to worry. The Delta chip's in and transmitting normally."

The room turned silent as Lopez and Miller considered all they had learned.

Sampson broke the quiet. "May I ask what it is you're after?"

Other than their captive's association with Sidki and the likelihood that he was a member of the Blade, anything learned from hypnosis would be more than they knew now. The man the Crimson team had captured had no identification or other papers on his person.

Lopez took a breath, released it, and chose his words carefully. "We know that Mr. Anonymous is part of a Middle Eastern terrorist group that has kidnapped two American citizens." Lopez chose not to explain why. "But besides that, one of the two is an old colleague of mine. He saved my life once. Whatever it takes, I'm determined to find him and repay that debt."

Lopez caught Miller's eye. He had reacted to this final statement. Lopez interpreted Miller's response in one word. *Finally!*

CHAPTER 49

FORESHADOWED

Blade of the Sinai safe house, Cairo, Egypt
30° 07'56"N latitude, 31° 25'45"E longitude
Sunday, 5:55 AM, August 9, 2009

Silverstein awoke and stared at the ceiling. The distinctive sound of jet aircraft resonated through the window. He couldn't be far from the airport. He had spent a restless night on his cot. Nearly two full days of nonstop flying had taken their toll. He tallied his time in the air and calculated he had flown over fifteen thousand miles since Thursday morning.

In between nightmares that shifted between motel rooms and airplanes, with plenty of guns and strangers to add interest, he had lain awake considering his options. Option one—breaking out of his cell, rescuing Kipling, and fleeing the country—had been high on his list. But it was also ludicrous. He adjusted his head on the pillow and blinked, surprised to see breakfast on the adjacent table. He must have been dead to the world if he hadn't heard the door open.

Option two seemed more practical. The odds were arguably better. If his parents could see him now, they would tell him to go for it. That was because they had been his biggest fans and trusted his judgment. He had gone out on a limb when he was eight years old, back in 1967, and it had paid off. Of course, at that age, the stakes had been low—at least for him.

"Sick toes, Daddy. She's got sick toes." That's what he'd said that made the difference. Silverstein smiled and reminisced.

The Silversteins had adopted Victor when he was three years old. It hadn't taken long before they realized they had a unique child in their charge. At the age of four, he could read his Dick and Jane books easily. That wasn't noteworthy. What was remarkable was that he had to read them only once. Victor Mark Silverstein had a photographic memory. All the way through school, this ability alone made him a formidable study.

But it was more than this special talent that made his teachers take notice. Behind his skills in memorization lay a mind for which intelligence tests of the day rated him in the top one-tenth of 1 percent of the population. Learning new principles and developing solutions to new or existing study problems came easily to him. Recognizing the gifts of the child they had unexpectedly received from Victor's mother, the Silversteins provided him with encouragement, private schools, and the wherewithal to make the most of his talents.

Victor had never ceased to amaze his parents with his mental shenanigans. It was a rare party or get-together with friends of the Silversteins that did not transition to one question: what had Victor done recently? One of their favorite stories had a life of its own and continued for years after Victor left the house in 1975 to attend Pennsylvania State University. That tale illuminated Victor's ability to make use of the tiniest grain of wheat in a mountain of chaff.

Ivan Silverstein, Victor's adoptive father, was a physician, a general practitioner. He operated a small practice out of his home. His office sat between the garage and the kitchen, with a small waiting room that fronted a sidewalk that ran directly to the street where patients parked.

Early on, the adventurous young Victor would find himself playing in the waiting room, often to the chagrin of patients, black and white, who did not know that the Silversteins had an African-American child. The cute and affable Victor made friends easily and often ended up in remarkably adult conversations with the flabbergasted patients. He would sit on the floor, look up with those big brown eyes, and soon have even the shyest patient won over.

The person for whom Victor's attention to detail would become legend was Mrs. Wilma Fenderson, a forty-five-year-old woman who had found her element in the sexually permissive, carefree 1960s. She dressed casually, with no pretense, stockings, or makeup, her only concession to vanity her brightly colored fingernails. Victor, newly aware that males and females were different, took note that she wore no brassiere.

Wilma had used Dr. Silverstein as her general physician for years, long before she married for the first time in her early forties. Her name then was Williamson. Her parents were people of means, and she inherited considerable wealth when they passed away. When she married, she became a Fenderson.

Dr. Silverstein became increasingly concerned when Wilma started coming to his office frequently, each time complaining of new maladies. Nausea, dizziness, stomach upset, and a variety of other complaints stacked up on her medical record over a two-month period. Because Wilma had never been one to complain or have hypochondriac tendencies, the elder Silverstein assumed her ailments were legitimate. He was at a loss, with none of his remedies or suggestions having much effect. It was one evening at the dinner table when a diagnosis crystallized in his mind.

Little Victor had started the conversation. "I saw Mrs. Fenderson today. She says she's still sick. What's wrong with her, Daddy?"

Sara Silverstein interjected. "You know, dear, I ran into her yesterday at Sears, and she even mentioned it to me."

Dr. Silverstein finished a bite of mashed potatoes and frowned. "That is a tough one." He shook his head. "I don't know."

Sara Silverstein knew her husband well and recognized his frustration. He prided himself on being an excellent diagnostician, which he was.

Victor blurted out. "Why not?"

Ivan Silverstein responded in a way he thought his son would understand. "She has all kinds of symptoms that don't go together. She seems to be sick all over, and that doesn't make sense."

Without hesitation, Victor responded. "I know one thing."

"What's that?" Dr. Silverstein smiled.

"She's got sick toes." Victor nodded his head up and down with vigor.

Victor's mother and father laughed. Dr. Silverstein then asked him why he would say such a thing.

"Her toenails are funny, Daddy. They have white lines all over them."

Sara noticed her husband flinch and his eyes open wide. He paused and asked sternly, "How would you know that, Victor?"

Victor sat up straight. "She said her feet hurt. She took off her shoes and rubbed her feet. I saw her sick toes then. She doesn't wear any socks."

The elder Silverstein leaped up from the table and ran down the hall to his office. Sara and Victor followed and found him poring through a medical book.

The rest, as they say, is history. Mr. Fenderson went to jail for attempted murder, and it made the papers. He had been slowly poisoning Mrs. Fenderson with arsenic. The white lines on her toenails were a symptom, and Dr. Silverstein had not thought to inspect her feet. She had similar lines on her fingernails but had covered them with nail polish. Little Victor had literally saved Mrs. Fenderson's life.

The sound of someone outside the cell door reminded Silverstein that he was far from home. He needed to move beyond the hired help. It was time to trust himself and make use of the one unique fragment of information he had garnered over the past two days—just like he had done once as an eight-year-old.

Silverstein stood, marched to the door, and yelled loudly. "Is anyone there? I need to talk to someone."

It wasn't long before the mustached one opened the wired window and peered in. Silverstein had no idea whether he spoke English. He made his statement short and to the point.

"Tell your boss if he wants to know about Caliph, he needs to talk to me."

CHAPTER 50

EXIT VISA

Blade of the Sinai safe house, Cairo, Egypt
30°07'56"N latitude, 31°25'45"E longitude
Sunday, 6:10 AM, August 9, 2009

Fortunately for Silverstein, his mustached handler spoke reasonable English. "Eat your breakfast and clean up. I will return."

Silverstein eyed the repeated assortment of meats and fruits and obeyed. He ate, showered, shaved, and dressed in the same clothes he had worn since three days earlier when he last awoke in Monterey, California. He was sitting on his bed, waiting, when the door opened.

"My name is Fuad. You will come with me."

"Where are we going?"

"My boss wishes to speak to you. We will drive to him, but I must ask you to wear this hood."

Silverstein obliged. His handler had been pleasant so far. There seemed to be little point in taking him on. First, Kipling might or might not be in the building. Second, Fuad no doubt had backup. And third, if they had wanted him dead, it would have been easy enough to poison him with the food.

Fuad led the way, his right hand gripping Silverstein's arm above the elbow. Silverstein knew immediately when they stepped outside. Even though it was early, the blast of hot air made its way through the dark mask within seconds. No surprise there; after all, this was Cairo during the scorching summer heat. Fuad escorted him to an air-conditioned vehicle, a welcome relief because breathing under the hood proved difficult.

By Silverstein's estimation, they rode for ten minutes. Again they stepped into the stifling heat, but the walk outside was short. As was the case from his cell, he could hear jet aircraft not far away. The conditioned air they entered felt cooler than in the car. They continued a short distance and made a right turn. Silverstein felt the movement and sound of an elevator ascending.

Fuad removed the hood. Silverstein squinted, his eyes adjusting to the light. A combination of dark wood, mirrors, and brass exuded elegance. The occasional writing, Arabic, he assumed, was indecipherable to his eyes. He watched as the circular buttons lit up progressively. The elevator came to a smooth halt at the last of them.

The door opened. There was no hallway. They entered directly into a room.

Fuad led the way and pointed to a chair in front of a desk. "Please sit. I will be nearby." He left the room through a doorway to his left.

Silverstein glanced around the large room, which was rather like a corporate office, with a desk and conference table. He had the space to himself and was amazed at the lack of security. At several points during his transport, he imagined that he could have escaped. Even in the building, once Fuad removed his hood, they had been alone. There were no handcuffs, nor was it evident that Fuad carried a weapon. Was he so inconsequential that his escape would mean nothing to them?

Silverstein stood, ostensibly to walk to the window to take in the view. He moved to the right of the desk and glanced down. It wouldn't hurt, for future reference, to have some idea of where he was. Damn! Again, indecipherable Arabic writing. Wait! Not all. *Sphinx Petroleum.*

He continued up to the window and stared outward. Expecting a robust cityscape, Silverstein instead saw only a barren landscape. As he looked off farther into the distance, however, he realized that he had an all-encompassing view of Cairo International Airport.

Silverstein considered the information he had assembled in between the nightmares of last night and realized he had little to go on. Until he'd arrived in Monterey and met the likes of Nicholas—a.k.a. Caliph, Silverstein had concluded—and Francis, he'd had no idea that anyone other than Rafferty, by way of Dickey, had an interest in Kipling. Since then, it hadn't taken a rocket scientist to conclude that foreign interests were involved.

The door through which Fuad had exited opened, and a distinguished-looking man entered. His suit and appearance, particularly an impeccably manicured beard and mustache heavy with twinges of gray, gave a sense of wealth and stature. Silverstein imagined him as someone's kindly uncle or grandfather. "Please have a seat, Dr. Silverstein." He walked to the chair behind the desk.

Silverstein did as he was told. "You know who I am?"

"Oh, yes. Your name has been making the rounds for some time, but I never imagined I'd get the chance to meet you in person."

Making the rounds for some time? "I'm afraid you have me at a disadvantage. I have no idea what you're talking about." He looked his host in the eye. "Who *are* you?"

"It's not in my best interest to give you that information."

Silverstein nodded. "Can you tell me *anything?*"

"The reason you are here in this room is for you to tell me something."

With those words, Silverstein knew that he had guessed right. "You're interested in Caliph."

"That is correct. Do you know where he is?"

"Sir, are you aware that he killed a man and then tried to kill me too?"

His host ignored the question. "I assume you realize that both of them were after the same thing."

"Yes. I figured that out."

His host's voice turned less tolerant. "Again, do you know what happened to Caliph?"

"I'm sorry, but I do not." Silverstein recounted his fight with Caliph in Carmel, his leaving him and his colleague there, and their flight to Mexico and on to Cairo. "Back in Monterey, when Linda and I arrived back at my plane, Aziz told us that Caliph—who was going by the name of Nicholas … you may or may not know that—had called to tell him we were on our way. It seems to me that you should question his partner, the one that Nicholas—I mean Caliph—called Francis. He'll know more than I do."

"I must tell you, Dr. Silverstein, that I hold your life in my hands. It would benefit you to tell me the truth. Listen carefully to my next question. Do you know of anyone who could have kidnapped him?"

Silverstein held his expression in check. He hadn't even considered that possibility. *Son of a bitch! It had to be Lopez.* It was possible that he could have arrived in Monterey after Silverstein and Kipling departed.

"I've told you what I know. Have you considered that he just went off on his own?"

"That's not possible."

Silverstein now had the opening he needed, the underhanded reason for which he had planted the Caliph seed.

"I don't know what happened to your man. My whole concern all along has been for my friend, Linda Kipling."

"She's a unique individual, you know."

Silverstein nodded. "It's taken me a while, but I've figured that out. I honestly cannot help you with Caliph, but I think I have something to offer instead."

Silverstein's captor's eyes widened. "Oh?"

"Tell me if I understand correctly what's going on. You say she's unique. Is that because she has this special gene—a prophecy gene, if you will? Is that correct?"

"Yes."

"Do you think that this gene gives her certain powers?"

"That's what we're going to find out."

"I've worked with Dr. Kipling for more than six years. Although I've sensed that she had premonitions at times, I am convinced that nothing she gains from this gene benefits her. I do not think that her ability could help you."

"That may be true, but our scientists are not convinced that all bearers of this gene, a prophecy gene as you call it, are the same. There may be degrees of premonition."

"Then why not let her go?"

"Two reasons. First, this will be the first time we can actually test for the gene in a human being."

Silverstein saw reason for hope. "You've probably done that already."

"That's correct. The DNA testing is ongoing as we speak."

"What's the second?"

"Although what you say may be true, we need to document her actual abilities, whatever they are. She may have more than what you give her credit for. Have you discussed this with her?"

Damn! He's made a good point, thought Silverstein. Not having broached the subject with her, in retrospect, might have been a mistake. "No, I haven't."

"Then you see my point."

Bad news! That could take years. "I don't know how these things work, but that could take a very long time." Before he said it, Silverstein knew his next statement was lame. "Can't she just tell you that she's had premonitions, or whatever, that have come to pass?"

Silverstein's interrogator stood. "There's no documentation."

Silverstein looked up. "I doubt she would lie to you."

"Dr. Silverstein, do you take me as naive? Do you know how rare this condition is? And you want me to give her up? For us to move forward, we need documented proof that she has any ability at all."

Silverstein could have asked why, but he knew the answer because Weaverman had indirectly alluded to it. The next step in the process was to create a designer gene identical to the prophecy gene Weaverman had discovered. That would cost dearly and take years. You wouldn't make that sort of commitment based upon the unsubstantiated say-so of one person. Nonetheless, Silverstein knew that this line of questioning gave him an opening. He had to act fast. His interrogator was walking away.

Silverstein stammered. "What, what, what if I could provide you the proof you're looking for? What if I could give you documented DNA evidence from someone in the past who could predict the future? Would you then let Linda go?"

The man came to a halt, obviously not expecting such a query. He slowly retraced his steps and leaned forward with two hands on the desk. "How could you possibly do that, Dr. Silverstein?"

Thank God, he had kept the article. Silverstein opened his wallet, removed the newspaper story from Johnstown, Pennsylvania, and handed it across. A moment passed.

"This is all very interesting, but I hardly see how this benefits me."

Silverstein's tone turned severe. "What if I told you that the envelope in which the letter was found has been tested and that the saliva used to seal it contains the prophecy gene? What if I also told you that I can provide you not only that envelope but the original letter? You could then inspect everything for yourself." Silverstein couldn't contain himself. This was his only shot. "If I did this for you, would you release Linda?"

The office fell silent. Only a hint of outside traffic noise permeated the walls and windows of the high-rise. Silverstein's proposal had obviously revealed an unexpected opportunity to his interrogator. He had walked into the room expecting information on Caliph and had received something altogether different. Silverstein kept his gaze direct.

The man standing opposite Silverstein stared back, obviously in thought, and sat down. He brought his right hand to his mouth. "What you've shown me is just a newspaper article. How is it that you, of all people, would have access to such information?"

"Before I even suspected Linda, I was aware of our government's research into this gene. Linda, in fact, gave me this article. I telephoned Peggy Houston, that woman in Johnstown who found the letter." Silverstein pointed to the article. "She forwarded the envelope to a friend of mine at the Smithsonian Institution in Washington, DC. He performed the DNA testing and confirmed the gene, but returned the envelope. She has the envelope and the letter. It's a long story, but I assure you that what I'm saying is true."

More quiet. Silverstein assumed that the bearded one was struggling with himself, unsure of what to do with this new information. The letter and DNA confirmation could save him a lot of time.

Silverstein pressed forward. "Release me now, and I will fly to Johnstown and bring back what I've told you."

The interrogator leaned back in his chair. "What you propose is very interesting, and I'm tempted to take you up on your offer. But there is a problem. I have superiors."

Several beats of time ensued. Silverstein couldn't wait. "Then talk to them."

He shook his head. "I'm sorry." He looked at his watch. "In a little over thirty-one hours from now, Dr. Kipling leaves Egypt, and you'll never see her again."

CHAPTER 51

DEAD MAN FLYING?

Headquarters, Sphinx Petroleum, Cairo, Egypt
30° 05'44"N latitude, 31° 22'60"E longitude
Sunday, 9:00 AM, August 9, 2009

Mohammed Abu Saada sat quietly in his office, pondering the agreement he had struck with the black American some seventy-five minutes earlier. *Victor Mark Silverstein.* He had actually come face-to-face with the man who had single-handedly thwarted their hurricane operation two years earlier. Had Kipling not tied her cooperation to his well-being, he would have been dead by now.

He peered out toward the airport, his eyes drawn to a jumbo jet as it took to the air. He swiveled around to catch the time from the wall clock. Five more minutes until his call to Cleopatra.

Abu Saada hoped he had made the right decision. Could Silverstein be trusted? Could he provide the documentation he promised? Abu Saada sighed. In any event, he had played the odds, choosing to hedge his bets.

Abu Saada had told the truth when he said Kipling would be leaving the country at three tomorrow afternoon. The Blade of the Sinai was nothing if not punctual. The council, as his three superiors called themselves, had made the decision even while Kipling was in the air to Cairo. DNA work would begin immediately upon her arrival, followed by extensive testing outside Egypt at one of the Blade's secure remote locations: one in

Venezuela, a second in Niger, and the third in eastern Turkey. Blade biologists and geneticists had earlier set up shop at their Turkish site to follow up on the Russian mice experiments. It made sense for Kipling to go there.

Still, thirty hours was enough time for Silverstein to fly west, obtain the materials he said he could provide in exchange for Kipling, and return. Abu Saada knew the only way that Silverstein could make the deadline was by using a Blade aircraft. He telephoned Aziz Riad and ordered him to prepare immediately for a return trip across the Atlantic.

Silverstein leaped out of his chair when told that Aziz could be ready in thirty minutes. Fuad hustled him to the plane.

Abu Saada considered the possible outcomes of this gamble. In terms of the Blade's interests, none posed a risk. If Silverstein returned in time with both the envelope and letter, Abu Saada would make the case to the council that they consider Silverstein's materials in exchange for Linda Kipling. Abu Saada had not promised Kipling's release, only that he would try. If Silverstein returned late, events would play out as programmed. There was another possible outcome, and Abu Saada informed Silverstein accordingly. If Silverstein failed to return to Cairo, Abu Saada would order that Kipling be eliminated once her usefulness had run its course.

But what if Silverstein returned with the materials he promised after Kipling had departed? Silverstein would make the case that Abu Saada should convince his bosses to return her. Abu Saada was inclined not to give in, although it would weigh on his conscience to take what Silverstein had to offer and give him nothing in return.

There was another complication. Silverstein had been involved in the deaths of the Ishmael twins. Caliph had made it clear that he wanted revenge. Should Abu Saada sanction the death penalty to satisfy Caliph? Then again, from what Abu Saada knew of the incident, Silverstein's role had been peripheral.

Abu Saada checked the clock. It was time. He mentally subtracted seven hours. It was a little after two in the morning back in Washington, hardly an hour for a U.S. senator to be roaming the streets, but a time he had chosen nonetheless. He took out the list from his top right drawer and dialed the telephone number adjacent to the two-digit identifier, number sixteen: 202-289-9157.

Only a single ring elapsed before he recognized the voice. They exchanged the required word sequences to assure both parties that their exchange was legitimate and without coercion. Because Cleopatra had never attained real fluency in Arabic, the conversation continued in English.

This was no time for idle chitchat. Abu Saada began abruptly but then waited for quiet as he heard what he knew to be the sound of a subway train. "What can I do for you?"

Cleopatra's response was immediate. "Have you located Caliph?"

"No. He and Sidki were planning to fly to Mexico City to catch up with Aziz. At the airport, Caliph disappeared. Sidki searched for some time before giving up."

A hesitation on the American side of the conversation. "You need to know this. I was on the telephone with Caliph when he was at the airport. He called to ask if I would send you a summary of what happened in Monterey. During the call, he just dropped off. That's how I knew he went missing."

Abu Saada reflected on this new information. "Could his cell have—?"

Cleopatra cut him off. "Another man's voice came on the line."

Abu Saada's face contorted, and he clenched his teeth. The worst was true. Caliph had been taken. This was not information he wanted to hear. "Are you in danger?"

"No. I used a throwaway. I'm confident my location was not compromised." Cleopatra continued. "You have Kipling. Is that correct?"

"Yes. This Silverstein fellow as well."

Abu Saada heard frustration. "Why is he still alive? He nearly ruined everything."

"Kipling offered to be cooperative, but only if we didn't harm him. If it means keeping him alive to ensure her assistance for the short term, so be it. But there's more. It's a long story, but he was here in my office this morning. He's offered us something."

"What could he possibly have that would interest you?" Cleopatra's exasperation came through clearly in her question.

"He is convinced he has proof of another gene carrier who lived at the end of the nineteenth century. He says he has DNA documentation, an envelope, which proves this person carried the gene. If true, that would be enough to convince the council to expend the funds to produce the artificial version of the gene."

"So how are you getting this so-called proof?"

"As we speak, Aziz is flying him back to the States."

A pause. "I can't believe this. You've been taken in by a con man. He just wants to save his hide."

"I don't think so. There's no harm in our taking a look."

"Why would he do this for you?"

"He wants Kipling in exchange. He didn't say it, but I think he's in love with her. I led him to believe that if he gave me what he says, I would release her. There is a complication, however. The council has dictated that Kipling be moved to our Turkish site. I told Silverstein he had to return by three tomorrow, before she leaves Cairo."

"And if he makes it, you'd let her go?"

"I don't know. But if we had indisputable proof that the gene sequence could result in clairvoyance, that would save us a lot of time."

"I agree. But even if Silverstein comes through, I recommend you still eliminate him. You don't want that sort of loose end walking around. The government here wants Kipling as much as we do. Don't forget that. We were fortunate to get her first."

Abu Saada paused and then acted impulsively. "By the way, there's another reason why you might want me to follow through with your suggestion."

"What do you mean?"

Abu Saada chose to tell Cleopatra. Together with Caliph, she had delivered Kipling, no small feat. Caliph already knew the truth. She deserved a form of reward. "You don't know this. Silverstein was directly involved in the deaths of your brothers."

Abu Saada waited for a response but heard none. "Are you there? Did you catch that?"

"Yeah, I got it. I ask that you eliminate him. That's what I want."

Abu Saada continued. "Back to what Silverstein promised. You may be able to confirm what he told me."

"What was that?"

"He showed me a newspaper clipping."

"Give me the details. I'll check it out."

Abu Saada read the newspaper article.

"Johnstown, Pennsylvania. That's not far from here. What exactly is Silverstein going to get there?"

"The letter and envelope. But it's the envelope that's vital because it has the DNA from the saliva of the person who sealed it—presumably the clairvoyant."

"When will he arrive?"

Abu Saada counted on his fingers. "I'd guess twelve, thirteen hours from now. They have to refuel twice. If he turns right around, he'll make it back in time. Kipling's scheduled departure has given him incentive."

"You said Aziz is flying Silverstein?"

"That's right, with his copilot."

"Will they land in Johnstown?"

"I presume. He would want to land as close to that … what was it? … some sort of Flood Memorial, as he could."

"Okay, I'm glad we talked. I'll do some digging around. Anything else?"

"That's it. I'll keep you informed. Good-bye."

Abu Saada reset the phone and cursed his impulsiveness. He should never have told Cleopatra about Silverstein's involvement with the twins. She would expect him to follow through on her request.

CHAPTER 52

ALIAS

***Parking lot, Johnstown Flood National Memorial, South Fork,
Pennsylvania, USA***
40°20'59"N latitude, 78°46'14"W longitude
Sunday, 3:25 PM, August 9, 2009

Silverstein slipped the cabby an extra fifty dollars. It could be as much as thirty minutes, he told the driver. He would need a speedy return to the airport. Aziz was tending to the aircraft and would be waiting.

He scanned the long parking lot above the visitor center. Several cars sat near the ramp that descended to the building. A lone vehicle was parked at the far end—probably an employee concerned about his new car.

Silverstein walked to the downhill edge of the lot and took in the vista he should have seen two days earlier. He had read up on the flood disaster after Kipling gave him the newspaper article. Below him was where the dam that held back the waters of Lake Conemaugh—or what the locals called South Fork dam—lay, before that fateful day in May of 1889. And about a mile diagonally across the lake had sat the infamous South Fork Fishing and Hunting Club, where the likes of the Mellons, Carnegies, and Fricks took their leisure. Their culpability in the disaster was never proved in court, and not one penny was collected in damages from the club—even though more than 2,200 people lost their lives because of the organization's negligence in the maintenance of the dam.

Silverstein turned toward the visitor center to his right. He inhaled generous breaths to clear his mind. He had tried to catch some shuteye on the aircraft, but the short bouts of sleep came infrequently. He found himself continually checking his watch or asking Aziz about the winds. Headwinds had slowed their progress. Hopefully, going back, those same winds would repay the time they had stolen from him. To maximize their progress, the flight westward had traced an approximate great circle route, stopping to refuel in Dublin, Ireland, and Halifax, Nova Scotia. Each stop had cost them an hour. Silverstein's step quickened; more than fourteen of his thirty-one hours were gone.

Silverstein checked his cell phone. Fuad had returned it at the aircraft in Cairo. Silverstein told Aziz he would call before he returned. Because his own phone was useless over the ocean, six hours earlier he had borrowed Aziz's satellite phone. He had phoned Peggy Houston to beg her forgiveness for standing her up and asked if she would please meet him today, Sunday. This time, Silverstein promised, he would arrive as advertised. In the earlier message that Silverstein had retrieved at the Monterey airport, Jimmy Travers said he had overnighted the envelope back to Houston. She confirmed that she had it and the original letter as well. He promised an arrival time near four o'clock.

Silverstein's job was simple, to ask Houston to hand over the letter and envelope. He was being presumptuous to assume she would release the documents. If she refused, Silverstein didn't know what he would do.

Silverstein stared at the double doors, told himself to calm down, and entered. Behind the desk to the right stood a man and a woman, uniformed park employees.

"I'm Victor Silverstein. Ms. Houston is expecting me."

Before they had time to react, an attractive middle-aged woman appeared from a door to the rear. "Dr. Silverstein, I'm Peggy Houston." She held out her hand and smiled. "Please follow me." Silverstein observed that she carried a manila folder.

Silverstein was pleased that no time was lost on pleasantries. Every second of conversation was a second lost. They continued down a flight of stairs. He looked to his right and took in the table mock-up of the area and the route that the water had taken to Johnstown. He remembered having read that nearly an hour's time had elapsed from when the dam gave way until the first crest reached the town.

They proceeded through the lower floor into what first appeared to be a maintenance room but which was, in fact, Houston's office. Silverstein noticed the safe immediately, sitting on a workbench to the side. Houston closed the door behind them and pointed to a pair of chairs.

Houston came across as a no-nonsense sort of woman. She initiated the conversation. "What the hell is going on? Wednesday night you got me out of bed, saying it was urgent you see me. You stood me up. Now here you are." She folded her arms.

Although his nerves were near the breaking point, Silverstein controlled his demeanor, all the while knowing that minutes were ticking themselves away. "Ma'am, if I told you everything that's happened to me since then, you wouldn't believe me. I must beg you to trust me now. I am not exaggerating when I tell you that your cooperation is a matter of life and death."

Houston huffed. "Are you suggesting I have not cooperated so far?"

Silverstein hadn't expected this reaction and retreated quickly. "Ms. Houston, you've done everything I've asked. You couldn't have been more cooperative."

Houston backed off, her hackles lowered somewhat. "Your friend, Mr. Travers, basically told me I was a liar. His letter said that the DNA from the saliva showed that the person who licked the envelope was a man, not a woman."

"That's correct, Ms. Houston, but I think I know why. Could I please see the original letter?"

Houston's back straightened. "Listen, since we're about the same age, you call me Peggy, and I'll call you Victor. Agreed? Formalities don't suit me much."

"Yes, ma'am ... I mean Peggy."

Houston stood and opened the folder. She removed two sheets of paper held together by two pieces of cardboard. They curled immediately in her hands. She smoothed them out on the flat wooden top of the workbench, forcing the ends down using glass paperweights. She maneuvered an adjustable fluorescent desk light into position and stepped aside.

Silverstein placed his hands flat on the bench on either side of the letter and, for the first time, read the words of Augusta Schmidt:

Thursday midnight
May 30, 1889
Johnstown, Pennsylvania

My name is Augusta Schmidt, and I am nineteen years old. I live on Jackson Street with my parents, Heinrich and Frieda Schmidt, along with my eighteen-year-old sister, Annabel, and my fourteen-year-old brother, Thompson. Papa is a supervisor at the Cambria Iron Company, and I work with him there on occasion. I have an older half brother, William, who lives in town and is Papa's son, too. His mother died giving birth. He works full time with Papa at Cambria Iron.

If you find this letter—no doubt days or weeks from now—you discovered it in the safe of the Trinity Lutheran Church where Papa is an elder. More importantly, as you read this, my family and I are surely dead, the result of a terrible flood that will destroy our town tomorrow afternoon.

Today I tried to think of some way of tricking my family into leaving town but could think of nothing that would achieve a satisfactory result. I could have told them the truth—what I knew would happen—but they wouldn't have believed me. And besides, I would have had to warn the entire town.

I considered saving myself alone. Tomorrow I could walk across town, climb up the side of the hill, and watch the flood play out in front of me. But Papa always tells me that we must place ourselves in God's hands. For that reason, tomorrow afternoon I will walk to our church and make one final plea to our Lord and Savior. My curses, both of them, make me a freak of nature. I know that I will not be going to heaven. I want to die along with my family. Once my family has left this world, I would not want to live anyway.

The reason I know about the flood is that I have a curse, an ability to see the future. In my lifetime, I have had many visions. The ones that I could verify have all come true. Most of the time I can't predict when my visions will actually play out. But right now, I see the destruction of our town tomorrow.

I once asked our minister in Sunday school if there were people who could predict the future. He said that if there were such a person, he or she was possessed by the devil and would go to hell, as surely as the Lord Jesus Christ stood at the gates of heaven. Knowing that my soul is doomed to an eternity of fire and brimstone, and realizing that if I told my parents they would have driven me from the house, I never brought up the subject again. Rather than take my secret to the grave, I am writing this letter. Because my family will be dead, I can take some comfort in knowing they will avoid the shame of a child condemned to hell.

I see many things in my mind's eye. I see many graves, mine among them, high on a hill above the town, and the town rebuilding itself. I see our country involved in large wars that will kill many. In one of these wars, I see a cloud shaped like a mushroom, and it suffocates everyone and everything in sight.

Sometimes I believe that the things I see are only the product of a vivid imagination. Colored, moving pictures that appear on windows, boxes that talk, and large silver birds that are big enough to carry people. Far into the future, I see two of these birds flying into the Towers of Babel, which fall and kill many people. Most of what I see is so scary that I pray it never comes to pass.

Beyond the silver birds, I see many things I cannot understand. But as consolation for my isolation at this moment in my life, I take comfort in seeing someone, far in the future, searching for me, hoping to find me, thinking that I am someone special. I see him standing at my grave. From what I can make out, he may be the devil, having come to claim his due. With this letter and bottle, I open my soul to the future, leaving a part of myself for posterity. The devil will know what he sees.

Any other relatives that I have are in Germany, far away. I have no other family here, so you needn't look.

I ask only that whoever finds this letter takes a moment to pray for my soul, because I am among the damned.

In Christ's name, I sign this letter in the name I cherish as my own, Augusta Schmidt.

Even though Silverstein's photographic memory had already committed the letter to permanent memory, he reread it. Afterward he stood up and backed away from the desk, his legs trembling. "Peggy, this is amazing." He looked over at the safe. "May I see the bottle the letter came in?"

Houston opened a cabinet and removed a medium-sized, wide-necked bottle sealed with a large cork. "The cork kept the insides dry." With two hands, she passed it across. "Be careful."

Silverstein looked at it closely. "You replaced the cork after you removed the letter?"

"Yes."

Silverstein returned the bottle, also with two hands.

Houston became impatient. "It's time you told *me* something. What is it you know that I don't? Am I being played for a fool?"

"No, you're not. There's a good reason why Travers first questioned this letter." Silverstein explained the puzzle that Jimmy's last voice mail had solved. "Let me explain. As you know, Peggy, men and women have 46 chromosomes, 23 of which come from the father and 23 from the mother. Two of those 46 determine the sex of a child." He pointed his index finger at Houston. "You have two X chromosomes, and I have one X and one Y. If there's a Y chromosome, you automatically have a male child. Augusta's saliva had a Y, which meant for sure that she was a he. But there is something more, and Jimmy didn't see it at first."

He took a breath to slow his delivery. "Occasionally, nature throws in a ringer. When Jimmy looked more closely at the saliva, he saw an extra X chromosome. And by the way, the reason I know this is that my father was a physician, and he once had a patient with this condition. It's called Klinefelter's syndrome. Klinefelter babies aren't that uncommon. One out of every 500 to 1,000 births."

Houston took in every word.

"Many men with the extra X chromosome go through life never even suspecting that they are different in any way. But they are different. Their testicles stay small, and they can't father children. In terms of physical appearance, they are usually taller and rounder, often with fuller breasts and larger hips, female characteristics superimposed on a male body—from the extra female chromosome."

Silverstein paused and pointed to the bench. "This is the first time I've seen the letter, and all of it makes sense now." He scanned the letter in his mind. "Look at the clues. In the first paragraph, Augusta says that she occasionally works with her father at Cambria Iron. That suggests a man. In those days, you wouldn't see women working at such jobs. And listen to her final statement, 'In Christ's name, I sign this letter in the name I cherish as my own, Augusta Schmidt.' I think that Augusta felt he was born a man in a woman's body, or maybe vice versa. Maybe other boys made fun of him. In the mirror, he must have convinced himself of this. Most Klinefelter men don't think this way, by the way, but I can see how it could happen. Whatever Augusta's real name was, I bet you it was a man's name."

Silverstein and Houston stared at each other. Only the hum of air pumped through the ducting broke the silence. Houston spoke. "I can tell you exactly what Augusta's real name was. It was August, the male version of Augusta. That's what threw me off when I went through the records of the dead. I found an August Schmidt but no Augusta. And another thing. The letter has to be legitimate because a forger would not have known that Augusta had a half brother named William. I know that he survived the flood. In fact, I've heard from his descendents."

Silverstein glanced at his watch. Twenty-five minutes had elapsed. "I must—"

Before he could get in the next word, Houston followed up. "So if the letter is legitimate, what does that mean about Augusta? Do you think she was a clairvoyant?"

Silverstein knew the answer because Jimmy Travers had also completed the test for the prophecy gene, and it had been positive. He decided to hedge; it would give him a better bargaining position. "I think so, but I need the letter and the envelope to go forward. I can't go into all of it now, but it is very important. I beg you to give them to me."

Houston stood up, walked to the desk, and removed the weights from the two sheets, which she carefully placed between the two pieces of cardboard and returned to the folder. She handed it over. "I trust you, Victor." She smiled and nodded.

Finally! Silverstein let out an internal sigh. "That's fantastic. I promise you that you've made the right decision. If I could have Augusta's envelope, I'll be on my way."

Houston's face contorted. "The envelope?" Her eyes narrowed. "I assumed you knew that your assistant—Linda Kipling, is it?—picked it up two hours ago."

.

CHAPTER 53

BLACK WIDOW

Johnstown Flood National Memorial, South Fork, Pennsylvania, USA
40° 20'59"N latitude, 78° 46'17"W longitude
Sunday, 3:54 PM, August 9, 2009

Silverstein's eyes bulged, and his left hand with the folder involuntarily flew upward. "What did you just say?"

Houston drew back, surprised at his response. "I said that your assistant came by to pick up the envelope. She told me you had sent her on ahead. Did I do something wrong?"

Silverstein spun around, faced the door, and dropped his head to his chest. *Besides Cairo, who else knew he was coming here?* He had spoken to no one. He turned back to Houston. "I'm sorry, but something is very wrong here. What did this Linda Kipling look like?"

"Tall, blond hair, late thirties maybe, glasses, well dressed, gray-green suit."

"Anything else?"

"I think her hair was a wig because she had red eyebrows. She has a mole on her right cheek. That's not Linda?"

Why didn't she take the letter, too? "Peggy, did she ask for the letter?"

"No, just the envelope. Are you sure that's not Linda?"

Silverstein shook his head. "Linda's not even in the coun—" The electronic tone of his cell phone cut him off.

He snatched the phone from his pocket and checked the caller ID. *Caller unknown.*

"Silverstein here."

Columbia Pines Lodge, Johnstown, Pennsylvania, USA
40° 18'40"N latitude, 78° 49'35"W longitude
Sunday, 3:56 PM, August 9, 2009

"This is Linda Kipling."

"Like hell you are! You've got something that doesn't belong to you."

"That I do, Dr. Silverstein. But I did leave you the letter. Wasn't that nice of me? Would you care to join me? I'll consider returning your property in exchange for some information."

"Where?"

Thurston smiled and felt dampness form between her legs. This always happened when she had powerful men in positions of weakness.

"Tell your cabby to take you to the Columbia Pines Lodge. It's by the airport. He'll know where it is. Room 315."

"I'm on my way."

Thurston hung up the motel phone and stared out at the hills, vivid with the greens of summer. Pennsylvania truly was a beautiful state. She had arrived in Johnstown in the early afternoon, an optimum time for visiting Peggy Houston at the Flood Memorial. What with traffic out of Washington, it had taken nearly four hours to make the 180-mile drive. Her conversation with Uncle Mohammed had ended at 2:20 in the morning. She returned to her condominium for some sleep. Complete with her wig and the spectacles she rarely wore, she then began the long drive north—but not before a stop at a pharmacy to purchase a third, smaller item.

She planned her strategy on the way. Immediately upon arrival in Johnstown, she scouted out the airport and rented a motel room there. Next, she needed to acquire the precious envelope. Houston was surprisingly easy to manipulate. Acting as the submissive, loyal assistant she imagined Kipling to be, Thurston convinced Houston that Silverstein needed it before his visit. With that job done, she had two choices, to wait at the motel or the Flood Memorial. She chose the latter.

Thurston had parked in the corner of the parking lot, at a distance from the visitor center, and waited. It took a while. The tall black man arriving by taxi was easy to spot. Once he left her sight, she initiated the second stage of her plan. From a pay phone, she dialed Aziz's satellite phone number. He answered on the second ring.

She was taking a chance in contacting Aziz. Her cover was so deep that only Uncle Mohammed and his superiors knew of her exalted position within the government of the United States of America. Although their paths had not crossed since her marriage to Thurston, she remembered Aziz fondly from her teenage years. Their relationship as cousins notwithstanding, it was he whom she had chosen to take her virginity. At the age of fourteen, she had decided that this medically defined condition was not worth keeping. She later wondered why she'd waited so long.

Thurston called Aziz for two reasons. First, she figured that if Silverstein had a cell phone, Aziz would know the number. A simpler tactic would have been to leave a message for Silverstein with Houston. But such an approach lacked the dramatic impact that Thurston was looking for just now. Second, in the Blade's line of work, where violence occasionally had its place, Aziz had once told her that he kept a variety of weapons aboard his aircraft. She had never needed, or wanted, a gun for personal protection. Given the short notice, it made no sense to risk a gun shop. In this country, they asked too many questions.

Although surprised to see her show up at his aircraft, Aziz acquiesced to her requests. As for a weapon, he showed her what he had. She chose one that seemed particularly suitable for her intended scheme. He promised to forget he had ever seen her.

Once Thurston had from Aziz what she needed, she returned to the motel to make her call.

*　　　*　　　*　　　*

Houston stood there, nonplussed. "I take it that I gave the envelope to the wrong person."

"It's not your fault. There was no way for you to know." Silverstein turned to leave but stopped. He owed Houston big-time. "Peggy, you've been wonderful, and I thank you."

"Promise you'll talk to me after this is over?"

"I promise."

Silverstein sprinted from the building. Visitors admiring the flood displays stepped aside and stared at the black man running at full speed. Probably because Houston followed Silverstein up to the main level, the two park rangers at the desk chose not to interfere with her visitor's sudden getaway.

As he exited the doors, Silverstein glanced at his watch. More minutes had vanished.

Fortunately, he knew he could trust his patient cabby who sat waiting. Silverstein jumped into the front seat this time and grimaced at the woman's attempt at humor. "You scared the shit out of me when I saw you hightailing it this way. Tell me you didn't rob the Flood Memorial."

"Columbia Pines Lodge. Do you know it?"

"Yes, sir."

Silverstein opened his wallet and handed the woman one fifty, and then a second. "I want you to drive like hell. Do you understand me?"

"You're the boss."

Silverstein fastened his seat belt barely in time before the cabby executed a tire-squealing U-turn out of the parking lot. Thirteen minutes later, Silverstein hopped from the car but not before handing the cabby another fifty. "Wait, please."

"You're the boss."

*   *   *   *

From her third-floor window that faced the entry to the motel, Thurston watched the yellow taxicab screech to a halt. For the second time that day she watched Silverstein step from the cab, this time from the front seat. He seemed a taller man than she had perceived earlier from a distance.

Before closing the drapes in both rooms, Thurston checked to make sure all was in order. Her eyes would need a minute to adjust to the low light. When Silverstein entered, he would see objects, but the details would be fuzzy.

Room 315 was in fact a suite, with two entry doors, 315A and 315B. Walking down the hallway toward the suite from the direction of the lobby, one encountered 315A first; inside was a sort of living room with an easy chair, sleeper sofa, and television, and a bathroom through a door to the left. To the right, through double doors that one could lock to make two individual living areas, one gained entry to a bedroom accompanied by a second bath. A king-size bed dominated the far wall. A chest of drawers fronted the hallway wall to the left of the second entry door.

Thurston opened the double doors wide. She intended that Silverstein enter through the living room door, 315A. She planned to stand by the double doors and interrogate him from there. The envelope that Silverstein so desperately wanted, the weapon that Aziz had given her, and the item she had purchased waited in the top drawer of the chest.

Thurston relished the moments that were about to unfold. She hadn't yet decided what she would do once Silverstein gave her the information she wanted. She would make up her mind as her whim dictated.

A knock on the living room door drew her attention.

*   *   *   *

There was obvious risk in meeting this stranger on her terms. Silverstein decided to take no chances and made a stop at the front desk. The receptionist was friendly and cooperative. He took the elevator to the third floor, located the room, and knocked. He waited a few seconds and tried a second time. He would soon meet Linda's impostor and retrieve the envelope. What information could she possibly want?

He heard a voice beyond the door. "Come in, Dr. Silverstein."

The light from the hallway allowed Silverstein an outline view of the room. A chair and sofa to the left, covered windows straight ahead, a TV to the right, and a large doorway to the far right. He saw no one.

"Close the door and sit down." The voice came from the right beyond the large door.

Silverstein took a seat in the easy chair after closing the door. Although the draperies allowed some leakage around the edges, he could see almost nothing. "I don't know who you are, but I'm in sort of a hurry. Give me the envelope, and I'll tell you whatever you want to know."

Silverstein discerned movement and saw a figure by the doorway. He could see no details.

"I'm in no particular hurry. We can take our time."

"You may not be, but I am. Please, how is it I can help you?"

"Stand up. I want to get a good look at you. I'm sorry you can't see me well yet."

Silverstein stood as ordered. Even though he was at a disadvantage, he was becoming pissed. And when that happened, he couldn't always control his mouth. "I can see you just fine. You're tall and dressed in a gray-green suit. Your glasses and blond hair suit you well, but your red eyebrows tell me you're a natural redhead." He gestured with his hands. "You're right, though, the light is a bit dim. Is that a mole on your right cheek?"

*   *   *   *

Son of a bitch! Was he trying to piss her off? There's no way he could make out those details in this light. He was simply reciting the description Houston had given him. Well, she could play hardball as well. "I'd be careful, Dr. Silverstein. If you want the envelope, I suggest you treat me with some respect."

Thurston took time to admire the fine physical specimen standing in front of her. Over six feet tall, well proportioned, muscular, with a strong chest and narrow hips. Probably hung, too. Come to think of it, she had never bedded a black man. Would he be as big as stories made them out to be?

"I'm sorry, but I'm in a hurry here." A pause. "What's to prevent me from walking across the room and taking what's mine?"

A risk taker, huh? Two can play that game. "There's no stopping you. Come on. I have no weapon, if that's what you're getting at. But I'm not so stupid that I'd have the envelope here in the room with me."

Thurston stood her ground as Silverstein came closer. Her eyes had now adapted well enough to discern his features and form clearly. *Damn!* Her body shivered, and she felt her nipples harden. *Control yourself! This is not the time. Not yet, anyway.*

"You said you needed information. Here I am. What do you want?"

"In 2007 you murdered two men in Monterey, California. I want to know how and why."

*   *   *   *

Silverstein had imagined that Kipling's impersonator wanted information about the real Kipling. The last thing he expected was this. "What the hell are you talking about? I didn't murder anybody! Who told you this?"

"I understand it was near where you live."

"Are you referring to the accident? Yes, two men died, but I had nothing to do with it. They ran into a road grader, for God's sake."

Recalling that terrible day still made him shake. He could remember staring into the rearview mirror of his Porsche and watching the black Mercedes slide sideways into the grader. He had barely escaped death himself. What possible connection could this seemingly well-bred, English-speaking woman have with that horrible event?

"So are you telling me you weren't responsible?"

"You tell me. I arrived home to discover that two men had broken into my house. I didn't even have time to get out of my car. They shot at me as I backed out the driveway. Then they chased me. That's all there is to it. I never did find out who they were. Do you know?"

*   *   *   *

These details were new to Thurston. She wondered whether Uncle Mohammed knew them. But from what Silverstein had told her, it didn't change the outcome or her sense of his responsibility. Silverstein would like her to believe those fatalities resulted from nothing more than a traffic accident. No matter who was chasing whom, Silverstein was responsible for the deaths of her Ishmael half brothers.

Accordingly, Silverstein's account only supported her earlier decision. From the moment she had concluded her conversation with Uncle Mohammed this morning, she decided she would avenge her brothers' deaths. The decision rested only in the method that would cause Silverstein the most pain and anguish. She briefly considered killing him but decided it wasn't worth the risk. Too many years and too much effort had gone into obtaining her position. Uncle Mohammed could handle that unpleasantness. He had the resources to chase Silverstein to kingdom come. Besides, he'd promised her as much this morning.

No need to get her hands dirty. She had a better plan. She would have her revenge, and her strategy meshed nicely with her physical condition. She couldn't wait any longer.

Silverstein gestured with his hands. "Can I please have the envelope? I've given you what you wanted. We had a deal."

The thought of what would happen now made her body tingle. Sex was always more satisfying to Thurston when it involved absolute control. A dab of humiliation added spice.

She closed the distance between them. She then removed her suit jacket and threw it into the bedroom. Next, starting from the top, she unbuttoned her blouse. She had almost reached the third button when Silverstein stepped back, and she heard his delicious response. Her excitement proved unbearable.

"What the hell are you doing?"

Without reacting, but watching his eyes for hints of interest, she continued with the buttons, finally pulling out the shirttail to complete the process. She removed the blouse and threw it behind her. "What does it look like I'm doing?"

Silverstein was clearly out of his league. "Are you out of your mind? You're kidding yourself if you think I find you attractive. Just give me the envelope, and we'll call it even."

By now, Thurston had reached behind her back. She undid her bra, leaned slightly forward, and ever so slowly lowered it away from her breasts. She smiled when she caught his eyes checking out her luscious nipples. *Wait 'til you get even lower, lover boy.* She unbuttoned her skirt and let it fall to the floor. Only her panties remained.

She had him going now. He was breathing more heavily. His chest moved up and down faster, and this excited Thurston even more. She glanced down to check for the bulge. It wouldn't be long now, she thought.

The look on Silverstein's face changed suddenly from confusion to anger. Thurston considered the latter to be a scrumptious complement to passion. He grabbed her shoulders, squeezed hard, and shook her. "Give me the envelope, goddamn you!"

Thurston responded to Silverstein's grip. It felt good. She reached down with her cupped right hand and pressed between his legs until she had his scrotum firmly in her hand. She looked him squarely in the eyes and gave no quarter. "Give me what *I* want, and then you can have your fucking envelope."

Silverstein wrested her hand away and pushed her back.

*   *   *   *

Silverstein couldn't believe this was happening. He wondered briefly if he had entered the *Twilight Zone*, where characters found themselves in bizarre, often supernatural, settings. Everything fit. Unfortunately, Silverstein knew this situation had nothing to do with make-believe.

This nearly naked woman was blackmailing him. She wanted sex in exchange for something he desperately needed to save his colleague and friend, Linda Kipling. But how could he do something so despicable? If he did as she asked, he would lose all self-respect. Would he be able to look himself in the mirror tomorrow?

Silverstein turned and walked to the door.

*   *   *   *

He's leaving? Thurston couldn't believe her eyes. Her charms had never failed her. Was he gay?

Time to up the ante. Even more than what her body craved right now, she needed to see his reaction afterward when she pulled the plug.

"If you *ever* want to see your girlfriend again, I'd recommend you not walk away from me."

*   *   *   *

Silverstein stopped short of the door. *How the hell? She not only knows of Linda's existence but her predicament as well.*

Silverstein couldn't take it any more. He would ask for God's forgiveness later. Kipling's future, and possibly her very existence, rested on his returning the envelope to Cairo.

Silverstein's nerves and body exploded with rage. He turned, raced the few feet back to the woman, placed both hands on the sides of her torso, yanked her off the floor, carried her a few feet into the bedroom, and tossed her through the air onto the bed. In seconds, he removed his clothes and advanced. She had already removed her panties and glasses and was waiting—with a smirk-like smile on her face he knew he would remember for a long time.

*   *   *   *

Thurston's back arched one more time as the vibration in her thighs sent her into delirious climax. Silverstein had been slower and achieved climax in time to match her second orgasm. He rolled off to the side. For a moment, neither moved.

With her passion satiated and reality bearing down, Thurston suddenly leaped from the bed, flew to the chest of drawers, and opened the top drawer. She removed Aziz's weapon and held it straight in front of her. Aziz had given her rudimentary instructions on its use.

Silverstein sat up in bed and looked across in the dim light. "Now you're going to shoot me?"

"I hope not. Just stay put while I get dressed. Your envelope is here in this drawer. I'll give it to you when I leave. I don't particularly want you chasing after me. Agreed?"

Silverstein did as he was told. Thurston dressed and checked to make sure she hadn't left anything behind. Anything she had touched she would take with her. Finally, she stood by the bedroom door and smiled back at her short-term lover. She could scarcely contain her anticipation.

"Okay, this is it. Are you ready?"

"Ready for what? Where's my envelope?"

Her weapon now in her left hand, Thurston reached into the top drawer and removed the ancient envelope Houston had given her. She held it up for Silverstein to see. "Is this what you came for?"

Thurston wavered. She knew what she was about to do was wrong and that Uncle Mohammed would be furious. Her impulsiveness could get her into trouble, but she didn't care. Revenge against Silverstein was more important to her now. Watching him fall apart when he realized he had lost any chance to save his dear Linda would be elegantly gratifying.

She transferred the envelope to her left hand, holding it between the butt of the gun and her palm. She then reached into the drawer to remove the butane lighter she had purchased at the drugstore. She lit the flame and held it to the base of the envelope.

*   *   *   *

Silverstein could not believe what he was seeing and reacted without thinking. Still naked, he leaped across the bed to reach the envelope before it was consumed by flame. Unfortunately, he hadn't even cleared the bed on the opposite side when he saw two thin wires eject from the weapon and strike him on the upper half of his torso. It hadn't been that long ago that he'd seen a similar-looking weapon. The yellow stripes were the give-away.

The darts at the ends of the wires embedded themselves in Silverstein's chest, sending fifty thousand volts of electricity flowing from the Taser into his body. He convulsed to the floor in front of his attacker. His body writhed and jerked for what seemed minutes. He thought he was going to die.

CHAPTER 54

DEVIL WITH A BLUE SHIRT ON

Columbia Pines Lodge, Johnstown, Pennsylvania, USA
40°18'40"N latitude, 78°49'35"W longitude
Sunday, 4:46 PM, August 9, 2009

The convulsions finally abated. On his stomach, sprawled naked on the floor, Silverstein raised his head and immediately lowered it again. He endured several waves of nausea. At the same time, he felt liquid and a stinging sensation on his chest.

The room was quiet and dark. His assailant was long gone. He lifted himself to his hands and knees, waited a moment, and trusted his legs to lift him upright. As soon as he stood up, they wavered and gave way. He tried again. This time he was able to guide himself to the bed instead of the floor. He had once watched a demonstration video of a volunteer shot by a Taser. Silverstein now appreciated the full effect of the device.

He crawled to the head of the bed and turned on the bedside light. He looked down to determine the reason for his stinging discomfort. Two dart-like projectiles, about six inches apart, were wedged into the skin of his upper chest. Blood oozed. His eyes followed the two wires that ended at the base of the chest of drawers. Ever so carefully, he removed the darts and flung them to the floor in disgust.

Silverstein sucked in deep breaths to will himself back to a functioning human being and to relieve the vertigo. He leaned over and cried. He was ashamed at what he had done and even more angry with himself for being duped so badly. He couldn't help but look at his watch. He had fifteen hours left to save Kipling—but he had failed. He lowered his hands and looked to the right. The ash remnants of the envelope lay scattered on the carpet.

Sensing that he once again had his wits about him, Silverstein tested his legs. He could now function. He was down but not out. His clothes lay on the carpet where he had dropped them. He stepped gingerly, retrieved them, and dressed. He opened the draperies and peered outside. His cabby had not abandoned him. He scanned both rooms to see if his assailant had left anything behind. Except for the muddled bed clothing, the room looked clean. The top drawer in the chest of drawers was open and empty.

Within another minute, he felt more like himself. He entered the hallway with a brisk walk that transitioned to a jog. He stopped at the front desk to retrieve Houston's folder that contained Augusta Schmidt's letter.

Silverstein jumped into the front seat. The surprised cabby took in his general appearance and stared at his shirt. She did a double take. "What the hell hap—?"

Blood had seeped through both his underwear and blue shirt from one of the wounds. He cut her off. "Don't ask, please. Don't even ask."

Silverstein took out his wallet. He still had plenty left. He removed two fifties and handed them across.

The cabby nodded. "Two fifties mean you want me to drive like hell."

"You learn fast."

"Where to now?"

"Back to the Flood Memorial."

"You're the boss."

Johnstown Flood National Memorial, South Fork, Pennsylvania, USA
40° 20'59"N latitude, 78° 46'14"W longitude
Sunday, 5:12 PM, August 9, 2009

The taxicab made good time and squealed to a halt. Silverstein handed across another fifty. No words were exchanged. They knew each other well by now.

Silverstein ran to the door. It was locked. They had closed at five. *Please, God, let Peggy still be here!* He banged hard on the door and, to his relief, the female ranger appeared. As she opened the door, she noticed the blood and pointed.

"Just a scratch. Is Peggy still here?"

"Victor, you're back?" Houston appeared from the back office when she heard the commotion.

Silverstein reached across for her hand. "Thank God, you're here. Could we go downstairs again? Please!"

"Of course."

He led the way with a brisk walk. Houston opened the door to her office, and they returned to their earlier seats.

Houston just then noticed his condition. "Victor, you're bleeding."

Silverstein waved his hands. "Please, I don't have much time."

"What is it?"

"I think there's more to Augusta Schmidt's letter than meets the eye. I've been rereading it in my mind ever since I left."

Silverstein started to open the folder when Houston held up her left hand, while her right hand opened a drawer. "Those sheets can't take any more abuse. Here's a photocopy."

Silverstein looked at the second of the two sheets and motioned. "Look at this paragraph." He read it aloud.

> *Beyond the silver birds, I see many things I cannot understand. But as consolation for my isolation at this moment in my life, I take comfort in seeing someone, far in the future, searching for me, hoping to find me, thinking that I am someone special. I see him standing at my grave. From what I*

can make out, he may be the devil, having come to claim his due. With this letter and bottle, I open my soul to the future, leaving a part of myself for posterity. The devil will know what he sees.

Silverstein stared at Houston. "Do you see what I see?"

"Victor, you've lost me. Augusta knows she's unique. She's leaving the letter that she considers a part of herself. What else is there?"

"Before that. She says she sees someone searching for her." Silverstein pointed. "Look here: 'From what I can make out, he may be the devil.'"

"So?"

"She says, 'From what I can make out.' Look at me, Peggy. I'm black. Back in 1889, how many African-Americans do you think lived here? I doubt there were many. Can't you imagine that for a young girl who might never have seen one, a vision of a black man could be interpreted as the devil? Not so far-fetched, do you think?"

Houston's face became noticeably pale. "Well I'll be goddamned."

"But Peggy, that isn't what brought me back here. It's the last part." He read it again. "With this letter and bottle, I open my soul to the future, leaving a part of myself for posterity. The devil will know what he sees."

"Go on."

Silverstein elaborated. "Augusta doesn't just say that with this letter I open my soul to the future. She says, 'With this letter and bottle.' And then, to top it off. 'The devil will know what he sees.'" He stopped to let it sink in. "Peggy, can I please see the bottle again?"

It took a few seconds for his words to register. She retrieved the bottle and handed it over.

Silverstein lifted the corked container toward the ceiling, in the direction of the fluorescent lights above. Holding the glass container upright, he saw nothing. He then turned it ninety degrees so that the side of the bottle paralleled the floor. He rotated it slowly. When he saw it, his legs quaked and nearly failed him. *The devil will know what he sees.*

He lowered the bottle and held it for Houston to see. "Do you see it, Peggy? Can you see the two strands of hair?"

CHAPTER 55

STUPOR

On approach, Runway 05R, Cairo International Airport, Cairo, Egypt
Monday, 2:25 PM, August 10, 2009

Silverstein peered out the port window and recognized the cityscape they had departed some twenty-nine hours earlier. He stepped to the other side. An excellent view of the city. Aziz's voice resonated over the PA system. He had called ahead to alert Fuad, who would be waiting to provide transport.

There had been little conversation with Aziz on the return trip. Silverstein decided it was not in his best interest to explain all that had occurred in Johnstown, or that he had discovered something even more persuasive than the prized envelope that Abu Saada was expecting.

Silverstein glanced at his watch for the thousandth time. They had made excellent time on the return trip, with tailwinds cutting a full sixty minutes from their flight west the previous day. He would make it in time.

Silverstein allowed himself a brief smile. Everything that could go wrong had, but he had come through. Notwithstanding the humiliation he had experienced at the hands of Kipling's impostor, Silverstein felt vindicated. He had deciphered Augusta's letter puzzle, and the two strands of hair had been the prize, far superior to the saliva from the envelope. Following his discussion with Travers, Silverstein had surfed the Net and learned a thing or two about hair DNA. Rather than cut the hairs from her head, Augusta had pulled each hair out by the root, thus contributing its individual root ball. By doing so, she had provided a robust set of DNA— even better to confirm the existence of the prophecy gene.

On the seat beside him lay Houston's folder that contained Augusta's letter. Dating the paper to confirm its age would add proof that the writer was legitimate. He had stored Augusta's hair inside his wallet. Back at the Flood Memorial, he had fashioned a tiny envelope to store the priceless strands. Fuad's boss, whatever his name was, would be pleased indeed. It was a win-win situation. Silverstein had upheld his end of the bargain. Through trial and tribulation, as the Scriptures say, Silverstein had persevered. The forty minutes remaining would provide ample time to drive to the offices of Sphinx Petroleum, lay out his treasure, and secure Kipling's release.

As Silverstein had come to appreciate, Aziz did a fine job of landing. Silverstein scanned the tarmac from both sides of the aircraft as Aziz taxied to his private corner of the airfield. Silverstein searched for Fuad's car. Yes, there it was, and there was Fuad. He couldn't make them out, but there were other passengers in his vehicle.

Both Aziz and his copilot remained forward with the cabin door open. The jet aircraft taxied to a stop and, with Aziz's nod, Silverstein opened the hydraulically activated hatch. He was about to descend the steps when Fuad appeared and motioned him back inside.

Silverstein was excited. "We've got to get a move on."

Fuad entered the cabin, frowned, and displayed the hood that Silverstein had earlier been forced to wear for his commutes.

Silverstein nodded. "I understand. Let's get going, please."

Fuad lowered the hood, and all turned black. He waited for Fuad to guide him off the plane. Instead, without warning, Silverstein felt two sets of hands grab his wrists and force his arms behind his back. He heard and felt metal handcuffs applied immediately.

"What's going on? I won't try to escape, I assure you."

No reply.

Silverstein began to panic. He had naively assumed that their agreement was sacrosanct.

In the next seconds, Silverstein felt himself being pushed backward into a seat. Next, a strap or other restraint immobilized his lower legs.

"What the hell, Fuad? Aziz! Help me! Your boss is expecting me. I have what he wants."

What was going on? Did they think he had failed in his quest for the envelope?

What was that? A sharp jab into his left arm. It was becoming hard to breathe inside the hood, and his mind was going woozy. He had to let them know he had the strands of hair.

"Please, I have what you want. I have the hai, hai—." Silverstein spit to clear his mouth. It felt like cotton, and he couldn't enunciate.

Finally, the mask came off, and he could breathe. "I ha, ha, ha." He shook his head, trying desperately to clear the stupor spreading through his head. The words wouldn't come, and he was losing consciousness. *I must let them know. I must! I have to save Linda.*

Consciousness was leaving him, and he had trouble holding his head upright. The best he could do now was move his lips, but nothing came out.

Is that you? Silverstein's eyes rose slightly, and he saw Kipling enter the aircraft and rush toward him, kneeling at his feet. "What have you done to him?" she asked.

Silverstein closed his eyes and fell into a deep sleep. The last sound he heard was the intense whine of jet engines on takeoff.

CHAPTER 56

SPOOK

Headquarters, Sphinx Petroleum, Cairo, Egypt
30° 05'44"N latitude, 31° 22'60"E longitude
Monday, 2:38 PM, August 10, 2009

Mohammed Abu Saada, fourth in command within the Blade hierarchy, lowered his phone to its cradle and cursed his earlier decision. Although not a religious man, he considered himself moral and of impeccable integrity. He knew he had done wrong. If there was a God and a hell, he had added one more check mark on the negative side of his ledger.

Silverstein had returned to Cairo as promised. According to Aziz, who had witnessed his takedown in the aircraft after landing, Silverstein made a valiant attempt to explain that he had completed his end of the bargain. Abu Saada ordered Fuad to confiscate the letter and envelope from his person. In Turkey, they would handle Silverstein as deemed appropriate. Kipling's demand that Silverstein be kept alive would likely spare his life for a few more weeks. But once Kipling's usefulness had been expended, so would Silverstein's life.

Blade scientists had reported some initial findings. DNA results from Kipling's blood confirmed that she possessed the gene sequence that made her a unique human being. However, the standard tests to ascertain her ability to infer symbols displayed in an adjacent room hidden from her view produced results no better than chance. Brain scans using an MRI (which a few years back had been proven superior to traditional lie detectors) reassured Blade scientists she had not tried to deceive them.

From detailed interviews, Kipling admitted to occasional visions, most of which had come true. However, she could never foresee them coming, nor were they regular. From her experience, she stated that the interval between occurrences could be as short as minutes or as long as years.

With this information, Blade scientists prepared for the next phase, during which they planned to use every scan known to humankind to probe her body and brain. Blade scientists intended to observe and document any physical or mental changes that accompanied her visions. That, together with the letter and envelope from Johnstown, would be enough to convince Blade bean counters that work should begin on the creation of an artificial gene to reproduce this trait.

Some aspects of this mission had exceeded expectations. On her first assignment since she had ascended to her senatorial position, Cleopatra had proved her mettle. She had made them aware of U.S. interest in the rogue gene and then guided Caliph to Kipling. Silverstein's delivery of critical physical evidence from the teenage girl of the nineteenth century had been gravy. Unfortunately, from Abu Saada's perspective, Caliph's disappearance outweighed these positives. Had he been careless, or worse, foolish? Abu Saada knew him to be headstrong. Had government agents in America apprehended him? If so, could they make him talk? Impossible, thought Abu Saada. Caliph was tough and would die before giving away any of the Blade's secrets. In that regard there was no concern.

Abu Saada flinched at the sound, his nerves taut. He squinted toward the telephone. The fourth light from the left meant that the call originated from his secretary on the ground floor. Yusif Heikal, a male subordinate, had served him faithfully for more than twenty years. In light of the gravity of today's activities, Abu Saada had asked that his schedule remain clear. Neither Aziz nor Fuad would call through the switchboard. They had his direct number.

"Yes, Yusif, what is it?"

Heikal's voice sounded hesitant, unusual compared to his normal, forceful tone. "Sir, you have a visitor."

"Yusif, I told you to clear today's schedule."

"Sir, a gentleman just walked in and asked for you directly."

"Who is he?"

Abu Saada tried to make out Heikal's words, and another's, in the background.

"Sir, he told me to tell you that his name is Hector Lopez and that he works for the American Central Intelligence Agency."

CHAPTER 57

REQUITAL

Headquarters, Sphinx Petroleum, Cairo, Egypt
30°05'44"N latitude, 31°22'60"E longitude
Monday, 2:50 PM, August 10, 2009

Over the course of his twenty-some year career, Hector Rodriguez Lopez had occasionally found himself in tight and dangerous situations. In those instances, he had worked under the auspices of the Central Intelligence Agency. Unlike the fictional James Bond, whose double zero designation gave him considerable authority to act on his own, including a license to kill, Lopez had no such official power. Still, the Agency had backed him on those occasions when situations turned south. Today, August 10, 2009, was different. He would have no official sanction. He had acted on his own.

At five o'clock the previous afternoon, Lopez had boarded a Delta flight to Cairo from JFK Airport. Three hours earlier, Marc Miller had driven him to National Airport in Washington, DC, for the short flight to New York. Three hours before that, Lopez had written his leave slip. As far as the CIA was concerned, he was going on vacation. His superiors at Foggy Bottom had not approved today's operation, nor would they have if he had asked.

To protect Miller, Lopez chose not to divulge his itinerary or plan. It hardly mattered. Once their temporary guest, whose name they now knew to be Caliph Ishmael, had spilled his guts under the diabolically clever hand of Dr. Philip Sampson, Miller could read Lopez's mind without benefit of brain surgery, retrograde amnesia, or hypnotism. Miller understood that Lopez wanted desperately to repay his debt to Silverstein. An opportunity had presented itself.

If Lopez's plan succeeded and he returned to Washington—not a foregone conclusion—he told Miller he would apprise him of what happened. The astute Miller agreed but pointed out that Lopez needed him for at least one part of his plan. Lopez laughed at Miller's insight and acquiesced.

Until Ishmael's awareness caught up with itself during hypnosis, he had willingly divulged who he was, why he had gone to Monterey, and various other pieces of useful information—including the Cairo address of his superior, Mohammed Abu Saada. Lopez had the pertinent information he needed. He knew that Ishmael's organization was actively involved in researching the prophecy gene. They had discovered that Linda Kipling possessed the gene and had come to the United States to kidnap her. Ishmael was unaware that Silverstein and Kipling had arrived back in Cairo. Lopez had deduced that fact from Ishmael's plans—and by tracking Sidki's Delta chip to Mexico City and then on across the Atlantic.

"Mr. Abu Saada will see you." The male secretary still had a look of incredulity. Greeting a Latino walk-in who claimed to work for the most powerful intelligence service in the world was not a common occurrence. "Take the elevator to the eleventh floor."

Lopez approached the elevator with nothing in hand, either suitcase or briefcase. He was not surprised when a fit-looking young man intercepted him and patted him down. Except for a satellite cell phone, Lopez carried nothing—not even identification, having stored his luggage and all personal papers, including his passport, in an airport locker. Except for the cell phone, Lopez passed muster for the elevator ride.

When the door opened, Lopez entered, followed by his escort. Looking across a large, elegant office, Lopez observed a bearded man sitting at a desk. Lopez assumed he had come face-to-face with Ishmael's boss. Ishmael had disclosed that Abu Saada held a significant position within the Blade of the Sinai. In fact, he revealed that it was Abu Saada who had authorized him and Sidki to seize Linda Kipling. Silverstein's involvement had been peripheral and unexpected.

Abu Saada motioned Lopez toward a chair. For an awkward moment, tension and uncertainty held thick in the air. Lopez could only imagine the disparate thoughts going through Abu Saada's mind. Foremost among them would be these: how did this stranger from the United States know Abu Saada, and worse, how had he found him? Lopez's handler relinquished the cell phone to Abu Saada, received a few words in return, presumably in Arabic, and left the room.

A ripple of fear shot down Lopez's spine. A significant impediment to his strategy would exist if Abu Saada spoke no English. He breathed easier when Abu Saada's first words, although thickly accented, made sense to Lopez. "How may I be of assistance? Mr. Lopez, is it?"

His goal was not to create animosity. "Forgive me, please. I apologize for barging in on you like this. I can imagine how I would feel if you did the same to me."

Abu Saada leaned forward, placed his hands flat on the desk, and then folded them, still probably trying to understand the significance of this visit since his secretary had called moments earlier. He unfolded his hands and gestured. "May I offer you some coffee or tea?"

Lopez was thirsty and responded instinctively. "Thank you. Tea would be nice. I didn't drink as much water on the flight over as I should have."

Abu Saada lifted his phone and placed the order.

Seconds of silence elapsed before Lopez initiated the exchange. "Mr. Abu Saada, my name is Hector Lopez. I do, in fact, work for the Central Intelligence Agency in Washington. However, you must understand that I am not here on an official basis. In fact, if my bosses learn of this trip, I might lose my job. I came here using my own money on a commercial aircraft." For the moment, Lopez chose not to divulge that one other person, waiting nervously back at headquarters, knew of this trip.

On edge, Lopez reacted to a sudden sound. The elevator door opened, and the secretary whom Lopez had first approached on the ground floor entered, a silver tea set in his hands. Abu Saada stood, motioned him forward, and accepted the platter. The secretary departed. Abu Saada poured two cups and offered Lopez his choice of the two, no doubt to reassure his guest that neither had been drugged.

Lopez took a sip and nodded. He set the cup and its saucer on the desk.

It was time. "I'll get right to the point. You have two American citizens in your possession, Victor Silverstein and Linda Kipling. I am here to ask for their return."

With Lopez's words, Abu Saada shot to his feet. "Mr. Lopez, I'm astonished that you are so well informed. Why do you think your two Americans are here?" A hesitation. "And how did you find me?"

"Mr. Abu Saada, I will tell you many things, but you must appreciate that there are limits. I will not betray my country. I am here to strike a deal with you, one that will benefit us both. I have come to you because I understand that you are an unusually ethical and practical man." Under hypnosis, Ishmael's description of Abu Saada made Lopez wish there were more with his character among his own country's elected officials.

Lopez leaned forward to retrieve his cup and took additional sips. He wanted time for his words to register before he continued. "I am willing to make you a trade. In exchange for Silverstein and Kipling, I can offer you two things." Lopez paused. "But before we discuss those details, I propose an agreement between us on a matter of greater importance."

Lopez could imagine the thoughts racing through Abu Saada's brain. *Is this man a renegade? But if so, how would he possess so much information? What could he possibly offer me in return for the two Americans? And now he suggests that there's something even more important to discuss?* Abu Saada said nothing.

Lopez continued. "Sir, I assume you know the significance of the science behind the reason we're sitting here together now. The special gene. In fact, you probably know more than I do. From what I understand, whoever has this gene sequence in his body possesses some unusual talents, perhaps even an ability to foresee the future. I also understand that with today's science, geneticists may be able to duplicate this biological anomaly." He hesitated. "May I ask you? Is this your understanding as well?"

Lopez waited for a reply and knew that it would be positive—unless Abu Saada chose to lie. Everything that he stated he had learned from hypnosis, from Caliph's memory of conversations with Abu Saada. The information retrieved from Ishmael's subconscious by Leopold had been exhaustive.

Abu Saada nodded. "Go on, please."

With minimal feedback thus far, Lopez was becoming concerned. Here he was giving away the store. He decided to elicit a response. "Are you a religious man, sir?"

Abu Saada's face revealed surprise at such a question. "As you might surmise, I grew up Muslim. Along the way I lost faith." Lopez appreciated Abu Saada's honesty and his next words, "And you?" Lopez had not answered his earlier questions and now had an opportunity to reply.

Lopez downed the remainder of his tea in two swallows. "Much like you, I must say. My family is Roman Catholic, but I no longer attend Mass. Certain relatives of mine are now convinced I will burn in the fires of hell."

Lopez had the beginnings of a rapport. A hint of a smile flowed across Abu Saada's features.

Lopez decided it was time to make his first point. "I think you'd agree with me that much of today's world is affected by religion. All you have to do is read a newspaper to see that." He held up his index finger. "I've thought about this for my entire adult life. I honestly can't decide whether religion creates a net gain or loss for human society. I guess I'm an optimist and assume that it does benefit our small planet. Either way, if this gene is real and provides a scientific way to explain the roots of religion—in particular, the prophets—we're in for a big change.

"You must have thought about this. My personal view is that this gene may simply be God's way of invoking his presence in our lives. And to tell you the truth, that doesn't bother me. But the conservatives of the world's religions, particularly yours and mine, could never get their minds around this concept. There's no doubt in my mind that if this information becomes public and proven, these religions would descend into chaos. And what would replace them might be even more disastrous for society than what we've got."

Lopez stopped speaking and waited for a reaction. Did Abu Saada understand what he was saying? Did he have the mental capacity to understand the implications of what this research could unleash?

Lopez continued, realizing he had forgotten something central to his argument. "One more point that I think is important. I doubt that the gene will be useful to any of us. The recipient may not be able to control its benefits. From a practical standpoint, that would make it useless. If someone in history had continuous clairvoyance and used it to his own advantage, I'm sure we'd have heard about it."

"Are you suggesting that my organization stop its research?" Abu Saada queried.

"Yes, that's what I'm asking. You and I are in unique positions where we might be able to influence what happens next. I suggest we say that a rogue scientist doctored the original data, and some of the world's best scientists got caught up in the hype." Lopez recognized that his point had the ring of truth. "That sort of thing's happened before, you know."

"What about the American government? Will it do the same?"

"From what I can tell, the information about the gene is limited to a few people within an American research facility. I'm not 100 percent certain I can stop it, but there's a good chance. One thing that my agency is good at is disinformation."

"And if you don't succeed?"

"If I can't stop it, you'll undoubtedly find out. And if that happens, all bets are off, and you would continue with your work. I'm willing to do my part to make sure that doesn't happen. I ask you to do the same." Lopez paused. "If there is a God—and despite my lack of church attendance, I do believe there is—I think that he would look favorably upon our actions."

Abu Saada was obviously mulling over the enormity of this suggestion. To break the tension, he motioned toward the teapot. Lopez nodded, and Abu Saada refilled his cup. Abu Saada then stood and paced back and forth. He ended up facing the Cairo airport, which Lopez saw for the first time. Lopez stood and positioned himself to Abu Saada's right. He took in the panoramic view.

Abu Saada faced Lopez. "Although I have some importance, I am not the leader of our organization. Earlier you said you had something you would exchange for Silverstein and Kipling."

With this comment, Lopez felt that he had gotten across his more important point. It was possible that Abu Saada agreed with Lopez's sentiments regarding the gene. Now would come the bargaining to free Silverstein and Kipling. "I can offer Caliph Ishmael's freedom in return."

Lopez saw no reaction. Abu Saada would make one hell of a poker player. Whether he had known or suspected that Ishmael was under American control, he didn't reveal it. He had to know he was missing, because Sidki had returned solo.

Abu Saada motioned Lopez toward a leather sofa against the far wall. Lopez sat back in the deep folds of the scented leather and waited. The second part of his offer would prove to be of far more interest to Abu Saada than the first.

Abu Saada had a good memory. "I recall you mentioned the number two. What else can you offer me?"

Lopez chose his words carefully. He had practiced them dozens of times on his trip across the Atlantic. "You may not consider my second offer much of a gift, but if you think beyond your initial reaction, you will see that it is. Only I and one other person with whom I work know what I am about to tell you. I do not have to tell you what would happen if this information were leaked."

Despite Abu Saada's keen ability to hide his thoughts, Lopez knew that he had his attention. "I am intrigued, Mr. Lopez."

Lopez locked eyes with Abu Saada. If he reacted, Lopez wanted to see it. "I know that you have a spy within our government, at a very high level. I'm sure that her code name, Cleopatra, means something to you?"

This time, anyone who possessed vision could tell that Lopez had struck a nerve. Not only did Abu Saada's eyes widen, but his face turned ashen. Thereupon he stood, turned his back to Lopez, and uttered a few indecipherable words under his breath. He returned to his desk and sat immobile for what seemed minutes. Lopez remained seated on the couch.

When Abu Saada came up for air, he motioned Lopez back to his chair. "Mr. Lopez, tell me exactly what it is you propose?"

"First, I suggest that we both do what we can to stop research on the gene. You and I know that is the right thing to do. Please tell me if you disagree about this." Lopez swallowed hard and continued. "In exchange for Drs. Silverstein and Kipling, who will return with me to the United States, I will give you Caliph Ishmael's freedom. With regard to Cleopatra, I'll give you something crucial to your organization: I'll give you my silence. In exchange for that, I expect you to extract her so that she no longer presents a threat to my government. She can resign, and you can fabricate any reason you want that would minimize suspicion and save face for her."

Abu Saada listened to every word with rapt concentration. Lopez figured that Abu Saada had no choice but to agree. If the scandal of a U.S. senator's role as a spy came to light, the President and Congress would authorize any expense necessary to locate those to whom she reported. The investigation could go on for years. Until Ishmael's revelations, Abu Saada's organization had operated well under the radars of Western intelligence agencies. Abu Saada had to know that this invisibility would be lost if he did not agree to Lopez's demands.

"Mr. Lopez, I must check with my superiors."

"Mr. Abu Saada, I suggest you do it now. This information regarding Cleopatra cannot stay secret for long."

"What about Caliph?"

"Give me my cell phone, and I'll coordinate his release. You can talk to him yourself."

Abu Saada reached for his own telephone and then stopped, a frown settling into lines that had taken a lifetime to create. "Mr. Lopez, everything you've told me makes sense—except for one thing. It seems that you are giving far more than you are receiving from me. Why?"

"During your life, have you ever felt beholden to one man, who may have saved you from disaster, perhaps death?"

Lopez sensed that Abu Saada knew exactly what he meant. "Yes, I have."

"Well, then, you understand. For me, that one man is Victor Mark Silverstein."

CHAPTER 58

DELTA CHIP

Reagan National Airport, Washington, DC, USA
38°51'21"N latitude, 77°02'35"W longitude
Tuesday, 6:30 PM, August 11, 2009

What was that all about? Lopez finished his short conversation and snapped his cell phone shut. Miller, who had earlier offered to drop by the airport to give Lopez a ride home, said he'd be waiting outside security. He said Lopez should hurry but wouldn't say why.

Lopez had been in New York, ninety minutes earlier, when they last spoke. No indication of trouble then. Miller explained he had purchased a ticket for Ishmael to fly to Cairo by way of JFK. He reported he had driven him to National Airport the previous evening. Even though his plane from New York to Cairo wouldn't leave until 6:15 on Tuesday evening, Ishmael seemed anxious. Probably fearing that someone might change his mind, Ishmael wanted to leave town as soon as possible, Miller figured.

Lopez exited the Jetway, walking confidently, a spring to his step. No matter what news Miller was bringing, it wouldn't deprive him of his good mood. His mission to Cairo had been 100 percent successful. Not only had he and Abu Saada negotiated a reasonable end to the prophecy gene odyssey, but Lopez had used his hole cards to secure the release of Silverstein and Kipling. It was somewhat troubling that he had acted on his own without Agency blessing or consultation. Still, at the end of this day, he knew he would sleep well.

The icing on the cake had occurred at JFK. Before they separated, Silverstein had taken Lopez aside and thanked him for saving him and Kipling. Had Lopez not acted, Silverstein said he was sure no one would ever have seen them again. He said he owed his life to Lopez.

At CIA headquarters the day before, Miller had waited for Lopez's call. Once he struck his deal with Abu Saada, Lopez instructed Miller to release Ishmael. Lopez decided the risk was low in offering up his hostage first. His knowledge of Cleopatra posed a much greater threat to Abu Saada and his organization.

Lopez rushed past the security checkpoint and saw Miller, who looked worried. "What's up?"

Miller steered him into a corner. "Where are Silverstein and Kipling?"

Lopez looked at his watch and subtracted mentally. "They should land in San Francisco in about an hour and a half. Why?"

"Can you call them on their cells?"

Something had happened! "No. They lost them. Why?"

"When will Silverstein get home?"

Again, Lopez did the math. "They'll land in Monterey at 9:30 our time. Figure another half hour to take a taxi home." Frustrated, Lopez repeated his question a third time. "Why?"

Miller stared grimly. "We have trouble."

"Spit it out!"

"I took Ishmael to National yesterday. His flight from JFK to Cairo doesn't leave until this evening." Miller noted the time. "About now, as a matter of fact."

"So?"

"You remember we implanted the Delta chip?"

"Goddamn it, Miller! Of course I know. You told me it was working just fine."

"After I drove him to the airport, I went back to work. As I did before with Sidki, I programmed my computer to forward updates on his position to my cell phone. Because it's nearly impossible to receive a Delta signal from inside a building or airplane, I wasn't expecting any messages for a while. We did pick him up briefly at JFK."

"So? The next transmission we get will be tomorrow morning sometime, in Cairo."

Miller swallowed. "On the way over here, my phone beeped. Ishmael's already landed."

Lopez looked at his watch. "That's impossible. Where?"

"San Francisco."

CHAPTER 59

FINALE

Runway 10R, Monterey Peninsula Airport, Monterey,
California, USA
36°35'26"N latitude, 121°51'18"W longitude
Tuesday, 6:30 PM, August 11, 2009

The flight from San Francisco touched down. They were home at last. Silverstein stared out his window and said a prayer of blessing for himself and for Kipling. Through eyes glazed with emotion, he said another prayer for a departed friend.

Less than a week had passed since Silverstein had departed the same airport, ostensibly heading to Johnstown, Pennsylvania, with Dickey in tow. Given all that had happened since, it seemed a lifetime ago.

He leaned to his left, grabbed Kipling's hand, gave it a reassuring shake, and smiled. "We're home and safe." She had been through a lot. They both had.

Monday afternoon had proved interesting indeed. The last thing Silverstein remembered after landing in Cairo was calling out to Fuad and Aziz as the drug took hold. That injection kept him comatose for hours. When he awoke, the plane was landing once again in Cairo. Kipling later told him they were supposed to fly to eastern Turkey but never made it.

Silverstein's friend, Hector Rodriguez Lopez, had pulled off a miracle. After their return to Cairo, a hostage transfer occurred without drama.

Lopez stood waiting and took possession of Silverstein and Kipling. They stayed at an airport hotel before the flight home Tuesday morning. They flew direct to JFK, where Lopez said goodbye. He flew south to Washington. Silverstein and Kipling headed west to San Francisco and then to Monterey.

Before going to bed in Cairo, Lopez explained what had happened—mostly. He had traveled to Egypt on his own to appeal to the same individual whom Silverstein had convinced to allow him to return to Johnstown to retrieve the letter and DNA—a man Lopez knew as Mohammed Abu Saada. Lopez admitted that, following Silverstein and Kipling's departure from Monterey, he had captured Nicholas. During questioning, Nicholas revealed that he worked for Abu Saada and that his real name was Caliph Ishmael. Silverstein wondered how they had gotten so much information from him. From Silverstein's experience, he would have expected Ishmael to be a tough nut to crack. Lopez then flew to Cairo to offer him in return for Silverstein and Kipling. "Nicholas" was free to return home.

Lopez explained that Ishmael was only half of what he had to offer Abu Saada. He said that once CIA scientists began to investigate what they had called the prophecy gene, they discovered that the uproar over a potential gene that could give humans unusual powers had been a sham. First, he said, an overly ambitious scientist had doctored the statistics for the Russian mice results; there had been no clairvoyant mouse. He said the situation was analogous to the stem cell debacle in South Korea a few years back.

Second, when CIA scientists studied Weaverman's descriptions of the genetic code that described the gene, they discovered that, in his zeal to believe it to be true, he had made mistakes. The excitement generated by its mind-boggling potential had caused scientists to scrutinize the genetic data with less than their usual rigor.

When Lopez presented this information to Abu Saada, who apparently had also been duped by the Russian mice experiments, the latter realized there was no point in keeping Kipling.

During Lopez's discourse on Monday night, Silverstein listened with mouth agape. He was shocked, not because of his amazing story, but because Silverstein knew that most of what he said was bullshit. He couldn't believe that Weaverman, *in his zeal to believe it to be true,* had produced flawed results. Furthermore, Lopez knew nothing of Augusta or Silverstein's Johnstown escapade. Silverstein decided to keep it that way. He would decide later how much he would confide to Kipling. He understood what Lopez was doing—putting out disinformation. Whether on his own or dictated from above, someone had decided to squelch the prophecy gene.

Unfortunately, some of what Lopez told them was true. Using his connections with the FBI, they found Weaverman—but too late. Silverstein shed tears when told that his friend, Dr. James Peter Weaverman, had been murdered, probably not long after Silverstein received the faxed photograph from Dickey, Silverstein concluded. Over the weekend, police implicated his boss, Dennis Rafferty. Lopez said that he didn't understand the full extent of what happened, but it seemed that Rafferty, who had also been taken in by the promise of the gene, wanted no competition from his underling. It was clear that Rafferty was taking orders from superiors. It was only a matter of time before he ratted them out.

Silverstein and Kipling exited the aircraft and headed to the street. No need to stop at baggage. They had left with nothing and returned with nothing. Several taxicabs stood waiting.

Kipling was not herself. Although she had stated that her captors had treated her well, she seemed to exist in a world of her own. He knew that her psychological recovery would require his compassion and understanding. "Do you want to go out for a bite? I can see you home then."

Kipling's response caught him by surprise. "Do you mind if I spend the night at your house? I'm on edge, and I'd feel better if you were nearby."

Silverstein raised his hand to hail a cab. "Good idea. I'll cook dinner."

On the ride from the airport, out Route 68 to the Boots Road turnoff, and finally into his housing development, Halcyon Heights, Silverstein watched Kipling out of the corner of his eye. He asked the cab driver to pull into the upper driveway. He settled the fare with his remaining fifty-dollar bill and escorted Kipling along the walkway into the enclosed courtyard that fronted the door. He glanced about the neighborhood. A car and occupant parked on the street above the house. Probably a Realtor scoping out his next sale.

Silverstein reached into his pocket. After all that had happened, he wasn't surprised he had lost his key chain. Like most people, he kept a spare key hidden for times like this. An imitation rock in an adjacent flowerbed served that duty. He opened the front door. The pre-warning alarm bell for the burglar alarm sounded. He walked to the keypad on the interior wall and entered his code, ending the obnoxious high-pitched screech. He looked back for Kipling. She remained in the entryway. "Come on. There's no one here except you and me." He checked the alphanumeric display on the keypad and pointed. "If anyone had set off the alarm while I was gone, it would say right here. Everything's fine."

Silverstein walked outside, returned the key to its hiding place, put his arms around Kipling, and drew her close. This was worse than he thought. She was an emotional disaster zone, afraid even to go inside his house.

While Kipling cleaned up in the bathroom, Silverstein whipped up an omelet with cheese, onion, and sweet peppers. Together with some Ciabatta bread from the freezer and a Napa Valley Merlot from Silverstein's wine cellar, they had an acceptable dinner. Practically no conversation accompanied the meal. He decided there would be time later to discuss the implications of Lopez's account from the night before.

By nine o'clock, Silverstein decided that bed was in order. Along with a new toothbrush, he handed Kipling one of his old shirts to wear to bed. He pointed her toward the guest room and offered her a sleeping pill. She declined. He hugged her one more time. "Sleep as late as you can. Okay?"

Silverstein decided to check messages at work. He lifted the receiver, but there was no dial tone. With exhaustion drawing him to bed, he didn't have the strength to investigate further; he'd address his phone situation in the morning.

Silverstein brushed his teeth, donned his pajamas, and slid between the sheets. Consistent with his standard procedure when guests visited, he didn't activate the burglar alarm. You never knew when someone might open a window or take a walk in the middle of the night.

Before nodding off, Silverstein glanced at his bedside clock. It was 9:15.

On approach to Monterey Peninsula Airport, Monterey, California, USA
Tuesday, 9:30 PM, August 11, 2009

On the drive to Dulles, where the CIA kept its aircraft, Miller had repeatedly called Silverstein's and Kipling's home numbers. He left numerous messages on Kipling's answering machine. Calls to Silverstein's phone rang unanswered. Lopez knew he had an answering machine. For that reason, and a second, Lopez and Miller chose to fly to California immediately.

If the first reason caused concern, the second provided impetus. Dr. Sampson's mental and physical analysis of Caliph Ishmael had been nothing if not thorough. One detail proved startling. Portions of his DNA matched Senator Thurston's; they shared one parent. A week earlier, when they first suspected Thurston, they had discovered that she and the two hit men who had tried to kill Silverstein two years earlier also shared a parent. Now they knew that Ishmael and the hit men shared the same parents. They were blood brothers. Ishmael's decision to fly west raised a scarlet flag.

The plane touched down, and Lopez glanced at his watch. It was 9:42.

Halcyon Heights home subdivision, Monterey, California, USA
36°33'30"N latitude, 121°46'28"W longitude
Tuesday, 9:46 PM, August 11, 2009

Silverstein sat up bolt upright from a deep sleep. The red numbers from his digital clock told him that only a half hour had passed.

This had happened before; he would hear a noise during the night, wake up, and not know whether he had imagined the sound in his dream or if it was real and had awakened him. He had heard breaking glass. As a check, he stumbled out of bed and padded to the burglar alarm display on the adjacent wall. Even though the alarm was unarmed, the indicator light would signal whether a window or door was open. On the way there, he recognized trouble—the green light was out. Perhaps Kipling had opened her window for ventilation. He pressed the button to check for the open circuit. *Shit!* Silverstein read the alphanumeric display: *Theater.* This was not good news.

Silverstein walked quietly across the carpet to the bedroom door, into the hallway, across the entryway, and into the living room, from which a spiral staircase descended to his home theater. He tiptoed closer to the staircase. If someone had broken into the theater through the back windows, they were now standing beneath him one level down. They could walk silently, but without knowing the room's layout, they would need a light. His eyes already adjusted to the darkness, Silverstein focused his gaze on the staircase leading down to the theater. His heart nearly stopped when a flickering light revealed itself.

He stepped backward into the entry foyer, nearly tripping over the coffee table. Someone had broken into his house. Only one scenario made sense. Burglars had noted his absence over the past week and figured this was a good time for a heist, not realizing he had returned home. The theater windows that sat away from the street provided an optimum location to enter.

Silverstein thought quickly. Aziz had confiscated Silverstein's weapon when he first boarded his plane in Monterey. Before Silverstein left Cairo, Aziz had returned it, but because Silverstein had no luggage in which to transport it, Lopez had taken it home in his own checked bag, offering to mail it to California later.

Standing in the entryway by the front door, Silverstein concluded he had two choices. He glanced around the corner toward the guest room at the end of the hallway. Kipling's door remained closed. She hadn't heard anything. Option one was to bolt out the front door, making sure the intruder noticed this when he appeared at the top of the spiral staircase. Simultaneously, Silverstein would turn on the overhead and outside lights from switches on the adjacent wall. The chances were good that the intruder didn't know anyone was home. Wanting to avoid a confrontation, he would escape out the door and make a clean getaway. It would be a win-win situation. Option two was to deal with the burglar inside the house. Even considering that he was standing barefoot in his pajamas, option one made more sense. No burglar would risk an altercation.

Silverstein reached for the light switches, watched as the faint shape of a head became visible at the top of the stairs, switched on all four lights, opened the front door wide, and ran into the patio. He scampered left toward the side of the house where the entry had occurred. He peeked around the corner and waited for the prowler to exit. It would soon be over.

*   *   *   *

Linda Kipling stood with her ear to the locked door, listening—and completely clothed. She had heard the breaking glass and had chosen to stay put. The situation she had foreseen in her vision was coming true. Her decision to stay at Silverstein's house had been the correct one.

She turned and faced the window. *What has Victor done?* From her bedroom window, which faced the walkway they had used to enter the house, she saw light. Had Silverstein exited, hoping to draw the intruder outside? Probably. Made sense. But she knew this was not to be.

Suddenly she noticed a light along the bottom of the door. From the outside lights that lit up her room, she saw the doorknob turn against the lock. Seconds later, the solid door burst open in an explosion of sound. In her plan to save Silverstein, she hadn't even considered that she could end up as collateral damage. Nicholas gestured with his weapon for her to walk in front of him. From Lopez's briefing the previous evening, Kipling knew that his real name was Caliph Ishmael.

*   *   *   *

Silverstein crept closer to the still-open front door. The crack of splintering wood resonated loud enough for him to hear it. *What the hell?* He had guessed wrong. Whoever this was, he wasn't interested in Silverstein's possessions. Inadvertently, Silverstein had placed Kipling in danger. This was no time to be outside, looking in. He sprinted inside, made a quick right turn into the living room, entered the dining room, and turned left into the kitchen. With luck, the intruder had not heard him and assumed he was still outside.

*   *   *   *

Ishmael directed Kipling into the hallway.

Why had Ishmael returned to Monterey? To capture Kipling again? Unlikely. Also, she could think of no reason why he would want to harm Silverstein. Silverstein's role in Carmel had been peripheral. Yet rather than fly back to Cairo, Ishmael had returned to Monterey. Why?

Ishmael approached Kipling from behind, put his hand on her shoulder, and placed the gun to her neck. He spoke softly. "Don't do anything stupid, and you will probably live." He pushed her to the front door, and they faced outward. Much louder, he projected his voice into the patio. "Victor Silverstein! Come inside, and let us have it out. Will you run away from your woman like you ran away from my brothers? Are you a coward, Victor Silverstein? I will give you ten seconds to appear, or I will fire a bullet through your friend's shoulder."

"One ... two ... three ... four ... five ... six ... seven ..."

Suddenly, a voice to the rear. "Why are you shouting outside? I'm standing right here."

*   *   *   *

Silverstein had proceeded through the kitchen, grabbing a large kitchen knife along the way. He continued through the adjacent breakfast nook and into the family room. When the man began counting, Silverstein made his decision instantly. He would not place Kipling in any more danger. He walked into the open, faced the foyer and the stranger's back, and made his statement. He followed it with two more words, "Run, Linda!" To his left, a three-foot wall separated the family room from the hallway.

In an instant, the stranger thrust Kipling hard out the front door, slammed the door behind him, locked it, and rotated to fire.

The first shot barely cleared Silverstein's right shoulder as he dived for protection behind the wall to his left. Once on the floor, a shallow corridor existed in the room, bounded by a sofa to his left and the solid wall to his right. He crawled frantically to exit the family room and enter the breakfast nook to his right. But during his adrenaline-fueled panic he dropped the knife he had so cleverly retrieved earlier. He slid along the floor to his right as the second bullet dug into the oak flooring behind him. He jumped to his feet, turned into the kitchen, and heard steps behind him charging into the family room.

At the end of the kitchen lay two alternatives: the long hallway to his right and the dining room straight ahead. Both avenues offered temporary protection, although the living room was better, he concluded. The only light illuminating these rooms came from the overhead chandelier in the entry. He needed to position himself where he'd have an advantage.

Silverstein decided where that advantage lay: the home theater at the bottom of the spiral staircase. Unless the intruder knew to flip the switch at the top of the stairs, it would be dark down there.

Silverstein flew to the staircase and descended two steps at a time. He could hear loud steps across the floor above. The stranger would know this path because he had ascended this staircase just minutes earlier.

Silverstein had seconds to decide on a plan. At the bottom of the staircase, he faced a door opposite the windows. Through that door lay the wine cellar. In the corner to the left of that door stood a stand-up bar. He dashed forward and opened the door. He then dropped to his hands and knees and backed in behind the bar, counting on it to hide him from view.

*   *   *   *

Kipling hit the patio hard when Ishmael pushed her out. She rolled over a step and came to rest shaken but uninjured. Being fully clothed with shoes on had helped. She tried the front door but found it locked. Luckily, the outdoor lights did a good job of lighting up the patio. It took a few seconds, but she found the fake rock where Silverstein had hidden his key. She opened the front door, peeked inside, and let herself in. She could hear the creak of the metal staircase to her right. The action had relocated to the lower level.

Before she could help her boss, Kipling needed to return to her room.

*   *   *   *

From behind the stand-up bar Silverstein lay prone on the floor, parallel to the wine cellar door three feet in front of him. Seconds earlier, the stranger had found the light switch that trained a spotlight down the staircase. The room lit up slightly. Still, Silverstein's position on the floor was low enough so that as the footsteps descended lower, he remained hidden from view. Silverstein was glad he had not chosen to hide behind the theater seating. A look from above, with even minimal light, would have given him away.

Silverstein listened as the metal staircase creaked with each descending step. He counted fourteen steps. Whoever it was that wanted Silverstein's hide now stood on the carpeted floor at the bottom. Light from the flashlight careened about the room. Silverstein considered his attacker's thinking. He might figure that Silverstein had escaped through the open window. But if so, why was the wine cellar door open in front of him, since it had been closed earlier? Leaving the door open had been stupid—although it had seemed like a good idea only seconds earlier.

The light from the flashlight bore straight past Silverstein, through the door, and into the wine cellar that curved off to the left. If his adversary walked by and shone his light to the left, Silverstein was a dead man.

Silverstein's heart hammered. Only one occasion matched this one in terms of tension and fear—when Ghali had cornered him at the Mountain High Inn in Fort Collins two years earlier. Ideally, his attacker would walk into the wine cellar. Silverstein would jump up, slam the door shut, lock it, run from the house, find Kipling, and escape.

Absolute quiet. The stranger proceeded slowly, much too slowly. Silverstein lay crouched. The flashlight continued to shine ahead, exploring the recesses of the cellar. Silverstein realized he had no choice. Hesitation could be fatal.

With the muscles in his forearms and legs quivering, Silverstein lifted himself inches off the floor, ready to pounce. At once, he knew it was time and lunged forward. He grabbed both of the stranger's ankles and pulled backward with all his strength. His opponent, with his center of gravity now in front of his backward-moving feet, had no choice but to fall forward. Instinctively, the stranger fired his weapon downward in an attempt to hit his attacker. By then he was flying too far forward and could not rotate his weapon backward quickly enough. The explosion resonated in the small room, but the bullet hit harmlessly in the carpet.

Silverstein considered himself lucky. The stranger's body was now falling toward the opening of the door, his head and weapon pointed away from Silverstein. In an instant, that advantage vanished. He had the sense to turn sideways as he fell, allowing him to point his weapon in Silverstein's direction. Silverstein jumped to the side as another shot flew by him and lodged in one of the theater seats. Instinctively, both of Silverstein's hands raced to the attacker's right hand. What Silverstein hadn't anticipated was the left hand that was now free. That hand went to Silverstein's throat, fingers plunging into skin and veins. Silverstein drew back at the assault. Feeling confident his left hand could control the stranger's right wrist and the firearm, Silverstein's right hand grabbed hold of the stranger's left wrist, wresting it to the side.

It was now strength against strength. As they struggled on the floor, Silverstein's exhaustion caught up with him. His pajamas offered little protection. His attacker used that advantage to kick at Silverstein's legs and bare feet with his shoes. Each blow sent shivers of pain through Silverstein's lower extremities. He needed to turn the tide in his favor. His strength was ebbing.

During this nightmare of a fight to the death, Silverstein's thoughts shifted to Kipling. Where was she? He prayed she had followed his advice and fled.

Knowing that the stranger's weapon gave him the ultimate advantage, Silverstein concentrated on removing it. In a microsecond of lull in the free-for-all, he grabbed his adversary's wrist again and thrust it backward against the metal footrest of the bar. Accompanied by a satisfying crack, the weapon flew five feet away, in front of the bar. The odds had shifted in Silverstein's favor.

Furious that Silverstein had temporarily gotten the best of him, the stranger flew into a rage, striking Silverstein furiously with his fists, legs, and feet. By now, Silverstein's pajamas had been torn from his body, and he was fighting nude. He had no strength left. In one final thrust, the stranger connected with his left hand, catching Silverstein squarely on the jaw and throwing him against the wall. He followed up with a kick to the groin.

Silverstein knew then that he was a dead man. Stunned from the blow to his head and writhing in pain from the kick to his genitals, he could do nothing more than lean against the wall and wait for the inevitable.

His vision fuzzy from the jolt his head had suffered, Silverstein watched the end unfold in slow, surreal motion. The stranger leaped to the side and lunged for his gun. There was no reason for him to hurry, thought Silverstein.

With his eyes fixated on the attacker's descending body, Silverstein almost failed to notice a blurry form at the bottom of the stairs.

*   *   *   *

Ishmael hadn't noticed her descent down the spiral staircase. Like an Amazon, Kipling's five-foot-ten frame stood erect and statuesque. Calm and deliberate, she pulled her right arm back steadily, her upper body strength overcoming the severe sixty-pound pull of Silverstein's bow. She waited until Ishmael placed his hand on his weapon before releasing the tension in the compound bow. She had to be careful. She had only one arrow, a target version with a smooth, pointed tip.

Kipling's target lay ten feet distant. At nearly two hundred miles per hour, the arrow penetrated to the left of Ishmael's right shoulder at a downward angle and did not stop even after it had pierced his heart. It exited the opposite side of his body, exploding tissue and splintering itself along the way.

Caught off guard by a sudden stab of pain, Ishmael rotated toward her and stared. His sudden realization constituted his last connection with the earthly world.

Seconds later, Kipling heard shouts from upstairs. "Victor! Victor! Where are you? It's me, Hector. For God's sake, answer me!"

EPILOGUE

From *The Washington Post*, Monday, August 17, 2009

Senator found dead

By Jim Manheim
The Washington Post

WASHINGTON—Samantha Thurston, junior senator from Kansas, was found dead early Sunday morning on the Metro platform at Union Station. According to police spokesperson Sgt. Jack Murphy, foul play is suspected, and an autopsy is pending. Sen. Thurston had been married to Sen. Maxwell Thurston who died from a heart attack only nine months after his 2006 election to the Senate. Samantha Thurston had replaced her husband in office ...

From *The Washington Post*, Wednesday, August 26, 2009

Senator MacDonald announces retirement

By Greta Winningham
The Washington Post

WASHINGTON—Clifton MacDonald, senior senator from Wyoming, announced his immediate retirement, effective Thursday, citing personal and family considerations ...

Grandview Cemetery, Johnstown, Pennsylvania, USA
40°18'56"N latitude, 78°55'39"W longitude
Thursday, 12:30 PM, September 3, 2009

Silverstein and Kipling took in the expanse of the huge cemetery situated above Johnstown. He had suggested that they make this trip to pay their final respects to Augusta Schmidt.

Earlier that morning, while Kipling slept at the motel, Silverstein had visited Peggy Houston. He asked for directions to Augusta's gravesite and explained to her most of what had happened, as well as Lopez's decision to squelch the information concerning the prophecy gene. She said she could not disagree with that decision.

Underneath a sky speckled with puffy cumulus clouds, they stood motionless, their thoughts on Augusta. On the way to the cemetery, Kipling had purchased a solitary red rose. Sweat moistened the handle of the spade in Silverstein's hands. He would wait for Kipling to give the signal.

The past two weeks had been healing times for them; he, with physical wounds that would mend soon enough; she, with the psychological trauma of having killed a man, a shock that would take longer to dissipate. Although her demeanor at work remained uneven and strained, he had begun to see more of the fire and drive from the Kipling he knew well. In the back of his mind, he hoped that this visit to Johnstown would provide closure.

The entry marker in this section of the cemetery provided the grim summary. *In memory of the unidentified dead from the flood May 31, 1889.* Not far from the graves of the unknown stood the markers for the Schmidt family: one for Heinrich and Frieda, and one for each of the children: Annabel, Thompson—and August. *August Schmidt, March 26, 1870–May 31, 1889.*

Silverstein had shared the contents of Augusta's letter with Kipling. They agreed that the psychological torment from the two curses—as Augusta called them—must have been unbearable. Bad enough was having a body that didn't conform to the male sex. More terrifying would have been the realization of the impending flood and not being able to do a damn thing about it.

Silverstein's thoughts returned to Monterey. Kipling had saved his life for the second time in as many years—in addition to her heroics at the Carmel motel. At the house, the intruder—whom Silverstein recognized following the fight in the dark as Nicholas, and thus Caliph Ishmael—had taunted Silverstein about the two men who had died trying to kill him in 2007. Wanting to hear Lopez's version, Silverstein asked why Ishmael had come gunning for him. Lopez confirmed what Silverstein had heard in his entryway, that the two men and Ishmael were brothers. Silverstein considered telling Lopez about the woman who had assaulted him in Johnstown, but because he then would have had to explain why he had flown to Pennsylvania, he chose not to. The topic of interest there had also been those same two men. How the woman fit into this complex puzzle was a mystery Silverstein hoped he would eventually piece together.

And although Kipling's actions at his house had saved the day, Silverstein had to admit that Lopez's arrival had been timely. He arranged for the removal of Ishmael's body and its transport back to Egypt. Lopez said he was not looking forward to explaining to Abu Saada what had happened.

Silverstein would have loved to discuss the prophecy gene with Lopez but decided not to bring it up. At the hotel in Cairo, Lopez had recited his version of events. Silverstein believed that Lopez knew the truth and had decided on a cover-up, perhaps with Abu Saada's concurrence. Putting himself in Lopez's position and considering the implications of the genetic discovery, Silverstein agreed with Peggy Houston that Lopez had acted appropriately.

More difficult was Silverstein's interaction with Kipling. Did she know she had inherited the prophecy gene? Consistent with his earlier decision, he said nothing. She had no knowledge of Rafferty's DNA analysis that confirmed Kipling's unique genetic makeup. She may have suspected that Silverstein knew, but that was not the point. From the beginning, he had chosen to shield her—at all costs. And that protection involved hiding that secret from her if there was even the slightest chance she did not know.

With that choice firmly made, Silverstein was careful not to let his conversation stray. She had asked about his trip to Johnstown. He told her about Kipling's impostor and how she had burned the envelope. He left out the gory details. They discussed Augusta Schmidt, her genetic gift, the puzzle inherent in her letter, and the strands of hair she left behind. They also debated Lopez's decision to describe the gene as the fabrication of careless scientists and those eager to believe the hype. The death of Weaverman, the source of the original scientific evidence, inadvertently helped shut off further publicity regarding the genetic aberration.

As the Johnstown sun neared its zenith, Kipling knelt, placed the rose by the marker, faced upward, and made a point of looking Silverstein in the eye. "Do you mind if I do it?" Her question caught him off guard. "Augusta would consider it appropriate."

Silverstein nodded. She had thrown him a bone. Her last five words answered the foremost question in his mind.

"Of course not." On the flight to Pennsylvania, they had agreed on what they would do.

Silverstein handed her the spade. He opened his wallet and removed the paper packet he had made back in Peggy Houston's office. Silverstein was glad that he had never been given the opportunity to tell Abu Saada what Augusta had left inside the bottle. The priceless samples inside his billfold had escaped Egypt undetected.

Silverstein removed one of the staples, pulled the papers apart to look at the hairs one last time, and handed them to Kipling, who also took the opportunity for one final glimpse.

She laid the packet next to the rose, drove the spade into the soft soil in front of the stone, removed a sizable section, and set it aside. She repeated the process until she had dug a foot-deep hole. She placed the packet deep inside, reversed the procedure, and tamped down the sod.

The two strands of hair that had traveled through thousands of miles of space and more than a century of time had finally caught up with their owner. Augusta's body—and her secrets—had been laid to rest.

Silverstein closed his eyes, felt the tears well up, and did as Augusta had asked. He said a prayer for her soul. If only she had known that two of her predictions were totally off the mark. The person who had come looking for her was not the devil. And Augusta need not have worried. From Silverstein's point of view, she would not be going to hell.

GLOSSARY

a.k.a.—also known as

base pair—any of the pairs of the hydrogen-bonded purine and pyrimidine bases that form the links between the sugar-phosphate backbones of nucleic acid molecules; the pairs are adenine and thymine in DNA, adenine and uracil in RNA, and guanine and cytosine in both DNA and RNA.*

Celera—a molecular diagnostics business with powerful discovery platforms dedicated to the practice of targeted medicine. Located in Rockville, Maryland, and Alameda, California, the company employs about 300 people and has the full capability to discover, develop, manufacture, and secure registration for in vitro diagnostic products.

chromosome—any of several threadlike bodies, consisting of chromatin, that carry the genes in a linear order; the human species has 23 pairs, designated 1 to 22 in order of decreasing size, and X and Y for the female and male sex chromosomes, respectively.*

CIA—Central Intelligence Agency

Cooper—a quick-change outfit that allows three different outward clothing appearances; developed by CIA Mensa team member Chris Cooper.

Crimson—a technique developed by the CIA to apprehend a solo individual, developed by agent Joseph Crimson.

Delta chip—a chip implanted in the skull that allows an individual to be tracked geographically using satellites; developed by the Mensa team at the CIA.

Diptera Muscidae—the order and family of the common housefly

DNA—deoxyribonucleic acid: an extremely long macromolecule that is the main component of chromosomes and is the material that transfers genetic characteristics in all life forms, constructed of two nucleotide strands coiled around each other in a ladderlike arrangement, with the sidepieces composed of alternating phosphate and deoxyribose units and the rungs composed of the purine and pyrimidine bases adenine, guanine, cytosine, and thymine; the genetic information of DNA is encoded in the sequence of the bases and is transcribed as the strands unwind and replicate.*

EDT—eastern daylight time

FBI—Federal Bureau of Investigation

GPS—Global Positioning System. The GPS consists of a series of satellites positioned in earth orbit. Developed by the U.S. Department of Defense, this system allows users to determine their positions anywhere in the world. Anyone can make use of this system, although location information for civilians is not as accurate as that for the military.

HGP—Human Genome Project. Begun formally in 1990, the U.S. Human Genome Project was a thirteen-year effort coordinated by the U.S. Department of Energy and the National Institutes of Health. The project originally was planned to last fifteen years, but rapid technological advances accelerated the completion date to 2003. Project goals were to

    —identify all the approximately 20,000–25,000 genes in human DNA;

    —determine the sequences of the three billion chemical base pairs that make up human DNA;

—store this information in databases;

—improve tools for data analysis;

—transfer related technologies to the private sector;

—address the ethical, legal, and social issues that might arise from the project.

ITE—image transformation expert; a makeup artist.

Johnstown Flood National Memorial—the National Park Service's facility for commemorating the great Johnstown Flood of 1889. From the memorial's Web site: "There was no larger news story in the latter nineteenth century after the assassination of Abraham Lincoln. The story of the Johnstown Flood has everything to interest the modern mind: a wealthy resort, an intense storm, an unfortunate failure of a dam, the destruction of a working-class city, and an inspiring relief effort."

Klinefelter's syndrome—an abnormal condition in which at least one extra X chromosome is present in a male; characterized by reduced or absent sperm production, small testicles, and in some cases enlarged breasts.*

LED—light-emitting diode; a semiconductor diode that emits light when conducting current and is used in electronic equipment, especially for displaying readings on digital watches, calculators, etc.*

MDT—mountain daylight time

NRL—Naval Research Laboratory, located in Washington, DC. NRL operates as the Navy's full-spectrum corporate laboratory, conducting a broadly based, multidisciplinary program of scientific research and advanced technological development directed toward maritime applications of new and improved materials, techniques, equipment, systems, and ocean, atmospheric, and space sciences and related technologies.

NRL Monterey—Marine Meteorology Division of NRL, located in Monterey, California. The division conducts a research and development program designed to improve the basic understanding of atmospheric processes and the atmosphere's interaction with the ocean, land, and cryosphere; to develop and implement automated analysis, prediction, and weather interpretation systems for Department of Defense users; and to study the effect of the atmosphere on naval weapons systems.

Romguard—a mechanical fly-like device, developed by Peter Romguard of the CIA's Mensa team, for conducting reconnaissance on a human-to-human level.

* *Random House Webster's Unabridged Dictionary*, 2nd ed. New York: Random House, 1998.

CAST OF CHARACTERS

Abu Saada, Mohammed: fourth in command within the Blade of the Sinai

Anchor, Billy: CIA subordinate of Lopez and member of the Crimson team

Blade of the Sinai: shadowy Middle Eastern organization committed to resolving political and social problems in the Middle East; although ostensibly opposed to terrorism, it has resorted to violence in the past

Cannon, Fred: backhoe operator for Goliath Construction in Johnstown, Pennsylvania

Cooper, Chris: CIA agent, part of the Mensa team, who invented the Cooper, a quick-change outfit that permits agents to have three different appearances

Crimson, Joseph P.: legendary CIA agent who invented Crimson, the method for capturing a solo individual, now a standard Agency apprehension technique

Francis: alias of Ali Sidki

Fuad: Victor Silverstein's handler in Cairo, Egypt

Ghali (a.k.a. Ahmed Abu Hamasay): Blade of the Sinai agent who died during a previous operation, friend to Abu Saada

Grafton, Cynthia: Senator Thurston's executive assistant

Hansley, Averill: CIA agent who reports to Hector Lopez

Heikal, Yusif: secretary to Mohammed Abu Saada in Cairo, Egypt

Houston, Peggy Sue: curator of the Johnstown Flood National Memorial, in Johnstown, Pennsylvania

Ishmael, Caliph: up-and-coming member of the Blade of the Sinai, brother to the Ishmael twins

Ishmael twins: hit men for the Blade of the Sinai, killed during an earlier operation; brothers of Caliph Ishmael

Jamieson, Dick: employee of Senator James MacDonald

Johnson, Timothy: Silverstein's roommate during his sophomore year at Penn State

Kipling, Dr. Linda: Silverstein's assistant at the Naval Research Laboratory in Monterey, California

Leopold, Dr. Craig: CIA agent, hypnosis expert, member of CIA's Mensa team

Lopez, Hector Rodriguez, Jr.: CIA senior investigative officer in counter-intelligence

MacDonald, Clifton: U.S. senator from Wyoming

Mensa team: CIA subgroup that designs advanced techniques and tools for field operations

Miller, Marc: CIA agent, Hector Lopez's principal colleague

Myra: Jamieson's first female associate

Nicholas: alias of Caliph Ishmael

Rafferty, Dr. Dennis: Weaverman's supervisor at NRL, linked to Senator MacDonald

Ramos, Joaquin: CIA subordinate of Lopez and member of the Crimson team

Riad, Aziz: chief pilot for the Blade of the Sinai and cousin to Samantha Thurston

Romguard, Dr. Peter: CIA Mensa member who invented the Romguard mechanical fly

Sampson, Dr. Philip: CIA scientist and surgeon, member of the Mensa team

Sanfold, Margaret: CIA specialist in speechreading

Schmidt, Augusta: teenager who died during the Johnstown flood of 1889

Shafer, Max: pilot of Silverstein's rented jet on his return flight to California

Sidki, Ali: Blade of the Sinai employee, gofer; implanted earlier with the Delta chip

Silverstein, Dr. Ivan: Victor Silverstein's adoptive father who died in 1997

Silverstein, Dr. Victor Mark: principal protagonist, preeminent Navy scientist

Silverstein, Sara: Victor Silverstein's adopted mother who died in 1997

Smith, Herb: construction supervisor for Goliath Construction in Johnstown, Pennsylvania

Sphinx Petroleum: Mohammed Abu Saada's official employer and cover

Strauss, Byron: CIA subordinate of Lopez and lead agent for the Crimson Team

Thurston, Maxwell: deceased spouse of Samantha Thurston and former Kansas senator

Thurston, Samantha: U.S. senator from Kansas

Travers, Jimmy: Silverstein's anthropologist friend who works at the Smithsonian Institution in Washington, DC.

Violet: Jamieson's second female associate

Warner, Dr. Clement: a mole of the Blade who had previously infiltrated the Office of Naval Research; he died during an earlier operation

Weaverman, Dr. James Peter: NRL biologist who discovers the prophecy gene, friend to Victor Silverstein

Winston, John: CIA agent who reports to Hector Lopez, operator for the Romguard

978-0-595-43444-2
0-595-43444-4

Printed in the United States
85987LV00010B/73-90/A